DANETHRALL

By Gwendoline SK Terry

Danethrall Trilogy
Danethrall
Rise to Fall
Ashes Remain

DANETHRALL
GWENDOLINE SK TERRY

TWO RAVENS PUBLISHING

Copyright © 2018 Gwendoline SK Terry

All rights reserved.

ISBN-13: 978-1-7339996-1-8

This is a work of fiction. Names, characters, places, and incidents either are the products of the author's imagination or are used fictitiously. Any resemblance to actual persons, living or dead, businesses, companies, events, or locales is entirely coincidental.

Frail as the lily's stem so slender,
Yet like spring roses fresh and fair,
As Freyja's troth-plight, warm and tender,
Thou as the will of the gods art pure.
Kiss me and let my burning passion,
Kindle thy soul to perfect bliss,
Of earth and heaven I lose the vision,
Enraptured by thy melting kiss

Fridthjof's Saga
Esaias Tegnér

CONTENTS

PROLOGUE 11
CHAPTER ONE 18
CHAPTER TWO 29
CHAPTER THREE 36
CHAPTER FOUR 55
CHAPTER FIVE 62
CHAPTER SIX 70
CHAPTER SEVEN 83
CHAPTER EIGHT 96
CHAPTER NINE 107
CHAPTER TEN 118
CHAPTER ELEVEN 127
CHAPTER TWELVE 138
CHAPTER THIRTEEN 146
CHAPTER FOURTEEN 160
CHAPTER FIFTEEN 175
CHAPTER SIXTEEN 193
CHAPTER SEVENTEEN 208

CHAPTER EIGHTEEN	225
CHAPTER NINETEEN	242
CHAPTER TWENTY	259
CHAPTER TWENTY-ONE	268
CHAPTER TWENTY-TWO	280
CHAPTER TWENTY-THREE	288
CHAPTER TWENTY-FOUR	298
CHAPTER TWENTY-FIVE	313
CHAPTER TWENTY-SIX	324
CHAPTER TWENTY-SEVEN	333

DANETHRALL

PROLOGUE

KINGDOM OF THE EAST ANGLES, BRITAIN
Autumn, 865

THE DAY BEGAN much like any other. I hauled a heavy bucket filled with icy water from a nearby stream. With small thin fingers, I struggled to push away the stray locks blown into my face by the cool breeze.

The warmth and brightness of summer had vanished long ago. The emerald leaves of trees were now faded red and orange, the bright wildflowers that blushed across open fields had browned and crumpled, the balmy breeze had cooled. At that moment, however, the crisp wind was welcomed on my damp skin as beads of sweat slipped down the side of my face.

My village came into view, wattle and daub cottages with deep sloping thatched roofs. Smoke drifted from the chimney pots, animals grazed in the pens and people ambled along the dirt paths.

I reached the sheep pen attached to the side of my home, water sloshing and spilling over the bucket's edge. I plopped it to the ground, opened the gate and heaved the bucket again, slamming the gate shut behind me. I staggered to the empty trough and poured the refreshing water into it for the bustling, bleating flock.

"Aveline," my mother smiled kindly, looking up from her weaving as I entered our home. "Get some porridge, child."

Wisps of steam drifted from the aged black cauldron, hung above a low fire; orange tongues of flame gleamed as they licked the bottom of the pot. I grabbed a wooden spoon and gave the porridge a quick stir before ladling a helping into my bowl, breathing in the scent. My stomach growled fiercely as I shovelled a heaping spoonful into my mouth, immediately absorbing vitality and comfort from the bland breakfast.

I quickly finished my bowl and started scooping more from the cauldron when, suddenly, we heard screaming.

"Hide!" My mother hissed.

Her eyes were wide, and her face had lost all colour. Alarmed, I froze – I couldn't move! Fear had erupted in every fibre of my being. The yelling and screaming grew louder, foreign voices roared and laughed and bellowed, the familiar tongue of my people screamed and shrieked in terror. Somewhere outside I heard the long, low, eerie howling of a horn.

My eyes locked on my mother. I clutched the bowl and spoon so tight my hands began to tremble. Silent and panicked, she waved vigorously towards the far end of the house where a loose panel on the wall led to the sheep pen attached to our home, just big enough for my scrawny frame to fit through.

"Go!" She barked as she lunged toward me and shoved me roughly towards the end of our home.

The bowl and spoon dropped from my shaking hands and crashed onto the dirt floor.

Then I moved.

My body worked faster than my brain could register what was happening. I pushed the board aside and clambered through the gap, scraping and scuffing myself on the wood and nails as I awkwardly scrambled through. My mother swiftly shoved the board back into place, hiding me away.

I did not feel the searing little red scratches scattered across my arms and legs until after I'd dropped to the filthy floor of the sheep shed. The sheep were agitated and squeezed into the shed with me, bleating frantically.

I shrank into a corner, sitting down as low as I could, hidden by sheep. Between their jostling bodies I could peep through and see the horrors befalling my village. My whole body was shivering and shaking as the cool white sun slowly scaled up the sky. The porridge had climbed up into my throat and I instantly regretted eating so much so quickly. I desperately wanted to throw up, but I had to keep my mouth closed for fear of being found.

Then I saw one!

This invader, he was huge – he was a bear! Like a man-eating ogre of the tales my friends and I had squealed and giggled at. He was unbelievably tall, broad, strapping and muscled.

No laughter fell from my lips now as I studied the monster across from me. He had in one hand, a large, well-used, colourfully painted, round shield, with a domed iron boss in the centre. His other massive hand curled around an axe – a massively long post with a curved blade atop, spattered in dripping red. As he swung the horrendous weapon, his icy blue eyes glittered with excitement and his thick blond hair blazed like yellow fire from his head. His snarling jaws roared ear-piercingly from beneath the mass of his thick reddish blond beard.
He raised the axe.
He jeered.
He cleaved my brother, Kenrick, in the head.
I heard the sickening crack, saw the splash of scarlet erupt from the deep, gaping rend in my brother's skull. Half of Kenrick's face was crushed in; the other half still gasped in horror. The stench of blood filled my nostrils and the copper taste was thick upon my tongue.
That's when I threw up.
I doubled up on my hands and knees and vomited into the straw. Tears streamed down my cheeks, vomit cascaded from my mouth. My stomach wrenched in pain until, finally, it was empty.
Still trembling, still filled with terror, I peered my tear-blurred eyes through the legs of the sheep thankful that my brother's broken corpse was not in sight. The smell and taste of his blood lingered in my nose and at the back of my throat, but I couldn't see him.
My head throbbed from the screams that stabbed my ears. The foreigners' weapons crushed and cracked and slammed and slashed upon my friends and family ... all the people I knew ... I squeezed my eyes shut, unable to stop the tears from pouring, but all I could do was keep my mouth closed, my body shuddering from my silent agony.
My mother screamed.
I whipped my head toward the wall of my home. Thuds, slams, and crashes boomed inside. I heard my mother scampering and screeching, trying to get away. The deep voice from the intruder cackled and taunted her in his strange, foreign tongue. My mother

wept.

"*Modor?*" I whispered. "*Modor? Modor?*"

My mother, my dear mother, she screamed again, a sudden thump and her heart-wrenching cry told me the monster had hit her. Her screaming transformed to wailing and hysterical sobs.

"No, stop!" My mother howled. "No! Aveline, run!"

A shard of icy coldness impaled my spine, I felt my muscles tense fiercely at the mentioning of my name. I heard fabric tear, the cadence of fleshy thumps and steady blows, my mother sobbed and bawled uncontrollably.

"Run, Aveline, run!" She screeched again, before howling out an ear-splitting scream.

There was a sickening crack.

There was silence.

I ran.

I plunged through the sheep, flung myself through the gate, and launched myself through the village as fast as my little legs could take me. My mother's screams echoed through my mind, urging me onwards, motivating me to get as far away from this hell as I could.

I darted through the maelstrom of violent turmoil that devoured my everything around me. I raced so hard my lungs burned, my chest tightened like a vice, my mouth was desperately dry and sore from my gasping breath, and my throat still burned from vomit and bile.

As I bolted through our village, I spotted the tiny, limp hand of my baby niece, streaked with red, collapsed in front of my brother's home.

I ran.

I dashed.

I sprinted as hard as I could!

But unfortunately, I was just nine years old.

I was no match for these huge, full-grown monsters.

Suddenly, one of the beasts appeared before me, and I collided into him. He scooped me up from the ground with his arm around my waist. He laughed a deep, bellowing laugh. I hammered my little fists upon him, writhing and wriggling, kicking, and punching. The monster only laughed harder and cooed something to me in a high, jovial voice. He hauled me over to a group his companions, and all of them laughed and mocked me.

I was a rabbit caught in a trap, descended upon by wolves.

I saw them raping girls only a handful of years older than me, I saw them raping women my mother's age. I saw them beating and murdering men and boys ... women and girls ... I saw the bodies of dead children ... I wept but stopped flailing; I had given up hope of my own survival, instead I tearfully prayed that I wouldn't be tortured and that my death would be quick.

But I did survive.

They didn't beat me, they didn't molest or rape me, they didn't hurt me at all, physically. I screwed up my eyes and my body shuddered as I cried, and the man - the foreign beast, carried me away.

When I opened my eyes, I saw the dirty grey smoke rise from my village. I saw the ethereal orange and red flames grow taller, saw the homes and farms I'd known all my life fade to black and cinders. I watched as the blazing inferno devoured everything I'd ever known. I dropped my head against my captor's chest and heard his heartbeat, steady despite the chaos. I hated everything about this horrid man. I squeezed my eyes tightly shut again, and tried to imagine my father's embrace ...

The foreign man smelled an odd mixture of blood, musky sweat and strong soap, and his large, muscled arms were covered in a thick sweep of dark bushy hair. My father had been covered from head to toe in fuzzy hair, also ... I tried imagining this all not to be real, tried to believe that it was my father who held me and that this all was a dreadful nightmare.

But then he spoke.

His deep guttural voice uttered strange and bizarre words I couldn't understand. I listened to his peculiar language reverberate in his chest as it fell from his wide, thin lipped mouth, killing my wishful dream.

Another tear slid down my cheek as I yielded, heartbreakingly, to this abysmal, devastating event. With no energy left to sob or fight I simply stared forward, not seeing anything, not hearing anything, just staring into nothingness.

A long time went by and my captor dropped me inside a long, narrow ship, waking me from a slumber I didn't remember falling into. Panicked, I whipped my head around, and glimpsed terrifying, ugly beast heads perched at the tip of either end of the ship, and my body began to shudder and shake all over again. My captor snorted a laugh at me before he jumped into the ship and stomped down to the end to talk with another of his kind. His companion – I recognised him. He was the one who had killed my brother!

I tried to fathom my surroundings. The blood splattered foreigners swarmed the shores, their ships either moored or bobbing on the waters, so great a number, we hadn't stood a chance. My heart sank painfully in my chest. I turned my eyes away from the shores of my land and gazed down the length of the ship.

To my utter surprise I spotted some familiar faces huddled together down the deck from me. They were mostly women and were all older than me by six years or more; their clothing was torn, and fresh wounds and bruises swelled from their pallid flesh.

My heart stopped, and their mouths fell agape at the sight of me. I ripped my way down the deck towards them, and one of the women, Mildritha, opened her arms to me.

I collapsed into her embrace and bawled and sobbed into her chest, my cries muffled. Mildritha hushed me and stroked my hair, squeezing me closely against her as she prayed quietly.

"O Lord God Almighty,
Pity us the highest favour by preserving and guarding our bodies,
Free us from the savage heathens who devastate our realms.
Though we are lowly sinners, we beg of you, please take us under Thy shelter.
Repel the evil from us, we altogether implore thee.
We plead on our knees, to the king of glory,
Give us protection.
Praise be peace and glory, to the Trinity who is wholly most magnificent for the people.
Amen."

"Amen." I whispered.

When I had no more tears left to cry, I soberly peeked down the deck of the longship. There were chests brimming with coins, glittering jewellery, golden goblets, crucifixes, silks, and countless other treasures presumably stolen from monasteries they'd attacked before my village. They lowered yet more chests and trunks inside, things they'd stolen from my village before they'd burned it to dust and ashes. They even stole livestock!

The foreigners carefully and calculatedly loaded the goods onto their ships before they boarded, their clothes stained with my family's blood, with my village's blood. They arrayed their heavy, round, fantastically decorated wooden shields along the topmost planking of the ship's sides. The rowers got in position on benches, sixteen men on each side, they raised the vertically striped sail and the longships began to move.

"Mildritha, where are we going? Who are these people?" I stammered, clutching the fabric of her dress so tightly my fingers turned white.

"These are the Danes – the Norsemen!" She said gravely, her eyes darting amongst the foreigners. "And they're taking us to their land."

CHAPTER ONE

ROSKILDE, DENMARK
Winter, 870

MY EYES SNAPPED open, darting to the large rectangular raised fire pit in the centre of the room. The flames that had roared there the night before had smouldered down to nothing more than embers and ashes, allowing the bitter coldness to permeate my home.

Lifting my gaze to the small smoke hole in the ceiling above the pit, I spied snow whipping and whirling in the grey morning sky.

This was my sixth winter in Roskilde, Denmark.

The warriors of Roskilde had attacked my home in the Kingdom of East Angles in autumn, five years ago. They had slaughtered most of my village but had spared a few lives to take as slaves, and I had been of those few.

It had taken two terrifying weeks at sea before the Norsemen moored their ships in the harbour of Roskilde Fjord. We had arrived on the cusp of winter, on my tenth birthday. Afraid and with aching eyes, I had watched the Norsemen unload the stolen goods before they forced their captives to disembark.

My fifteenth birthday had passed just a month or so ago. I lived in a small farm, the adopted daughter of the very man who had kidnapped me, a warrior named Birger Bloody Sword.

I sat up in my bed, groggily acclimating myself with the cold. I had slept in a linen shift, thick woollen socks, and was swathed with fur blankets, but still I shivered. The chilled air raised goosebumps upon my flesh and clouded breath streamed from my shivering lips. I took one of the furs and wrapped it around my shoulders. My back ached faintly from sleeping on the hard, wooden bench, but it was better than the unforgiving packed dirt floor.

This time five years ago, I had been a captive in the Jarl of Roskilde's hall. There had been no space for me to sleep on the benches with the thralls, so I was forced to sleep on the cold, hard dirt floor.

I'd lived in the Jarl's fine hall for almost two months while my fate had been debated and bartered over by Birger Bloody Sword and the Jarl, Alvar the First One, the chief of the town.

The Norse had many kings – Guthrum, Ivar and Halfdan, for example – and then there were the jarls.

The jarls were rich, and held their wealth in property, followers, treasure, ships and estates. Alvar the First One had a mighty fleet of ships and owned masses of land in Roskilde. He also owned many thralls who had been taken and enslaved from different raids in various countries, to work it for him. When Jarl Alvar died his son, Vidar, would become the next jarl of Roskilde – should no one manage to gain enough support to oppose him, that is.

Karls were the next down – the 'average' people, the landowners, the freemen, the farmers, the smiths. Birger was a karl, a farmer by trade but more revered as a warrior.

Birger and Jarl Alvar were childhood friends and the closest of companions, which afforded Birger the ability to argue my fate with the Jarl. Though I hadn't known any of their Norse tongue, from Birger and Jarl Alvar's staring eyes and pointing fingers, I knew they were speaking about me.

It wasn't until the final night of their twelve-day long winter celebrations when Birger, a victorious grin blazing from his face, took me to his home. Alvar had finally *allowed* me to live with my kidnapper.

Birger had not taken me as his thrall, though. I had seen how thralls were treated by these people ... I may have cooked, cleaned, and tended his livestock, but I wasn't a thrall like the other Anglo-Saxons that had been captured.

Thralls were the lowest of the Norse societal ranks. They were slaves with no rights, or bondsman working off debts or crimes to those they'd wronged. I was somewhere in between, a thrall by my Anglo-Saxon heritage and a karl through my adoption to Birger. Some townspeople would refer to me as *Danethrall*, a cruel name that mocked my 'thrall' heritage and Birger's determination to have me accepted as a freewoman.

Birger had spent hours every evening carefully and patiently tutoring me in his language, among other things, to help me adapt to my new life. He had been patient with me, kind, his voice gentle and soothing. Within two years of his tutorage, I had finally become proficient in the Norse tongue and I had immediately asked him was why he had taken me.

"Well, little Aveline," Birger had said, gazing at me with his huge, deep blue eyes. "A long time ago, I had a daughter. You and she are incredibly alike ... same button nose, same big amber eyes, same dark hair ... same high cheekbones." He'd examined my face with fond reminiscence glazing his eyes – it was not me he saw before him. "By the gods, you even had my Astrid's scowl! You were so much like my daughter I couldn't leave you. Astrid died from sickness when she was nine ... four winters later, I raid a foreign country and find my daughter there already! I couldn't leave you."

Birger Bloody Sword hadn't taken me to be his thrall, he had taken me to be his daughter. At first, I was horrified he'd stolen another man's daughter to replace his own, but in a twisted sort of luck, his yearning, mourning and heartache for his beloved dead daughter had saved me.

"Is – is that why you and Jarl Alvar argued about me when I first arrived?" I had asked him meekly.

Birger nodded to me.

"Alvar refused to let me adopt you at first, because he was sure I would be driven mad. He thought I was chasing the ghost of my daughter. As I said, you and she are identical ..." Birger had explained. "Alvar also thought it too dangerous to give you freedom, my people and I had just raided your village and I had stolen you away from your home – what if you sought vengeance against me?

"I was willing to take the risk. I know you're not Astrid, but seeing your face brought me a happiness I hadn't known since she had fallen sick. It took a lot of convincing, but Alvar finally granted me permission, and I'm glad he did."

Steady, deep snores rumbled from the bed closet across from me. Birger was still asleep. I was glad Alvar had given Birger permission, too. Birger was the only person in this town who was kindly towards me.

Sure, Jarl Alvar had warmed out of respect for Birger, and Freydis the Jarlkona – 'Jarl's wife' – had been very welcoming to me, but others in the town also thought Birger mad to be so eager to adopt me, believing the same as Alvar, that Birger was chasing his daughter's ghost.

I rose and shuffled to the chest where my clothes were kept. I dropped the fur, unlatched the chest, and slipped my long, ankle length dress over the top of my shift. I shook the fur and folded it, before placing it neatly on the bench then I stuffed my feet into my leather shoes. Finally, I grabbed my thick woollen cloak and wrapped it securely around me, snuggling into its blissful warmth.

Quietly, I pulled open the door just a crack and the frigid air tore through. I lingered in the doorway for a moment, shielding myself from the ferocious wind with the door, reluctant to step into the frozen morning. With a longing glance back toward the fading embers, I took a deep breath and timidly stepped outside.

The snowflakes were small and hard, like smashed white pebbles tossed through the air. I clutched my hood tight with a shivering, naked hand, and charged through the relentless weather to the sheds a little way from the house, in search of chopped wood so I could tend to the fire inside my home.

I banged the door of the woodshed shut and leaned against it, recuperating from my arduous walk. I panted; puffs of white cloud streamed from my quivering lips. My cheeks, nose and hands were pink, throbbing and bitten by the chill.

"Aveline, *góðan morgin*." A soft voice said.

My eyes darted around the shadowed shed and I spotted the tall, broad, fur covered silhouette of a man. He stood by the high piles of split wood, basked in charcoal-grey darkness.

"Vidar ... *góðan morgin* to you. I was just coming to collect the–" I stuttered from nerves more than trouble with the language or the coldness of the season.

"Let me help." Vidar offered warmly, taking a log from the pile.

In the dim light his icy blue irises seemed almost white. Mesmerised by his gaze and the sweet, subtle curve of his smile, I stepped towards him and reached out to take a split log from the large stack. My shivering hands, dry from the coldness, stupidly let slip the log and it clattered to the ground.

"I'm sorry!" I squeaked, lunging down to pick up the wood.

Vidar chuckled softly at me as I rose, the firewood cradled in my arms like a baby. My face felt suddenly flushed and was significantly warmer than when I'd entered the shed. In embarrassment I avoided his gaze, instead I maintained a firm stare with the shadowed floor of the shed.

"Did I scare you?" Vidar asked, his concerned voice barely a whisper.

Vidar was double my age, an experienced, successful, well-travelled Dane, a remarkable warrior, an incredible hunter, and the Jarl of Roskilde's son. Vidar Alvarsson was an icon in his world, he was the apple of his father's eye and was in line to take his father's place as jarl when the time came. I was a fifteen-years-old Anglo-Saxon, young and clumsy, foreign, and unimportant. *That* was why his kindliness intimidated me.

"*Nei, nei.* I'm – I'm just cold." I finally said, still staring at the floor.

The cold, dry tips of Vidar's long fingers gently urged my chin up, until I looked him in the eye. And what beautiful eyes he had: around the outer edge of his ice blue irises was a cerulean ring, such a stark but beautiful contrast in colour, and the golden eyelashes that framed his eyes were long and thick.

In awe of Vidar's handsomeness though I was, nervousness still gripped my heart, and my fingertips had turned white from how tightly I grasped the firewood. It wasn't safe for me to be alone with a Dane.

Though Birger was my protector, I was constantly apprehensive around the Danes, especially without Birger by my side. What if one were to disregard the immunity Birger had bestowed on me? Thralls weren't protected from attack like Danish women were …

"I have a meeting with your father this morning," Vidar said as he reached for another split log. "And I realise, though our fathers are good friends, this is the first time we've ever truly met."

"*Já* – it is." I agreed, picking at the bark of the log I held.

"I wonder why that is?" Vidar continued, arranging the firewood in his arms.

"Poor timing?" I peered shyly at him.

"It must be." Vidar said, a crooked grin beaming from his face.

Unable to stop myself, I lowered my eyes to the firewood in my arms and smiled

"Let's hope this is the end of our bad timing." Vidar said.

He rested his hand on mine and, so surprised by his sudden touch, I dropped the wood. Deftly, Vidar caught it and smirked at me again.

"I caught it this time." He winked at me. "Our timing is improving already!"

Vidar took a few steps backwards, his eyes sparkled with mischief and that roguish smile still curved his lips. He turned and left the woodshed. I stared at the closed door for a few minutes, my lips parted slightly.

Suddenly I realised my arms were empty, Vidar hadn't returned the log to me. I rushed to the door, whipped it open and saw Vidar disappearing in the snowfall, in the direction of my home.

I stared, unbreathing, for a few moments as his bulky silhouette disappeared before I snatched a few more logs from the pile with numb fingers. I clung to them with one hand and gripped my slipping hood with the other, trudging outside after him.

The snowstorm had grown fiercer. Vidar's legs were long and strong, he had marched through this whirling nightmare with ease. I, however, stumbled slowly through the blinding snow as it whirred in a ferocious vortex about me. The howling wind thrashed my skirts against my freezing legs and my face and hands throbbed from the piercing cold.

Finally, I staggered through the door of my home, shivering, and thickly frosted with snow, to find Birger and Vidar standing beside the fire pit in peaceful conversation.

Vidar's faded bronze flesh glowed from the radiant copper of the flames in the pit. His long, thick golden hair dripped with melted snow, and tiny droplets slid down the side of his face. His head had been shaved but for the thick, dark blond hair on the top of his head, which he had grown long and had braided back.

Upon his strong, square jaw was a thick, neatly trimmed beard, full of gold, white-blonde and pale brown hues. Vidar was thirty years old and subtle lines were beginning to show around his icy blue eyes, more from the stress of life than from age.

He had removed his furs and hung them over a low beam close to the fire to dry. Without the thick bear skin cloak encasing him, Vidar's figure was less hulking but brawny still. He was broad in shoulder and his tunic sleeves were tight around his large, muscled arms.

The men laughed softly about something Vidar had said in a tone low enough I couldn't quite hear his words, then both turned to face me, beaming.

"*Góðan morgin*, Aveline." Birger smiled, striding to me. He took the wood and tossed it onto the fire. "How are you today, my *dóttir?*"

Birger had called me *dóttir*, meaning 'daughter', soon after the Jarl had granted him possession of me. I used to prickle uncomfortably every time he referred to me as such, the image of my real father appearing in my mind, but I never argued with Birger over it. As time went by, I found that I didn't begrudge the word anymore, instead I felt an odd mixture of comfort and guilt.

"I'm good, *pakka*. I'm fine." I murmured, eyeing the floor, and avoiding Vidar's warm gaze.

Birger squeezed my shoulders quickly with his worn, calloused hands, before pulling the sodden, bedraggled fur from me. He tossed the fur over the beam, beside Vidar's. I smiled appreciatively to him and rubbed my pink hands together briskly. I glanced around the room, briefly catching Vidar's twinkling eyes and half-smiling lips, before clearing my throat and hurrying to the back of our home.

Birger watched me, smiling, as I went about my chores. Thankfully he didn't comment on the pink glow that burned on my cheeks – he must have mistaken my blazing blush for the bite of cold on my face.

Livestock pens were located through a doorway by Birger's bed closet at the back of the small house. After quickly peeping through, I realised Birger had already let our little herd of sheep out for the day, so I rushed back to begin breakfast, gathering from the pantry cheese and bread and dried fruits to prepare, my wet skirts slapping against my lower legs.

"Vidar, eat with us, would you?" Birger said, waving a large hand in the direction of the bench by the fire. "Aveline made a delicious stew last night and we have plenty leftover to share for breakfast."

"I'd enjoy that a lot." Vidar replied, seating himself on the bench closest to me, watching me cut the bread and cheese and arrange them neatly next to the dried fruit on wooden plates.

The stew simmered in a plain, handcrafted clay pot, hung on chains above the fire that Birger had lit while I was out. The flames grew considerably as they ravenously devoured the logs Birger had added, the damp logs spitting and hissing occasionally. I glanced in the pot and carefully tossed a few of the heated cooking stones into the stew, to help it warm up faster.

Quietly I handed the two men their laden plates, nodding to their thanks. Vidar's finger grazed mine discreetly. I blushed fiercely but ignored him and rushed to retrieve bowls from the cupboard, and a ladle for the stew, all the while hiding my burning cheeks. Once the stew began to bubble, I scooped some into the bowls, and Birger began speaking again.

"Vidar has come to me with an offer." Birger said slowly, his voice muffled by a large bite of cheese.

"Oh *já*? What offer?" I replied as I handed Vidar his bowl.

I stole a glance at the blond Jarl's son as Birger paused to swallow. Vidar's ice blue eyes glinted with the firelight and his handsome face was covered with a vague contentment, a small mysterious smile, nothing more.

"There's to be another raid ..." Birger said carefully, avoiding my wide-eyed stare. "I have the honour of attending it. You will have to stay here, however."

"Where are you raiding?" I asked softly.

"Since I have no living kin to look after you, Vidar and Freydis have kindly and graciously offered to watch over you while I am gone." He said, ignoring me as he began to pace around the room, ingesting huge mouthfuls of his stew from the bowl clasped in one hand.

"Where are you raiding?" I repeated sharply.

Vidar's effect on my nerves waned as I grew agitated with Birger.

"I don't know if these bastards will leave you be with me gone, so Vidar will take my place caring for you. This way I know they will not touch you. With the Jarl's son and the Jarlkona watching over you, you should be fine."

"Where are you raiding? Why isn't *he* going?" I interrogated, much like an impudent daughter.

Luckily my cheek was ignored.

"My father is going on the raid. He's left me to run Roskilde in his place." Vidar explained nonchalantly.

"Where is the raid?" I glared eye to eye with the thirty-year-old warrior and Jarl's son.

"You know bloody well where." Birger snapped suddenly, pausing his pacing. "We're going to the Kingdom of the East Angles."

Hearing my old home's name out loud made my blood run as cold as the blizzard outside. Heinous memories flooded through my mind. I squeezed my eyes shut for a long moment, slowly opening them to give Birger a steely glare.

"You'll be staying at the hall with Vidar."

"I want to stay here."

"*Nei*, you'll stay with him. It is safer for you." Birger answered, pacing again.

"How ironic it is that you speak of my safety considering you are going to attack my homeland." I spat.

"In the name of all the gods, quiet girl, and know your place!" Birger barked, slamming his fist upon the tabletop. "You'll do as I command!"

I gawped at him, horrified. He'd never spoken to me like that before.

Vidar stretched his back and rolled his shoulders, apparently not at all bewildered by Birger's outburst. He tossed a dried strawberry into his mouth and chewed it quietly, eyeing Birger and me amusedly.

Fury surged through every fibre of my being.

"*Do as you command?*" I scowled at Birger. "Like a thrall? What happened to *dóttir*? Or am I only your child when it suits you?"

"*Dóttir* or thrall, I should whip you for your disobedience." Birger said sharply, glowering at me as deeply as I scowled at him. "Can't you see I'm trying to look after you? Whatever the irony, whatever the anguish you're feeling, you're mine! As my *dóttir* or my thrall, it doesn't matter which, you will do as I say. You will stay with Vidar while I raid your *old* land. That's it!"

Flushed red with rage, Birger stormed out of the house, the bowl of stew still in his hand, though most of it was sloshed across the floor. It was silent save for the howling wind outside. I could feel Vidar's gaze rest heavily on me.

"I know it's hard for you. It's hard for him too, you know." Vidar said.

I spun around and glared at him.

"He's racked with guilt over your past, but he's trying to protect you, as he has done for all of these years. You shouldn't be so quick to bite the hand that feeds." Vidar remarked.

A big, dark shadow of shame lowered over me. My hands began to shake slightly as I stared at the floor, my face still and lips pursed tightly. Vidar stood up silently and placed his empty bowl on the cupboard next to me.

"If you want to stay here while he's gone, you can. Wait until his ship has sailed from our view. Then you can return here, to your home. But you would do well to apologise to Birger and make things right before he leaves. They sail in three days to Skargerrak, to meet with the Norwegian fleet, then on to the East Angles. Make peace with this, Aveline, you can't change the past."

I stood cold to him, listening to his words but not moving. Vidar waited for a moment in silence before he left me alone in the house. I was frozen in spot for an age.

I hadn't wanted to anger Birger. Birger had always been kind to me. He had saved me from certain death in my village by taking me. I had never been a thrall to him, only his daughter. Those that had even referred to me as Birger's thrall in passing had received swift retribution from Birger – he was unafraid to defend me from anyone.

Most would only refer to me as Danethrall behind Birger's back – most were not stupid enough to say so to his face, lest they suffer the fury of Bloody Sword. One of Birger's friends had made the mistake of mocking me to Birger a few months after I had turned thirteen, and he had paid dearly for it.

Birger had taken me to Jarl Alvar's hall, where he, the Jarl and a few of their companions were drinking one evening.

"Bloody Sword, your little Danethrall is growing to be quite beautiful!" One of his companions had commented, taking a lock of my long, chestnut hair, and admiring it. "I see why you were so adamant to keep the girl; I wouldn't mind having her around either."

As his friend had begun to laugh at his crude insinuation, Birger had lunged at him and began pummelling him with his fists. It had taken Jarl Alvar and two of their companions to haul Birger from the one who had insulted me.

"Aveline is my *dóttir*!" Birger had roared. "Don't insult her again, or I'll rip out your tongue!"

That had been the first and only time I'd seen the 'Bloody Sword' side of Birger. His actions had terrified me, but deep inside me was relief – relief that I was protected, and this fearsome warrior was my defender.

Since then, no one dared touch me or say anything untoward about Birger's little *Danethrall* – at least not to my face, and if Birger had heard anything derogatorily said about me, he handled it and never told me. Birger was my shield, he was my shelter, he was the dearest person I had in this foreign land.

Snapping me from my thoughts, my large, long-haired, black cat Svartr crept out from Birger's bed closet, the door left slightly ajar since Birger had awoken. He twined himself around and through my legs, purring loudly. On the ground a little way from my foot was a hunk of stew meat, which had been flung from Birger's bowl during our argument. The gorgeous, fluffy feline spotted it and happily began to feast on it.

"Oh, Svartr." I sighed sadly, bending down to stroke him, his purring pleasure infinitely louder. "What am I to do?"

CHAPTER TWO

IT WAS NIGHT time before Birger finally returned home. I had changed into clean clothes, washed my filthy dress, scrubbed the bowls and cupboards, swept the floors, spun wool until my hands ached, made a fresh batch of stew, baked some bread, and fed and watered the sheep before herding them back into their pens.

I was combing out a wad of fleece on the bench by the fire, the occasional bleat of a sheep puncturing the silence, when Birger stomped through the door. He held the empty and cleaned bowl and spoon in his hand. I looked up at him, timidly.

"Stew?" I offered meekly, putting my work aside and rising.

"*Já*, please." Birger replied, matching my tone as he gingerly handed me the bowl.

I took it from him softly then stopped and looked up at him with big shining eyes.

"I'm sorry, *faðir*." I said, my voice just above a whisper.

Birger's mouth grew into a wide smile before he wrapped his arms around me, and I threw my arms around his waist returning his hug tightly.

"Me too."

After a long while in his embrace, I felt the weight of my sorrow lift from my shoulders. Comforted, our loving grips relaxed, and I skipped to the pot while Birger took a seat at the table. I ladled huge scoops of stew into his bowl and took it to him with a plate of the fresh, warm bread. I sat beside him closely; I was so relieved to have peace between us again.

"*Dóttir*," Birger said, cutting a slice from the loaf. "You must understand that your way of life and ours are different ... We raid because we must, it's part of us. We are a warrior people – war is in our blood, it's the only way we can reach Valhalla in the afterlife! To us, raiding is an honourable challenge to fight where I either gain my place in Valhalla, or I win the spoils." His deep voice explained in hushed tones. "We *had* to raid your village. My kings dream of ruling Britain ... so we raided the churches on the cliff tops and moved further inland, raiding the villages we reached ..."

"But it was my home." I whined quietly and pathetically. "My family ..."

"I know, child, but there was nothing I could do to stop their deaths. By the time I saw you, your family was already dead, and I knew I couldn't leave you. You saw what happened to the other women and girls – I wanted to save you from their fates. If I had left you alone, someone would've raped you and killed you. So, I took you."

Silence fell over us. Birger stared into his bowl on the table, absentmindedly tearing his bread into chunks.

"If I hadn't looked like your daughter, would you have saved me?" I asked tearfully.

"I may be called 'Bloody Sword', but I *don't* kill children or women, Aveline." Birger said staunchly. "Not all feel the same as me, however ... I bare not to think of what would have happened if you'd not resembled my Astrid ..."

I thought suddenly of Mildritha. She was the woman who had cradled me, a bawling nine-years-old child, on the ship as we sailed from our home with our heathen captors. Her three young children and her husband had been murdered by Danes. She had taken it upon herself to look out for me as best as she could on the ship and in Roskilde.

Mildritha had been in her mid-twenties when she was captured. She was very beautiful, pale as the moon with light brown hair and dark brown eyes and was bought as a thrall by the Jepson family. The older head of the family, Glúmr, was widowed. He had paid a decent amount for her, attracted to the lovely woman though she was decades younger than him, and had forced her into his bed every night.

He treated her badly, not caring if some other townsman would take her when they'd see her in the streets trading goods on his behalf, or when she was hanging washing to dry outside their home. Even Glúmr's sons, who were her age and a few years older and all of them married to Danish women, would rape her.

Mildritha became pregnant a few times within the first three years of living in Roskilde. In a rage, Glúmr would beat her. Another thrall in the town would smuggle some special herbs to her, to kill the child in her belly, and thus stop the beatings from her owner.

The herbs worked, but the fourth time Mildritha became pregnant was her last. I wasn't sure if it was the herbs or the beatings, or even the birth that killed her, but Mildritha had died and her baby was tossed to the wolves.

When news of her death had reached my ears, I remembered not being surprised. In fact, I had shockingly felt comforted by the news. Mildritha had lived in Roskilde for two terrible years, but thanks to her death, she would never be abused again.

"It's hard to understand ... This is our culture. I raised you Danish to save you." Birger said. "I know my lands and ways are still strange to you, but it's your life now. You must adopt it and accept it to stay alive. Nothing will take away the pain of losing your family, but I hope that one day you'll accept me as your family, just as I hold you as my daughter. All I want is to protect you."

"Aside from my appearance, I am not Astrid, but because of my appearance, you rescued me. Do you truly hold *me* as your daughter? Or do you just protect me to keep the image of your daughter alive?" My voice was brittle as I questioned him.

"Astrid is dead, Aveline." Birger replied in a low, husky tone. "I will always love her, but she has been dead for almost a decade. I may have rescued you because you look like her, but I love you because you are Aveline – *my* Aveline."

I didn't answer immediately. His words rang in my mind. The somewhat clouded faces of my mother, father and brothers swirled before my eyes. I understood Birger, I truly did – I had already accepted him long ago. But, as he had said, nothing would take away the pain of losing my family. As I gazed into his deep blue glistening eyes, I realised nothing would take away his pain of losing his family, either.

I sighed deeply.

"What would you have me do?"

Birger heaved himself upwards, straightening from his slumped position in the chair.

"I would prefer it if you stayed in the Jarl's hall with Vidar. He is a very honourable man and has given his word to keep you safe while I am away. I will be gone for a long time – this isn't just a raid; we are joining the Great Army. Many clans and towns are coming together to take on the Mercians and the Angles." Birger explained, still avoiding my gaze. "I need to make sure you won't be hurt while I'm gone. A lot of our people have accepted you as my daughter, but not everyone … I won't be here to defend you from the few who haven't – I need to make sure you aren't hurt. Vidar has promised to send thralls to tend to the sheep or at least aid you tending them. He's vowed he will do everything to assure your safety."

"Okay." I replied, hurriedly adding, "I appreciate that."

"I think it would be wise for you – for you to be married. You *are* fifteen." Birger said delicately.

My eyes shot open, as wide and round as plates.

"Married? To who?" I gasped.

"I won't be here to help you decide. Vidar could help you if you'd consider marriage a possibility … Is there – is there anyone you have your eye on?" A light pink rose on Birger's pale skin – he was completely avoiding my gaze.

"Ah, well, no." I stuttered, shocked to my very core. "I haven't even thought of marriage."

"Of course, not … well. Vidar can help." Birger cleared his throat gruffly.

"I'm the *Danethrall*. Who would want to marry me?"

"You're not the *Danethrall*. You are Aveline Birgersdóttir!" He said firmly. "I may not be a jarl, but I am a great warrior with a good name. I'm not rich, but we have land, a good home, livestock … you'd have a decent dowry. You've accepted the gods–"

My heart skipped a beat at this comment. I had hardly accepted his gods, I attended and participated in their rituals because I had to, not because I had faith in them.

"–You know our language, you have learned our ways, your maidenhead is intact – that in itself would fetch you a husband ... You'd be a good wife, Aveline. I'm sure Vidar will find you a suitable and acceptable husband."
I didn't say a word; I was far too surprised. Of course, even in my homeland marriage would be considered around my age. I had seen a lot of fresh-faced wives in Roskilde who were my age, or even a year or two younger. Some were with child, others had one already. I was of perfectly acceptable marrying age.
"How long will you be gone?" I asked.
"I don't know, *dóttir*." Birger sighed. "A time to be sure. Months, maybe a year or two. I'd like to be here for your marriage, but ... just in case the Valkyrie take me to Odin's table, I'd like you to be safely wed while I'm away."
"And you don't care to whom I'm wed?"
"Someone with money to them, would be nice." Birger chortled. "Someone you trust to protect you is what I want most. Be critical, be careful, be sure you're making the right decision." He nudged my arm with his elbow and added, jokingly, "The life of a divorced mother would be hard."
"Mmm." I murmured, giving him a small uncomfortable smile.
"Perhaps you'll meet Jarluf's oldest son? He is unwed, he's but a handful of years older than you – I'm sure you two would get along, he would make a fine husband! Perhaps Vidar will help, he's good friends with Jarluf's son – *já*, I'm sure he'll be able to help." Birger yammered, though I didn't know whether he was trying to convince me or himself.
I stood on tiptoe and kissed Birger on his cheek. He looked at me surprised.
"I'm going to wash the dishes, then go to bed." I announced.
The front door opened, and one of Birger's friends showed his head through the doorway.
"Birger! Come drink with us! In three days, we sail to war – we must celebrate!" The loudness and cheeriness of his voice suggested he'd already begun drinking.
Birger glanced at me, and I smiled and nodded my head. He

stood, dropped his spoon in his empty bowl and grinned at me quickly.

"Will be right there, friend." Birger said, grabbing his fur cloak. He turned to me. "Will you come, my child?"

I shook my head, smiling still.

"Enjoy your night, *faðir*."

Birger made his way to the door and paused to glance at me.

"I'll tell you more of Jarluf's son in the 'morrow." Birger promised with a grin.

I laughed and scuttled over to him quickly, placing another kiss on his cheek.

"Goodnight, *faðir*." I smiled, carefully closing the door on his beaming face.

I couldn't help but laugh, turning my back on the door. I unhooked the empty cooking pot from above the fire fetched the bucket of water from across the room. I hung it above the fire to boil so I could clean the items from dinner.

As I watched bubbles appear and pop on the surface of the water as it boiled, I thought of Birger's recommendation … Marriage. He thought it wise that I should marry …

"*Perhaps you'll meet Jarluf's son?*" I murmured under my breath as I pulled the bucket carefully from the fire.

Birger was right, I was of more than reasonable marrying age and I did have some qualities to offer my prospective husband. As well as speaking the Norse language and managing the farm well, Birger had taught me to hunt, read the sky and read runes, and had taught me the way of their gods. Whether I believed in the Norse pantheon or not, I could at least maintain the ruse that I did.

Birger did have a very good name, he was recognised far and wide as a loyal, fearsome warrior. Unfortunately, it was also well known that if anyone ever said anything disparaging to or about me, chances were high that he would beat them within inches of their lives. With that type of fearsome reputation, I wondered if anyone would dare agree to meet with Birger's daughter in fear of Birger's wrath if they decided they didn't want to marry me after all?

Even if Birger did manage to sway Jarluf's son to meet with me, the idea of marriage ... it was petrifying to me. I was fifteen, I was naïve – I had no idea how to find a suitor. I hadn't managed to even make a friend in Roskilde, how would I convince a man to take me as his wife? I had never been in a romantic situation before; I didn't even know how I was I meant to act in that type of circumstance. I had never kissed before, never even been alone with a man that hadn't been some form of family member ... Except for today when I was alone with Vidar Alvarsson.

Intimidated by his handsomeness, his station and the very fact that he was a Danish man, I had dropped every log I'd handled, stuttered through every word I'd uttered, and blushed ferociously throughout our entire conversation. Thank goodness it had been a short conversation ...

If my reaction to Vidar was anything to go by, I wasn't sure I'd ever marry unless I was lucky enough that my suitor would find my ridiculous clumsiness and shyness endearing.

I sighed deeply as I scrubbed a bowl with a dampened rag.

Would I be betraying my people and my deceased family if I married a Norseman?

What if I were to wed and discover my Danish husband had murdered my family when they had raided the Kingdom of the East Angles all those years ago? What if he had killed my brothers or father or had been the one who raped my mother? What if his father or his brother or uncle had murdered my kin and companions?

Though Birger concerned for my safety and saw marriage as the perfect way to guarantee me protection while he was away ... I couldn't. Among all these reasons, my naivety, my shyness, my guilt and my fear, the very reason for marrying hung heavily over my head.

What if Birger did die? What would I do without him? I didn't want to marry to replace Birger as my protector. Most of all, I didn't want to lose another father.

CHAPTER THREE

THREE DAYS PASSED quickly as I helped Birger organise for the raid. The town was buzzing like a hive in preparation for the raid – the men and women attending the raid had not been given much time to ready themselves. I appreciated the ability the Danes had to take everything in their stride, including the unexpected. At the drop of a coin, they were ready for anything.

During our preparations, Birger made me pack a chest with clothes and items I may want to take with me to the Jarl's hall. I assured him I could just go home and get what I needed should I need it, but he bade me to take things with me as a precaution. Rolling my eyes, I did as I was told, hoping to keep the day as light as possible before his departure.

Food and mead and beer were hauled onto the ships in great oaken casks, furs and weapons were also loaded. They were to meet King Guthrum and a fleet of Norwegians led by Norwegian Jarl Halvard Sturluson of Túnsberg at the Skargerrak, a strait that ran between the southeast coasts of both Norway and Sweden and the Jutland peninsula of Denmark, before sailing to the Kingdom of East Angles.

From conversations I'd overheard, the Norse army planned to surprise the Mercians and Angles by attacking in the middle of winter. Luckily the town of Roskilde was well stocked from a bountiful harvest, and we had a lot to spare to make sure that the raiders went on their voyage with no shortage of food.

It took the whole morning, but they were finally ready. At midday the mothers, lovers, wives, and children, plus more than a few thralls, had rushed to feed their raider men and women before they went aboard the long ships. Once their brave warriors were assuredly well fed, the farewells ensued.

Birger and I stood on the shore, watching the crowds embrace their warriors, watching the warriors take their places on the ships, their heavy, round, fantastically decorated wooden shields were arrayed along the gunwales. Already the intricately carved dragon or serpent heads were arranged on the bows of the ships, glaring over the waters ahead. Once the ships were in the open waters, they would fix the second head to the stern.

These Norse were a superstitious lot, believing the beast heads would frighten away spirits. The heads would frighten the evil sea spirits that might try to capsize their ships, but they were careful not to frighten the land spirits in case of negative retribution.

The time had come. Sadly, I turned to my adoptive father. Birger brought me against his chest, I wrapped my arms around his waist, and we squeezed each other tightly. I felt the sudden swell of tears in my eyes.

"I know we've had difficulties as of late, but I love you, my *dóttir*, and always have. Be safe while I'm away." Birger murmured.

"The same to you, *faðir* – Valhalla doesn't need you, yet." I replied, sniffing loudly.

Birger pulled away from me, his hands rested on my shoulders, and beamed down at me, before unleashing a raucous laugh from his thin-lipped mouth. He drew me to him again, still chuckling.

"The gods' already know my fate," Birger grinned, his cheek pressed against the top of my head. "We will see what they have decided, soon enough."

"Gods or no gods, please come home to me, *faðir*."

***

IT FELT LIKE an age had passed as I sat watching the ships glide through the water into the distance, my furs drawn tightly around my shoulders. Solemnly, my gaze followed the narrow but imposing long ships as they sliced through the sparkling white reflection of the pale sun on the glassy face of the calm, cold bay until they were nothing more than faded dots.

The sun slowly slipped down the pale lavender sky. It was still afternoon, but the light waned quickly and drew with it a bitter cold. The scenery around me was swathed in shadows of grey and the snow stretched across the land, twinkling silver and ivory. The trees around me and buildings behind were black and ash, even the townspeople were nothing more than faceless ebony shapes wandering hazily.

I crouched on a peak overlooking the bay, hugging my legs, my chin perched on my knees. Clumps of trees dotted the shore where I sat, dusted thickly with powdery white. The snow beside me has seeped into the neck of my little leather boots and melted from my body heat, soaking my socks. I was too consumed by thoughts to notice my freezing feet.

Lifting my gaze from the bay, dashing spots of light half-clouded my vision. I screwed my eyes shut and rubbed my forehead with the palm of my hand, sighing deeply. With a throaty caw, a bird flew close by to me, its skinny clawed feet tip-tapped towards me in the crunchy snow. It screeched at me again and beat its wings angrily as I stood up.

"Settle down! Are you *Huginn* or *Muninn*, little raven? Hurry and go find your brother." I snapped as a sharp streak of pain carved through one side of my head. "I have no news for your master. Go bother someone else!"

The raven glared at me with its glossy, beady eyes, and I noticed a milky cloud swirled in one of them. It cawed angrily again and noisily flapped off across the bay. I rubbed my forehead and began to stomp back to my home.

Along the way, I heard a commotion at a neighbouring farm. An older woman, Adhelin, and her husband, Hefni, lived there, childless, raising cattle for both meat and dairy. As I grew closer, I spotted Vidar Alvarsson talking with Hefni, who held a whip in his hand and a thrall crumpled at his feet.

Nervously I continued towards my home but couldn't stop myself peering nosily at the scene. Though my head was aching, I couldn't tear myself from the hubbub in the neighbour's pasture.

I grew closer and noticed a cluster of poorly dressed male thralls shivering in the snow a few feet away from Hefni and Vidar. One of the thralls held a rope in his shaking fingers, which was tied to the neck of a cow. All the thralls were watching Hefni and the Jarl's son.

Pausing at the perimeter of Hefni's land, I noticed that a fence panel on the opposite side was completely broken – there was a large, gaping hole, and the shattered remains of wood trampled into the snow. I strained my ears, eavesdropping into the conversation between the two men.

"He was meant to finish fixing the damned fence!" Hefni roared. "If he had done a good job, the cow wouldn't have escaped!"

"I agree, Hefni my friend. His work on the fence was inadequate." Vidar said, his voice soothing and smooth.

"I give him food and shelter and let him sell his hand carved rubbish at the market once a week!" Hefni continued furiously.

Hefni glared as he watched Vidar remove the furs from his shoulders and wrap them around the injured thrall. The thrall's legs and arms were covered in long scarlet welts and bloody wounds from the thrashing Hefni had inflicted upon him with the whip, and blood seeped through his ratty tunic from the lashes on his back.

"And he repays me by poorly tacking a broken fence together, rather than mending it, properly?!"

"You are most generous." Vidar nodded, rising to his feet. "But, Hefni, it is *winter*, and he is in rags."

"So?" Hefni kicked the thrall who quaked in the snow, fraught with pain.

"Tell me honestly, could you manage to mend a fence properly dressed as he? If you could, you're a better man than me, for I admit I could not!" Vidar grinned warmly, placing a hand on Hefni's shoulder.

"Well … the *slápr* lacks effort." Hefni spat.

"That may be, but when your flesh is shaking from your bones, with nothing but a dirty tear of flax wrapped about you, wouldn't you lack effort? I'm sure he wanted to mend the fence properly – didn't you, Holt?"

"Y-y-yes m-master Vidar-r-r." Holt the thrall stammered; a long, thin, bloody gash slashed across his face.

"I implore you, friend, allow the thralls to rest, give them something warm to eat. I will send a house thrall of mine to you, her arms filled with new clothes for your thralls. With warmer garb and a belly full of hot broth, I'm sure they will work harder for you!" Vidar said, his magnetic smile not faltering even for a moment.

Vidar's tone hadn't changed at all during this interaction. He was calm, he was friendly, he was kind.

"What if the cow had gone – or a pack of wolves had attacked it?" Growled the old farmer. "Do you know how much money I would have lost?"

"But the cow is here, safe and sound." Vidar pointed out gently. "I sympathise with you, really I do, Hefni. I will personally see to it that she is returned to her pen safely, after which I will fix your fence myself."

"*Nei, nei, nei*, you're Jarl Alvar's son – you can't mend my fence!" Hefni gasped, colour draining from his face.

"I assure you, though I am the Jarl's son, my work is indeed satisfactory." Vidar winked.

"Of course, it is!" Hefni spluttered, his eyes bulging from their sockets.

"Send your thralls inside for something warm to eat." Vidar pressed. "Let me see to your cow and mend your fence. I will even purchase your damaged thrall – he will not work well with the injuries you have punished him with, so allow me to take him off your hands."

Hefni stared in shock as Vidar took a hefty sum from the coin purse that hung from his belt and pressed the money into the farmer's hand.

"That should cover the thrall and any cost he may have caused you in the past. It should also cover what loss you *could* have suffered, had your thralls not managed to retrieve your cow. Now please, go and inform Adhelin and the house thralls to make a decent meal for the other thralls, while I take care of the rest."

The farmer stared at the glittering coins in his hand, astonished, as he staggered towards his home. He didn't even notice me, so surprised at his transaction with Vidar. I stifled a giggle as I watched the old man, before I turned back quickly to observe Vidar again.

Vidar harried the thralls together and lifted the injured thrall to his feet, tugging the furs to make sure they were tightly secured about him.

"Hefni is an angry, hard master, I can see." Vidar laughed, supporting the injured thrall as they stumbled towards the house. "Work hard and he will not thrash you. Though he is short tempered, he is prone to bouts of kindness that you can use to your advantage. Keep your heads down and do the best you can for the man, and he will reward you."

The thralls didn't argue, they only murmured in acknowledgment. They were all pink, blue, and white in the face from coldness, but all appeared to be hopeful by Vidar's speech.

"You're my thrall now, Holt; you will come with me to the hall." Vidar said directly to the injured slave. He then looked about the frozen faces of the other thralls. "Will one of you ready his belongings for when my house thrall comes with your furs and clothes? Hand them to her for her return."

They murmured in agreement.

Close enough now, Vidar noticed me. He winked and grinned at me, and I smiled back. With a stab of pain through my skull, I pinched my furs around my neck and hurried on my way.

By the time I returned home my head was throbbing; pain screamed in my eyes and ears. It was as though I had the blade of an axe wedged into my skull.

I blindly splashed cold water over my face from a bowl sat on the cupboard and threw myself onto the bundle of blankets on the bench. I snuggled into the blankets, laying on my side, and Svartr leapt onto the bed, gazing at me with his large yellow eyes. Cautiously, he padded over to me, purring softly. As tears trickled down my cheek and the bridge of my nose, Svartr peeped up at me and gently rubbed his head against mine.

"I love you, silly cat." I smiled weakly, as he licked a tear from the tip of my nose with his rough pink tongue.

He curled up next to me, I buried my face into his fur, and we slept.

***

IT WAS LATE the next morning when I woke. I'd forgotten to bring the sheep in and a nagging voice in the back of my mind demanded that I get up and check on them immediately. The delicious scent of food that had been cooked in the surrounding houses was still lingering in the air, even though breakfast should've ended a few hours before, from what I could tell of the noises outside and the light glaring in through the smoke hole.

The air was clear and fresh, and melted snow dripped from the rooftops in rhythmic taps. I would've fallen asleep to the gentle steady sounds had my stomach not began grumbling and growling.

"Oh Svartr, I think we're going to have to get up." I complained, looking at the fluffy feline.

He had encased himself in the fur blankets, perfectly spooned between my thighs and stomach, purring loudly. He opened one eye and surveyed me, as though he were not happy with the idea of leaving our warm cocoon. He shut his eye again, snuggled closer against me and purred even louder than before. I laughed quietly at his tender protest and reached my arm out of the furs to stroke him. I was hit by a surprising cold, realising quickly why he didn't want me to get up. The fire had died, there was a chill in the air, but hunger beckoned me.

"Sorry, darling." I cooed, trying to slip out carefully without ruining his little nest. "It's time for food."

I was still dressed in my clothes from the night before, but the icy air hit me hard when I exited the bed, as though I were wearing nothing at all. I quickly grabbed a few hunks of wood and tinder from against the wall and tossed them onto the pit, arranging them properly afterwards.

Shivering, I grabbed Birger's beautiful little fire steel, a basic C-shaped steel piece with ends curled into spirals, with a thicker hump on the inside surface of the long side. It took some effort, but the fire finally roared, gradually heating up my home.

I glanced around the room and melancholy settled over me. The house seemed a lot bigger and emptier now that Birger was gone.

Birger was a large man, phenomenally large. He was tall, he was thick around the middle, but not at all fat, he was muscled and strong. He had long reddish-brown hair, streaked with grey, always braided back. Birger had lines of age drawn over his face, and his beard was flecked with white and grey. He had big shining blue eyes, framed by crow's feet, and a slightly hooked nose, rosy cheeks glowing amid his pale flesh. Birger was a wonderful collection of contradiction, his face was kind and fatherly, but his body was that of a warrior.

He was a very capable and accomplished warrior, known far and wide as Birger Bloody Sword, due to the number of people he'd slain in battle. But for the one evening in Jarl Alvar's hall two years ago, I'd only seen him as the sweet, generous and intelligent man who'd carefully raised me into this Danish life, never as the fierce killer, Bloody Sword.

He had been married before and had lost his son and daughter to a sickness. Birger's wife had killed herself soon afterwards, consumed by the agony of the deaths of her children. I pitied Birger for his loss, truly I sympathised with him – I knew his pain.

My heart still wrenched at the loss my family, my parents, my brothers, my sisters-in-law, my three young nephews and baby niece ... I would never forget my niece's tiny chubby fingers, soft and lax, colour still fresh though I knew no life flowed, the long streak of her own scarlet blood trickling down her palm.

I pushed away those memories.

Though I had been in this place for just over five long years, I still had visions of my life before. Their faces had clouded, but I still saw my family. When I concentrated, I could remove the mist and picture them clearly. After our morning chores were complete, my mother and I would spend hours spinning and sewing, and after the evening meal was done, we would spin and sew again, squinting at our work by the firelight before bed.

I continued this routine in Birger's home, but every now and again my heart would stab as I looked up, expecting to see my mother beside me, but instead I would find nothing but empty space.

I wondered if Birger's warrior heart was hardened to memory, or whether he was also burdened with recalling the past at quiet moments? He'd saved my life due to my shocking resemblance to his lost daughter, but Birger never took another wife to replace his lost love …

I breathed out deeply.

Svartr's loud mew brought me back to earth.

"Right. Food then, shall we?" I asked the cat.

He brushed himself against my legs and mewed in agreement.

I loved this cat. He kept me stable and solid when the hurricane of emotions swept over me daily. He kept me sane.

"Aveline Birgersdóttir?"

I whipped around and saw a blonde slave girl's face peeping through the front door.

"Oh! Hallo, how can I help you?"

"Master Vidar sent this for you." She replied in Anglo-Saxon as she stepped into the house.

She carried a basket in her arms. I could smell the delicious food inside it from where I sat, freshly made bread and a rich stew. I met her by the door, taking the basket from her with thanks, peeking into it. A variety of cheese and dried fruits accompanied the stew and bread, plus a jug of icy buttermilk.

"Thank you so much." I smiled warmly, replying to her in my native tongue.

I hadn't heard a word of Anglo-Saxon since I'd been brought to Roskilde. It was wonderful to speak it aloud; my native language still so natural to me, though I hadn't spoken it in so many years. The thrall hardly returned my smile, though, instead she examined me shrewdly.

"You're a thrall like me?" She asked, her mud brown eyes narrowed into slits.

"Err, well. Not really, I–"

"*I know, I know.* Birger adopted you. But you were a thrall, captured from the East Angles, where they're raiding now?" She interrogated further, waving away my apparently insignificant reply. "Why would the acting jarl, the *Jarl's son* be sending a food basket to a *thrall*?"

I frowned at her, bothered especially by her emphasis of social positions. I straightened my posture, held my head high and glared at her.

"None of your business, is it? Thank you for the basket. You may leave."

I turned my back on her, dumped the basket on the floor next to the hearth, and sat next to Svartr, stroking his soft coat, and ignoring the thrall pointedly. She huffed then left, slamming the door as she went. Feeling somewhat victorious, I hurried to the basket and grabbed out the stew. I poured out a few hunks of meat and liquid into a bowl for Svartr then feasted ravenously on the rest.

The food was delicious, even if the deliverer was nosey and rude. I wasn't surprised at her reaction though, Birger adopting me was not something that pleased the others who had been stolen as spoils of war. I was free, they were slaves. I understood her anger, I understood her jealousy.

I was lucky.

I was protected.

All this thought of Birger, as I sat in our empty home, made me feel a pang of shame for not following his request to stay at Vidar's hall. I'd never been so completely by myself before and found myself craving the solitude, but I also wanted to honour Birger's wish. No matter the resentment I held over the past, he had done no wrong to me.

I chomped down on a clump of bread and thought for a long time. Many hours had passed, and evening was falling upon the land. I'd opened the door and let Svartr out, noticing the sky had darkened immensely.

I grabbed my fur cloak, wrapped it around me and raised the hood. From a split-second decision, I snatched up the basket and marched out of my home. I'd go and see Vidar before collecting firewood and returning home.

The streets were quieter than usual, most of the townsfolk were bustling around their houses, finishing chores, or looking after their children and setting them to bed. I noticed some thralls checking on farm animals, bringing them in to their homes or fetching wood for the houses' fires, doing the necessities to ready their homes for the night.

Most people paid me no notice. I was nothing but a faceless

inconsequence walking underneath a fur hood, heading meaningfully forth under the deepening darkness of the night sky.

I reached the Jarl's hall with no trouble, darting through the dirt streets, passed many houses. We lived in a small farm on the edge of the town, giving us plenty of room for our sheep to graze and peace when we wanted it, but still close enough to offer us conveniences, like Birger not having to stagger *too* far home after a joyful night of drinking.

The Jarl's hall was situated in the centre of the town, quite a winding walk from my home. I weaved my way through the well-trodden, labyrinthine streets filled with homes and shops. Rich-smelling wood smoke slipped upwards into the air through smoke holes, doorways and little gaps and cracks of the buildings. I bumped and squeezed by townspeople occasionally in the alleyways that thinned to nothing more than shoulder width.

The hall was a huge rectangular wooden building, much larger than any of the longhouses in Roskilde, with massive double doors at the entrance framed and sheltered by a finely carved portico. There were three wide, spacious steps that led up to the great doors under the portico, with ornate rails leading upwards on either side. The massive roof was wood shingled, unlike Birger and my turf roofed home, with large posts evenly spaced in tilted positions to support the huge outer walls.

Other buildings were littered around beside it, a bathhouse, a woodshed, the thralls' shed, plus a fenced in-area at the rear of the hall that was used as a peaceful outdoor sitting area for the Jarl's wife, Freydis.

The garden was the pride and joy of Freydis, it was filled with all sorts of beautiful flowers that her devoted and loving husband had snatched from the various places he'd raided and visited. When I had lived in the hall for two months, I would steal away into the garden when I had a chance, and examine every flower, admire every scent and every colourful petal. It truly was like heaven on earth.

I knocked on the door of the hall which swiftly swung open soon after my little fist had rapped upon it. The same blonde female thrall who had given me Vidar's message stood before me.

I was a step down from her, but I stared determinedly upwards to meet her glowering glare.

"You came then?" She asked snottily.

"Of course, the Jarl's son *did* ask for me." I replied snootily, pushing passed her.

I didn't care for this thrall. The words Birger had spoken to me before he left drifted through my mind, '*I need to make sure you won't be hurt while I'm gone. A lot of our people have accepted you as my Danish daughter, but not everyone ...*'. I'm sure whether I was born Dane or not, this slave would hate me regardless, considering her thraldom. I understood her emotions, I pitied her, but it was an awful world we lived in and her envy and loathing were a threat to me.

I shook my head quickly, attempting to shake away the horrid thoughts that had started creeping into my mind.

She's a threat to me ...

I knew where this thought process was leading and immediately blocked it out. I supposed I must've been more of a Danish daughter than I had realised. Half of me warmed, Birger would be pleased at my alertness and less-than-Christian consideration of dealing with this thrall, but the other half of me was disgusted at myself ...

"Aveline! You came, I'm pleased to see you." Vidar exclaimed upon sight of me, holding his arms out in welcome.

The walls in the centre of the hall bowed outwards, making it narrower at the ends than the middle, mimicking the shape of a longship. There were two rows of posts that ran down the length of the hall, supporting the roof beams. These columns separated the interior room into three long aisles, and two wooden partition walls divided the hall into several rooms.

The furthest room, to my left, was the Jarl and his family's sleeping area. I noticed the faint glow of the small circular fire pit in the room through the beautiful cloths that hung over the doorway, hiding the bedroom from view.

The commanding centre area was the main room, used to host everything from grand banquets and town meetings, to normal day-to-day happenings for the Jarl's family. It was entered from the double door entrance and held a huge, raised, rectangular fire pit in the centre of the room, that currently roared with copper and gold flames.

Two tables sat on either end of the fire pit, one had various spinning tools and an abandoned game of *Hnefatafl* forgotten on it. Lining the far wall were wide benches used as a platform, with a table and some finely carved chairs atop it. On the opposite wall were benches covered in furs and blankets.

It was very comfortable standing in this warm and welcoming room, with the furs and bits and pieces of cosy paraphernalia belonging to the family littered around.

In the main room the walls were smoke stained and bare, but for shields hung upon them here and there, and a warp-weighted loom that leaned against a far-side wall. I noticed in the corner near the loom, Freydis and two thralls were sitting in comfortable fur-covered chairs, spinning and laughing together.

To my right was the final room, the kitchen. There was another central fireplace there, with all sorts of pots and pans hanging over it, and yet another table where I could spy a thrall stood cutting and slicing vegetables.

The kitchen was full of casks and cupboards and bags of grains and oats, all sorts of different foods. There were shelves bursting with drinking horns and wooden cups and plates, and pots full of flowers littered everywhere, wilting from the fire smoke.

When I had lived in this hall five years ago, I would hide away from the Jarl's family in that kitchen. I aided the house thralls with their cooking, fetched buckets of water from the well or food from the store shed just outside of the hall, and spent a lot of time washing cups and plates.

I had been terrified of Jarl Alvar, nervous of Freydis even though she was gentle with me and scared of Vidar on the few occasions I saw him.

Soon after Jarl Alvar and his fleet returned to Roskilde from raiding Britain, Vidar had set sail in his father's stead, taking with him a fleet of refreshed warriors. He had been away raiding for much of the five years I'd lived here, so I had hardly seen him.

When I had lived in this fine hall, I had felt like a rabbit trapped in the den of wild predators. I couldn't understand their words, and they were the rulers of the murderous heathens who had destroyed my home. Birger had brought me to this hall on many occasions since I had come to live with him, and I wasn't afraid anymore.

"Welcome, my dear." Freydis smiled at me, catching my eye. I blushed and bowed my head to her as the tall, slender jarlkona rose and made her way to us. "I'm about to head into the garden. I'd be delighted if you two wanted to join me when you're ready."

Freydis was beautiful and tranquil, a welcoming looking woman nearing fifty years of age. Her long, soft, moonlight tresses were neatly plaited and tucked beneath her *hustrulinet* – a white, pleated fabric pinned to her hair, the symbol of a married woman. She was noble, elegant, graceful and intelligent, dressed in gorgeous finery, a serene smile painted upon on her beautiful face. She truly was the perfect jarlkona.

She winked one of her glittering emerald eyes at us, before she beckoned her thralls with a quick wave of her hand. The Jarlkona swiftly left with her thralls through the door in the kitchen area. Thankfully the hateful thrall went with her, too.

My mouth drew into a small 'O', surprised by her quick exit. Why was I suddenly alone with Vidar?

"I'm glad you've come." Vidar placed a large firm hand on my shoulder and ushered me into a seat. "Our fathers have set sail. Now it is time we talk about Birger's decisions."

Ah, *that* was why.

"Birger's decisions? Had we not made decisions of our own?" I asked, allowing myself to be led to the chair, nervous of what Vidar was going to say. "Did you speak to him before he left?"

"I did." Vidar admitted, sitting across the table from me and reaching out to fiddle with a stray *Hnefatafl* piece.

"And what has he convinced you of?" I asked stiffly.

Vidar laughed.

"For nothing more than a fifteen-years-old foreigner living in the land of the Danes, you have a very daring way of talking to a Jarl's son. Have you always been so bold?"

My face flushed scarlet.

"I can't tell if you're impressed or if you're threatening me." I replied.

"I would never threaten you. Never." Vidar said seriously.

I softened immediately, tilted my head and gazed at him; my lips parted slightly. Vidar blinked, but maintained eye contact with me, a smile curling at the corners of his lips after a few moments. I returned his smile and leaned back in the chair, wringing my hands in my lap.

"What have you and Birger spoken of?"

"He was insistent for you to stay in my hall while he is gone."

"Danes go on raids, leaving their women and children alone in their home for months or years at a time while they fight and plunder, risking never seeing their families again. Why are those loyal, beloved Danish women fine to leave alone in their own home, but I am not?" I said snidely.

"Because they were not Anglo-Saxons taken as plunder from a foreign land."

My jaw dropped.

"Those women have rights. If they are raped, they will punish their attackers, or their husband or father or son will avenge her, or the law will." Vidar was incredibly matter of fact. "As Birger has explained, some people have accepted you as his daughter, but not everyone. You are not officially a Dane until you've married a Dane."

"Ah, he spoke to you about his marriage idea, as well." I sighed, frustrated. "I cannot marry, I have no suitors and I have no interest in anyone."

"We will get to marriage. First, your living situation. He asked again if I could take you in and protect you while he's away and I agreed. I want to ask – why do you refuse to stay here?"

I dropped my gaze to my fingers entwined in my lap.

"I want to stay in my home. I have the sheep to tend to, my cat, keeping up the place while Birger is gone. I can't just abandon it." I said.

"You can do all those things during the day with a thrall to assist you. You don't need to be alone in that house all the time."

I rubbed my face with my hands before I looked up at Vidar.

"I don't want to live in your hall as a thrall, when I could live in my home as a freewoman." I admitted.

"We wouldn't treat you like a thrall." Vidar said firmly.

"*Já*, you would. I'd be better off in my home. Your little blonde thrall views me as a traitor to her and my heritage, and as you said, I'm not a true Dane 'til I have married a Dane – and I am *not* married." I said. "It would be a slow but sure process; I would become a thrall living here. In my own home I would remain free to tend my farm and my sheep, eat and sleep and live as a freewoman. Not here. Try as hard as you might, I would become a thrall, nothing more."

Vidar was silent for a long time, considering my words. I felt better admitting to him my concerns. He sat in quiet thought for a long time.

One of his mother's thralls slipped into the house, fetched a bottle filled with a liquid of some sort, glanced at us then scurried back outside to fill her mistress' glass.

The silence was as thick as the smoke pouring from each fire pit. My head began to spin slightly, and I heard the soft feminine laughter and muffled words of Freydis and her thralls outside.

I peeked at Vidar, who was lost in thought, lightly chewing his bottom lip.

Vidar wore a dark blue tunic, straight legged black linen trousers and leather boots. Fastened around his middle was a thin leather belt with a beautifully decorated silver belt buckle. Hanging from the belt was a leather pouch and his utility knife. A few shining silver rings adorned his fingers, and I could spy a silver arm ring wrapped around each of his wrists.

As I looked over him a blush rose to my cheeks. Vidar was extremely handsome. I began to feel awkward, having spoken to him so disrespectfully. He was calm and gentle, but the aura that he exuded … Vidar had the air of a king! He was beloved in his community and would be a powerful, magnificent jarl one day.

"Now we speak about marriage." Vidar finally said.

"I do not wish to be married." The words tumbled from my lips before I could stop them.

"In the name of all of Midgard, girl, you *are* demanding, aren't you?"

Vidar laughed exasperatedly at me, and I shrank back in my chair, embarrassed.

"You want to be a freewoman, but you understand that living alone would be dangerous with Birger not here to protect you. You understand you are not truly a Dane until you are wed to one, but you refuse to marry! What can I do to honour my promise to Birger, but make you happy at the same time? You're making this very difficult." Vidar was frustrated but not unkind.

It was my turn to think deeply in silence while he examined me. In the back of my mind my thoughts surprised me; I wondered what his opinion was on my appearance ... My plain, heart-shaped face was framed by wild chestnut curls that rolled all the way down my back to my buttocks. I was small and pale; my only great *womanly* assets were my wide hips – I felt like a tiny child in the presence of this worldly warrior.

"I don't know." I answered rather lamely.

"What if you were to just spend the nights here? You could wake in the morning, breakfast with us if you choose to, then the rest of the day is yours to do as you please, wherever you please. You won't be trapped here. But I will send a thrall with you, to assure your safety. Should anything arise he can protect you, or he can fetch me should you need me. You will return to the hall for dinner and stay the night here.?" Vidar offered. "Is that satisfactory?"

"So, for all intents and purposes, I will live with you, then?" I lifted an eyebrow up at him, suspiciously. "Who says anyone will even try to harm me, anyway? I haven't made any direct enemies since I *came* here."

"As you said, my thrall Hilda doesn't seem to like you." Vidar smiled and tilted his head almost victoriously. "Birger is a great man, very respected in our community. People know of his little Danethrall daughter–"

I glared at Vidar when he referred to me as 'Danethrall', but unfortunately, he had made his point.

"Just because they respect *him* doesn't mean they approve of you. And what of Birger's foes? Great men have enemies and those enemies usually hide in the shadows unseen until just the right time to strike."

"I shall remember that." I mumbled.

"Birger said you had a chest of clothing to bring here? You can stay tonight in your home to ready yourself. In the morning I shall send a thrall to carry your things here." Vidar suggested.

I nodded, relieved at least that I would get to spend one more night in my home alone.

"So, you agree to the terms?"

"*Já* ... I suppose Birger will be happy with this arrangement." I said tautly.

"I'm sure he will," Vidar smirked. "Birger was the one who suggested it to me."

My jaw dropped, and I stared at him in disbelief.

"You're very sly, Vidar Alvarsson."

"Have you ever played *Hnefatafl?* You must be cunning to win ... Here, let me show you."

Freydis, Hilda and the other two thralls returned a little while after Vidar had set up the game and had begun to explain the rules to me. Freydis took up some spinning with Hilda, who shot glares at me from across the table, envious of my enjoyment with Vidar. I glowed, basking in her jealousy for a moment, before I forgot her completely, lost only in my concentration for *Hnefatafl* and the pleasure of Vidar's attentions.

***

IT WAS THE dead of night by the time I left the hall. I'd eaten a delicious meal of boiled lamb with roasted root vegetables, buttermilk bread, dried apples and a large horn of ale.

The ale, though somewhat watered down, had made my head spin rapidly. I had stumbled a few times along the way before Vidar took my arm in his, holding my tiny hand in his large one. I blushed at this, but happily allowed him to lead me through the darkness to my home.

In my alcohol induced confidence, I chatted and giggled with Vidar as we ambled underneath the cold, star scattered sky, our footsteps crunching in the snow. At one moment I closed my eyes, listening to Vidar's voice, letting him lead me. My head spun again, so I quickly snapped my eyelids open and giggled quietly to myself, gazing up at Vidar. He beamed down at me and pulled me closer, wrapping his arm around my shoulders as we finished our journey.

The sheep were already crowding around the back side of the house, huddling together for warmth. Vidar and I entered my home, where the fire pit had settled down to a warm glow. He put some logs and kindling onto the fire while I opened the back door to the home and let the sheep into their pen.

I stood in the doorway bathed in shadows, watching Vidar build the fire. I smiled as I watched him bend to pick up wood, appreciating how he stuck his bottom lip out slightly as he concentrated on arranging the split logs just right, occasionally stealing an admiring glance at his firm, plump bottom ...

"There you go." Vidar said as he turned to me, the fire roaring before him, dressing him in dancing yellow, orange and red light. "You ought to know how to make a better fire, one that will last longer."

"Don't scold me after such a wonderful evening." I reproached, perching on the bench opposite him.

"I do apologise." Vidar smirked as he sat next to me.

He put his arm around me again, bringing me against him. I laid my hand on his hard thigh, closing my eyes and listening to the *thump-thump* of his heartbeat.

"You ought to get married." Vidar murmured.

"And who do you suggest?" I asked softly.

"You should be the one to decide that." Vidar placed a finger under my chin to raise my head to face him.

"I'm sure I'll find someone." I smiled as I stood up. "But – it's late ..."

"*Já*, it is." Vidar replied after a moment before rising from the bench.

Vidar kissed my forehead gently and my face turned pink. He chuckled quietly and stroked my cheek with the back of his hand, before swiftly leaving me to my solitude.

CHAPTER FOUR

Late Winter

"YOU'RE FROM BRITAIN? That's where they are currently raiding, is it not?" Kainan asked me as we trudged to my home.

Houses stirred with the quiet sounds of waking; the muffled clanking of pots and food being prepared, and the heavy plodding of sleepy occupants staggering around their houses. Kainan and I passed by a few thralls and farm owners, bundled up against the cold, tending to their animals.

It was early in the morning, three weeks since Birger had departed for Britain. Vidar had accompanied me to my farm and would assist me with my chores there, but today he had business to attend to elsewhere in the town. He had sent with me, instead, his field thrall, Kainan.

Still marred by sleep, I hadn't said a word yet to Kainan, and was slightly taken aback by the unabashed spite with which he spoke about the Danes. I understood his feelings, but his bluntness surprised me, nonetheless.

"Err – yes, I am." I said awkwardly, tucking a lock of hair behind my ear with my frozen pink fingertips. "W-where are you from?"

"Constantinople." The thrall smiled, shallow dimples appearing in his cheeks. "I believe these people call it *Miklagarðr* or some such nonsense."

I shot him a wry smile as I pushed open the door of Birger and my tiny house.

"When did you come to Roskilde?"

"I wouldn't say I *came* here, that implies I *wanted* to leave my land." Kainan commented. "It was eight years ago when I was sold to Alvar, though it was eleven years ago when the bastard Varangians stole me from my home."

"What happened?" I asked timidly as I began setting up a fire in the empty fire pit.

Kainan paused for a moment. I glanced at him; his slight frame bathed in the gloomy dimness of the house. He drew his hand through his ebony hair, which had been cropped short to signify his lowly position as a thrall, and beamed at me, a faint glint of light shining in his charcoal eyes. Shadows pooled in the hollows below Kainan's high, sharp cheekbones, making his gaunt face appear eerily withered.

"Constantinople is a great fortressed city – strong, magnificent! – but whilst my people were at war, we were left weakened ... that's when the Varangians attacked. They came so suddenly ..." Kainan explained, his Danish words marred by his Mediterranean accent.

I found his voice endearing, though at this moment his words brought goosebumps to my skin.

"It was summer – the sun was sinking down the sky and there were the longships – *so many of them* – stains on the water's surface ... The monsters leapt from their ships and pillaged homes, burned them, slaughtered so many of my people! But they took me and a few others as slaves.

"They worked us within inches of our lives, and they didn't waste their food on us. At night they beat us to unconsciousness, just so they wouldn't hear us groan or weep. One night I was sure I would die, and a terrifying sense of relief washed over me at the very idea of death ..." Kainan laughed, short and cold.

Meagre embers sparked to life in the pit, and I silently nursed them until the dancing flames had grown sufficiently. Svartr appeared and silently weaved between my legs, glaring at Kainan. I watched the fire as it devoured the dried-out wood logs, uncomfortably waiting for the thrall to continue.

"Alvar didn't give them much coin for me, so I wonder whether they'd wished they had killed me rather than let me live – was I worth the paltry money they received?" Kainan said. "But I survived. Being a Danish jarl's thrall was not what I intended to do with my life, but it is much better than being dead or in the clutches of the Varangians."

"What did you want to do with your life?"

"I wanted to be a sheep farmer." He admitted.

I couldn't stop the grin that erupted over my face.

"I'm glad to hear you say that – it relieves the guilt I felt over forcing you to accompany me for my chores." I giggled.

"*You're* not forcing me." Kainan remarked. "I'm happy to be here, regardless. But ... to be honest I don't have a clue what to do with sheep. My family and I were crop farmers, not livestock, and the Varangians didn't use me to tend to livestock, nor does Jarl Alvar."

I laughed at him.

"It's simple, come on. Beware of Audrey, though – she bites."

It didn't take long to tend to the sheep, most of our time was spent hacking the layer of ice that had formed in the water trough overnight and topping up the trough from the well.

When opened the door to the pasture and the sheep immediately trundled outside, seemingly eager to be released after being shut in their pens all night. The sheep were hardy against the freezing, snowy weather thanks to their thick woollen fleeces, but it was safer to keep them inside, away from predators and the dropping temperatures of the night.

Kainan and I huddled next to the fire, warming ourselves before our trek back to the Jarl's hall. Svartr glared indignantly and unblinkingly at us from the other side of the pit.

"Don't worry, silly cat, I'll be sure to bring you some warm food this evening." I cooed to the feline. He meowed angrily and turned his head from me. "I must bring something special for him tonight ... he's an ornery cat, but never usually *this* bad tempered."

"I'm sure Freydis will give you some stew or whatnot for him." Kainan said as he studied the fluffy black cat.

"She'd give me stew for a cat?" I laughed. "I didn't realise the Jarlkona would be *that* generous."

"She's an incredibly generous woman." Kainan confessed. "Though I despise these people and everything they stand for; I will admit that Freydis is a kindly mistress."

I knew that to be true. For the brief few months I had lived in her home, even though I had been nervous of her, I had seen how kindly she was to her thralls. She treated thralls better than any other mistress I'd seen. She would reprimand when needed, but was frugal with physical punishment, unlike other Danes. Freydis's thralls were careful not to betray or misbehave or risk losing their home with her.

Normally thralls would be fed fish, dried mostly, or porridge – any meagre meal their owner would toss to them. Freydis, however, fed her thralls well. She would make sure all her thralls ate vegetables and meat at least once a week. Freydis demanded every thrall in her possession received a decent breakfast after their morning chores and after her family had eaten – food of the quality she would eat her very self.

Freydis's house slaves were the lucky ones, though – they were allowed a hefty serving of whatever meal the family have leftover. Freydis befriended her house thralls, though they were still slaves the Jarlkona had a dear relationship with each girl in her home.

"A happy thrall is a faithful thrall." Kainan commented pointedly as he stood. "Come now, we should set off."

When Kainan and I returned to the hall, I reached out to open one of the double doors and paused for a moment.

"Thank you." I smiled timidly at him, only briefly glancing into his eyes.

"I look forward to tonight." Kainan smiled back, those charming dimples gleaming from his cheeks.

Kainan turned and began to walk towards the shed the field thralls were housed in, and I stepped into the hall. The Jarl's wife and son were sitting at the table enjoying breakfast together.

"*Góðan morgin.*" I said to Freydis and Vidar as I removed my snow-dampened furs from my shoulders.

Aaminah quickly scampered to me and took the furs. She whisked away around the corner, presumably to hang my furs to dry in front of the fire in the kitchen.

"Come, sit." Freydis patted the chair next to her. "Are your flock handling the cold well?"

"*Já*, they are." I nodded as I sat beside her.

"And Kainan was useful?" Vidar asked.

I smiled.

"*Já*, very."

***

Spring, 871

AND THUS, WAS my stay at Jarl Alvar's hall. I found myself spending most of my time there, much to the disapproval of Svartr. Though I had at first been dubious, Vidar was proven right – I was not treated like a thrall.

Vidar and I had grown very close, we had become friends, and he treated me like an equal, and I adored my time spent with his mother, Freydis, spinning and gossiping. Kainan and I had become steadfast companions quickly and easily, thanks to our daily excursions to my little farm to tend my flock of sheep.

"Feed me, woman, I am hungry!" Kainan whined.

The sun bore down upon the morning, hot and bright. Sweat dripped from our faces as Kainan and I stumbled into my home. We had just finished sheering my sheep, and the task had proved much more difficult and laborious without Birger's strong, capable aid. Though I appreciated Kainan's help immensely, it was his first time sheering a sheep, and it showed.

"The audacity of you – I should whip you for speaking to me like that!" I gasped in mock offence.

Regardless of his boldness, I fetched a dusty plate from the cupboard for him and wiped off the dust with the hem of my skirts.

"It wouldn't be the first time I've been lashed." Kainan snorted, helping himself to a fistful of the dried fruits in the pantry.

"Oh yes?" I commented, delicately arranging some dried fruit onto the plate.

Without saying a word, Kainan turned his back on me and lifted his shirt. My eyes followed the rough flax tunic as he raised it, gazing upon his naked torso as he revealed it to me. Shadows danced along his spine and pooled beneath his shoulder blades and in the dimples of his lower back.

Kainan's waist was narrow but his shoulders were broad, and there, like a spider's web stretched across his olive flesh, were the many silvery scars from his beatings by the Varangians. I clapped a hand across my gaping mouth, the plate wavering in my shuddering hand.

"I'm sorry!" I cried out.

Kainan murmured indistinctly as he pulled his tunic back on, hiding the deep, leathery white scars once more. He sat at the table and stretched his arms high above his head.

"I must say, though, that bite your sheep gave me hurt far worse than any of these." Kainan said adamantly.

I laughed softly and set the plate of dried fruit in front of him. I sat beside him and took his rough, calloused left hand.

"I told you, Audrey bites." I chided as I examined his hand.

The crescent shaped bruise on the back of his hand had healed to a faint grey shadow, but on his palm arched deep maroon scabs from Audrey's teeth. A week ago, the cantankerous sheep had bitten Kainan's hand as hard as she could, impaling every single one of her jagged, uneven incisors through his flesh.

Delicately I ran my thumbs along Kainan's palm, examining the healing wound on his hand. His hand was strong. It was calloused, rough and dry from the heavy labour he was set to everyday for so many years. There were many faint white scars marring his beautiful olive skin, accidental nicks from working with knives.

I gently ran my fingertip over each digit, watching his hand twitch every now and again as my tender touch tickled him. Kainan didn't laugh or say a word, though, he just silently allowed me to stroke his hand.

What was I doing?!

Suddenly I snapped out of my trance and looked up at him, horrified by my own forwardness. Upon his cheeks was a subtle rosy hue, and his lips were parted, curved into a tiny surprised smile. Immediately my face flushed to scarlet.

"Y–you need to be nice to Audrey. She's an old lady, you need to respect her." I stammered.

I dropped his hand quickly and jumped to my feet. I glanced around the room, urgently searching for something to do to relieve my nervousness and put distance between us, but I was frozen to the spot.

"I'll be sure to do better next time." Kainan promised in a soft, drifting voice.

I felt his fingertips graze my palm and glanced down to find him cautiously reaching out for my hand. The blush on my cheeks burned hotter as he entwined his fingers with mine. I squeezed his hand lightly, and he tightened his grip. For a few brief moments we gazed into each other's eyes, unblinking, our hands held tightly together.

"What is this, Aveline?" Kainan asked softly.

My lips parted, but no words came out. Slowly he leaned towards me, bringing his lips closer to mine, his shallow breath dancing on my lips. I couldn't breathe, my heart pounded violently in my chest and yet I felt myself drawn to Kainan.

What was this feeling inside me?

"We should return to the hall." I whispered.

The fantasy shattered as those words fell from my lips. Kainan pulled his hand away from mine and cleared his throat as he stood.

"Yes, of course." Kainan said, just as timid and nervous as me.

CHAPTER FIVE

KAINAN AND I did not speak of what transpired between us at my home that day. Not that I really knew what had happened to even speak a word about it. The next morning, we were equally skittish in each other's company. We hurriedly tended to Svartr and the sheep, quickly swept the floor where Svartr had disturbed the dirt whilst he chased mice, then we returned to the hall.

It took a few more days before we had overcome our shyness towards each other. Soon enough we were laughing and chattering incessantly with each other again, and that morning was quickly hidden away to the back of our minds.

"I must retire to bed." Freydis yawned, her dainty ivory hand covering her mouth. "It's far too late for a lady as old as me."

"Sleep well, *móðir*." Vidar chuckled.

"Goodnight," I squeaked.

"Have a wonderful evening, my darlings." Freydis cooed sleepily as she turned her back to us and stepped through the curtains to the sleeping area.

When Freydis disappeared, the curtains quietly swooshing shut behind her, Vidar rested his sword and whetstone upon the table and entered the kitchen while I continued to spin by the fire. It was bleak in the hall, so late at night that I could hardly see my spinning by the firelight, even as I squinted at it. I dropped the wool and the instruments onto my lap and rubbed my eyes with my fists.

"Aveline, come here, it's a beautiful night tonight." Vidar called.

I placed my things on the table and sleepily plodded out to him. Hilda crouched in the doorway of the kitchen, purposely blocking it by pretending to be too absorbed shuffling through a cupboard to move aside for me. I shoved passed her, and we shot each other a fiery scowl before I continued over to Vidar.

When I reached his side, I glanced up at the sky and, oh! It *was* beautiful! The pinprick stars were like tiny diamonds scattered across an onyx blanket, gently glittering their silver light.

"Hilda, fetch me a sheet." Vidar called without tearing his eyes from the sky.

Soon enough Vidar and I were lying upon a linen sheet on the grass in the garden, admiring the sky. Vidar had set a small fire a few feet from us, so we could see one another. It was so small we could feel none of its heat, but it flickered and radiated a pale orange glow, which we could see each other well enough by. Wrapped in the night, lying side by side, we chattered softly and meaninglessly about everything and nothing.

We spoke of Birger and Alvar fighting in the East Angles, we spoke of our futures, we spoke of our pasts. Vidar told me tales of his gods and goddesses, of his childhood, of his raids and battles, of his travel.

I told him of my family; of my brothers and parents and nieces and nephews, of the friends I used to play with, of the priest who used to travel to our villages and preach the word of God to us and taught us to pray and repent our sins.

"The Christian God admits being a jealous god, but commands that you don't covet your neighbour's belongings?" Vidar laughed. "How hypocritical."

"You're funny." I commented, rolling my eyes at him. "It seems hypocritical when you say it like that, but the two statements are not intertwined.

"Thou shalt have none other gods before me. Thou shalt make thee no graven image, neither any similitude of things that are in heaven above, neither that are in the earth beneath, nor that are in the waters ... Thou shalt not bow down to them, neither serve them: for I am the Lord thy God, a jealous God.

"God doesn't want you to worship idols of anything, because *He* is the only one you should worship. *Thou shalt not covet your neighbour's house, nor wife ... nor anything that is your neighbour's* is condemning theft and envy, greed, and jealousy in reaction to what other people have, and forbidding the intentional desire for immoral sexuality."

"But what if my neighbour's wife is beautiful, full figured, with amazing breasts and an arse worth dying for?" Vidar said.

"Then that is immoral sexuality and you must do everything you can to stay away from her, because she is a temptress and will lead you to sin." I replied matter-of-factly.

"I don't think I like your religion. If I saw a woman like that, staying away from her would be the last thing I'd do."

I burst out laughing at his comment.

"You would make a terrible Christian, Vidar Alvarsson."

"Thank the gods in Asgard that I'm an excellent Norseman, then." Vidar smirked, adding teasingly, "And what of you, Aveline? Are you a good Christian? Do you remember *everything* your priest told you?"

"I wouldn't say I'm a good Christian, but I do remember everything the priest taught, yes." I smiled to myself. "I lived in a small village with no church. The priest would ride to my village and preach to us every Sunday morning, rain or shine. It was very important for us to listen to him and absorb his words – he was our only link to God. Religion is very important to my people."

"Is Christianity still important to you?"

"I don't know … It used to be, but I haven't prayed to God in a *very* long time …" I replied quietly. "I have tried, but there was no sincerity or belief behind the words I said … only melancholy. So, I stopped praying. I fear spending eternity in hell, but if I did worship God with no sincerity in my heart, I would be condemned to hell any way."

"The Christian God will *not* send you to hell, Aveline. My gods will save you, fear not." Vidar promised.

I smiled at the determination that blazed from his handsome face. Our eyes were locked for a few moments, before turned his icy eyes back to the silver stars scattered above us.

"Maybe you should try to put your faith in the Norse gods?" Vidar suggested. "We aren't servants to our gods; you aren't forced to suffer. There is a sort of reciprocity between my gods and those that follow them, just as there is between a warrior and his jarl. If a warrior fights bravely and loyally for his jarl, then the jarl rewards him with his share of spoils from a raid.

"In the same way, if I want the gods to support me for whatever reason, then I make the appropriate sacrifice to them and they should give me what I ask for. My people have obligations to our gods, but our gods have obligations to us. The gods only ignore you if you're dishonourable or undeserving – if you don't offer a worthy gift to the gods in return for what you ask.

"They certainly don't punish you for lusting after a beautiful woman. Why, the gods themselves would admire her, too!"

I laughed softly but didn't speak any more about religion with Vidar. With fond reminiscence, I shared stories of my life before Roskilde, but it didn't take long for the memories to darken and my heart to ache.

For the first two years of living in Roskilde, I had prayed constantly. I wanted God to reach his giant hand from the sky, pluck me from Roskilde and place me back in my village in the Kingdom of the East Angles, where I would find my family, safe and sound.

For I know the thoughts, that I have thought towards you,
Saith the Lord, even the thoughts of peace, and not of trouble, to give you
an end, and your hope.
Then shall you cry unto me, and ye shall go and pray unto me, and I will
hear you,
And ye shall seek me, and find me, because ye shall seek me with all your
heart.
And I will be found of you, saith the Lord, and I will turn away your
captivity, and I will gather you from all the nations, and from all the places,
whither I have cast you, saith the Lord, and will bring you again unto the
place, whence I caused you to be carried away captive.

I prayed, but I wasn't heard. I sought Him, but never found Him. I wasn't returned to my homeland ...

I was angry for the longest time. Why did God let His people die? Why did He let me be taken here? I realised that I would never see my home again, never see my family again, and *He* had let it happen ... I was *so* angry! I felt betrayed by God and abandoned by Him. I felt like I had been disregarded by the one I'd spent my whole life worshiping, insignificant and discarded ...

The priest had told us many stories of those who had suffered because it was God's will. He said *ye are partakers of Christ's sufferings, that when his glory shall appear, ye may be glad and rejoice* ...

I was a child when I lost everything and everyone I'd ever known. It was cruel, it was painful, it was horrifying ... Why would it be God's plan to make a child suffer so? It was hard for me to rejoice for God and heaven, when all my family was dead.

As time went by, my anger turned to guilt for forsaking my faith ... I was scared. It had felt as though, like the flesh on my bones, Christianity had been with me from the moment I was born. Without the comfort of religion, I was lost, I was naked, I was incomplete.

Was I condemning myself to hell by not worshiping God? No matter how hard I tried to reach out to God, I was ignored. With every day that passed it became harder to pray until I just didn't even try anymore. Nothing changed, I wasn't punished, God didn't come to me even then.

I mourned the loss of my faith as I mourned the loss of my family. I had been angry that my family was gone, and I was angry at God. I had been scared to face the world without my family, as I had been fearful of life without God.

Though I missed my family, my heart ached from my longing for them, the agony of losing them gradually subsided. It would never truly disappear, but each day became easier. I had found comfort in Birger – he would never replace my family, but I loved him. He was truly my second father.

Slowly, it became easier to live without God, but there would always be an emptiness inside me from where my faith used to be. Losing my faith had been like losing a limb – agonising but slowly I had come to adjust. There would always be a scar, a shadow constantly in the back of my mind, but I could move on.

I could adjust.

The steady rhythm of Vidar's heartbeat beat in my ear and drifted my mind away from faith and religion. Nothing seemed to matter in that moment, but the star-studded black sky stretched above us and the night that cradled us. We had been comfortably silent for a long time before Vidar punctured our peace and broached with me the subject of marriage.

"For an unmarried man, you seem very obsessed with the idea of marriage." I scoffed.

"Firstly, I made a promise to Birger that I would look for a satisfactory husband for you. Secondly, I am a man; I can protect myself. You need a husband to defend you in case you ever need protecting." Vidar explained distantly, a light smirk playing at his lips.

My left eyebrow cocked upwards and my lips pursed tightly shut. I glared grumpily at the side of his head before I retorted.

"I have a jarl's son protecting me well enough, why do I need a husband?" I commented, feigning flattery, though a scowl was still fixed to my face. I turned back to the stars and released another deep sigh. "I suppose there are other positive reasons for getting myself a husband ... A man to defend me, a man to share my bed ... I can't just go around and *rape thralls* when I feel the need for sexual gratification, like a male Dane can."

"I'm offended!" Vidar gasped, choking on his laughter. "I'll have you know; I don't *go around and rape thralls*!"

"Oh no? What do you do then? You don't have a wife warming your bed, so how do you deal with your urges?" I goaded, a vivid blush glowing on my face.

"Though it's legal to rape thralls, I don't support it. Nor do I support the rape of any person, whether they are a thrall or an enemy of a land we're raiding – or *whoever* they are." Vidar said sternly.

He must have felt my gaze, for he turned to me. Noticing the teasing expression upon my face, Vidar grinned.

"My father taught me that it is better to lay with a woman who *wants* to lay with you, rather than one who doesn't." Vidar winked at me. "It's much more enjoyable when she's willing."

I rolled onto my side; my lips pursed into a failing attempt at hiding my smile.

"Then why do you not have a wife? Have you not found a willing woman, yet?" I sneered playfully.

"I've found *many* willing women." Vidar said, not rising to my bait. "So many, in fact, that it would be hard to pick *just one* to make my wife. Not to mention, I don't wish to pick just one – I enjoy wooing! I enjoy chasing! Roskilde is filled with so many beautiful women, I couldn't possibly settle for just one, yet. You have heard of 'the thrill of the hunt', *ja*? Well there is a thrill when hunting women – a thrill from earning my place in a woman's bed ... When I take a wife, my life will be dedicated to her, wholly and fully. I'm not ready for that yet."

"Oh, how *honourable* you are, Vidar Alvarsson!" I laughed. "Though I'm sure the women of Roskilde swoon over you for your morals, what do the men think of them?"

"My tales of conquest are much more impressive when women swarm to me for carnal affairs, rather than me forcing them to open their legs ..."

I laughed again and stared back up at the stars. My teasing grin fell from my face as I thought of the words he'd just spoken. I believed what he said.

He was Vidar Alvarsson, I doubted there were many women (or many men, for that fact) who would need convincing to share his bed. And even though I had teased him and mocked him, I knew he was true to his honourable morals – in fact, I was secretly one of the many women who admired him for his morals, in addition to his other traits ...

"What are you thinking about, Aveline?" Vidar asked after a while.

"Wooing, chasing, romancing." I said, closing my eyes. "I really ought to start considering marriage ..."

A noise of agreement hummed from Vidar's throat. His hand snaked across the linen sheet and clasped mine.

"Vidar?"

"Hmm?" He squeezed my hand briefly.

"I may tease you, but I really do hope my future husband holds similar morals as yours."

Vidar pulled me into an embrace in reply to my statement. My eyes snapped open and my heart jolted violently in my chest; I was shocked by his embrace but filled with an indescribable warmth as

I felt my body melt against his. He held me firmly against him, and I was not at all eager to be free.

I peered at his face and saw he hadn't torn his eyes from the stars. I closed mine again and enjoyed being wrapped in his arms, meekly laying my hand on his chest to reciprocate his affectionate gesture.

We didn't speak anymore that night, so lost in our own thoughts were we.

CHAPTER SIX

Late Spring

A FEW WEEKS had passed since that night, but still I could not stop thinking about Vidar. I smiled as his handsome face drifted into my thoughts, when I closed my eyes, I could even feel his warm embrace, feel his arms wrapped around me.

I could feel a blush burn on my cheeks. I shook my head as though trying to dislodge the memory from my mind before I rose from my bed and dressed.

Vidar was affectionate towards me, but never offered himself as a suitor to me. And why would he? I was brought to Roskilde as a captive and held for two months as a thrall. I doubted very much that I was marriage material for the future Jarl of Roskilde.

Vidar was a flirtatious man by nature, admired by so many, I was surprised that he was not wed considering the number of women he had to pick from. As he had said, though, he enjoyed chasing women too much to settle down.

Vidar would gift me the occasional kiss and embrace, but nothing more. We had spent an increasing amount of time in each other's company, he had even escorted me to my farm every day for the last few weeks, in Kainan's place. There was never an awkward or horrid moment when we were together, every word and action felt so natural when I was with him ...

No, I needed to stop.

Vidar would never offer himself to me as a suitor. Vidar was the Jarl's son, of course he wouldn't offer himself to me! But it was easy for my mind to drift to him, to fantasise about him ...

I shook my head again and sighed deeply, pulling open the door. I glanced passed the sleeping thralls at the doorway to the sleeping area, veiled by beautiful cloth curtains. Freydis was deep in slumber in her bed closet when I had awoken, and Vidar had been absent from the hall entirely.

I stepped out of the house without waking a soul. It was deliciously bright and warm this early morning. I was dressed in my tunic and apron dress, two turtle shell brooches, given me by Birger, were pinned to the straps at the front of the apron. There was a string of little amber beads hung between the brooches, also gifted to me by Birger. In one hand I held a small basket I'd woven myself; a jug of buttermilk and a bowl of fish stew carefully and tightly packed inside.

Birds twittered and chirruped in the hornbeam, fir and birch trees that were littered thickly around the town, flittering here and there in the branches as I walked closer by them. Luscious verdant grass grew thickly, covered in diamonds of the early morning dew. The sky was periwinkle, dotted here and there with a soft ivory cloud.

The shops were still as I passed them, but in a few houses, I heard muffled sounds of a few families stirring awake.

"Aveline! Aveline, hold on." I heard a male voice call.

I stopped and turned around to see Kainan's long handsome face beaming at me as he scurried to catch up with me. His olive flesh seemed to shine in the early morning light and his deep brown eyes glittered with happiness.

"*Góðan morgin*!" I cried excitedly, a huge smile spilling across my face.

"You didn't wait for me." Kainan said, offering me his arm.

"Vidar has been accompanying me. He was gone this morning, so I just left on my own." I explained. I was so elated to see Kainan after such a long time, I lost my inhibitions and laced my arm in his and leant my head against him. "Oh Kainan, I have missed you! It has been far too long since I've seen you."

Kainan took my basket and carried it for me as we walked together towards my home. We chatted happily together, laughing and grinning like fools. I hadn't realised how much I had missed Kainan and could feel a deep blush burning upon my cheeks as I gazed at his handsome bronze features.

When we arrived at my home, Svartr mewed indignantly and darted away from me when I reached out to him. He sniffed at the basket, excited for the meal I'd brought him, regardless of his surly mood.

"I'm sorry I haven't seen you lately." Kainan said.

I loved so much that he retained his accent through his years of living here. Sometimes on our walks I'd make him speak to me in his foreign language, though I couldn't understand it, I just loved to hear him talk.

"Vidar said you were busy working, that's why he had has been accompanying me here instead." I grabbed the broom and began sweeping the floor. "I – I've missed you."

Without the adrenalin of surprise, I was suddenly shy to admit this to him again. I glanced at him, my heartbeat racing in my chest. I sucked in a quiet, shaking breath to try to calm myself, but felt my throat constrict.

Beneath his thick black brows Kainan's dark eyes gazed at me in surprise.

"I missed you, too." Kainan strode over to me in just a few wide steps. He took my hand and pulled me against him. "Very much …"

I dropped the broom to the ground, and it hit with a soft thud. Svartr jumped and meowed angrily, before attending to his meal again, tail flicking irritably.

"I – err–"

I didn't know what to say.

My body was suddenly filled with a burning warmth, goosebumps prickled over my flesh leaving a trail of tingles where he touched me. Kainan's words made my heart skip a beat, his touch sent shivers through every part of me, but I felt a conflicting mixture of excitement and anxiety.

Kainan was a thrall. I was Birger's daughter! As Vidar had told me a long time ago, I wouldn't truly be a Dane until I married one … What would I be if I loved a thrall?

Kainan stroked my face with his long brown fingers, drawing his fingertips over my cheekbones and jaw. My eyes closed, and lips parted as he ran his fingertips down my neck in a delicious wave of sensation.

A shadow covered my face. The shining morning light dimmed through my eyelids as Kainan drew close to me. I realised I was holding my breath, but I could feel his, warm and shallow as it danced over my lips, before he placed a kiss upon them, as soft as a whisper.

Butterflies whipped like a hurricane from the pit of my stomach and my heart thrashed against my ribcage, almost painfully, as his mouth pressed against mine. Hesitantly, I returned his kiss, slow and unsure — I had never kissed a man before and I knew that I shouldn't kiss a thrall. I needed to step away from him, I needed to stop this, but ...

Kainan embraced me closer, clasping me against him firmly. My shaking fingers curled around fistfuls of his rough flax tunic. I pulled him against me, and refused to let go, overcome by the temptation of his flesh.

Kainan slowly slipped his tongue between my lips in a bid to open my mouth. Instinct took over me, and I opened my mouth to him, suddenly craving him with a desire I'd never known. I was sixteen years old; I had never been betrothed, had never engaged in any sort of romance before. I had been told of the dangers of being carnal with a man, especially out of wedlock, but all those who had warned me had underestimated the intensity of lust ...

I ran my fingers through his soft jet-black hair, my other hand still clutching his tunic. Kainan caressed and squeezed my body. As our kiss grew more passionate so did his hands, slipping over every inch of me. I felt the hardness of his desire against me, his sudden need for me.

Kainan took a step back, pulling me with him, taking me to the bench. He turned me, I felt the bench on the back of my legs and broke our kiss long enough to register where we were. I understood what Kainan wanted from me and fear began to mingle with my desire. He kissed me again and my mind emptied, focused on nothing else but the sensation pouring into me from his lips and his hands ...

I fell onto the bench.

Kainan climbed on top of me, using one of his knees to open my legs so he could kneel between them. I gaped at Kainan, gawping at the angular features and sharp cheekbones of his determined face, as he snaked a hand beneath me, grasping the back of my neck. He kissed my lips, my neck, my chest ...

I ran my hands down his arm, feeling the movement of his muscles beneath his taut skin as he slid his hand down my thigh and squeezed it through the fabric. Cool air suddenly danced over my naked flesh and I realised Kainan had lifted my skirts over my stomach. My eyes snapped open to see his bare thighs, covered in a soft down of black hair. His cock was against me, but not inside. In a panic, I jerked upwards, accidentally slamming my head into his nose.

"Argh!" He wailed, clapping a hand to his face. "Oh, Aveline!"

He rubbed his face, a trickle of blood leaking out of his nostril from where I'd head-butted him.

"I – I heard someone." I panted, scrambling out from beneath him.

I leapt from the bench to beside the fire pit and briskly smoothed my hair with shaking hands. My heart raced painfully in my chest, overwhelmed by all that had happened and what had *almost* happened.

"Are you okay?" Kainan's thick black eyebrows were drawn together as he frowned at me, sat on the edge of the bed with his trousers hanging from one ankle. "I'm sorry if – I just ... I wanted you, and I thought you–"

"It's just – I'm not, I *can't*–"

Kainan beckoned me to him with a wave of his hand and slowly I stepped towards him. He gently held my hips and pulled me closer to him until I stood between his legs. I rested my shaking hands on his shoulders, and he laid his head on my breasts. Our bodies squeezed together tightly; I could feel Kainan's erection pressed against me.

"I understand, you must wait 'til marriage." Kainan kissed me tenderly, but his disappointment was obvious. "But I'm nothing more than a thrall ... Would you even consider marrying me?"

"I'd have to ask Birger. I don't know whether I'd be allowed to or not ..."

My voice trailed off as Kainan cupped my face and brought me into a kiss.

"I want you, Aveline. There is a connection between us, I've felt it since we first met." Kainan pressed. "Have you felt it? Do you want me, too?"

I nodded slowly, unsure of what to do or say. Yes, I had felt *something* between us. Kissing Kainan, holding him, feeling his touch upon my skin – yes, I wanted him ... But, as Kainan himself had pointed out, he was a thrall.

"I'll buy my freedom and give you everything I can." Kainan whispered, unnerving me, it was as if he had read my mind. "I'd be a good husband to you, Aveline. Until I am a freeman if you feel for me as I feel for you ... Will you be mine? Will you wait for me?"

I didn't answer him, just closed my eyes, my forehead pressed against his, thinking wildly of all the words that weighed heavily in the air. Did I feel the same as Kainan? I didn't know – I didn't even know the name of what I felt. The carnality that had just burst between us, did it come from love? Whatever it was, I had enjoyed it. But ...

The title of 'Danethrall' hung over me like a heavy mantle. All Birger wanted was for me, his Anglo-Saxon adoptive daughter to be accepted by all, but I was still disapproved of by some. He had spent the last few years trying to dispel that name. By sending me to live in Jarl Alvar's hall I was protected from those who would treat me like a thrall and marrying a Dane would surely solidify me as a Dane ... but if I married a thrall?

"We mustn't tell anyone until the time is right." I finally murmured. "Just – just in case."

"Of course," Kainan smiled. "Just in case."

"Aveline, are you there?" Vidar's voice called through the door.

I leaped out of my skin, whipping my head to the door.

"Err, yes, one moment, please!"

I was frozen staring at the door, as Kainan attempted to pull up his trousers as quickly and silently as he could. I waved my hands at Kainan, panicked out of my mind, silently indicating for him to hurry. He pulled his trousers off his leg and dashed to the sheep pens, hidden. I stared at the pens for a moment, before scuttling to the door and opening it, hoping beyond hope that Vidar didn't notice a thing.

"Hello there." He said.

Vidar's lips curved into that damned smirk, and his eyes creased in the corners, blue and twinkling. My heart fluttered at the sight of him, my face was hot and hands damp and clammy from nerves.

"What are you doing here?" I shuffled aside so he could enter.

"You didn't wait for me." He replied airily, smiling but examining me quizzically.

"Ah, you're not the first man to tell me that today." I said quietly to myself, thinking of Kainan.

"Who else told you that?" Vidar asked.

"Oh, err—"

"I did," Kainan said, appearing fully dressed and tidy.

"Oh, you're here." Vidar said in an unimpressed tone.

My eyes darted between the two men, frantically.

"Yes, master Vidar." Kainan was unfazed. "Following your directions to accompany Aveline when she comes here."

"Good ... good. Well, you may leave now I'm here. I need you to go to Hefni's farm and herd their cattle. Hefni is in Britain and he took a few thralls with him. His wife is alone at the farm and some fences have broken but there are not enough thralls there to mend them and catch the cows." Vidar clapped Kainan on the shoulder as he approached, pushing the thrall towards the door. "I appreciate you accompanying Aveline."

Kainan nodded unsmilingly at Vidar and offered me a short glance before he left. Vidar shut the door tightly behind him and silence fell over us for a few long, nerve-wracking moments.

"So, the sheep?" Vidar turned to me. His smile was fixed to his face, but there was no sincerity about it. It made me tense. "How far did you get with them?"

"He had just gone to check on them." I rubbed the back of my neck anxiously. A swift *déjà vu* swept over me; Kainan's hand grasping the back of my neck, kneeling between my legs as I lay on the bench, kissing me lower and lower ... shivers ran down my spine. I cleared my throat quickly. "We hadn't started yet, just talked and saw to Svartr."

Speak of the devil and he will appear. I thought glaring at Svartr as he padded over, mewing and rubbing his head against Vidar's leg. The little demon feline had no issue showing his preference between the two men.

"Shall I help, then? Since I'm here." Vidar didn't wait for my answer, instead he strode over to the back of the house, glancing at the disturbed, ruffled furs on the bench as he went.

I raced to catch up with him, reaching him in the pasture. There was a large trough in the centre of the field, and a well not too far from it. Vidar had stopped by the trough, apparently absorbed by it, scrutinising something as he stared into the shallow puddle in the trough.

I didn't look at Vidar but inspected his reflection instead. His arms were crossed over his broad chest, his forehead furrowed, and he chewed his bottom lip as he always did when lost in thought. Nervously, I turned my back on him and made my way to the well. I tossed the bucket down inside the well until it splashed, the noise echoing up to me.

"So, what were you and Kainan so busy speaking about?"

I jumped, startled at the sudden proximity at which Vidar stood to me. He was immediately behind me, so close that if I moved an inch, I would've been flat against him.

"Why we hadn't seen each other in the last few weeks." I replied honestly. "We caught up with each other, we joked with each other, we …"

My voice trailed off as Vidar's hand rested upon my hip. I closed my eyes, unsure, uneasy. My flesh tingled as though a thousand bolts of lightning were weaved beneath my skin. With his other hand Vidar drew back my long, dark curls and bent over me to whisper into my ear.

"If you marry a thrall, you'll *be* a thrall forever." Vidar said darkly and softly.

I didn't answer. All manners of sharp-tongued replies floated around my mind, but I was still, unable to move or speak even if I wanted to.

"Birger wouldn't approve of that arrangement, you know that … and I can't approve of it, either."

"I know …" I breathed.

I felt Vidar's warm breath dance upon my ear; my flesh cropped up in goosebumps from the eerie way he spoke to me.

"If you've given up your honour, it won't make it easy for me to arrange a marriage to a Dane for you." Vidar continued, his voice still low, but somewhat musical, his nails digging into the soft flesh of my hip. "A Dane will certainly not marry a whore thrall."

"I haven't given up my honour." I growled. "I'm not betrothed to him, either."

Vidar traced a fingertip over the edge of my ear and down my neck, the fingertips of his other hand still pressing into my hip. I would've enjoyed his touch, but at that moment the hand on my hip was a vice, his fingertip on my neck and ear like the cold tip of a dagger being dragged across my flesh.

"Good." Vidar jumped back happily, a cheerful smile upon his face.

He walked to the opposite side of the well, gripping its aged stone mouth. Vidar smiled innocently at me, his eyes sparkling … he reminded me of Svartr moments before pouncing on a mouse; handsome, elegant and sleek, until the moment came when he'd strike …

"What are you thinking?" I asked suspiciously.

"Nothing," Vidar replied brightly, taking the rope and hauling the bucket upwards. "Nothing at all."

Vidar practically skipped over to the trough, pouring the water into it. He smiled at me jovially as he came back to the well to fetch more water, but we spoke no more as he went back and forth.

I didn't know what my opinion was of Vidar anymore, but I didn't trust him.

***

Summer

TWO MONTHS WENT by and our conversation by the well was not mentioned at all. I tried to avoid Vidar. I would try to sneak off to my home, alone, to tend to my flock and I'd remain there for the whole day, much to Svartr's delight, before reluctantly making my way back to the hall for dinner.

Of course, Vidar was up before me most mornings, and would take me to my home. If she saw me trying to sneak away before Vidar had woken, my darling Hilda would let Vidar know I'd left, but if he knew Kainan's whereabouts and mine did not correspond, Vidar seemed content.

Other than purposely keeping Kainan and I separated, Vidar was pleasant. Occasionally Kainan and I would have a chance to bump into one another, stealing a kiss or two while we were able, but nothing more, and not frequently at all.

One night, Freydis and Vidar brought up in conversation Birger's wish for me to be wed to a Dane. Obligingly, Vidar found a few suitors and over a couple of weeks he hosted a dinner for each of them to make my acquaintance.

Fortunately for Kainan and me, nothing came to fruition from any of these little meetings. To my surprise, Vidar had been extremely supportive and amiable during all three meals with my possible suiters.

The first prospective suitor was much older than me, only a handful of years younger than Birger. He was kindly and amusing but far too old for me to want to marry him.

The second was young, seventeen years old, lanky and skinny with an abnormally strong resemblance to a cockerel. He was dull but sweet enough, I supposed, but I could not imagine spending any longer than that evening with him, and that was long enough.

"May I introduce," Vidar said, his icy eyes glinting with mischief. "Jan Jötunnson, son of Jarluf."

I smiled. So, this was the man that Birger had mentioned all that time ago.

"Some prefer to call me Jan the Handsome." My third suitor winked.

Jan, the third of my suitors, was very attractive; he had deep blue eyes, long, light brown hair and skin as white as snow. He was ten years Vidar's junior, and the two were close friends. He was handsome and tall – so tall, he towered over all of us. He stood at least a head higher than Vidar, and Vidar was a tall man in his own right

"I'm pleased to meet you Jan the Handsome, son of Jarluf ... *Jötunnson?*" I couldn't help but laugh.

"I am called 'Jötunnson' because of my phenomenal height and strength – like an offspring of the *jötnar*." Jan bragged.

"By chance, was your mother a *jötunn*, or did she take one to her bed?" I teased.

"The *jötnar* blood runs through both sides of my kin." Jan smirked. "Though no one could blame my mother, had she bedded a *jötunn*, for there are many positive reasons for doing so. Even the gods took jötnar to their beds."

"And what are these many reasons, Jan Jötunnson?"

"Rather than tell you, I will show you, should we wed." Jan grinned.

Jan was the only suitor out of the three that interested me. Usually reserved in my manner, Jan brought out the playful side in me immediately. I had to admit, Birger was right. Jan and I got along wonderfully; we slipped into conversation easily and laughed sincerely and joyfully together for the whole evening. I even found myself delighted by his flirting and thrilled by his flattery.

By the end of the night I could muster no reasonable explanation as to why I didn't want to marry him, unable to confess my affair with Kainan.

Freydis sympathised for me, disappointed that none of their match making efforts had been successful. She promised me they would find an adequate suitor to my liking, questioning every so often why I decided against Jan considering how compatible we seemed, and how naturally we got along together. I could only smile and change the conversation.

Occasionally Vidar would offer to arrange more meetings for me, asking me questions about what I was looking for in a man to help him on his quest to find me a satisfactory husband.

He did not mention Kainan.

Vidar had been kind to me again, since his warning (or was he threatening?) me in the pasture. I wondered whether he might, in a very crude and offensive way, have been legitimately looking out for me? I remembered his bizarre, mischievous behaviour, the dark tone of his words ... If his intention was to frighten me from marrying a thrall or intimidate me from ruining my marriage prospects by losing my maidenhood before marriage (especially by giving it to a thrall), it had worked!

Vidar had vowed to Birger that he'd marry me to a Dane, and Vidar's honour was on the line if he did not keep his word ... Maybe scaring me was the best way, in his mind, to keep me from moving forward romantically with Kainan?

But ...

Though Vidar had never admitted that he had any serious romantic interest in me, I thought of the affection he would bestow upon me in tender, solitary moments ... These moments had lessened since our discord in the pasture, but fleetingly he would steal a gentle touch of my hand or sweep the hair tenderly from my face.

I thought of the occasional gentle kisses he would press against my forehead ... Did he harbour any fondness for me or was I just a prize from another chase, another hunt? Did he gain nothing but a thrill from trying to add me to his list of conquests, or was there any tender, sincere emotion behind his actions? Was it my best interest he was looking out for, or his?

Regardless of the reasoning, Vidar had become a knot in the otherwise straight thread of Kainan and my relationship.

I weighed my emotions towards Vidar.

I cared for him; he'd become a dear friend. His usual warm, caring manner to me had made his insult – deliberately labelling me a 'thrall whore' – hurt me more than I thought possible.

As much as I missed Kainan – missed being alone with him, missed him holding me, kissing me – I found myself missing the peaceful closeness and the compassionate rapport between Vidar and I, so much more.

***

"AVELINE! WAKE UP!" A voice hissed into my ear, excitedly.
"What are you doing?" I groaned.
"Shh!" Vidar held a finger to his lips. "Be quiet! You'll wake someone."

I got up noiselessly, rubbing an eye with my fist, trying to wake myself up. I glared at Vidar with blurry vision and realised he was fully dressed.

"Let me get dressed." I muttered, turning my back towards him to fetch clothing from my trunk.

Unexpectedly he was by my side in an instant, holding my hand.

"*Nei*, just come." Vidar urged, pulling me towards the door with him.

I glanced down helplessly at my white linen night gown and naked feet, before giving in to him. It was like arguing with a child – he had already made up his mind. I was groggy and irritable, in no mood to start an argument with him.

Before I had a chance to snatch up my cloak, Vidar pulled me out of the room and out of the hall entirely.

Vidar's hand was secured around mine tightly, leading me rapidly down the winding trail. I could hardly see a thing in the darkness, it must've been midnight or later. Vidar led me towards the wooden wall that surrounded the town. Pushing open the gate quietly, he took me towards the shore, the gentle waves lapping close by.

The moon and stars were dazzlingly beautiful, but the darkness obscured everything around me dauntingly. It took my eyes a while to adjust to the night thanks to Vidar's dizzying speed, and I was incredibly impressed by his agility in the night. After a while of scurrying down the dusty road that wound from the town to the outskirts of the fjord, we finally stopped at the entrance of a forest that edged and overlooked the bay.

I glanced at Vidar. Even in the darkness, I could see his pale eyes alight with anticipation and eagerness. He turned to me, smirking, and squeezed my hand excitedly.

"Are you ready?"

CHAPTER SEVEN

WE SLOWLY STEPPED into the forest; my hand still clasped in his. Vidar was noiseless and watchful, making his way through the trees directly and knowledgably.

I stumbled behind Vidar like a blind woman, stepping on all sorts of sharp sticks, twigs and stones; the pointed fingers of tree branches slicing my bare arms and yanking my hair. I groaned and grumbled and muttered all sorts of horrid things about Vidar as we ventured through the forest on his mysterious mission.

"Where are we going?" I demanded, panting breathlessly.

"We are going–" Vidar said distractedly. "Right ... Here!"

Vidar pulled me through a final tangle of branches to a small clearing that was raised upon a hillock, framed by a thick litter of shrubbery and arching trees. He tugged me to his side, embracing me with one arm.

"Vidar – what? *Oh!*"

Before us were the shadowed waters of Roskilde Fjord, a long and narrow sea inlet surrounded by the most incredible landscapes, dotted with many little islands and islets. Sandy dirt shores lined the bottom of the inlet, and hilly slopes and open fields bordered it, gradually rising above the level of the water. Bunches of woods were dotted sporadically about, and there was a vast forest of deciduous trees only a short distance from the city.

I could roughly spy the dark line of land on the other side of the fjord thanks to the pure, radiant glow of the full moon lighting up far more than I'd ever expected, its reflection wavering on the softly sloshing waves. My eyes had adjusted enough to the pitch darkness to make out shapes, but colour was near impossible to decipher accurately.

Suddenly, through the beautiful opaque surface of the fjord waters I saw movement – large bobbing blobs cut through the moon's glimmering reflection. I pressed my body closer against

Vidar, watching the blobs grow and grow, outlines defined. They became long and smooth, darkly coloured and glistening in the moonlight. Suddenly a deep, low noise emanated from the waters before us.

"What is that?" I whipped my arms around him and clung to him, terrified.

"Whales." Vidar grinned proudly. "Usually they don't come this far in. I was out here tonight and saw them, I thought of you immediately."

"You thought of me?" I asked, pleased to hear I had been on Vidar's mind, though my voice was faint.

I could not tear my eyes away from the smooth, streamline beasts protruding from the waters, splashing and dipping up and down, rolling around and singing that sound ...

"I've never seen whales in the waters of your land in all the times I've been there." Vidar said, holding me with both arms. "I thought you might be interested to see them."

I watched in awe and amazement as these monstrously huge creatures played before me, delicately they rose to the surface from the depths of the dark, glittering waters, to flop and glide peacefully together.

Vidar was right, though I had eaten whale here in Roskilde, I had never in my life seen such beasts. I couldn't imagine them to be true even as they frolicked before me! In their largeness, in their abnormal and bizarre appearance, the whales held a sort of grace and elegance that I couldn't explain. These magnificent marine monsters ... they were extraordinary.

When I was first brought to Denmark, I was told tales of thralls who would try to flee Roskilde by stealing boats, and their punishment terrified me ... I avoided nearing the fjord as much as I could and dared not get too close if I couldn't avoid it completely, in case I was mistaken for a runaway and dealt with in the same manner ...

"Do they ... do they eat people?" I asked.

"*Nei*, not at all." Vidar laughed.

"Then they are wonderful." I squeezed him appreciatively. "Thank you *so* much for showing them to me!"

After a while longer of absorbedly staring at the creatures, he guided me to sit beside the fire that I hadn't noticed was burning. The heat that radiated from it was strong, cutting through the mild night air and the tepid breeze that blew over us from across the waters.

I still embraced Vidar; my enthrallment of the whales consumed me to the point where I was too entranced to do anything else. Vidar didn't seem to mind. We sat beside each other at the foot of a fat tree trunk, leaning back against it, each of us entwined in the other's arms.

A long time had passed in complete silence until the whales began to glide downstream. In a while they would reach the open sea. The fire still burned hotly, but the reach of its glow had shortened.

"How often do you come here?" I asked, looking up at him.

"Often. I've come here ever since I was a boy. I'm sorry you were cut up along the way, I like to keep the path to this place as discreet as possible. The trees and shrubbery below us hide this spot from view from the water." Vidar said, glancing down at me. "In fact, you're the first person to come here with me."

I gaped, shocked. He chuckled at me and kissed my forehead gently.

"When I was a young boy, my father gave me a sword. It was fairly sharp but a tiny thing, and I thought it was the greatest weapon in the world. Well, one night, he and my mother were copulating – and loudly at that." Vidar scowled playfully as I giggled at him. "I'd had enough of listening to them, so I grabbed my little sword and left. I walked and walked through the darkness until I heard a noise."

Vidar was a keen and gifted hunter. His eyesight and hearing were incredibly acute. I could imagine him hearing the whales' song and by all curiosity following it. Their song was so unlike anything ever heard; beautiful and eerie in its haunting strangeness, so hard to ignore or to forget.

"I made my way through the forest, hacking away with this pathetic little sword." Vidar snickered, turning his gaze back to the waters. "I finally made it. I was lucky the whales remained; it had taken me so long to get here. I saw them, and I sat and stayed, shivering into the night, but I didn't care. I stared at them, mesmerised, until they left, then I returned home. I have come back most nights ever since."

"You're going to have to bring me along, now, too." I said seriously, answered by a snort of laughter.

"I'm so glad to have had such an impact on you, Aveline." Vidar grinned. "Though the whales don't come this far inland that frequently. Most times it is nothing more than sitting under the trees beside a fire, watching the water."

"Then we will do just that, together."

"I'd like that."

Vidar rose for a moment, grabbing his sword from seemingly out of nowhere. He grabbed a few logs of firewood and placed them onto the fire, poking at the ashes with the tip of his blade. As he carefully tended to the fire, I noticed he also had his shield, a bow and a quiver full of arrows on the ground next to where he'd been sat.

I tutted at him and teased him for having left them here while he fetched me.

"I had to make my way to you quickly, so I took the risk." Vidar said carelessly. He sat behind me this time, situating his legs on either side of me and pulled me against his chest. Though it wasn't a particularly cold night, autumn had only just begun, it felt nice to be nestled together with Vidar. "While we're here, at least, if a bear or wolf or boar come upon us, we'll be somewhat safe. Do you swim?"

I gaped at him for a moment, terrified at the thought of those vicious wild animals hiding in the dark, and snuggled against him nervously. His body encased mine, lending me a sense of safety, and he squeezed me gently, noticing my unease.

"*Nei – nei*, I can't swim, not really. I can paddle around like a dog, and float on my back, but that's about it."

"We will have to fix that." Vidar smiled warmly.

Silence fell over us for a few minutes before we began talking again. The whales had long since disappeared, it was as though

Vidar and I were the only people left in the world, and it was magnificent.

The breeze blew gently over us, growing gradually cooler as the night deepened, bringing with it the strong scent of salt from the water below. I closed my eyes, partially listening to Vidar, partially listening to our surroundings – the rustling and whispering of the trees and bushes surrounding us, the sloshing of the waters before us, my heartbeat gently thumping in my chest, calm and rhythmic, our breathing unified to the same pace.

I shivered slightly and regretted not brining my cloak. I glanced down at my nightgown; it was thin and had only mid-length sleeves that stopped above my elbows. Flowed before me, I noticed that dirt from the ground covered the hem all the way to my knees. There was a deep 'V' opening from the neckline to just below my breasts, and the breeze wafted the opening, occasionally showing a good view of the soft flesh of my cleavage.

Though it was summer, the night air was cool and covered my arms in goosebumps. I shifted in Vidar's arms, huddling deeper into his embrace. It was as if nothing had changed, as if the wedge between us didn't exist.

We spoke of our past *Hnefatafl* games, for we had not played it in months. We spoke of my weaving and sheep, and of the town duties he'd been attending to recently. He told me about previous raids and future ones and explained to me the aims of Alvar the First One.

"Why is your father called 'The First One'?" I asked, repositioning myself in his arms so I could rest my head on his shoulder and look up at him as we spoke.

Vidar chuckled for a moment before he answered me.

"My father is a leader; he always has been. On all the raids and battles he was the first one to lead the attack, shouting out 'I am the first one!' before going forth. He would always volunteer to be the first for everything. Soon enough he was 'Alvar the First One', and he did not need to volunteer anymore, it was accepted and expected, and he was happy." Pride emanated from the smile on Vidar's face.

"What do they call you?"

"Me? Sometimes I'm referred to as 'Jarl's son', but not much else – I don't have a byname like my father."

"Do you want one? Is that something special here?" I asked interestedly.

"Having a byname can be great or terrible, depending on what stands out with you most." Vidar explained. "My father, for example, was always the first one, so that's what he was known for. Bynames can be drawn from what you wear – like in the case of King Ragnar Loðbrók and his 'hairy breeches'. As you know, Jan is incredibly tall – as if he is the offspring of a human and a giant – so he is called Jötunnson, 'son of a Jötunn'. Bynames can be drawn from your age, where you're from, your kinship, your looks, the list goes on and on. They can be praising, or they can be condescending, whatever stands out most in connection to you as a person."

"I wonder what my byname would be had I been born here. Something better than *Danethrall*, I'd hope." I speculated bitterly, turning to face the fjord in front of us.

Vidar laughed at me and sat up. He leaned his head over my shoulder and wrapped his arms around me, squeezing me briefly.

"Perhaps, *Aveline Thrall's Wife*? *Aveline Once a Dane*?" Vidar teased.

I slapped his arm.

"That's enough from you!" I snapped. "I don't even know why you care about my friendship with Kainan. It hardly affects *you*."

Vidar carefully stood up and walked to the fire, holding his hands out to warm them. I rose to my feet but remained in the shadows of the trees, glaring at Vidar with my arms crossed over my chest.

"It affects me when Birger slices me from neck to stomach," he said, pointing at the base of his neck to his bellybutton. "For allowing his daughter to wed a *thrall*."

"Is that all you care about?" I demanded.

"I definitely care somewhat for my survival, yes. He is called Bloody Sword for a reason, you know." Vidar replied facetiously.

I rolled my eyes and sighed sharply, turning my head away from him.

"But I also care that you don't marry *him*."

"I'm not betrothed to Kainan." I sighed exasperatedly. "Who should I wed, Vidar? You offered me a man who could be my grandfather, a boy as exciting as filth on the floor of a horse shed, and Jan. Should I marry Jan, then?"

"*Nei*, of all the gods, *nei*! I only introduced you to Jötunnson because he and Birger both asked."

"I got along well with him – he is *very* handsome. I'm surprised he has spent three years a widower, rather than marrying again quickly ... Birger is very eager to have Jan as a son-in-law." I taunted, glaring at Vidar. "That's it, I have decided, I should very much like to marry Jan."

Suddenly Vidar was beside me, his hands enclosing my wrists in a vice grip.

"*Nei*." He commanded.

"Get off!" I tried to wrench my arms from him. "Why can't I marry him? Birger would be very pleased with that match! Jan is a *true* Dane – exactly the type of man you've been tasked with marrying me to. If you won't allow me to marry Jan, then, for all the damn angels in heaven, tell me, how do I please you?"

Vidar's lips crashed onto mine faster than I could blink. He held me against his chest with one arm, securing me against him with no hope of moving. His other hand was on my buttocks, squeezing, pressing, pulling my lower half against him.

I returned Vidar's kiss. I recognised the warmth of my desire growing, just as it had from Kainan's kiss. The moment Vidar's lips parted I did not wait for his tongue to probe mine, I parted my lips and met his tongue in a passionate clash. Vidar's arm around my shoulders slackened enough for me to wrap my arms around his neck.

I stumbled backwards, back to the tree we'd been sat at moments before. Vidar shoved me against it; the rough bark grazed my back painfully, but I didn't care.

We kissed and kissed until he suddenly broke away and staggered back a few feet.

I gazed at Vidar questioningly, my body tingling, my mouth thirsting for his. My hands trembled, still stretched out from holding him only seconds ago. My eyes darted over his body hungrily, as I gazed at his face, I noticed his expression – he examined me with the same craving as I had for him. He rubbed his bottom lip with his finger and thumb, shaking his head slightly.

"What's wrong?" I whispered, slowly lowering my hands.

"I won't dishonour you ... You're a Danish woman, I won't dishonour you." Vidar breathed, as though trying to convince himself.

I straightened my posture and slowly approached him. Vidar gazed at my breasts, my erect nipples pressed against the pale linen dress, easily spied through the thin fabric. I rested my hands on his chest and tilted my head to the side.

Vidar couldn't stop himself from touching me – delicately he glided his hands over my arms and back as he lowered his face close to mine. One of his hands rested on my hip, gripping it gently, and he brought the other up to hold my jaw as he examined my features.

Closer and closer his lips came to mine, before he paused in reluctant self-restraint, our lips only inches away. Vidar chewed his bottom lip, his ice blue eyes flickered as his mind raced with thought.

"Marry me, Aveline ..." Vidar said suddenly.

"So, *that's* why you hate Kainan and don't want me to marry Jan?" I asked evenly.

"*Já.*"

I furrowed my eyebrows at him as I stared into his eyes, my lips drawn together tightly in a faint frown. Tenderly Vidar leant forward and kissed me. Lost only for a moment in the sweetness of his kiss, I shoved him roughly away.

"Why didn't you just tell me that, rather than call me a 'whore thrall'? Why were you so wicked at my home?" I scowled at him fiercely.

"Because at that moment I wanted to kill you both." Vidar sighed flippantly.

"*What?!*"

"I heard you both. I heard the muffled moans and the movement. I've seen thirty-one winters, Aveline, I know what it sounds like when a man and woman fornicate." Vidar explained, turning his back to me as he slowly walked towards the edge of our clearing.

Vidar dropped himself lazily to the ground and dangled his feet over the edge. The hillock had a long, sharp fall ending in a thick cluster of trees and foliage on the bank, perfectly placed to conceal the clearing from those sailing on the fjord but offering an incredible view for us to spy from.

"Obviously you don't, since I didn't share my bed with him." I snapped, striding towards him. My desire for Vidar had vanished; I felt nothing but a horrid mixture of apprehension and fury. "I should push you into the fjord to drown!"

Vidar laughed and continued to stare at the waters, bouncing the heels of his feet on the muddy face of the steep earth wall below him. I wavered for a moment, tempted to actually shove him off the edge, but instead I collapsed to the ground beside him, rage radiating like an inferno from my body.

"The moment I entered your home and saw how dishevelled you and your blankets were, then when *he* walked out from the pens … I wanted to rip him apart with my bare hands." Vidar said.

He was very matter-of-fact and indifferent. I knew Vidar was serious, but what terrified me most was the carefree tone he used. Death – to kill and to die – was not at all a scary thing in his culture. But hearing someone tell me they wanted to kill me … that was horrifying to me.

"I wanted to take you on the bed he'd just made love to you on … then strangle you."

I shuddered; my eyes were as wide as plates as I gawped at him. Vidar looked at me and smirked at my reaction. He took my shaking hand to his lips and kissed it tenderly.

"I didn't make love to him." I repeated firmly, ripping my hand away from him.

"Then what did you do?"

"We kissed." It sounded ridiculous out loud. "He took me to the bench to … *go further*, but I made him stop."

"You hurt him? That's why he cried out?" Vidar asked, visibly attempting to smother his amusement.

"I – I head-butted him in the nose …"

Laughter streamed from Vidar's mouth. While he calmed himself down, my hands had stopped trembling and my face had turned scarlet, burning hotly with embarrassment.

"Then what happened?" Vidar asked.

"He asked if I'd consider marrying him."

"And you said?"

"Maybe."

It was his turn to gawp at me.

"Do you love him?" Vidar asked faintly.

I paused.

Memories of Kainan flooded through my mind. I stared across the fjord, remembering our time spent together in my home laughing or confiding in one another; the butterflies that whirled inside me from Kainan's touch; the brief moments of intimacy we stole every chance we could ...

"I don't know."

Vidar whipped his head around to face me, a small smile curling the corners of his mouth. His eyes were so wide, and his blue irises were so light, he looked sinister in his happiness. I was amazed by how quickly emotions could flash across his face and was unnerved that he could make even a positive expression so unsettling.

"You don't know?" Vidar inched closer to me.

"*Nei*." I replied stiffly, recoiling from him.

"Then marry me." Vidar urged. "If you loved him, you'd know it in your bones, as I know in mine that I love you."

"*Nei*. I don't know how I feel about you right now, Vidar." I sighed deeply. "I do know that I don't intend on losing my maidenhead to anyone before marriage, and I don't intend to marry just yet."

"I could offer you far more than Kainan or Jan or anyone else could."

"*Nei*." I repeated, staring into the darkness spread before us.

Another hour passed silently by; the fire had died so we began our journey back to the hall. I stumbled along slowly, my feet were bloody and aching from rocks and splinters. Vidar stopped suddenly and touched my arm.

"Let me carry you." Vidar said.

Hesitant, I glanced at my bleeding feet and nodded reluctantly. Vidar gave me his quiver to hold as he lifted me into his arms and carried me carefully through the tangles of the forest. His bow was hooked over his chest, the shield on his back and his sword on his belt.

I rested my head against his, my body safely cocooned in his arms. I could think of nothing but this bizarre man. A man who, out of jealousy, wanted to kill me for making love to another man, yet took no offence to my not loving or wanting to marry him.

Vidar carried me through the winding trails, passed many houses, and stopped at a well on the way to wash the stones, splinters, thorns and blood from my feet. With cupped hands Vidar poured the refreshing water on them, sliding his wet hands over my feet smoothly, wiping the dirt and debris with his large, strong, calloused hands. I enjoyed the sensation of him cleaning my feet, but I had nothing to say to him. His hideous words at the clearing still plagued my mind, repeating endlessly.

"Because at that moment I wanted to kill you both ..."

The sky was beginning to lighten.

We reached the hall and Vidar reached out to open the door, but I put my hand on his to stop him. He glanced at my hand rested upon his, before looking at me questioningly.

"You said it's better to lay with someone who wants to lay with you, rather than someone who doesn't. Yet you said you wanted to rape me? You wanted to *take me on the bed he'd just made love to me on?*"

"I didn't want *you* to enjoy it." Vidar said simply. "I also wanted to strangle you, don't forget." He added with a wink.

"I thought you were different to the beasts here." Offended, I ignored his ghastly humour, furious with him.

"I have never raped a thrall, but I have enjoyed many thralls' bodies. I have never raped a woman, but I have made love to many. I have never raped a foreigner, but I did share a bed with a few on my second raid in Northumbria who willingly offered themselves to me for their survival."

"That sounds like rape to me." I spat.

"They survived. It was a deal that we made together – an agreement. They honoured their end, I honoured mine." Vidar said.

"Vidar – you wanted to rape and murder me!"

"*Já*, I did *want* to."

I gaped at him.

"Want to, Aveline, doesn't mean that I would. I was under the impression the woman I loved had given herself to a thrall ... I was furious and heartbroken, and I wanted you to feel the hurt that I felt." Vidar shrugged his shoulders, glancing at me, his face innocent and plain.

"You don't love me if you wanted to do those things to me." I growled.

"I do love you. I want you as my wife."

Vidar bent down and lowered his face to mine, tilting his head so his lips could meet mine. Softly, gently, kindly, sweetly, he kissed me, and I was unable to stop myself from returning his kiss. My lips tingled as he pulled away from me. I staggered, appalled by his confessions, lightheaded from his tenderness, dizzy from the whirlwind of emotions engulfing me.

"I can't marry you, Vidar. There's a terrible darkness inside you ... I fear it – I fear you." I whispered.

I immediately regretted meeting Vidar's gaze. The pale morning light glinted blue and silver in his piercing, unblinking eyes as they flickered over me searchingly. Fierce and beseeching, sorrowful and intense ... I glanced away, unable to face him any longer.

"You asked why I was so wicked to you, and I answered you truthfully. Those were the thoughts in my mind when I caught you and Kainan. They were just empty words; I could never hurt you ... I'm sorry I scared you, I shouldn't have said those things."

"Would you kill me, Vidar?" I asked weakly, my mouth was dry, and my lips quivered.

"*Nei*, never ..." Vidar said softly. "I could never kill you or rape you. But, Aveline ... I *will* murder Kainan if he takes you away from me."

"You promised you'd never threaten me!" I cried.

"I'm not threatening *you*, Aveline. And I'm not threatening at all – I'm promising."

Vidar pulled his hand from mine and stepped into the hall, disappearing to the kitchen.

My breath was caught in my throat.

Slowly, I made my way to my bed and laid down in my filthy dress, slipping under the blankets in shock. I closed my eyes and didn't realise I'd fallen asleep, reliving our conversation even in my slumber.

CHAPTER EIGHT

Winter

AND OUR LIVES carried on. During the snowy months, I'd have to see to the sheep twice or thrice a day, to feed them, break the ice of their frozen water trough and make sure no starving wolf had attacked them, locking them up safely in their pens at night time. During the rest of the year, though wolves were still a threat, I didn't bring them in at night.

Surprisingly, Vidar had allowed Kainan to accompany me to my home again. Though I was happy to see Kainan again, my happiness was bittersweet. Since Vidar had promised to kill him, I felt uneasy being alone with Kainan. I tried to avoid being affectionate with him, but he was persistent.

When we were alone together, on and on Kainan would attempt to woo me with his fantasies of our marriage. Poetically he would describe all the ways he would love me and satisfy me, and how me loving him would bring him no greater pleasure ...

Though he was trying to romance me, his every mention of marriage and increased pressure for me to relinquish my body to him overwhelmed me. Kainan's lyrical, amorous words were daunting and made me apprehensive – rather than persuading me to lay with him, his words would deter me instead. What if Vidar was lurking outside listening?

I couldn't encourage a romance between Kainan and me for so many reasons ... What would Birger do if he found out a thrall had been wooing me? What would happen to me for accepting the advances of a thrall? What would Kainan do if I told him of Vidar's promise?

I was so young and naïve ... Though I shuddered under the pressure he'd exert on me, he was one of the few companions I had in Roskilde and I was scared to lose him. Kainan was an ally, he had walked the same path as me. I tried to avoid any physical interaction with him but the more I pulled away, the more tenacious Kainan became.

Mentally exhausted from evading Kainan's affections, a huge wave of relief would wash over me when Vidar would announce that he would accompany to my home in Kainan's place. Vidar hadn't today, however. Too busy at the shipyard, he had sent Kainan with me instead.

I released a deep sigh and leaned the long handle of the broom against the wall, dragging the back of my hand across my damp forehead. Finally, my chores were complete!

Like a spider, Kainan's hand crept over my shoulder, delicately sweeping my chestnut tresses aside. My body froze as Kainan's breath began to dance over my neck as he drew his lips against my flesh, the short ebony bristles of his stubble gently grazing me.

My eyes darted across the room – I glanced at the broom, the bucket by the fire, the cupboards of food, the sheep pens – but I could not find a valid excuse to evade his sweet touch. I squeezed my eyes shut and clenched handfuls of my skirts into my fists as he snaked a hand around my waist.

"Kiss me." Kainan whispered.

Involuntarily I turned, clamping my eyelids shut. Lightly his rough hand cupped my jaw and brought my face to his. Excitement fluttered in my stomach, I yearned for his lips to press against mine, yearned for his arms to hold me, but Vidar's words had struck a deep, uneasy tension through me. I was terrified that by being intimate with Kainan I might cause his execution.

Thankfully, Svartr's mewing pierced the heavy silence.

"Oh! I forgot to feed Svartr." I cried out, diving out of Kainan's arms.

I lunged across the room and snatched the jug of buttermilk and Svartr's bowl, hurriedly busying myself with the feline. I shot Kainan a few fleeting glances, my heart racing. His shoulders had slumped, his brown arms were crossed over his chest, and he shifted agitatedly where he stood.

"We haven't kissed in a long time." Kainan complained, his thick black brows knitted in obvious frustration. "There always seems to be some reason."

He sighed shortly, and a faint irritated laugh slipped from his frowning lips.

"I just – I remembered Svartr." I licked my lips nervously. "I've been busy – I–"

"Yes, yes, I remember every excuse, you don't need to repeat them." Kainan flung his arms behind his head and stomped back and forth. Suddenly he stopped and glared at me. "Your eyes might be orange like fire, but there has been no warmth from you for some time now!"

"Kainan!" My jaw dropped, and eyes grew wide. "I just–"

"*I know!*" Kainan snapped as he stormed to the door.

"I'm sorry!"

I dropped the jug with a clatter and splash and scurried towards him. Kainan's glare softened and, though his forehead was still furrowed, his mouth had relaxed

"I'm sorry." I repeated, squeezing his hand between both of mine. The itchy fibres from the hem of his flax shirt scratched my fingertips, but I ignored the unpleasant sensation and gazed at Kainan pleadingly. "Please forgive me."

A tender smile curled his lips and his eyebrows lifted.

"Always."

And Kainan kissed me.

For the first time in weeks, Kainan kissed me. I couldn't avoid his touch any longer – and yet … this kiss, it was … different.

I felt no passion; no wave of goosebumps swept across my flesh. My heart did not skip a beat, instead, like a ship destroyed by a furious sea, my heart sunk heavily in my chest. I returned Kainan's kiss meekly, but he didn't mind or seem to notice.

A kiss was a kiss.

I had pacified him.

Thank the gods in Asgard, for weeks I had pacified Kainan! With a tender sweep of my hand upon his, a timid kiss placed upon his eager lips, the warmth of our bodies enclosed around one another … He was placated.

Allowing Kainan the affection he craved and deserved, fleeting moments of breathlessly kissing, embraced together tightly, calmed his confusion and frustration. Though my mind still raced with worry and anxiety when he and I were alone together, I tried to make him happy.

Sometimes it wasn't enough for him. My sudden distantness was noticeable, and occasionally Kainan would become irritated by me and say hurtful things. I reasoned his tantrums – of course he was upset. Not long ago, we were lovers; I happily participated in our forbidden affair, stealing kisses from him in the shadows, holding him in my arms behind locked doors ...

The sudden change in me was not Kainan's fault. I couldn't even offer him an explanation or tell him of Vidar's promise, lest Kainan do something foolish like challenge Vidar ...

Kainan's tantrums filled me with guilt, other times he intimidated me with the tenacity and assertiveness of his affections. Though Kainan knew where my boundaries were for sharing my bed outside of marriage, in the heat of the moment he would try to take me. Driven by fervour, he'd lift my skirts or try to undress me, and I would shove him away. Emblazoned by lust, I wanted him, but I refused to abandon my inhibition.

"That's enough," I panted, pushing Kainan away and stumbling to the kitchen cupboard.

With trembling fingers, I took the torn strap of my dress and briefly examined it – even with my head spinning I could see the frayed rip. Kainan's gaze was heavy upon me, with a glance I caught him staring, longingly, at my breast – the pink of my nipple delicately peeped through the almost sheer white fabric of my shift. He had torn the strap of my dress when he attempted to undress me.

"It's hard to resist you, Aveline. I want to feel the warmth of your body against mine ..." Kainan murmured, watching me attempt to pin the strap back to the dress with the brooch. "I dream of our wedding night – dream of your beautiful body beneath me, mine to admire and to touch ..."

In less than a handful of steps Kainan was beside me, pulling me against him once more. He pressed a pining kiss against my tingling lips. In my fist I squeezed the brooch. He ran his hand over my breast and held the frayed end of my broken strap.

"It maddens me that I cannot call you wife, yet." Kainan complained, resting his forehead against mine. "How blessed I'll be to lay beside you in our wedding bed, to be able to call you mine! To feel the soft flesh of your thighs clasped around my body as I–"

"You must be patient!" My face burned hotly at his words.

"I am trying, I truly am." Kainan fiddled with my broken strap between his finger and thumb. "I'm sorry for tearing your dress. I'm just a feeble man."

"Then maybe we should stop?" My quiet voice was lined with hope.

"No, I couldn't stand that!" His dark eyes gazed into mine imploring and impassioned. "Could you?"

A noncommittal sound hummed from my throat as I frowned at him. So small and slight was the shake of my head, but enough for him to notice. Quickly I kissed him. A smile crept across his face and a light laugh tumbled from his lips.

"You impress me with your strength to not surrender to lust. I understand why you won't give yourself to me yet … how wonderful it will be when I finally get to be with you, fully and completely."

Kainan pulled me against him once again and forced me into yet another kiss. His hands began to wander over my body, and hastily I broke away from him.

"As much as I'd like to stay, I – I have to meet with Freydis." I lied, pulling myself out of his arms.

Reluctantly, Kainan released me.

"At least we will have tomorrow."

"*Já*, of course." I said.

I had answered so quietly that Kainan didn't hear the dismay in my voice.

***

WITH EVERY DAY that went by, I began to lose my fear of Vidar. With my emotions growing more strained with Kainan, I found myself strongly missing Vidar. I pined for the ease of Vidar and my past comfortable friendship. I missed our laughter and playful teasing of each other ... I yearned for his tender touch.

Though his words had shocked me to the core, I believed Vidar when he said that he would never hurt me. I also appreciated that, though Vidar had confessed his feelings towards me, he had said nothing more on that subject since. Vidar hadn't tried to pressure me into reciprocating his feelings, he hadn't tried to force or coerce me to his will – I said no only once, and Vidar complied immediately.

Kainan however ...

When his attempts to undress me would fail, Kainan would beg me to allow him to love me completely, but as always, he was met with my coldness and fear. He would chastise me, and I'd further distance myself from him, emotionally and physically, so disheartened by his disregard of my wishes.

Every unpleasant moment with Kainan softened my heart towards Vidar.

It was evening time, snow was gently falling outside, and Vidar and I were alone in the hall. Freydis had gone out to visit a friend, thankfully taking that damned Hilda with her, and the other thralls were quietly eating their dinner in the kitchen.

As I sat by the fire mending the strap that Kainan had torn, I watched Vidar arrange the Hnefatafl pieces on the board as he sat at the table across the room from me. The silence between us was suffocating, I couldn't bare it any long. I glanced from the strap to Vidar and saw my chance. Taking a deep breath, I gathered my courage, silently rose from my chair, and meekly approached him.

"*Hnefatafl* would be a lot more enjoyable with another player ... Could I join you?" I asked shyly, turning bright red as Vidar's sparkling blue eyes darted up at me in surprise.

"I'd like that a lot." Vidar replied, offering me the chair beside him.

From that moment on, we quickly slipped back into our old ways, immediately comfortable together once more. It was as though that evening had never happened. We would talk with each other for hours, we laughed together again, and even in silence we were at peace, contented just to be together.

We played *Hnefatafl* together every evening again, and I had become an extremely decent player, strategising like a seasoned warrior. I hadn't beaten Vidar yet, but he dedicatedly taught me everything he knew.

Vidar had also begun teaching me how to fight like a Dane. He would take me to the garden or to an expanse of clear land in the town and teach me swordplay or how to use a shield to benefit me, not just as protection but also as a weapon. Vidar was surprised at how well I fought with a sword, impressed at the knowledge I'd remembered from my father's teachings, and when we hunted, he delighted over my skill with a bow and arrow.

As winter thawed, and the snow melted away, Vidar started taking me to the fjord and teaching me how to swim. It was a long and arduous process; I was not quick to learn, but I was getting there. The waters were chilly and biting, and it took me a long time to get used to the awful temperatures. Should I ever fall out of a boat or ship on warm, calm waters, I had a good chance of swimming to safety, but if the waters were even slightly choppy or cold, I would flail and panic dreadfully.

Vidar would always dive in and save me.

I hadn't forgiven him for what he had said, but I was so thankful that our closeness was returned.

***

Early Summer, 872

VIDAR AND I were walking through the busy marketplace. A woven basket hung from my arm, full of items we'd bought at various shops and stalls, and one of Vidar's hands rested on my shoulder. We were in the middle of a playful disagreement. The night before I had finally won a single game of *Hnefatafl* against him – for the very first time, might I add – and Vidar was of the extreme belief I'd somehow cheated.

As I laughed at Vidar for his hilarious indignation, I noticed Kainan across the crowded way from us. He saw me and urgently beckoned me to come to him before he curiously dived out of sight behind the crowd of shoppers at a pottery stall and a cloth merchant's stand.

Just as Kainan vanished, Jan and a few of Vidar's other friends appeared behind us, drawing Vidar's attention from me.

"I'll return in a moment." I muttered to Vidar, then flew through the townsfolk to find Kainan.

I reached the cloth merchant's stand and hastily pretended to look at the different fabrics for sale. I briefly touched linens and silks that hung from the stall's beams, careful not to bump the shelves that held huge rolls of fabulous fabrics, while I subtly glanced over my shoulder in search of Kainan.

"It's good to see you." Kainan said quietly, appearing beside me.

"Good to see you, too." I whispered back.

Kainan discreetly reached for my hand and tangled his fingers with mine, smiling warmly at me. Our clasped hands were hidden from view by the tables and racks laden with rolls of material. Slowly and inconspicuously, Kainan led me to the back of the stall, and we stepped behind it, hidden in shadow.

Unnoticed, we faced each other and Kainan immediately swooped down to kiss me. Our hands still entwined, he crept to the edge of the stall to sneak a glimpse of Vidar through the bustle of the marketplace. After a few moments of bobbing around combing the crowds, Kainan spotted Vidar and noted that his back was turned to us. Satisfied, he pecked a small kiss on my lips again.

"I see you and Alvarsson are getting along well."

"Ah? Yes – we're doing fine." I said awkwardly.

"Is he still trying to find you a *suitable* husband?" Kainan asked.

"Once in a while Freydis introduces me to someone new, but not lately, no."

"I'm glad to hear that. I shouldn't like you wed off before I get a chance to marry you myself." Kainan laughed.

"I – I don't want to speak of this right now."

I took a step back. Kainan noticed my movement and narrowed his eyes at me briefly before urging me closer again with a gentle tug of our clasped hands. Hesitantly, I shuffled forward, staring at him dubiously.

"It's alright, I have something else to speak of." Kainan promised. "I want to know if you can meet me tonight? Late, after the hall has gone to sleep. We'll meet at the dock."

"Sneaking away in the dead of night? We can't do that." I scoffed.

"I promise, it's worth the risk." Kainan winked.

"You won't be saying that when we get caught. Tell me why you want to meet me there and I'll tell you if it's worth the risk."

"But that will ruin the surprise." Kainan pressed, bringing my hand to his lips and kissing it softly.

With a small smile on my lips, I carefully stepped around him, out of our hiding spot. I glanced across the road and immediately found Vidar's tall, broad form in the crowd. I watched him for a few moments, he seemed to be parting from his friends.

"I have to go back to Vidar." I said and tried to pull my hand from Kainan. "I'll see you tomorrow morning?"

"Meet me tonight, please?" Kainan asked.

Kainan wouldn't release my hand, instead he squeezed it tightly.

Kainan was only slightly taller than me, whereas I had to gaze neck-achingly upwards to face Vidar. Vidar, like most Danes, was broad and muscular, with large strapping arms. The Danish men were incredibly active – from sports and games to fighting, raiding and working – which made them large and muscled. They also ate a varied diet of meat, poultry, fish and huge amounts of vegetables, cheese, breads and fruit.

The thrall diet consisted of fish and the occasional root vegetables, which, melded with their horrendously long days of gruelling labour, made most thralls very lean and slight. Kainan was no different – he was slender, but firm from his long hard days of excruciating labour.

The contrasts of the two men did not end there. Vidar was the personification of a bright summer day, long, flowing fair hair, glowing golden skin and eyes like glaciers. Kainan was the night, with deep olive-brown skin, dark chocolate eyes and short ebony hair ... they were two very opposite men and I was caught between them both.

"Kainan, we *can't*. What if we're caught?"

"You're with Alvarsson a lot, I see." Kainan commented, leaning over me to peer through the crowds at the Jarl's son.

"Well, yes." I watched Kainan through narrowed eyes.

He increased his grip on my hand, painfully. I winced and tried to wriggle it free, but he didn't seem to notice nor care that he was hurting me, he was still too absorbed in watching Vidar. His stare had turned into a scowl – I didn't know what he was thinking, but I could see frustration and anger rising in his onyx eyes.

"I'm surprised by how affectionate you are towards me right now. What's changed you?" He said icily.

"*Excuse me?*"

"Don't think I haven't noticed your dismay when I try to woo you. Is he the reason? Do you share his bed now?"

"*What?!*"

With no more care to be discreet, I tried to snatch my hand from him again. He let me struggle a few moments before he finally released my hand. I stumbled backwards, out of the shadows, and held my throbbing hand against my chest, glaring at him.

"You're not as sly as you try to be, Aveline. Your reluctance to marry me is paralleled by the increased amount of time you spend with *him*." Kainan finally looked me in the eye.

"I do not share his bed." I growled.

"I saw his hand on you. You seem very intimate with each other – if you're to be my wife then I would like to know if you've given yourself to another man."

"I haven't given myself to anyone." I said through gritted teeth. "You're the only man trying to take me to bed!"

"If we're to be wed–"

"No, stop! I *do not* want to speak of marriage!"

"Do you want to marry me or not?" Kainan asked flatly.

I stared at him in shock for a few moments. Kainan's voice may have been steady, but he couldn't stop himself from glowering at me.

Unable to bare his gaze, I silently turned away from him and stared at the ground, my forehead furrowed, and lips pursed together tightly. The noise from the packed market street was muted to my ears, nothing but Kainan's question rang in my mind.

I could feel him examine me as I tried to find the words to answer him with but unfortunately the heavy, awkward silence that blanketed us seemed to say everything.

"Why didn't you tell me sooner?" Kainan's voice was faint, and his expression faded to disappointment. "Why would you treat me like a fool?"

"I wasn't – I didn't ... That wasn't my intention." I stammered.

"Then what was?"

"I enjoyed being with you ..."

"What changed?"

"I still don't know how to tell you." I whimpered.

"Vidar?" Kainan murmured.

"*Já*, but–"

"Just as I thought."

"I don't share his bed, Kainan!" I exclaimed tearfully.

Kainan shook his head slowly. He was done listening to me.

"Hallo, Kainan. How are you?" Vidar appeared towering behind me, his hand on the small of my back. "I've come to reclaim Aveline."

I glanced between the men, who glared at one another amidst their cordial pretence.

"Of course, master Vidar." Kainan glanced at me, his face absent of all emotion. "She's yours to keep."

He turned and walked away.

Kainan was finished with me.

"I can keep you?" Vidar asked as I slowly turned around.

Bewildered, I looked up at him.

"I suppose so."

Vidar raised his eyebrows and smiled. He didn't say a word as he wrapped his arm around me, and we began to walk.

CHAPTER NINE

Autumn

THE HORNS ECHOED across the bay, growing louder as the ships drew closer. Crowds plunged through the streets like rushing water from a flooded stream, cheering and hailing as they arrived at the docks. Filled with excitement and exhilaration, I ran along to join the flurry.

Vidar was there before me as his father's ship moored. Alvar the First One was unmistakable even from where I was standing. He was a bear of a man, huge and broad, with saffron yellow hair and a thick, reddish blond beard on his pale face. I watched the Jarl of Roskilde and Vidar embrace, grinning and laughing together. Within an hour all the ships were moored, and families were reunited.

"Birger? Where's Birger?" I muttered, dashing frantically amongst the swarm that still buzzed on the shore.

I managed to run into Vidar, unfortunately it was literally. I tripped over my own feet as I tried to stop myself, but with an agonising thump my head thudded against his chest. He staggered back but expertly managed to stay on his feet and catch me, clasping me tightly against him to save me from toppling to the ground.

Alvar watched our crash and boomed with laughter. Red-faced and catching my breath from our surprise collision, I gazed up at Vidar.

"Where's Birger?" I asked.

"I don't know – *faðir*?" As Vidar turned to Alvar, his grin dropped from his face.

"The injured are being brought off the ships over there." Alvar explained solemnly, pointing across the shore at one of the longships. "Birger—"

"Injured?" I cried, staring at the great bear-like jarl. "He's injured?"

"*Já*, he—"

But I did not wait for an account.

I saw where Alvar had pointed and tore through the people. As I grew closer to the ship, I saw bodies being pulled off on stretchers constructed of rough wooden posts with animal skins affixed to them. There were also persons haphazardly carried down to the shore, supported by the arms of their loved ones.

I paused, shocked, waiting to see Birger's face materialise. I noticed the tears of women bawling, having heard their men were not to return. '*He is dead, but fear not, for his is seated at the great table of Odin*', and other sympathetic consolations were uttered to comfort the widowed and orphaned.

I was somewhat comforted with the knowledge Birger was injured, I was glad not to be one of the mourners, but I was terrified of what 'injured' had meant. The grave look upon Alvar's face had worried me greatly. I had heard and seen many men return to Roskilde injured, then succumb to their wounds later.

Then I saw Birger.

Carried on a stretcher, he was covered in a woollen blanket. It was draped over his upper body; I could see his legs and large bare feet but not his torso. I could see his head, his long hair greasy and dank, noticeable even from this distance. As he grew closer and closer, I saw a thick sheen of sweat slick upon his face.

"*Faðir!*" I roared. "*Faðir!*"

I watched Birger groggily trace my call. Hearteningly his expression lightened immensely when he finally found my face. I ran to his side and watched him wince in agony as he tried to rise from the stretcher to embrace me.

"What happened? What's wrong?" I panted, trying to keep up as the two men carrying him continued their way to the shore.

Birger said nothing, moving his lips and grunting as though trying to find the words, but to no avail. I tried to find his hand under the blanket but couldn't. Alarmed, I stared at him and reached to pull the blanket away. Birger grabbed my hand quickly, staring back at me with wide eyes, slowly shaking his head.

He was lowered to the ground. The men spoke calmly and supportively to Birger, offering him praise for the successful raid and assured him they'd be back to take him to his home. Birger gripped them each in turn with a one-armed embrace, then turned to me as they left.

"Where are you injured?" I demanded, fear rippling through my body.

Birger said nothing but pulled the blanket away. He wore no shirt; his torso was naked. I couldn't bring myself to look – I examined the different aged tattoos that were etched in green-black ink upon his torso before I gained enough courage to look at his injury. I lifted my eyes slowly to his shoulder–

Birger's right arm was completely missing!

"Oh, *faðir*." I sank to my knees beside him, my body quivering, bile surging up my throat. "Oh *faðir*!"

"I killed the whore's son who did this to me." Birger bragged, coughing, spittle flying from his lips. "I'll be fine, my *dóttir*, my Aveline." He soothed.

"How did this happen?" I asked, unable to take my eyes from the stub that used to be his right arm.

It was gruesome, a jagged cut just below his shoulder. It was thickly crisped with a coal black layer, and horrendously deep maroon blotches surrounding the angry wound. They had cauterised his arm to stop the bleeding ...

"Some bastard Saxon managed to catch me unawares – he swung his sword at me and cut my arm! After he had struck me, I swung around and cleaved him with my shield; struck it straight through his skull! Serves him right for trying to chop off my sword arm." Birger laughed painfully. "He only made it halfway through, though – damn Alvar had to cut the rest off for me ..."

"Why are you laughing, *faðir*? Your arm is gone!" I howled, tears streaming down my face.

"I will have to learn to fight with my left." Birger barked stubbornly. "We led a successful raid; we have many treasures brought back and a few of our men who fought gallantly and honourably are celebrating in Valhalla. I am home to you, alive, my Aveline. There is no need to shed tears!"

I sucked in my breath and held back my sadness. I gazed down at the sand beneath me, silently wallowing in distress.

Soon enough, Vidar appeared by my side, and greeted Birger proudly. He quickly glanced at Birger's wound before meeting his eyes. Birger tried to rise, pushing himself up one-handedly, grimacing as he struggled. Vidar put his hand on Birger's shoulder and rested his forehead against Birger's.

"Alvar said you killed many of the Christians." Vidar soothed, carefully forcing Birger to lie back down in the stretcher and covering him with the blanket. "You did well, Birger. Now, you need your strength, you need to heal."

"I do not intend to leave Midgard for the halls of Hel, Vidar Alvarsson." Birger panted, but allowed himself to rest.

"Valhalla is the rightful place for a warrior like yourself." Vidar agreed, grinning. "But you will not go there if you die from wound sickness. Rest easy! Alvar tells me he plans to return to Britain again, and soon. You need to heal so you may fight again."

My head rung, his words crashing in my mind.

Birger die?

Return to Britain?

Fight again?

I had no words. I was dizzy, I felt sick. I swallowed the vomit that inched up my throat, shakily facing Vidar. He met my gaze but said nothing, turning back to speak more with Birger.

Alvar the First One made his way across the shore in our direction, frequently stopped by congratulators and friends. Freydis hung from him lovingly, one of his sizeable arms wrapped around her, her pale face flushed pink and her lips beamed with bliss and glee at her husband's return.

"Birger, come, man, let's get you to the hall! We need to celebrate our victory!" Alvar thundered joyfully, nodding to his son.

"I love you, brother, but I don't want to go to your hall. I've spent too much time in your company; I want to go to my home!" Birger chortled.

"I'm insulted!" Alvar shot a quick offended expression at Birger before the men laughed together. "We must celebrate, you must celebrate with us!"

"Later, you fiend." Birger replied, gazing at me. "For Frigg's sake, let me spend some time with my *dóttir*. It has been more than a year since I saw her last."

"I understand." Alvar said, glancing warmly at his wife and son. "I have also been reunited with my family – I have a wife to love, and a son to regale to me what has happened in my absence."

Freydis, Alvar and Birger chuckled together as Alvar coiled his arm around his crippled friend and hoisted him from the ground. Vidar caught my eyes and smiled sympathetically, understanding my fear and devastation. I just blinked at him numbly, stumbling silently beside Freydis as Vidar and Alvar carried my injured *faðir*, between them.

"I will join you this eve, my friend." Birger promised. "For now, I want to go home."

***

OUR HOME WAS silent for a while. It was long passed midday and the bitter chill of night drew ever stronger. I stood beside the table, chopping carrots to toss into the bubbling pot, bathed in the orange glow of the fire the pot hung over. Though we planned on attending the celebration and eating at the feast, I needed to busy my hands.

I glanced at Birger. He was lying on the bench opposite the fire pit, watching me work. Svartr purred contentedly upon his lap, caring not that Birger was missing a limb. Svartr was happy as long as he was cuddled and scratched under his chin with Birger's remaining hand.

"So, have you found anyone suitable to marry?" Birger asked spritely.

"You come home to me with one less body part than you left with, then you ask about my marriage prospects?" I replied evenly.

"I came back to you, *alive*, like you asked. You didn't dictate what condition I came back in, you only demanded that I lived." Birger quipped.

I raised my eyebrows at him and smiled slightly. Birger grinned sheepishly in return.

"You're a terrible man, *faðir*."

"And you love me despite that, *dóttir*."

I kept a steady gaze upon him, warming to him again. I smirked at his comment, took a handful of herbs I'd spent a few weeks drying and sprinkled them into the pot. I stirred the stew carefully for a moment, before settling down on the bench next to him.

"I'm angry that you were injured." I pointed out flatly. "I'm angry that you are sick from your wound."

"I assure you, I didn't allow the Saxon to chop my arm off on purpose." Birger winked.

"Regardless," I stressed. "I'm still angry at you for it. I'm going to care for you and make you well, and I will not allow for you to die in the next raid! You will not get injured like this again, either."

"I can't say anything about dying in the next raid, but I refuse to die from this wound. Dying in battle is a very honourable thing – far more respectable than dying of sickness."

"I don't care how respectable a battle death is." I snapped childishly, taking his remaining hand and squeezing it. "I refuse to let you die, especially after I've healed your wound."

Birger laughed at me. He brought my hand to his lips and kissed it briefly, beaming at me.

"Enough about this. You didn't answer me about the suitable husbands ... has any man been able to steal your heart while I've been away?"

"I fell for a thrall and was almost ended up betrothed to him." I revealed.

"Ha! You tease a man weary from battle and gravely injured! What a wicked girl you are!" Birger laughed. Like an after though he added in a sterner tone, "You cannot marry a thrall! You're–"

"Good job I'm not marrying a thrall, then, hmm?" I interrupted, smiling weakly at him.

He chuckled at me.

"Tell me of your suitors!"

So, I told him. I told him of the old man, the cockerel looking boy, the handsome Jan.

"Jan Jötunnson is a fine warrior, from a very good family! He's not much older than you either – you'd have a long life with the man. He would make a grand husband – I'm glad you met with him!" Birger gushed excitedly.

I agreed with him before I quickly carried on, telling him of the other unsuccessful suitors Freydis and Vidar had introduced me to. I told him how much time I had enjoyed in Vidar's company, though I didn't divulge much more. Birger didn't need to know of Vidar's proposal, I had already refused him.

After another hour of talking, Birger and I heard a commotion outside. The town was alight with excitement – the celebration was beginning!

"You'll have to tell me more about your life in the Jarl's hall later. I certainly want to hear more about your interests in Jötunnson!" Birger yawned. "But for now, I am tired, and I must rest."

"You won't go to the celebration?" I asked, slightly surprised.

Birger had stopped sweating as profusely as before. I had cleaned him with warm water and a soap I'd made from animal fats, ashes and crushed flowers I'd harvested from the forest. He was still pale and sickly, regardless of his humour, and was too weak to raise himself from his laying position on the bench without my assistance.

"I am tired, *dóttir*. I need rest. I will join later." Birger replied as I eased him into his bed and covered him with his fur blankets.

"I will stay with you."

"Don't even think of that!" Birger exclaimed. "You can't stay at home with an old cripple when you could be celebrating. Go! If you see Jötunnson there, perhaps you could talk to him again?"

I smiled and placed a gentle kiss on the top of his head.

"Food will be ready when you wake." I murmured before leaving my Birger alone.

Svartr, disgruntled at being disturbed, slunk away into the sheep pens and far from sight. I sent a half-smile to the cat through the darkness, before stepping out of our home and making my way down the noisy streets of Roskilde.

The streets were bathed in lavender. Evening would fall soon, but not yet. There were many lanterns hanging from hooks and posts, their dim orange glow glimmering in the late afternoon light. They were many and frequent, the only non-lit areas were the thin alleyways, but I slipped through them with no fear of what may have been hidden in the shadows.

I arrived at the hall and saw the doors were wide open, people walking in and out freely. Extra benches and tables had been pulled from the rafters and shed and filled the main room with plenty of people sat laughing upon them, joking and drinking, telling their tales, kissing their women.

These people, the Norse, had no issue with their women going to raid with them. Most women would not fight, however. They would set up camp and cook their food while their men fought, and care for them when they returned. A few women might partake in the raiding itself, but that was not a common occurrence.

The table nearest me held a few men speaking and laughing loudly together, and a couple who were passionately absorbed in each other. I watched, longingly, as the pair of sweethearts held each other, kissed each other – I missed being held.

Playfully, I toyed with the idea of being in Jan's arms, before my mind led me to memories of Kainan. I hadn't seen him in months, and I wondered where he had vanished to. I regretted my coldness towards him, I regretted not telling him of Vidar's threat … I regretted leading him on in his belief that we would marry, yet I regretted not holding onto him a little longer.

Vidar had not told me where the thrall had gone, maybe Kainan still lived in Roskilde and I had not seen him? I doubted that, and I worried deeply, but I asked no questions about Kainan's whereabouts.

By leaving me, Kainan had protected himself, though he didn't know it. I only wished I hadn't been so afraid to tell him why I was distant, though I knew had I explained it to him, he would've wanted to run away together, or he would've challenged Vidar …

I sighed.

Vidar ...

Hilda appeared, shoving me carelessly as she went by. I glared at her back but carried on wandering slowly around the room.

I hated that thrall girl ...

A while had passed, and I stood in the shadowed doorway of the kitchen, my fingers wrapped around a cup of sweet mead, examining the people in the room. As the cup touched my lips, there was a rousing roar of "*Skål!*" from the table closest to me. Surprised by the sudden outburst, I leapt out of my skin and spilled half the cup's contents down my face and front.

"You may need this?" Vidar chuckled at me, suddenly appearing behind me and offering me a rag from over my shoulder.

I blushed and muttered my thanks while reaching to take the rag, but instead he began to dab my lips, chin, neck and chest. I closed my eyes, enjoying the tenderness and delicacy of his help, leaning my head against him as he gently wiped the fabric over my flesh. I turned my head, eyes still closed, feeling his chin against my forehead. He lowered himself slightly and kissed my forehead gently.

"You must be more careful." Vidar chided warmly, the hairs of his fair beard tickling my face.

I rubbed my head against him, snuggling into him.

"Why should I when I get such wonderful attention afterwards?" I purred, feeling his arm snake around my waist, clasping me against him.

Vidar replied with nothing more than a laugh and a few kisses on my neck that sent shivers through me. We watched the happy celebrators for a while before he silently urged me back to the kitchen. I held his hand firmly as he led me to the door at the back of the room that led to the garden.

The flowers were mostly dead or dying thanks to the season, but I noticed the rich pungent scent of freshly dug soil. I looked around and spotted a new plant in Freydis's collection: inside a large wooden pot were a cluster of tall, leafy stalks topped with bunches of pink-orange mouths.

"Snapdragons!" I gasped, dashing to the pretty flowers.

"*Já.*" Vidar smiled, as he stepped to me. "Alvar brought them home for Freydis. They were raiding a very grand monastery and there were many pots filled with them – these 'snapdragons' – decorating the edge. He took this whole thing and brought it home for her."

I prickled at his explanation, knowing the fate of the monks without needing to ask. I cleared my throat and crouched down beside the pot. I plucked one of the little dragon head flowers from a stalk and squeezed the sides of the mouth to make it snap.

"My father went away when I was very little … he came back home after a while and brought my mother this same plant, only one though. They were pretty for a while. I used to go to them and pull off the flowers and play with them for ages." I reminisced. "My mother was angry because the flowers kept disappearing. She caught me plucking them one day and beat me half to death. She really loved the flower. Unfortunately, it never grew back."

"Try not to kill this one, *já?*" Vidar smirked as he took my hand and brought me to him, the little snapdragon mouth still held carefully in my fingertips.

He put my arm on his chest and kissed me softly, gently, squeezing my waist as I clung to him, returning his kisses with tender ones of my own.

"They originally come from the Mediterranean, you know? The snapdragons? I want to go there one day … maybe you would join me?" Vidar said.

With sudden realisation I pulled away from Vidar and glared at him.

"Did you kill Kainan?"

Vidar's eyebrows rocketed upwards and his lips fell into a frown.

"Kainan?" Vidar asked blankly.

"*Já,*" I answered firmly. "Did you kill him? I haven't seen him for months."

"I did not kill him." Vidar declared, taking the flower from my fingers and twirling it in his.

"Then where is he?"

"I sold him." Vidar crushed the snapdragon blossom and flicking it to the ground. "He came to me and asked me to sell him.

He didn't want to be here anymore. Jan was going south to trade, so I sent Kainan with him."

I gaped in shocked silence. Vidar released me from his grip and stepped away from me. I was suddenly cold, not realising how much warmth was dependent on Vidar's embrace.

"I didn't know a little flower like that would remind you of him." Vidar tipped his head carelessly in the direction of the snapdragons.

"He wanted to leave because I didn't want to marry him." I whispered, coming up behind him and resting my head on his back, his fur cloak soft against my cheek.

"I can't say I'm unhappy to hear that." Vidar confessed, turning to face me.

We held each other, blissfully warm again in his embrace.

"I still don't know how I feel about you, Vidar. I enjoy being with you, but I still fear you."

"I didn't kill your lover." Vidar reiterated, running his hands up and down my back. "I said I'd kill him if he ever stole you from me. He didn't, he *gave* you to me."

"I didn't realise I was his to give away." I remarked. "That doesn't even matter – you said you wanted to kill me!"

"*Wanted* to. It doesn't mean I would." Vidar teased, a tiny smile on his face, his blue eyes blazing with mischief.

"You're maddening, Vidar Alvarsson!" I barked childishly.

"I know." Vidar smirked.

"I'm not ready to marry you, Vidar."

"Tell me when you are." Vidar said.

And then we kissed.

CHAPTER TEN

FIRST THE DRUMS began. Then the horns and bone flutes chimed in. Poignant voices entered the rugged music, deep and foreboding – the tiny, fair, downy hairs on my arms stood on end, my flesh bathed in goosebumps. Haunting alto voices joined the throng of baritones in song, and the music echoed to the skies.

Suddenly Alvar appeared cutting through the crowd in front of the hall, the stern, elderly male *hofgoði*, the temple priest, at his side. Together they slowly marched through the people, a thrall dressed in a loose white linen tunic staggering immediately behind them. His shoulders were slumped as he stared at the ground with a blank face, empty of all emotion.

Alvar the First One wore the gigantic pelt of a black bear, its roaring head mounted on his like a crown. He and the *hofgoði* were dressed in brilliant blue robes, wide leather belts buckled at their waists, golden finery adorning their wrists and fingers, with slick black makeup smeared over their faces.

Upon his shoulders, the *hofgoði* wore a long grey wolf fur cloak. From his belt hung pouches and amulets and tied over his wrinkled brow was a leather strap. His hair was long, and his beard had never been cut – silver hairs sprouted from high on his cheeks and fell to his middle.

Behind the *hofgoði,* the Jarl and the thrall, were the *hofgoði*'s sons and his wife, who wore a goat's skull crown, and three of the wealthier and more respected karls of Roskilde. The karls each walked beside a thrall.

The Roskilde freeman were dressed in ritual garb and makeup, and the thralls were dressed identically in ghostly tunics. Each thrall led an animal – two horses and a cow – through the busy town streets. The musicians followed in the back, singing and playing their music, drawing the town to follow.

And follow we did.

Through the dusty streets we strode, fires left unattended in houses, more important was the call. We were an army, marching down the dirt paths weaving through the buildings, passed the farms and homesteads.

We filed across Roskilde to the huge forest outside of the town walls. We reached its mouth where a passage had been hacked and carved out by the ancestors of Roskilde. Massive, smooth grey rocks, mottled by verdant moss, lined the wide dirt path in an even distance from each other. Aged branches arched overhead as we followed the path to the heart of forest.

A mixture of skeletal white, umber-brown and ancient grey tree trunks loomed around us, gnarled with age, the arthritic boughs' fingers stretched outwards. Above us autumn had painted a rich, brightly coloured dappled roof of scarlet, gold and orange; and gaps in the foliage exposed the steely sky.

A few red leaves fluttered down, landing on my head and shoulders. I shivered, and goosebumps skidded across my flesh – the leaves foretold what was to come: the blood of the sacrifices.

The path we trod was covered in centuries of snapped branches and fallen leaves that had crashed to the ground and rotted, a carpet of soft, natural death under our feet. The smell of compost, age and nature, a haunting invisible miasma of scent rising to my nostrils, intermingled with the sweetness of sap. The smell of decay …

Only a short way down the path, almost hidden behind the trees, was the *hof*, a hall used for indoor rituals and preparing sacrifices, it was also the home of the *hofgoði* and his family. It had elegant carvings decorating the outer wood planks and posts and was almost camouflaged in its surroundings. Its secretive position sent shivers down my spine, but I carried on, taking comfort from the crowd.

I flowed forth with the chanting walkers, like lifeblood surging through the veins of a single being. The music danced through the branches. I focused on the sound; the deep, steady heartbeat thump of the drums, the loud, roaring commands of the horns …

We carried on away from the *hof* and it quickly hid away in the brush and foliage and trunks; a silent, stealthy sentinel watching us pass. The rocks kept us on our path, leading us forward, deeper and deeper.

The further we went, the more mystical and darker the forest became. Huge roots spread across the ground; vast, solid, dark tangles of creaking, wooden webs knitted across the forest floor. The thick and lush foliage had woven itself into a blanket of emerald, ruby, gold and amber. The light shining upon the forest roof gave nothing, but a dampened glow to brighten our way and cast deep charcoal shadows over us.

I heard the snuffling noises of a boar or two foraging for food under crispy piles of leaves and carpets of feathery moss in the distance, their appearance hidden by the knots of thick brush and overgrowth.

Finally, we arrived at a large, perfectly circular glade, lined with the same large, evenly sized and spaced boulders. Four ancient, massive trees with huge, thick naked branches rose in the centre of the clearing, long, fat ropes hanging from six of the branches.

The sunlight above cast a honeyed sheen over the four ominous trees, but it did not dispel the knowledge of their horrifying use. On one of the trees branches I spotted the raven with the blinded eye and its companion, their feathers glimmering blue-black in the dappled sunlight.

The music grew to a huge crescendo as Alvar and the *hofgoði* strode to their spot in the middle, two of the mighty trees on either side of him. The *hofgoði*'s family stood behind them and the singing, the pipes and the horns halted, only the steady beat of the drums prevailed.

Obediently, without being ordered, the thrall leading the cow tied it to a post in front of the Jarl and the *hofgoði*. A long, low rectangular stone trough stood on the ground beside the cow. The ravens cawed raucously as the other thralls attached the ropes to the horses' necks, and stood behind the remaining ropes, staring at the ground. The karls that had walked with each thrall, stood in the shadows of the trees next to their thralls.

The *hofgoði* brought his arms up into the air. Following suit, everyone in the crowd brought their arms into the air. I watched, my arms at my sides, paralysed by the mystical atmosphere.

"Odin, Villi, Ve,
Odin, Villi, Ve,
Odin, Villi, Ve!"

The *hofgoði*'s voice was surprisingly strong, loud and commanding, and streamed through the entire forest.

I was frozen, still and unspeaking. I had not believed in the Christian God for years, but I didn't worship the Norse gods either. Birger made sure I knew of them, taking me to *blóts* when they occurred, seasonally.

From years of knowledge and attendance I noticed the difference with this *blót*. Animals were ritualistically slaughtered at the four annual *blóts*, occasionally if Roskilde was in dire need of help from their gods then they would slaughter thralls. I was confused – the raid had gone well then surely Roskilde was not in need? Why were there so many thralls stood, emotionlessly, ready to be sacrificed?

Alvar the First One stood solemnly in the middle of the crowd as the *hofgoði* began walking to the left. He made his way to the tree line and halted, turning swiftly to face his previous direction.

"Hammer of Thor, hallow and hold this holy stead!"

He made the sign of a hammer as he walked to the right side of the clearing. He repeated his command, making his way back to the left, then silently came to the middle again, standing with Alvar, the cow shifting on the spot before them.

"Hail the Æsir! Hail the Vanir!
I bid you welcome, high ones,
Stand with us.

Hail the gods of the north,
We give honour to you, holy kin,
Our troth is true.

> Hail the álfar! Hail the dísir!
> We bid you welcome, honoured kin,
> Stand with us.
>
> Hail the ancestors of our lines,
> We give honour to you, worthy kin,
> Our troth is true.
>
> Hail the landvættir!
> We bid you welcome,
> Stand with us.
>
> Hail unseen ones, greetings I give,
> Holy vættir, we give honour to you,
> Accept our offerings of gratitude."

Vidar and Jan appeared beside the three karls in the shadows behind the trees. They wore blue robes and the same black makeup smeared over their eyes.

I shuddered – Vidar's pale eyes were wide and unblinking. Usually enchanting and beautiful, the black makeup accentuated the coldness of their colour, and the glint of excitement burning inside them lent him a sinister air. His lips were drawn together, but even from this distance I could see the tiny lift of a smile on one side of his mouth.

They made their way down the line of men and horses, tightening the ropes around their necks. Vidar and Jan stood behind the furthest thrall on the left, the other two karls beside the second thrall. The third karl waited by the horse.

With a wave of Alvar's hand, Vidar and Jan took hold of the rope and swiftly yanked it, pitching the male thrall into the air. I flinched as the thrall was hauled off his feet, his choking and gurgling struck through the air like thunder. Then he hung still. Dead.

Alvar waved his other arm and the two other Danes pulled the rope on the next thrall, while Vidar and Jan stood behind the braying horse. The redheaded thrall's body writhed and with a quick *crack!* she died.

The horse was beautiful, large and white. It could smell the thick, pungent stench of death in the air and began to panic. The five burly men stood behind the horse and began pulling the rope higher and higher. They panted, the horse struggled as it rose off the ground, screeching out in pain and fear. Soon enough the poor creature was suspended a few feet off the ground and slowly hung to death, flailing and whinnying until finally life left it.

The other gorgeous white horse was in full panic by this point. It tugged and yanked at the rope as the men strode over to it. The final thralls at the end remained surprisingly still and calm. Tears cascaded down my face silently for them.

Vidar, Jan and the three karls held the rope mightily to stop the horse from bolting. Another man from the crowd swiftly dashed over to assist them. Alvar watched them carefully, patiently waiting for one to nod to him in a sign of readiness.

As soon as Vidar had given the signal, Alvar raised his arm and the six men forced the flailing horse into the air. Thankfully the animal flung sharply and snapped its own neck, a quick death. The men tied the rope to a post, keeping the horse suspended like they had done with the other horse and two thralls.

The process continued until all four thralls and both horses were dead. All eyes were on the cow in the centre. Alvar the First One pulled out a large, terribly sharp dagger. Golden flashes of light glinted from the deadly blade. Then the *hofgoði* began chanting again;

> "Hail the Æsir! Hail the Vanir!
> Hail the gods of the north,
> Hail the álfar! Hail the dísir!
> Hail the ancestors of our lines,
> Hail the landvættir!
> Hail unseen ones and holy vættir,
> Accept our offerings of gratitude!"

Alvar the First One slit the cow's throat with a sickening spray. The blood poured, covering a huge radius around them, spurting into the massive rectangular stone trough beside the cow. Alvar's hands were scarlet, and the copper taste of the cow's blood tingled sickeningly on my tongue.

Quickly, the cow died, collapsing with its head in the long, low basin. The ravens finally quit their horrendous noise and swiftly flew up into the sky and vanished from sight. A hangman stepped forward and retrieved the dagger from Alvar, handing him, in return, a branch covered in a shell of lush foliage.

Alvar dipped the branch into the blood and began asperging Vidar, Jan, the four men, and the horde of townsfolk with the blood.

> "Praise and thanks to you, Odin the Allfather,
> Son of Bor and Bestla;
> Husband of Frigg;
> Father of Thor, Baldr and Váli;
> Father of Vidar.
> Accept our offerings of gratitude!"

Vidar stood proudly, shoulders back and chest puffed out, his face solemn, at the hearing of his godly namesake.

> "Praise and thanks to you, Frigg,
> Wife of Odin;
> Mother of Baldr and Höðr.
> Accept our offerings of gratitude!
>
> Praise and thanks to you, Thor,
> Son of Odin and Jord;
> Husband of Sif;
> Father of Magni, Modi and Thrúd.
>
> Praise and thanks to you, Freyja,
> Praise and thanks to you, Týr,
> Praise and thanks to you, Ullr,

Praise and thanks to you, Forseti,
Accept our offerings of gratitude!"

When the *hofgoði* had finished his thanks, the mass roared "Hail!" on the top of their lungs. I, and everyone around me, were sufficiently spattered in the cow's blood. Every man, woman and child, with blood splashed over their flesh and staining their clothes, cheered for their pantheons of gods, cheered for their Allfather, cheered for their goddess of the home, cheered for their gods and goddess of war, battle and justice.

"From the gods to the earth, to us,
From us, to the earth, to the gods.
A gift for a gift.
Hail!"

With that, the ritual was complete.

A shudder ran through my body as the music began again. I waited for the throng to disappear, waited for the townspeople to follow Alvar, the karls and the musicians back to the town. The *hofgoði* and his wife watched their sons, Vidar and Jan load the animal bodies onto two wagons, to push back to the town for the feast.

The four thralls' bodies were loaded onto a separate wagon, tossed upon each other in a gruesome pile, and taken to the *hof*, ready to prepare to be burnt for the gods.

I watched them load the thralls. I recognised the red headed woman. She had been only a few years older than me when I had been kidnapped, I'd met her on the longship that brought us to this land. She was Anglo-Saxon, from a farming community not too far from my own.

I watched her body flop and fall as they released her rope, yanking the noose carelessly from her neck before they hurled her onto the wagon.

I felt no sadness.
I felt no pity.
I felt no fear.

I was empty.

I watched them take her body, and the others, to the *hof* hidden in the trees. I followed quietly, unblinking, ignoring Vidar and Jan's pleasantries when they spotted me. I stood at the tree line and watched the *hofgoði* and his wife wash the bodies of the murdered thralls.

The thralls had been so empty of life, they'd not feared their deaths. Instead they accepted them easily and willingly.

I saw the square pyre that had been prepared for the thralls. I watched them align the men evenly on the pyre. The red-haired thrall was tossed across the male carcasses, her pale white breasts facing up to the sky, her head lolling unnaturally, legs strewn carelessly apart.

I watched them light it. I watched the first few licks of flame begin to consume the structure. The flames grew into an inferno, blazing up to the grey heavens.

I stayed for hours until the red-haired thrall began to burn.

I turned my back on her and made my way to the celebration. I had not tried to save her, a fellow countrywoman, a kidnapped child like me.

I had not tried to save her life.

I had watched her death, but I refused to watch her burn.

CHAPTER ELEVEN

"WHERE WERE YOU for so long?" Vidar asked, handing me a plate laden with tender beef, horsemeat and honey roasted vegetables.

"By the pyre." I said simply.

Vidar stared at me, his brow knitted, and lips drawn tightly together. I looked at him blankly and offered no further explanation. I glanced at my plate, examining the meat from the sacrificed animals. "From the Gods to the earth, to us; from us, to the earth, to the Gods. A gift for a gift ..."

"The thralls? Are they what bothers you?" Vidar asked quietly. "You've seen thralls be sacrificed a number of times since you came here–"

"Since I was brought here." I corrected.

"You've seen the sacrifices before." Vidar said firmly, taking me by the wrist and pulling me aside, away from listening ears. "Why are you acting like this? What is it, Aveline?"

I turned my vacant eyes to him, but I didn't speak. Vidar's voice was low and concerned, but not angry, and he surveyed me through narrowed eyes, as if searching my face for answers.

Suddenly, I did not see him.

Images flashed before my eyes, the redheaded thrall on the top of the pyre – the wooden wall of my home I had stared at as I listened to my mother's rape – Birger's warm and loving smile – Kainan drenched in shadow, gazing down at me with animalistic hunger – the axe wedged in my brother's head – Vidar kissing my wrist as we lay curled into each other beneath the dappled forest roof, the fjord's water singing softly in the background ...

"I don't think I'm hungry." I finally said to Vidar, looking up from the plate.

I could taste the cow's blood still, as though it were fresh on my tongue. My timid hand touched the crusted splatter on my cheek, it crumbled onto my fingers like scarlet snowflakes.

"I'd like to go home." I said quickly before Vidar could speak.

I dropped the plate onto the nearest table and turned to him again. He looked at me, worried and concerned. I smiled and began to walk away.

"Aveline," Vidar called, grabbing my hand and pulling to him.

We clung to each other and kissed, I could taste the sweetness of the honey mead upon Vidar's tongue, before I stepped into the night and walked to my home, alone.

***

I HEARD EACH uneasy breath that fell from Birger's lips as he slept. I crept to his bed closet and placed my hand on his forehead, feeling the heat that radiated from him. His skin was clammy and hot, but he slept on, deeply.

I tiptoed through the darkness, the embers glowing in the pit, thinking of Birger and his sickness as I stoked the fire and removed the pot of stew from the fire. He hadn't eaten the food, the pot was still full, simmering untouched as it hung above meagre flames. The delicious smell filled our home – it would serve well as breakfast in the morning. I wasn't hungry, consumed by fear for Birger's wellbeing.

He would die in battle before allowing his sickness to take him. Unfortunately, the chances of a one-armed man dying in battle were great and he would get his wish sure enough if he survived until the next raid. I hated the idea, I wanted him to live a long and happy life, but death by old age was not regarded as honourable in this culture.

Silently, I changed into my bedclothes and slipped beneath the thick heavy furs. I stared at the ceiling, mindlessly examining the wooden planks.

I thought of the Jarl's hall, how I had searched for Vidar and waited, listening to the conversations floating around me. The men, sat next to the kissing couple, were loudly talking (presumably to drown out the sound of the voracious lovers).

They spoke of the Great Army. I knew a lot about the Great Army from the lessons Birger had given me in his effort to turn me into a Dane. Jarl Alvar and the warriors of Roskilde had supported the Great Army when they first attacked Britain – when they raided and burned my village to the ground all those years ago.

The Great Army was an army of Danes led by three of the sons of the great King Ragnar Loðbrók, who had made their first attack on East Angles back in 865 – the year King Ragnar had fallen, hurled into a pit of snakes at the command of King Ælla of Northumbria.

Alvar the First One and his men had been there with the sons of Ragnar – they had stormed my country's shores with the Great Army and raided my village in the autumn. They destroyed it and kidnapped me and a few of my people – but, like a few other Danish clans, Alvar and the warriors of Roskilde had travelled back to Denmark after they were satisfied, and their ships were full.

The Great Army had stayed, however, that much I knew. Led by Halfdan Ragnarsson and his men, they stayed and caused havoc, raiding and killing.

A year after they had landed in my village, the Great Army had travelled to Northumbria and conquered Jorvik – what my people called Eoferwic. Later they invaded Mercia and took Nottingham, but after agreements with the Anglo-Saxons they withdrew to Jorvik and remained there for a year.

Less than two years ago they attacked the Kingdom of the East Angles again and captured and killed King Edmund.

Over the six years of the Army's invasion, Alvar the First One had taken his men over every few years to join the battle. They would leave to take home their spoils and rest up, then ventured back again. He had no intention of settling in Britain, preferring to return to his home, to his land, to his Roskilde.

Vidar had raided the isle many times with his father, but had missed the last raid, to protect Roskilde. There was bad blood between Alvar and the Jutland town of Aros. Long ago, the Jarl of Aros attacked Roskilde, the day Alvar and his young son had set sail. Luckily Roskilde survived, but Alvar made sure to leave able-bodied men to protect it while he and the others were gone.

The three men had spoken of the last few battles in the past year alone. Alvar and his men had followed the brothers Halfdan and Ubba Ragnarsson who led the Army's attack. They had defeated King Æthelred I in Reading, causing the Anglo-Saxon king of Wessex to suffer a heavy loss. They went on and fought at Ashdown, but unfortunately lost the battle and returned to Reading. They went on to win at Basing and Merton, however.

At Wilton a huge battle was fought, and the Danes defeated King Alfred, but the king made a deal with them, offering to pay the Danes tribute, danegeld, in lieu of further attacks.

At that point, Alvar The First One eagerly brought his men home, and within hours of arriving he arranged the blót to thank the gods for their great luck and even greater winnings and finally holding their beloveds in their arms again.

Assumedly, Birger had lost his arm at Wilton – the wound was relatively fresh and, as I had thought before, a one-armed man would not survive long in war.

A deep sigh fell from my lips, and I rolled onto my side.

Poor Birger. Every time I thought of him, I thought of his low chances of survival. I did not want him to die. I couldn't lose another father!

I had lived with a constant guilt these last few years. Upon first hearing of him leaving to raid my homeland I was outraged. But I soon realised that most of my outrage was not for my people, but due to my fear of Birger dying …

Birger was a kind and loving father. Seeing him so critically injured and sickly had made me realise that I felt the same love towards him as I had towards my own father! I felt like I was betraying my blood father, but I couldn't stop myself.

At the feast with Vidar, when memories had flooded my mind, I had felt a frightening detachment to the images of my family, the thrall and Kainan. My life in the Kingdom of the East Angles seemed so long ago. Memories of my family had blurred and faded, and I realised my fury had too ... a shadow of resentment towards the heathens who murdered my family remained, yet, when the thoughts of Birger and Vidar has passed through my mind, I felt ... warmth.

Inside me the kidnapped Anglo-Saxon child, the only remnant of my past, was quiet and still. I wasn't her anymore ... I was the Danish daughter of a grand warrior, with the heart of a Jarl's son beating in my hand, eager to see the future and quickly disconnecting from my past.

I had realised at the pyre, and during my occasional, accidental meetings with Hilda the thrall, that I was not the Aveline I had been all those years ago ...

I was not my father's child anymore; I was Birger's.

I may have been from the same lands as the redheaded thrall who was sacrificed, like Hilda who was owned by the Jarl, but I was changed.

I was thankful for being brought here.

I was glad of meeting Kainan, which never would've happened should I not have been kidnapped ... Kainan had been empathy, he was tenderness, he was the key that opened the door to new passions.

Kainan was my attempt to pacify my guilt; I felt I was a traitor to my family and people, for loving those who had murdered them. Though his advances had become frightening, Kainan had been my secret, my spite, my rebellion against Birger and Vidar and all those trying to convince me to love the 'new life' that they'd forced upon me.

But truly, the revolt I waged was not against Birger and Vidar. It was a revolt against the comfort of my new life. When wrapped in the Mediterranean thrall's arms he became the perfect blanket to shield myself from my love of these people ... I had been ashamed of my love for them, but I realised at the sacrifice that, though I held similarities to Kainan, Hilda and the red-headed thrall, we were far from being the same.

I was not a thrall.

I was a Dane.

***

"BIRGER! BIRGER!" I gasped. "Please, Birger!"

Morning had not long struck, silvery rays slipped through the cracks of the house. Birger's breathing was noisy and rasping, he was struggling for air. His flesh was ghostly white, but his cheeks were flushed scarlet, and sweat poured from every ounce of his flesh. Heat blazed from him, but his body quaked and shivered.

"Birger! Wake up!" I bellowed, my voice shaking with fear and anxiety.

I ripped the furs from him, gaping at the burned stub that used to be his arm. It had swollen immensely and oozed with disgusting, slimy pus. Ugly red streaks snaked from the edge of the burn and a putrid stench exuded from his wound. In horror, I whipped a hand to cover my nose and mouth, as I lunged to the pens, vomiting onto the dirt floor.

Birger did not stir even from the noise of my retching.

"Birger!" I cried, wiping my mouth with the back of my hand as I crawled back to his side. "Birger – oh please, *faðir*, wake up!"

He didn't move. Blinded by tears, I burst from his side, leapt through the door and let it crash shut behind me.

"Help!" I screamed, banging on the doors of houses I ran by. "HELP!"

A few people answered their doors, calling after me, demanding to know what was wrong with me. I whipped around, shaking and pale, my eyes bulging from their sockets.

"Birger! I need help – *Birger!*"

I rushed back to my home, collapsing to my knees at Birger's side. I grabbed his hand with one of mine, pressing the palm of my other on his forehead.

"For all the wretched gods in Asgard, *faðir, wake up!*" I begged, tears burning my eyes.

"What's wrong with him? What's happened?" Adhelin of the cattle farm gasped, coming up behind me, staring at Birger urgently.

"He came back from raiding – he lost his arm – he's sick!" I whimpered.

Three children, two aged between eight and ten, the youngest was only perhaps four, were in the doorway staring horrified. Swiftly, the dark haired Sighni, mother to the children, and Hefni, Adhelin's husband, a short man with long hair wet from being freshly washed, appeared and shoved through the children, arriving at our sides.

"What–" Hefni began.

"Sickness from the wound." Adhelin explained, pointing at Birger's swollen stub. "We need the healer."

"Healer!" The man barked at the children over his shoulder.

The mother rushed to the children.

"You, get the healer – you, get the Jarl!" Sighni grabbed each child by the shoulder as she tasked them with a duty. "You," she added softly to the youngest, "go fetch water from the well."

The children nodded to her silently, dashing in full flight to accomplish their missions. I watched them shakily, so grateful for their help but too worried for Birger to feel in any way reassured.

I turned my gaze to my *faðir*, his body still shivering, the hideousness of his wound and the greenish-yellow pus seeping from his burn … I'd seen and heard of this before, and none who had suffered it survived.

Turning my grief glazed eyes to Birger's still face, my heart crushed in a fist of fear, I held his damp hand in my own, whispering encouragement and assurances to him. Encouragement and assurances that I didn't even believe. But I hoped, and I prayed silently … and I found myself praying not to God, but to Frigg.

> "Beloved Frigg, weaver of fates,
> Share with me Birger's destiny,
> Please let my *faðir* live!"

Then I wept. I wept and wept.

Sighni forced me to the bench, covered my shoulders with a fur, and left me alone so she could tend to Birger. The husband and wife conferred together, but their words were muffled – even if they spoke louder, I wouldn't have heard them; my mind was racing, and I was too consumed by anxiety and dread to acknowledge anything around me.

Damp locks of hair, slick from sweat and my sorrowful breakdown, stuck to my face. My hands were drenched in tears and snot had streamed from my nose. I heard the door slam again, and hurriedly used my gown to wipe my grief-stricken face.

Blurred figures walked past me – I recognised one as the youngest child hauling a bucket of water. It sloshed and splashed, leaving muddy puddles on the dirt floor.

I blinked a few times to clear the remaining tears from my eyes and noticed the poor boy's hands had turned bright pink from the weight of the bucket. He panted heavily, but he hauled the bucket gallantly to his mother Sighni, and she took it from him quickly.

Within moments Adhelin appeared from the kitchen with rags in hand. She gave them to Sighni, who dipped the rag into the cool water and began wiping Birger's face with it. Once his face was clean of sweat, she rinsed the rag in the bucket and laid it on his forehead.

"You need to get yourself together." Adhelin said sternly to me. "Hefni and Sighni are doing their best for your father. Crying will not help."

"Adhelin, where is the damned healer?" Hefni, who had been examining Birger's stub, demanded from his wife.

Before Adhelin had time to answer, the door swung open. Appearing forebodingly, his face drained of colour, was Alvar the First One with the tiny healer behind him, engulfed in his huge shadow. Alvar didn't say a word, he reached Birger's bedside in but a few fast, long strides, and the healer scurried after him.

"Wound sickness." Sighni explained timidly. "The pus—"

Before she said more, the healer bustled passed her. She was a tiny, ancient looking woman with wrinkled flesh, a bulbous nose and squinting eyes, and her hair was hidden beneath a tightly knotted handkerchief.

She looked over Birger's stub, shrewdly, prodding and pocking, seemingly noting everything down in her mind. She turned and looked at the doorway where the child who had fetched her stood, holding in his hands a small, aged wooden chest. She beckoned him over with a wave of her gnarled hand.

He handed her the box, which she snatched and searched through frantically. A strong, bizarre smell emanated from the box – I spied a greatly varied collection of different sprigs of herb and plant, tied with frayed threads. She seemed to know the difference between each item, occasionally sniffing them to be sure, before removing them from the box.

She took her fistful of sprigs into the main room and foraged around for a knife, a bowl and a pot of honey. She chopped the herbs finely on the tabletop, tossed them into the bowl and began to grind them down with the wooden hilt of the knife. She poured in a little honey and stirred the mixture with the knife tip, slicing through it occasionally should she spot an herb or plant not ground down finely enough to her liking.

"I need rags – strips of linen." The old goblin woman croaked, leering at me from beneath her heavy eyelids.

I jumped from the bed and fetched a dress of mine. I grabbed a knife, slit into the dress and cut the fabric into long rectangular strips. She snatched them from me and began towards Birger again.

Suddenly she paused.

"Come. You must learn." She rasped. "You! Leave, take the children." She added, dismissing my neighbours.

Sighni herded her children and left, Adhelin and Hefni shuffling out behind her.

I followed the healer the moment she beckoned me and knelt beside her when we reached Birger. I watched her every move attentively. She explained to me the mixture – comfrey, yarrow, honey and bistort to heal the wound – and taught me how to wrap the bandages appropriately around the wound.

"Tomorrow I will come and show you how to change his bandage and make and apply the mixture." She said. "You will clean his wound daily, only use clean strips of linen on it. Keep a cold, wet rag upon his head to ease his heat. Though he shivers, he isn't cold, his body quakes from the battle against the sickness that rages inside him."

She rose and sat at one of the wooden chairs by the table, inhaling a deep breath. I noticed that she was missing many teeth, and her cheeks were so gaunt, they were nothing but loose folds of flesh hanging from her sharply protruding cheekbones.

"You will want to pray for Eir's help to heal him." The healer continued. "There is a small rite you can do to urge her to come to his aid, as well. I recommend you do both and continue the medicines and cleaning of him."

I nodded, my eyes and cheeks still stung from my unrelenting sadness. The tears had stopped, their tracks were sore on my cheeks and my dress was filthy, but I had a goal, now. I had absorbed all the healer's information, her words echoed through my mind clearly.

I *would* make Birger better!

"Tell me the rite." My voice was low and steady.

She told me the rite, she repeated to me the instructions thrice over, so I'd be sure to know exactly what to do and how. She told me a prayer to say, as well as the rite, knowing full well my background. She assumed my Anglo-Saxon upbringing gave me the inability to create an appropriate prayer to her Nordic goddess.

I knew many prayers to ask of this goddess – I'd been praying to every deity I could think of since I'd found Birger this morning – but her words, her prayer, gave me a sense of comfort. This was the healer's prayer.

She left me a bundle of herbs on the table, along with various squares of green and red cloth, and red thread. Alvar strode to her and pressed a few coins into her hand. She accepted the payment with a short nod of her head and scurried to the door.

"When he wakes," she seemed to suddenly remember, turning to me, quickly. "When he is strong enough, take him to one of the sacred springs. The water from the springs will heal his mind as much as his body."

I didn't have a chance to reply before she turned on her heel and left. I was alone with Jarl Alvar. Birger slept on, his breathing harsh, noisy and shallow. Svartr was nowhere to be seen.

"Aveline–" Alvar the First One started.

"We must do the rite." I interrupted, gazing behind him at Birger. "Someone must stay and watch over him while I do the rite."

"I will send a thrall." Alvar said firmly. "I will do the rite with you."

I nodded, meekly stepping to Birger. I bent down to my knees and rested my head against him, gently, careful not to put any pressure on his chest as he struggled for every single breath.

"I love you *faðir*." I whispered, kissing his damp cheek. Then I looked at Alvar, directly into his icy blue eyes – identical to his son's. "Please, Jarl Alvar, don't send Hilda."

Alvar looked at me questioningly for a moment, before thinking better than asking me anything. He left, storming to his hall. I didn't know who he would send, but I knew it would not be the bitter, hateful thrall Hilda.

Taking the rag from Birger's head, I rinsed it in the bucket, before laying it upon him again. He was still hot, like a blacksmith's forge, his skin was still pale as the moon, cheeks flushed with fire, body shivering. I worried, I feared, and I prayed the healer's prayer.

> "Maiden of Lyfja,
> Mighty healer,
> Mend Birger's wounds,
> Grant relief for his pain,
> Alleviate his sickness,
> Grant the return of his health.
> Eir, of all the maidens mighty,
> Oh, hear my plea!"

CHAPTER TWELVE

ALVAR, VIDAR, FREYDIS and I stood hip deep in the freezing waters of Roskilde Fjord. The fjord was vast and spread like a velvet sheet around us, smooth but rippling lightly around our bodies. The clear sky was as blue as a robin's egg, free of clouds, just the jetting white light of the sun's beams dashing through it. It was a beautiful autumn morning, but the world inside my mind was black.

Two of Freydis's beloved thrall girls watched over Birger in his and my home, so we four could perform the rite together. I looked between the three of them, they met my gaze equally serious and ready. So, I began:

> "Hail to the healer of the holy well,
> Friend of Menglad on her high mountain,
> Friend of Frigg on her high throne,
> Friend of the fallen warrior who asks
> For mending and surcease from pain.
> May blood be stanched, may flesh be whole,
> Look upon us with generous eyes."

There were a few small knots of people upon the shore watching us. We paid them no heed; we were focused.

Alvar had brought the thread and cloth the healer had left with me. The cloths – green and red – all had Eir's *bind-rune* sewn into them. The healer explained that the red cloth was used for wounds and acute conditions that needed immediate treatment, whereas the green was for remediation of long-term illnesses.

Vidar held a large bowl of water, filled from the fjord we stood in, and Freydis had a small wooden bowl filled with different coloured pebbles in her hands, which she had brought to assist with the rite. She had done this before.

We each took turns and made a prayer to Eir for Birger's health, before reaching into the little bowl, begging in our minds to Eir, *please, goddess, place the right stone inside my hand!* We placed the chosen stones inside the cloth and tied them shut with the red thread.

Finally, the stones were wrapped, and we were ready for the next step. I began to invoke Eir again, dropping my stone into the crystal fjord waters that swirled inside Vidar's bowl.

"Goddess Eir,
Wash us with your waters,
And wash our loved ones as well.
May all be made whole,
May all be made healthy,
May all be made well."

"May all be made well." Freydis, Vidar and Alvar echoed.

Vidar handed me the bowl with the wrapped-up stones and fjord water. Carefully I held it, careful not to spill even a single drop. He squeezed my small shoulder with one of his large hands, gazing at me with reassurance.

Together in silence we made our way back to the shore, the fjord water sloshing gently against our legs. We walked to the forest, close to where the *blót* had occurred, but we took a different path.

Our clothes were soaked and dripping, the sun was bright but cold and the dirt from the roads stuck to our shoes and garments. It was cool inside the ancient forest; the trees blocked the gentle but bitter breeze. I did not feel the nervousness as I had the day of the *blót*.

At that moment I felt comforted to be travelling into the forest, away from society, hidden among the brush and the bushes and the tall trunks. Brilliant russets, cadmium yellows, mushroom browns and scarlet reds, thick and lush foliage blanketing above our heads, giving me solace and warmth. More leaves had fallen over the night, crunching and crisping loudly under each step.

The trees had seemed a bloody prophesy of the deaths about to occur, each leaf like a drop of the cow's blood splattered across us by Alvar. The anticipation of the blood sacrifices filled me with anxiety: I knew the thralls' deaths were to happen, this Norse culture was drenched in blood.

I thought suddenly of the number of creatures that had died in this forest. Human thralls and animals sacrificed at each *blót* for so many years, and all the other rituals demanding blood sacrifices – the incalculable number of animals hunted and killed, by humans and beasts alike – the sickly or rejected new-born babies who were left, abandoned at the bases of trees for nature to take …

I scrunched my eyes tightly and opened them again, staggering silently, but careful not to spill anything from the bowl. Today I didn't want to think about blood and death, I wanted to think about life and health.

> "Eir, please heal Birger back to health
> Frigg, protect my household from death
> Hel, you cannot take him!"

We came to a part of the wood that opened into a small surprising glade. The sun shone directly onto the clearing; white beams illuminated the lush, verdant grass. I hadn't expected to find such a stunning clearing – it peeked over the edge of Roskilde Fjord, like Vidar and my secret spot. I looked to him and caught him gazing at me – identical sparks flashed in our eyes, he'd thought of our clandestine rendezvous spot, too.

"This is the spot." I said, breaking the silence.

I made my way to the centre of the green and carefully placed the bowl down, the long blades of grass cradling it. I stood and stared at the bowl for a while, watching the light dance upon the glassy face of the water, examining the somewhat frayed edges of fabric that held the stones …

Vidar stood behind me while his parents stood back quietly and respectfully, watching us. Vidar placed a hand on my waist, and took my hand with his other, holding it to his lips and kissing it softly.

"We return in an hour to bury the stones." I said, turning to him.

Vidar kissed the tip of my nose before nodding in agreement. We returned to his mother and father, our hands still clasped together.

"I'll go back and get a shovel. I will stop by Birger before we return." Alvar the First One said, taking his wife's hand in his. "Freydis, accompany me, my love?"

"Of course." She nodded slowly, her luscious green eyes sparkling with wonder as she examined Vidar and me.

And they left.

Vidar and I were silent, listening to Alvar and Freydis's crunching footsteps disappear into the distance. I let go of Vidar's hand and sat on the grass, my legs tucked beside me. I straightened my skirts before I leant back on one hand and a deep sigh cascaded from my lips. I stared at the bowl in the centre of the clearing, sunlight glistening in the still water captured inside it.

"I'm sorry about Birger." Vidar said in a low voice as he sat beside me.

Vidar didn't touch me, he didn't look at me as he spoke, he just stared at the bowl as well.

"He's sick. He will become better." I replied tautly.

"Aveline–"

"*Nei*, he will become better ..." I said, adding grudgingly, "He *has* to if he is going to battle and reach Valhalla." I screwed my eyes shut and breathed out deeply. "He *will* become better."

"*Já.*" Vidar said. "*Já ...*"

Vidar took my hand from my lap and held it tightly, examining the tiny little lines on my skin, my neatly trimmed nails, stroking my small knuckles with his thumb. I closed my eyes as Vidar dragged his fingertips over the soft flesh of my inner arm, reaching my elbow then back to my thin wrist. I enjoyed the explosions of sensation radiating through me from his tender touch.

"Come to me." Vidar tugged my arm softly, urging me towards him.

I did as he asked, and curled up into the grass with him, his arms folded around me, mine pressed against him. I listened to his heartbeat through his chest, steady and calm as was his expression.

We would have to wait at least an hour until the final step of the rite, then all would be complete, and I could return to Birger, ready to begin nursing him to health.

As we laid in the grass, unspeaking for a very long time, I thought of the rite. I thought of Christianity, I thought of the Norse paganism.

I thought of Norse *blóts*, the Christian priest's mass.

The Allfather Odin and the Almighty God.

I thought of the Christian's kneeling, genuflecting, and blessings; I thought of the rites and sacrifices performed by the Danes. Equally stubborn and loyal were both the Christians and the Danes to their respective religions, and here I was caught in the middle, a Christian by birth yet here I prayed to Eir and performed her rite ...

"Marry me, Aveline." Vidar whispered.

Vidar's unexpected request caught me off-guard, my heart skipped a beat.

"*Nei.*" My voice was soft and light, drifting from my lips. "Not now."

"Why not now?" Vidar asked in disbelief. "Now *is* the right time. If Birger doesn't make it, you will need a protector. I would be–"

"You would be *perfect*. But Birger *is* going to make it, with my help. I need to dedicate my time to being by his side."

I sat up and gazed into Vidar's piercing blue eyes. His mouth was pursed tightly shut, frowning slightly at the edges, his forehead was furrowed. I stroked his cheek with my cold fingertips, studying his incredibly serious expression.

"You're so handsome." I traced his lips and face with my fingertip. "We would have such beautiful children ... you'd make a wonderful husband and father."

"Then marry me and bare my child." Vidar leaned up on both arms, and his expression softened. "I know you intend to bring Birger to health – and I hope to all the gods of Asgard that you do ... but in case, *just in case*, you should be wed. And *I* should be the one you marry."

"*Nei.*" I repeated firmly. "I can't think of children and marriage when Birger needs me. I must be with *him*, dedicate myself to him. I have to pray, and care for him, watch over him—"

"You sound like one of your Christian monks." Vidar scoffed.

"Call me what you like," I said, stung by his comment. "That doesn't change the fact I need to spend all my time with Birger and make him well.

Vidar pulled me against him, kissing me lovingly, warmly. I returned his kiss, as tender and soft as his own.

"I haven't seen anyone survive from his type of wound. I love your *faðir* dearly," Vidar said. "But I also love you."

"I always said I wouldn't marry you." I said, the hint of a smile playing on my lips.

"I was hoping you would change your mind." Vidar winked.

"Well, I did – I did change my mind." Our eyes locked. Vidar looked hopeful and excited for my next words. "I love you, but I will not marry you – not right now."

Vidar was confused and crestfallen, I watched his shoulders sink, his expression dropped and the light in his eyes faded a little. We were silent for a while – I felt awkward and ashamed for disappointing Vidar. I rose and walked from him, standing by the edge of the clearing, overlooking the water.

"Not right now ... that means you will marry me at some point?" Vidar asked suddenly.

"When Birger is better, yes." I said, turning to face him.

"Accept my proposal now – we can be betrothed until the day Birger is well." Vidar suggested, smiling up at me from his spot on the tree line. "The wedding will be planned by then and he can celebrate our union with us."

I bit my lip and shook my head.

"Vidar, I *can't*. I can't think of marriage or engagements or anything but Birger! I can't have thoughts of marriage in the back of my mind, distracting me. I want to marry you, I do! But I – I can't. Not yet ..."

Vidar gazed at me with disappointment but nodded: he understood. He came to me, wrapped his arms around me, and pulled me into another tender kiss. I could sense his sadness at my decision through the touch of our lips.

"Well at least you've changed your mind." Vidar said brightly. "I can look forward to marrying you in the future?"

"*Já.*" I smiled, my eyes glistening with unshed tears. "*When* Birger is better, I will wed you."

"Tell me that you love me, again." Vidar grinned, the sparkle of mischief reborn in his eyes.

I was bemused by his reaction but released a loose laugh, bowing my head for a moment before I looked him in the eye again. I pushed my shoulders back and held my head a little higher.

"I love you." I admitted.

"I love you too, my little *Danethrall.*" Vidar grinned.

"Urgh, don't call me that again." I rolled my eyes, shoving him back with annoyance, to which he laughed.

"May we interrupt?" Jarl Alvar's voice floated over to us, causing me to jump slightly.

"Birger's condition has not changed. He sleeps still. The thralls are caring for him, replacing the rag on his head regularly." Freydis said sympathetically, placing a hand on my arm when Vidar and I reached her side. "Let us finish the rite."

I crouched by the bowl and picked it up, pouring the water out gently. I stood and nodded to Alvar, who started to bring the shovel to me until Vidar halted him. A brief glance of understanding passed between the father and son, and Alvar gave the shovel to Vidar. Vidar stood beside me and pressed the tip of the shovel into the ground, glancing at me for approval. I nodded my head, and he began to dig.

It only took a little time before the hole was ready. It wasn't shallow but was not incredibly deep. I bent down and gently placed each wet, wrapped up stone into the ground, then stood back and allowed Vidar to cover them with dirt. The rite was done.

I breathed out deeply, staring at the hole. Now it was time to be with Birger. Alvar and Freydis walked ahead, returning to their home. Vidar accompanied me to my farm but stopped me before I could open the door.

"I love you." He whispered.

"I love you, too."

I placed my hand on Vidar's bearded jaw, the neatly trimmed golden hairs were soft like threads of silk, and I kissed him gently. Vidar's honeyed lips were bittersweet, for this was our kiss goodbye. I moved his hand and pushed open the door to my home, shutting the door firmly behind me, leaving him outside, alone.

CHAPTER THIRTEEN

ROSKILDE, DENMARK
Mid Spring, 874

FRESH LEAVES HAD budded and bloomed from the trees, and their vibrant colours grew brighter every day. I breathed in delicious gulps of the fresh, crisp air – my nostrils filled with the scent of new flowers, bright and dazzling, their scent strong from their recent birth.

Hanging from my arm was a basket full of herbs I'd plucked from the fields and from the foot of trees. I had bought many bunches of medicinal herbs from the healer during the winter, but when spring and summer began, and Birger was thankfully awake, I would spend hours hunting for the wild herbs that the healer had recommended.

I would comb the fields and livestock pens for snails, which I would crush up into a disgusting mixture alongside fenugreek, grease and flaxseed to spread over his stub. The healer explained that this salve would soothe the inflamed wound. I would take armfuls of yarrow, drying the dainty little flowers for weeks, to brew with hot water and honey for Birger to drink every night for his pain.

I had dedicated myself, as I had vowed to Vidar, to tending Birger. Within a month of my obsession-like care and the aid of the healer, Birger had woken. He was weak, incredibly weak, but his fever had broken the day before and he had finally opened his eyes. It took a few more months after that until he was able to hobble to the sacred springs, however.

Shortly after I had said goodbye to Vidar after completing the healing rite, Vidar had left for Britain with a fleet of ships. There had been a rebellion in Jorvik, and Vidar had gone to aid his Scandinavian kings against the Anglo-Saxons.

Vidar had been gone for almost two years.

I hadn't heard of his departure until a month after he'd left. I hadn't attended any feast or *blót* since the night Birger had returned, I had refused to leave Birger's side. I had disassociated myself from the outside world unless it pertained to Birger. I had only found of Vidar's departure when Birger had asked Jarl Alvar of Vidar's whereabouts after he had woken.

Alvar had come to visit Birger, which he did once a week, bringing with him his beloved *Hnefatafl* game. They had not yet played it but intended to play each other as soon as Birger could rise from the bed.

After a particularly full, strong cup of his yarrow tea, Birger had fallen asleep. He drank deeply from his wooden cup as he listened to Alvar speak and had drifted peacefully to slumber.

I had been busy preparing a late dinner for us all, prickling at Alvar's news, and Alvar had been so wrapped up in his monologue about Vidar, staring at his hands entwined in his lap, that neither he nor I realised Birger was sleeping until a mighty honking snore burst from him, scaring Alvar and me half to death.

We looked at each other and erupted into a fit of laughter, both of us cautiously trying to quiet ourselves so as not to wake Birger.

"So much for that conversation." Alvar scoffed. "I suppose I ought to leave."

As he began to pack away his *Hnefatafl* board and pieces, I picked up one of the figures and examined it. It was the little white *Hnefi* – the king.

Alvar said nothing, he took the other figures and gently laid them onto the table and slipped the beautiful eleven by eleven square wooden board, inlaid with walrus' tooth, inside the game bag Freydis had made for him, before slowing putting the figures into the bag with the board.

Alvar was very proud of the bag, she had sewn intricate little pictures into the hem and gifted it to him alongside the handsome game the day they were married. It was immaculately kept, even after all these years.

"Why did you not tell me of Vidar's travels, sooner, Jarl Alvar?" I asked lightly, gazing at the *Hnefi*. "I would've liked to have known."

"I know you would've." Alvar the First One replied quietly. "But I was of the understanding from Vidar that you'd already said goodbye."

I stood in shock and silence for what seemed like an age. My jaw had dropped, and heat swelled in my eyes – tears threatening to drop. I swallowed with difficulty, before I lifted my head and stared at Alvar. With shaking fingers, I held out the game piece and offered it back to him.

"Is that what he said?"

"That is." Alvar said somewhat uncomfortably, delicately accepting the *Hnefi*. "It is no business of mine what occurred between you and my son. I just … I did not want to cause you any upset."

I tilted my head and a damned tear dropped from my lash and tumbled down my face.

"I appreciate that." I said pathetically, watching him place the *Hnefi* into the bag and tying it shut.

Alvar made his way to the door but paused and turned to gaze at me.

"I think you should also know you're very dear to him … he truly loves you." Alvar said quietly, leaving without waiting for my reply.

When Alvar left, I crawled into my bed, under the furs, and wept, shoving my fist into my mouth to silence my wails.

But a long time had passed since that night.

Birger and I frequented the springs, as recommended by the healer, and cleansed his wound with the waters. He claimed the refreshing water did better for his pain and sore than any of the 'filthy stinking slime' I rubbed on his wound, and he somewhat resented the tea. Even though the tea helped ease his pain, he despised the sleepiness that came with it.

Before long, life had gone back to normal. There were only a few differences; Birger would go to the Jarl's hall and practice fighting with Alvar frequently. The two men – friends since they were young boys – would practice their battle techniques; Alvar was teaching Birger to fight again, left-handed and without a shield, at Birger's insistence.

His right arm had been his strongest, but now it was gone, and he had optimistically decided he needed to learn to fight with his left. Birger did abysmally, leaving Alvar's home steaming with self-resentment and rage. Birger would roar in fury; he had once been one of the fiercest warriors ...

"Now," Birger would exclaim, "I'm nothing more than an invalid – a cripple!"

I wallowed in his depression; he was furious with himself for being less capable, and agonisingly punished and chastised himself for it. I detested his depression more than I'd been distraught by his wound. Birger's amputation wound had been incredibly hard to heal, but his emotional wounds seemed incurable.

But Birger carried on. He kept trying. He was a proud man; he was a stubborn man and his stubbornness helped him live. He grew better every day that he practiced with Alvar, though he was far from the warrior he used to be. Birger still drank the yarrow tea, no longer needing the wretched mixture of snails and grease and herbs to be spread across his wound.

And so, there I stood, in the middle of spring, collecting the beautiful yarrow flower, two years after Birger had returned to me, almost two years since Vidar had left ...

I drifted from my original quest, having blanketed the basket half-full with the pretty little flower, I began collecting other flowers and herbs, enjoying the music of the forest, the silky tunes and twittering songs of various birds that fluttered among the branches around me.

I stumbled my way through the forest, lost in a gorgeous haze of scent and gleaming light, the sun baring down so brightly above the trees, it made the forest shimmer and twinkle with viridian, emerald, jade, juniper, shamrock, olive – so many radiant and incandescent shades of green, I felt as though I were in a dream.

I closed my eyes, inhaling deeply through my nose, my mouth slightly open. The flavours of delectably sweet tree sap and, somewhere, beehives dripping with honey danced upon my tongue, blended with the glorious scents of the flowers that were so strong I could almost taste them, too.

I hadn't felt so alive in years.

I stumbled my way through the forest, drunk on sensation, not caring where I went. I found myself entering a clearing – the same glade I had performed the rite to Eir that long time ago! I laid down my basket at the tree line and slowly stepped into the centre of the meadow where I had buried the stones.

My mind flashed with the vivid memories as I sat upon the spot the bowl had been placed. I gazed at Roskilde Fjord, sparkling, clear, beautiful.

"Thank you, Eir, thank you, Frigg, for healing my faðir... and thank you, Hel for not stealing him from me." I thought as I smiled at the wondrous view.

The sky was a clear, sheer sheet of cyan; it was bright and stretched for miles before me. The viridian waters were still, dappled by pure white sunlight and outlined by the expanse of forest and field; dappled with the dark green and brown shadows of islands further out. It was beautiful.

I laid down on my side, feeling the warmth of the morning sun, phenomenally glorious considering it was still only spring. I closed my eyes, drenched with peace and tranquillity, and fell asleep.

I dreamed.

I dreamt of the horns echoing across the fjord, filling every crevasse in Roskilde. I dreamt of the magnificent longships, crafted from hardy, elegant oak – Odin's preferred tree. The ships were graceful, long, narrow, and light, pointed at both ends, with a shallow draft hull designed for speed.

The heads of dragons or serpents were mounted on the prow to scare away sea monsters and spirits – easily removable so as not to scare away the land spirits as the seafarers approached their destination. The seafarers' round, painted shields were arrayed along the gunwales of the ship, a fantastic visage of wonderful decoration, useful storage and convenient protection.

As the ships grew closer their horns grew louder, a vivacious announcement: they were home! And upon the first ship, leading the small fleet, I could spy the handsome, weathered face of Vidar Alvarsson, beaming across the fjord.

I opened my eyes, suddenly woken, greeted to the actual sound of horns reverberating across the fjord! My dream bloomed in front of me – I rubbed my eyes with my fists, lurched onto my feet and stumbled to the edge.

Yes – there they were! Vidar had returned!

I rushed through the woods; my basket forgotten. I lunged through branch and twig, bush and scrub, thorn and vine. Colour and light whizzed passed me, my heart pounded in my chest achingly, my lungs seared, and my mind raced. Vidar was home. *Vidar was home!*

I was eager to see him but feared the consequences of two years apart. Two years of Vidar at war. Was he healthy? Was he wounded? Was he dead? Though I could see the ships, I could not make out the faces as I could in my dream. I hoped beyond hope that my dream had been a vision and Vidar was safe and well.

The shores were filled with townsfolk by the time I had reached it, the longships were moored and emptying. And there – thank the gods! – there, standing by Alvar and Freydis, was Vidar, *my Vidar*! I stopped, my heart stopped, my breath was jammed in my throat, my hands shook. Then Vidar saw me.

Before I knew it, my legs began to run, and I dashed towards him, panting. And to my immense happiness and surprise, he sprinted to me. Vidar's hair had grown much longer, still shaved on the back and sides, and the lengths of the top were tied and braided back, whipping behind him.

We met, colliding into each other in a fervent embrace, squeezing so tightly I couldn't breathe, like a python crushing a tiny mouse. And we kissed – our lips crashed upon one another's in a gush of incredible passion: delayed of each other's touch for two years, it poured from us now, a volcanic eruption of desire.

I could not hear nor see anything but him – the crowds, the sounds, the entire atmosphere had faded. I couldn't feel the sun or the breeze, couldn't hear the gentle slosh of the water, nor the noises of the people. It was just Vidar and me in our zeal and fervour, reunited at last.

We paused, forehead pressed against forehead, panting heavily. Vidar leaned forward, biting my lip gently and tugging my mouth to his, kissing me tenderly. His kiss, though gentle, was intense, bursting with ardour, lingering on my lips. He kissed the tip of my button nose, the bridge of my nose, the centre of my forehead, holding me tightly against him.

"I've missed you." Vidar whispered.

"I've missed you, too." I replied earnestly, tears slipping down my cheeks.

I felt ridiculous for crying, even as silently as I was. So full of emotion: I was ecstatic he was back, overjoyed to be held in his arms, delighted to be in his presence, so regretful of the time we had been apart. I was resentful I'd missed him before he'd sailed and had constantly feared that something had happened to him but was so appreciative that nothing had.

I savoured his every touch, my skin tingled where his hands caressed me, where his lips kissed me, where our bodies pressed together.

The atmosphere began to return, voices and cheers and laughter, a few tears ... We woke from our daze and realised neither of us were dreaming, we were here, on the shore of Roskilde Fjord, holding each other.

It was real!

"Is Birger well?" Vidar asked cautiously.

"Oh, he is, Vidar, he is!" My voice cracked from my tears; a grin exploded on my face. "He is well! He is healthy!"

Vidar beamed at me, and we began to laugh together, our giggles punctuated by kisses. We said nothing more, Vidar fastened his arm around me, and I clutched a tight hold on him, and we walked to his parents, greeting them with our childish chuckles, both of our faces rosy and eyes bright.

"Together at last, I see?" Alvar smiled. "Unfortunately, you'll have to wait to make up for lost time with your woman. You must come and tell me the news from Britain, my son."

"Of course, *faðir*." Vidar agreed, a little disheartened but a cheerful tune lighting his words, nonetheless.

"Let them be, Alvar." Freydis chided, stepping towards me and taking my hands in hers. She placed a soft kiss on my cheek and smiled down on me warmly before she turned to her husband. "Let them be together while we welcome the rest of the men. Then you and he can speak of Britain."

Alvar nodded his head, beaming kindly at us, before taking his wife's hand and making his way through the crowds, welcoming his people's return.

"I left my basket in the forest. You could come with me to retrieve it?" I suggested, giddiness fluttering in my chest.

"I'd like that." Vidar grinned.

We walked quickly to the forest, eager to be completely alone together.

Birds twittered and chirruped overhead, flapping away as we grew closer to them, squawking indignantly at our interrupting them. Thrushes and tits, robins and blackbirds and so many songbirds flittered among the treetops, I could even hear the loud, hollow hammering of woodpeckers drilling into tree trunks close by.

We did not speak of sickness; we did not speak of the battle he fought in Britain. We simply laughed and joked and spoke of nothing important, and yet everything was significant at the same time – a wonderful mixture of contradiction where even the most trivial comment was incredibly special. We laughed and giggled, ecstatic to be reunited with nothing standing in our way.

"So, you'll be my wife, now Birger is better?" Vidar asked as we strode arm in arm.

I laughed at how casually he had asked brought up the subject of marriage.

"What would Alvar and Freydis think to you marrying an Anglo-Saxon? I was a captive here, a thrall in your very home. Do you truly think they'd let you marry me?"

"Alvar has already given me permission. So *já*, I do think they'd let me marry you." Vidar winked.

I stared at him, astonished.

"Alvar had been reluctant to allow Birger to adopt you, but as time went by, he saw how happy you made Birger. That was all it took for them to accept you – they accepted you years ago." Vidar smiled. "Alvar was surprised to say the least when I told him I wanted to marry you, but your birth and how you came to Roskilde wasn't mentioned. He recognised you as the daughter of his most treasured friend and that was it. He was overjoyed to unite his and

Birger's families with marriage. Just as overjoyed as I was to have permission to marry you."

"Why do you want to marry me so much?" I asked playfully. "Do you want to share my bed that badly?"

Vidar smirked, casting a sideways glance at me, an eyebrow raised.

"You can't blame a man for following his heart, can you?" He answered innocently.

"Following his cock, more like." I teased, shoving him gently in the ribs with my elbow.

"Well, when a man's heart and cock both point in the same direction, he can hardly refuse to go the way they lead." Vidar winked.

I scoffed at him, feigning offence. He grinned and pulled me against him and kissed the top of my head. I released him and leapt forward a little, skipping through the trees.

"Where are you going, little fawn?" Vidar called teasingly.

I turned and faced him, walking backwards. I'd been through these trees so often in the past two years, I could practically make my way to the clearing blindfolded.

"Follow your heart … and your cock." I called playfully.

I grinned before I skipped away, deep into the forest.

Like children, we dashed! Vidar chased me, and I slipped away, hidden, giggling to myself quietly like a fool, my heart pounding in my chest.

I concealed myself behind a massive oak that loomed upwards from a bed of tall ferns and tangles of shrubbery. It was massive in girth, its many swollen arms bursting with new foliage, its fat, ancient roots, like a pit of snakes, coiled into the plush, moss carpet of the forest floor.

I rested against the gigantic trunk, the rough bark scratching my back through my linen dress, snaring my hair as I panted, breathlessly.

"Come out, come out, wherever you are." Vidar sang, though I couldn't tell from where.

Stifling my giggle, I crouched down, heart thumping, pulse racing. I felt like a rabbit being hunted by a fox, but I enjoyed the excitement. I naturally wanted to run to Vidar every time he called, but I enjoyed the thrill of the hunt. Conceitedly I savoured my skill of outsmarting him, though a part of me realised Vidar was toying with me.

Carefully I rose, stealthily continuing my way to the clearing, listening to him rustling through the trees as he tracked me.

I was close to the clearing when I couldn't hear Vidar any longer. I paused and frowned. I glanced around and listened carefully, but I couldn't find him. I abandoned my stealth and pushed through the brush, crunching and rustling noisily as branches snared my skirts.

"Ullr, mighty hunter, you can come out now." I called, wondering if I truly had lost him.

I kept walking, however, scanning the area in search of Vidar as I paced to the clearing, which opened wide only a few feet in front of me. I could hear nothing but the birds, the rustling of my own steps and the slosh and ripple of the fjord.

Standing at the edge of the clearing, I paused, spotting my basket conveniently close by, exactly where I had left it. I breathed in deeply, the gilded rays of sunlight piercing the azure sky, illuminating the clearing magically.

The deliciously balmy heat warmed my face, my chest, my breasts and my legs. The back of my body was cool from the shadow of the forest, a delightful contrast of temperature. I closed my eyes as the clement breeze caressed my flesh, the skirts of my dress dancing softly around my ankles.

"I've found you, little fawn." Vidar's voice whispered in my ear.

I lurched in surprise, my shoulders thudding into his torso. He grabbed my hips and pulled me against him, though my feet were cemented to the ground. Vidar slipped one hand over my stomach, maintaining pressure to seal me against him as his other hand slid upwards to rest on my chest, feeling my heart pummel against my ribcage. Vidar snickered at my racing heartbeat and goosebumps erupted over my skin where his warm breath danced.

I tilted my head in reaction to him, and he nuzzled my chestnut hair aside, revealing the soft, taut, milky flesh of my neck. Vidar glided his lips across my skin, from my shoulder to my ear, taking my earlobe between his teeth delicately. I shuddered as Vidar drew the tip of his tongue along the edge of my ear.

"I thought I'd managed to lose you." I purred as he nibbled my neck, his hand squeezing my breast.

"*Nei*, I knew exactly where you were ... my heart and my cock are very good navigators."

Together we laughed, and I turned to face him, draping my arms around his neck.

"Your cock seems to be pointing you to another course." I grinned, feeling his hard member pressed against me.

"I know exactly where it's leading me, and I plan on following it directly." He smirked, pulling me into a kiss.

Vidar's lips were full, warm, pressed against mine in a wave of tender, lingering pecks. They were rough and cracked from his time at sea, and his gold and brown beard scratched my chin, softly. He held my face with one hand, his thumb pressed along the edge of my cheekbone, his fingers curved around my neck.

Tenderly, Vidar nipped my bottom lip, and I smiled as he took my lip between his teeth and tugged gently. My lips parted, and he slipped his tongue quickly into my mouth; our tongues grazing in yearning jabs.

I trembled with anticipation, my body on fire. We stumbled backwards, our tongues dancing harmoniously, interrupted only by quick soft presses of our lips. Vidar's hands caressed my back, waist, hips, buttocks, his touch pressured by longing.

As we kissed, I slid my hands down to the belt around his waist. I couldn't get the damned thing undone! Sensing my frustration, Vidar hurriedly undid his belt and yanked off his tunic. I gazed at his gorgeous body: his shoulders were broad, his muscles defined beautifully. Maroon slashes of various size and bruises ranging from purple to black tainted his tight bronze flesh: mementos of war.

I stroked his torso with both of my hands, drifting them over his tattoos and the light covering of soft fair hairs that dusted his chest, and ran my fingers, delicately, over his hard, dark rose nipples.

"I don't want to shame you ..." Vidar said, gently gripping my hips.

"You won't shame me. I want you, I want *this*."

"Will you marry me now Birger is better?"

"*Já.*" I smiled. "I love you."

"I love you, too." Vidar said, kissing me.

When I saw Vidar on the shore after two years of separation, there was nothing I wanted more than to be in his arms. Vidar was constant, noble, considerate of me. There was a darkness to him, and yet I was drawn to him despite that. With Vidar I was comfortable, safe, happy.

With faith in the Norse gods, the rituals and rites, Birger was healed and healthy. Now Vidar was returned to me and I was ready to put my faith in him. I was ready to marry him, to be with him. Even though we weren't married, I was ready to give myself to him. I was ready.

Vidar opened the brooches from my gown and tossed them aside gently. He slipped the straps of my apron dress over my shoulders and slid the rest of the dress down. It pooled at my feet, like a puddle of golden sunlight, quickly forgotten.

I pulled my arms from Vidar. His eyes were wide, and his expression was full of wonder and eagerness as I began to undress.

I pulled my arms out of the sleeves of my ivory linen dress. I shimmied slightly, lifting the dress upwards to slip over my head. He reached out a hand and took a fistful of the dress, bunching up the fabric, and pulled it off me.

I stood naked before Vidar. I was self-conscious, I'd never been completely naked in front of a man before and I hoped beyond hope that Vidar liked what he saw.

I was short, with wide hips and small breasts. When I was young, my mother used to proudly comment that my hips were perfect for child-birthing. I'd been embarrassed when she'd told me that, but at that moment all I wanted was for Vidar to enjoy the sight of me.

Nervously I crossed my arms and my cheeks bloomed pink. I gazed at the grass at my feet and avoided Vidar's eyes as he gazed me.

Suddenly Vidar lunged at me, like a wild beast attacking its prey. He kissed me and scooped me off my feet. My heart jumped, I whipped my arms around his neck, my legs wrapped tightly around his waist. Vidar chuckled into our kiss and my face burned redder.

Vidar carefully lowered me onto the soft emerald grass, some patches still damp with the delicate drops of morning dew. I gazed at him, knelt between my legs, excitement pouring out of me. Vidar smirked – his eyes were alight, the palest of blue, like the winter sky, rimmed with a ring of sapphire, tinged with mischievousness. I couldn't help but smile back.

I closed my eyes and pushed my shoulders into the ground, gripping wads of grass. I curled my legs around Vidar's body as he lowered himself onto me. He held me with one hand and his other hand grasped and squeezed my breast as we kissed.

I lifted myself onto my elbows as he shifted further down me, tenderly sucking the nipple of my breast, his hand still clutching the other, rolling the nipple between his finger and thumb, sending delicious sparks of sensation to pulsate through my body.

I lowered myself back to the ground, the blades of grass tickled and scratched my bare flesh. A quiet purr wispily escaped my parted lips and Vidar continued to suck my nipple eagerly until I gasped. He lifted his face, concerned, but I gently took Vidar's jaw between my hands and urged him upwards, smiling.

I brought him into a kiss and felt his cock press hard against me. I removed my legs from around him and planted my feet firmly on the ground. With every little movement Vidar made, he nudged me, his cock rubbed between my legs and sent little explosions of bliss rippling through my body.

Vidar shifted his lower body and slipped his hand downwards, over my mound of silky, dark hairs, rubbing a fingertip between my legs. I gasped, and my body shook as his finger danced over me in delicate circles.

He kissed me gently, lovingly. I caressed him, stroked my hands over his hard nipples and the soft down of fair hairs that dusted his chest. A warmth grew inside me, boiling and boiling and our kisses grew more fervent. He added the slightest of pressure to the constant rhythm of his fingertip and jerky snaps of lightning flashed through my body before euphoria crashed over me like waves in a storm.

The breath I didn't realise I'd been holding fell from my lips in a quivering gust of pleasure. Vidar slipped his hand from between my trembling thighs and gripped my hip tightly, kissing me once before he rested his forehead on mine.

"Do you want—"

"*Já.*"

"We're not wed yet."

"I want to."

"Are you sure?"

"*Já!*"

"This might hurt." Vidar whispered.

With one hand, he tugged his trousers down and took his cock in his hand. Gently, he pressed its head against my virgin opening.

"Are you sure?" Vidar repeated.

"Be gentle." I breathed, squeezing my eyes shut tightly, inhaling deeply.

Vidar eased himself into me. Maintaining a careful pace, he slowly increased his pressure until he was finally inside me. I gasped, so filled with him, I thought I might burst!

"Are you okay?" Vidar murmured between kisses.

"*Já,*" I replied breathily. "Keep going!"

Vidar grinned and began to thrust, slowly. Sharp jabs of pain lined the delectable pleasure that rushed through my body. I gripped his firm, plump buttocks, digging my nails into his flesh as he began thrusting harder and harder. The pain was easily ignored as I writhed beneath Vidar in an abundant eruption of ecstasy.

CHAPTER FOURTEEN

WHEN WE REACHED the hall, it was already late afternoon. We'd taken much longer than planned and Alvar was noticeably impatient when we arrived. He clapped Vidar on the back with his paw-like hand and practically pushed him to the chair beside his on the wide platform.

"There are celebrations to be had for your and your men's return, son. But first, tell me what happened at Jorvik." I heard Alvar's booming voice command as he led Vidar to the platform.

I sighed, quickly looking around the room to find Birger in deep conversation with Jan. My heart jumped slightly, but I made my way to them, anyway, nervously appearing beside Birger. I shot a timid smile at Jan who winked back at me, grinning.

"Ah! There's the girl, now." Birger beamed, wrapping his arm around my shoulders.

"Here I am." I winced, my lips curled into a wonky smile. "You were speaking of me?"

"Birger was asking if I was still unwed." Jan grinned impishly, running a hand through his long, light brown tresses, his deep blue eyes glittering with mischief. "He was wondering why we decided not to marry each other all those years ago."

"Well, it was only two years ago." Birger pointed out, his eyebrows raised. "Not that long ago."

"It wasn't that long ago at all." Jan nodded to the relieved and hopeful Birger. "I also told him I had been very fine – overjoyed, even! – with the idea of marrying you." Jan continued wickedly, making my jaw drop. He innocently fiddled with the three plaits he kept braided in his bushy beard, which flowed to his chest. "It was you who didn't want to marry me. We were just trying to discern why you denied me."

"I realised you hadn't told me why – you hadn't even told me he wanted to marry you! I urge you to reconsider his proposal, whatever your reasons were to deny him in the first place! Jan is a skilled warrior, a strong man from a very good family – his farm is large, he could provide for you very well!" Birger sputtered.

I scowled at Jan furiously. As wonderful a companion as he was, Jan was quite the trickster when he wanted to be. He was a teaser, taking vast enjoyment from fooling his friends and comrades, yet it would be hard to find a more loyal man than him.

Hearing Birger sincerely try to convince me to marry Jan made me realise he had not seen Vidar and my scene on the beach. I assumed no one had spoken to him about it, either. I was positive that his daughter romancing with the Jarl's son would've been at the tip of his tongue to talk about, had he known.

Birger was not the social butterfly he used to be. He spent most of his time learning to fight after he had finally healed from his fever and hardly socialised much at all anymore. Though the two older men spent so much time together, I assumed the noble Alvar had not seen it his place to reveal Vidar and my relationship to Birger.

I placed a hand on my adoptive father's arm and gazed at him with a semi-smile upon my face.

"*Faðir* ... I've decided to marry Vidar."

"Vidar?" Birger gasped, staggering backwards onto a chair. He grabbed the closest mead and gulped it down noisily. "Vidar? Vidar Alvarsson? *The Jarl's son?*"

"He wants to marry me, as well." I smiled, before tipping my head towards Jan and adding rudely, "You recommended I marry well. I think marrying Vidar is far better than marrying him."

Jan laughed, loud and unrestrained, placed his hands on my shoulders and drew me into a deep embrace. His alabaster skin glowed in the firelight, and he smelled of lye soap and honey mead.

"Marrying Vidar may give you a better position in society, Aveline Birgersdóttir, but marrying me would give you far prettier children and much more enjoyment in bed." Jan quipped, planting a big smooch upon my lips.

I laughed and slapped him playfully.

"What is going on here?" Vidar had appeared, his father and mother behind him, bemused smiles painted on their faces.

Other celebrators had turned their focus to us now, wondering what had the Jarl and his family quite so interested.

"Aveline and I are to be wed." Jan quickly replied, resting his head on mine. He was one of the tallest men I'd ever met – I could see why he was known as Jötunnson, for he was gigantic – and had to bend himself absurdly to be able to rest his head atop mine. "Birger has just given us his approval!"

Vidar continued to look bewildered, both eyebrows slowly inching higher up his forehead, his eyes glaring at me for an explanation. People began cheering for Jan and my engagement – Birger was even more shocked than before.

"I'm just fooling you, man!" Jan cackled. Finally, he released me and opened his arms to Vidar. "Aveline just shared the news. Well done, brother, congratulations!"

"I'm glad you said that. I was wondering for a second if I was going to have to gut you here or wait until we arrived in Britain and do it there." Vidar winked, sighing with great relief as he embraced his friend.

"No gutting required." Jan grinned. "But I would like to reserve her, in case one of the Saxon bastards kills you."

"You'll have to ask Aveline and Birger," Vidar shot a quick smirk at me. "But don't keep your hopes up. You will have to outlive me to marry Aveline. You're a great warrior, Jötunnson, but I'm better – the Anglo-Saxons will slay you long before they're able to slay me."

"So," Birger interrupted as he rose to his feet, finally somewhat composed. "You want to marry my *dóttir*, do you, Vidar Alvarsson?"

"If that is agreeable to you, *já.*" Vidar answered, holding his arm out to Birger.

Birger gripped Vidar's forearm tightly, and Vidar enclosed his fingers around Birger's.

"It is agreeable, very much so." Birger said before yanking Vidar against him.

Vidar embraced Birger with his free arm and cheering erupted loudly from all around. It was agreed – Vidar and I had permission to wed!

The two men released each other, both grinning from ear-to-ear. Vidar took his place by my side, pulled me against him softly, and we kissed to the adoration of the townsfolk. Alvar clapped his enormous paws together, Freydis looked on us with silent happiness, ever smiling, gorgeous green eyes glittering.

"You knew of this, you fiend?" Birger barked at Alvar.

"I gave my approval long ago." Alvar smirked.

"And you didn't think of informing me?" Birger reproached.

"I wanted to see the surprise on your old ruddy face." Alvar chortled. "You're my oldest friend, Bloody Sword. And on the day, they wed we will be kin!"

"I take back my approval! I can't have *him* as my kin!" Birger exclaimed in mock horror.

Laughter streamed through the hall, and the two men continued to rib and scoff at one another. I turned to gaze at my future husband, and he pressed his forehead against mine.

Suddenly, I was ripped from his arms by a gaggle of gossiping women. In a whirlwind of chatter, the hoard of excited women went on and on about the when's, how's and undetermined what's of the future. It took some time, but I finally managed to slip away, in search of Vidar.

I found him on the main platform in deep conversation with Jarl Alvar and Birger, an empty chair beside him reserved just for me. My heart fluttered in my chest – it was real. It was real! I was officially betrothed to Vidar Alvarsson!

***

EVENING HAD FALLEN, and the meal was served. The feast consisted of delicious deer and wild boar, with stuffed pheasants and rabbits and mountains of various vegetables, cheese and bowls of steaming stew.

Vidar took a hefty bite of his pork, grinned at me with puffed-out cheeks and grease on his lips, and pecked a kiss upon my lips. I wiped the transferred grease from my face on the back of my hand, then cheekily cleaned my hand on his tunic.

"If you keep stuffing your face like that, they'll shove a stick up your arse and cook you on the spit with the swine." I said, poking him in one bulging cheek with my fingertip.

"*Ha-ha.*" Vidar sarcastically retorted after laboriously swallowing his mouthful with an immense gulp.

He wrinkled his nose and showered my lips with a flurry of greasy kisses.

"You're enjoying yourself, are you?" I laughed.

"I am, thank you." Vidar replied, wiping his mouth with his tunic sleeve. "It has been agreed and announced we're to marry, why wouldn't I be happy?"

I beamed at him and we giggled for a little while. Vidar ate while I plucked little bites from his plate, and we drank mead together until my head began to spin. We had just ended yet another conversation about our impending marriage when a sudden thought popped up into the forefront of my mind.

"Vidar – what did Jan mean, 'in case one of the Saxon bastards kills you next time'?" I asked. "When is the next time?"

Before Vidar had a chance to reply, Alvar stood, tankard of ale in hand, the air of announcement radiating from him. Vidar and I forgot our conversation and turned to focus on Alvar, as did the others in the hall. The Jarl's hall was filled to bursting, townsfolk stuffed into every inch of space within the walls. Even the double doors were wide open, faces crowded within the frames.

"Welcome home." Alvar bellowed proudly, gazing around the room. "After a long time battling the Christian bastards, you've returned! Odin, Thor and Týr fought beside you – favouring your efforts. You should be proud! The rebellion was beaten down! And Mercia has been conquered!"

The hall walls quaked from the uproar of victorious ovations and applause. Alvar found his son's face and stared at him pointedly. Vidar immediately rose to his feet. The townsfolk followed Alvar's eyes and looked intently at the Jarl's son.

After gaining all the attention in the hall, Vidar brought his horn of mead to his lips and threw it back dramatically, gulping the entire contents impressively fast.

"Brothers!" Vidar said, arms spread wide. "We are triumphant! The Anglo-Saxon King Burgred has fled, Mercia is ours! But the war has not ended yet. King Guthrum and King Halfdan have separated the forces – Guthrum continues the battle against Wessex, and Halfdan's men head north to Strathclyde to fight the Picts and the Britons."

Vidar began to move around the room, making his way to stand by his father. Faces followed him intently, men clapped him on the back as he passed them, women blushed. Everyone was enthralled by the Jarl's son.

"Though we have only just returned home," Vidar continued, taking his place beside Alvar the First One. "We must gather strength – we need more men! We go with Guthrum to Wessex! We are to join the Great Army again, and soon! Britain *will* be ours!"

Adulations and acclamations thundered. Horns thudded against each other, mead and ale and beer sloshed and splashed. The musky scent of body odour was seeping through the air, mingled with the sweetness of mead and the hoppy aroma of the ale and beer. I began to feel nauseous and wobbly. I slipped unnoticed through the crowds to the doors and out into the cool night air.

I breathed in deeply. My queasiness disappeared, but I felt dizzier from the sudden cool, fresh air mixed with my alcohol induced half-daze. I saw a group of women roasting two fat wild boar sows and four chubby young piglets on spits over a hot fire – they looked juicy and succulent, and the smell was a delectable mix of sweet and smoky.

I felt hungry suddenly and carefully made my way to the spits. Salivating, I watched one of the women begin to slice off meat from one of the piglets, and my stomach began to growl.

Before I had a chance to approach the women, a body shoved into me, causing me to stumble backwards, and with astounding luck I did not fall. The body paused, snickering at me.

"*Hilda?!*"

"Sorry, *Danethrall*." She spat sarcastically. "Or is it *mistress Danethrall* now your engagement to the Jarl's son has been announced?"

"I am sick of how you treat me! Why do you hate me so, Hilda?" I growled.

"Because you are a betrayer." She snarled. "You've forsaken your God and your people for pagan murderers!"

I stared at her, shocked and taken aback by her answer.

"Here you are, calling the monster who stole you 'father' – and you fornicate and sin with a murderer! How could you love the monster who has the blood of your kin drenching his hands?" Hilda hissed.

"*Vidar* did not murder my family." My hands had curled into fists and quaked with rage.

"He would've had he raided in his father's stead."

"The blood may be upon Alvar's hands, and Birger's, and the blacksmith's and the fishmongers, and every other damned Dane in this town, but I have moved forward!" I exclaimed. "These Danes are just like us! Our people are not innocent of murder, either – even a Christian's hands are not clean of blood! Can you not let go of your hatred?"

"I will *never* forgive what these God forsaken heathens did to me and my family!" Hilda roared. "And you – you are the worst of them all, you traitor!"

"Is it really so wrong of me to have found love?" I gasped indignantly. "You judge me and brand me a betrayer, yet God teaches forgiveness and mercy – even to your enemies!"

"'*Never take your own revenge, beloved, but leave room for the wrath of God, for it is written, "Vengeance is mine, I will repay!" says the Lord.*'" Hilda boomed victoriously. "Fear his wrath, Danethrall, for God will strike vengeance upon you!"

Before I could even register my movement, I slapped Hilda viciously across her face. She clapped her hand to her cheek, her face pale with shock.

"I have struck you! '*Since indeed God considers it just to repay with affliction those who afflict you ... they will suffer the punishment of eternal destruction, away from the presence of the Lord and from the glory of his might!*' – Now I will deserve his vengeance!" I growled.

I stared at her for a few moments, my whole body trembling with fury.

"I did not forget the Christian teachings my parents raised me by, nor any word the priest uttered at mass. I have remembered them ever more so since being brought to Roskilde!" I thundered. "I prayed every day since I was brought here – as I'm sure you have too – and God did not answer me! He never answered me. He did not save me – and he hasn't saved you! God forsook my village! God forsook me – and he forsook *you*! I prayed to the Dane's gods *once*, and they saved Birger from death, like I asked!"

I whipped my hand out and grabbed her wrist. Hilda flinched, expecting me to hit her again. Instead, I jerked her towards me and glared into her pallid, terrified face.

"Since you have called upon your god to strike me, I call upon two of my gods – Vidar and Vali, the gods of vengeance! – to aid me and strike you down!" My voice was low and steady, and I glared at her with dark determination.

Hilda ripped her arm from my grasp and sprinted away into the darkness, sobbing hysterically. I sighed deeply, my breathing was quick, and my chest ached.

"Are you okay, dear?" One of the women by the spit called to me.

"Uh, yes, thanks." I replied weakly, as the surrounding area began to materialise back into focus.

The woman beckoned me over, and I slowly stepped towards her and the collection of women at the spit, my mind spinning from the confrontation with Hilda.

"Hungry, dear?" An older woman asked, holding out a slice of meat from the edge of her knife.

"Thank you." I said feebly, accepting the scalding slice she offered me.

I bounced it back and forth between my hands, blowing on it, before finally being able to take a bite. The women giggled at me, but one rushed off and brought a plate to me, plopping a few more slices onto it. I smiled, embarrassed but appreciative, taking another bite of the meat. Though the confrontation with Hilda had diminished my appetite, I could still appreciate the delicious flavour of the meat.

"What happened with the thrall?" The older woman asked tactlessly.

"Oh, nothing." I dismissed, not wanting to divulge any further.

"She doesn't seem to know her place." She said. "You may need to show her it ..."

"You're right, she didn't ... I think she does now, though." I answered, taking another bite of the sweet pork.

"Mind my asking, love, but you're Aveline Birgersdóttir, are you not?" The younger woman interrupted, examining me rather shrewdly.

"Err, yes." I said, swallowing hard.

"Well done, lamb." The older woman beamed warmly. "The Jarl's son! What a wonderful match! Birger must be very proud."

I blushed scarlet, nodding and murmuring my thanks. All the women began cooing over me, reminiscing over their marriages, quickly pushing Hilda out of my mind.

The women gossiped and fussed and shared their tales with me. They all had been fifteen or sixteen when they'd wed, and a passing comment was made of my age, but swept away quickly. I began to realise the sudden respect I'd earned among the Danes from just announcing my betrothal to the Jarl's son. Birger was highly respected in this community, but he was still just a Karl.

"When do you plan to wed?" She repeated. "You've waited long enough, I'm sure you plan to marry quickly." She added, giggling a little.

"Oh, I'm not sure." I replied, honestly stumped. "With preparations for battle ... I'm unsure."

"Well of course you'd want to wed before he leaves!" She gushed.

"You can let him plant his seed in your belly before he's left. A son would be wonderful for him to return home to!" The older woman winked, answered by a storm of tittering.

"Is Alvar raiding or Vidar?" Another woman questioned, thoughtfully. "We cannot be without all our men, in case that damned Erhardt attacks again ... Alvar will want someone to stay and defend Roskilde – and Freydis!"

"Of course! Knowing Alvar the First One, he'd want to fight beside King Guthrum."

"But Vidar just aided Guthrum in the taking of Mercia, he may be eager to take Wessex soon, too."

"With a new bride, he may be preoccupied with other things needing his attention …"

"Oh, Anna, you have such a filthy mind for a woman so old!"

"Old and experienced!"

The women burst into great fits of laughter. My mouth had dropped at their comments, I stood awkwardly as I listened to their conversation quickly dissolve to crudeness.

"Good eve'," Vidar said, placing a hand upon my hip.

The crowing women stopped immediately, greeting the Jarl's son with faces the colour of beets.

"You have a gift at sneakily appearing when one least expects it." I admired quietly, bringing his hand to my lips to kiss.

"We were just talking to your bride, my lord." The older woman, Anna, said. "We were wondering how soon the wedding would take place?"

"After contracts between her family and mine have been agreed upon, gifts have been purchased and a *mundr* and dowry set, then we will celebrate our union." Vidar said pleasantly yet matter-of-factly. "It should not be long. But with the next raid being organised so quickly, I cannot be sure."

"When do you leave?" I asked.

"There are a few minor repairs needed on the ships, we need to restock the food and arrows, mend the weapons, make a few new shields, and decide whether Alvar will be leading the men, or I. Then we shall leave. Thirty days, I should think, then we'll sail." He replied thoughtfully.

"Thirty days?" I gasped.

"We plundered well, didn't lose many men. We came out quite well." Vidar explained, eyebrows raised and frowning slightly – almost like he was surprised at this realisation. Then he turned to the women, taking a bite of the wild piglet meat from my plate. "The meat is excellent. *Gott kveld*, ladies."

They bid their cordialities and Vidar began to lead me away, but not to the hall. We walked through the quiet streets, away from the noise and the smell of the feast, able to enjoy our own company.

"Do you intend to go back to Britain?" I asked bluntly.

"I'd like to." Vidar admitted. "But King Guthrum made mention he'd like to fight with my father by his side. He was glad to take Mercia with me, but it has been a while since he's fought with Alvar. He'd like to share this victory with my father."

I sighed with relief.

"So, you won't be leaving our wedding bed and leaping straight into battle." I smiled. "I was beginning to think you hadn't enjoyed me earlier …"

"I did!".

I recoiled slightly, not expecting such a fiery answer. He stared at me for a moment, but his expression cooled, and he tugged me against him.

"Of all in Midgard, Aveline, I did. I've been waiting a long time for you."

"How long?" I beamed playfully. "Since I was sixteen, I assume. Your reaction to Kainan hinted–"

"Don't speak of him." Vidar snapped. "I don't want to hear his name. I want to speak of *us*."

"Then speak." I said, somewhat shortly.

He paused for a moment. His brow furrowed as he rubbed his bottom lip with his finger and thumb as he carefully considered how to proceed with what he wanted to say.

"Aveline … I was married before; you know this?" He finally asked.

Shockingly, I hadn't known. The expression on my face must have said as much. Vidar thought in silence for a few moments longer, sighing deeply once or twice, before he continued.

"I was married to a woman from Lund, when I was sixteen." Vidar explained quietly, staring into the darkness ahead of us as we walked. "She was three years younger than me. We were married for ten years and she bore me no children. Our marriage was difficult … I raided a lot in those years – Britain, Francia, wherever. I would come home for a while, and still we had no child, no heir, no son. We realised quickly that she could not bare my child, so she refused to share my bed anymore. She was unhappy, I was unhappy … so, we divorced.

"She went back to Lund, married a widower and happily raised his children like her own … I stayed here. Alvar and Freydis wanted me to marry again, but I did not. Not quite so quickly … I wanted to lie with whores and remember how exciting sex could be … sex had, unfortunately, turned into a disappointing chore for my wife on the rare occasion that she would lay with me."

"Why didn't you tell me you were married before?"

My head spun, I was stunned by the news of this marriage I'd never heard of.

"Would it change anything?" He asked, turning to me.

I thought for a moment and shook my head.

"I'm just surprised no one said anything about it before." I commented.

"It was inconsequential; a childless marriage that ended over a decade ago. Why *would* anyone say anything about it?" Vidar pointed out.

"Then why are you telling me about it now?"

Vidar suddenly stopped walking. We stood at edge of the forest, but so deep was the darkness, we may as well have been standing before an abyss.

"Because you are to be my wife soon. I want no secrets between us, Aveline, and no omissions, only the truth – no matter how dreadful." He explained, holding my hands tightly in his.

"I agree." I replied, bringing his hands to my lips so I could kiss them. "For as long as you're honest with me and confide in me, I will always do the same for you. But Vidar, you asked for no omissions, but you silenced me when I began speaking of Kainan?"

Vidar smirked and pulled me against him, enveloping me warmly. He planted a kiss atop my head and chuckled to himself quietly.

"I am jealous he loved you first." Vidar admitted softly.

"I never laid with him."

"Loving doesn't just mean sharing a bed."

"Vidar?"

"Mmm?"

"I am jealous you married another before me." I murmured.

He laughed softly, and I squeezed him gently.

"And now here we are together, in each other's arms and engaged to be wed."

"Exactly where I want to be."

We kissed tenderly for a few moments before Vidar rested his head upon mine again.

"You asked me how long I've wanted you." He continued.

"*Já*, I want to know." I said, my cheek pressed against his chest.

"Well, four or so years after my divorce – Birger Bloody Sword stepped off a longship with a little thrall child at his side." Vidar smiled. "You slept on the floor of my home for a month, and I paid no mind to you at first. You were nothing more than a snot-nosed Christian child – but how significant you were to Birger! He desperately fought to keep you and adopt you. I was intrigued – why was Birger Bloody Sword so eager to adopt a dirty little Christian girl? Of course, you looked like his daughter but ... but there must've been more. I wondered whether you were here for a reason, if perhaps the gods had placed you into Birger's hands on purpose – but *why*?

"I remember seeing you the day you left the hall ... it was midday, and you were in the garden, gazing at my mother's flowers. The sun gleamed down upon you, and I saw all the colours of autumn glisten in your hair. You turned around and faced me suddenly, and I froze; before me was a Saxon child – a girl with fire in her eyes! You stared at me, horrified, your big, burning amber eyes so wide with shock ... then you dashed away ... I'd never seen eyes like yours before!

"I'd watch you sometimes. I'd watch Birger teach you to fight. I laughed in passing at your terrible Danish when you first began to learn ... noticed you weep, all ruddy faced and damp cheeked, at the *blóts* when we sacrificed the thralls and animals...

"When you became a woman, my interest in you began to grow into something more ...

"Do you remember bumping into me in the woodshed?"

"*Já*," I answered, finding my voice.

"I'd been pacing around the shed, trying to work out whether I should ask Birger for your hand or not. I didn't know if you were promised to anyone yet, and honestly, I didn't know if I should propose to you or not anyway – you were fifteen years younger than I, and I hadn't ever really spoken to you. Love comes after marriage, I suppose. Marriages work quickly; once contracts are signed and money paid, you have the ceremony and you're married – you can learn about each other and find romance together afterwards.

"Anyway, I digress.

"In the woodshed you stood before me shivering and even in the darkness, your amber eyes glowed like fire in the night. I was fascinated by you. But I was to be the next Jarl of Roskilde – I needed to know if you were truly a Dane or whether you were still a little Christian thrall child. A jarl cannot marry a thrall."

"How long until you decided I was *worthy enough* to marry you?" I asked mockingly.

"Very soon into your argument with Birger." Vidar winked. "Anglo-Saxon women are very meek; they do as they are told. You were fiery, stubborn, fierce … very passionate. Much like the goddess Freyja! I realised the gods placed you in Birger's hands so that I would meet you; we were meant to be together, I knew it – I felt it in my bones."

"So why didn't you ask him for my hand then, when you were sure?" I blushed.

"I hadn't asked Alvar if he would approve of the match, for one." Vidar said. "And when Birger asked if I'd guard you for him, possibly find a viable husband for you – without giving the impression he viewed me as a possible suitor … I just didn't ask. He was very intent on Jan." Vidar laughed. "Which is why I was so surprised this evening, when Jötunnson announced you both were to marry!"

"If you knew Birger wanted me to marry Jan, but *you* wanted to marry me, then why on earth did you invite Jan to dinner for me to inspect him?" I exclaimed.

"I had to honour my promise to Birger – I said I'd ask Jan, so I did. But after the dinner, when Jötunnson told me he'd like to marry you, I told him that I wanted to. So, he backed down."

"And it took you this long to ask me to wed you?"

"Far from it! I told you that I loved you and wanted to wed you many times – you turned me down!" Vidar retorted playfully, as we reached the edge of the forest.

"I can't disagree with you there." I smiled. "But I couldn't, because of Kai– because of the situation I was in."

"Because you wanted to marry the thrall." Vidar's smile dropped slightly. "Do you still?"

"*Nei*. I never did, Vidar …He … he helped me realise who I am and what I wanted, and I – I struggled to accept that for a long time …" I turned to him, my eyes blazing with steadfast resolve. "It's you, Vidar – only you."

Vidar kissed the top of my head.

"Come," he whispered. "I've something to show you."

CHAPTER FIFTEEN

WE DIDN'T SPEAK again until we had reached our clearing. Giddy with excitement, I spotted the whales meandering slowly in the fjord below. I rushed from Vidar's side and stood at the edge, eagerly watching the huge beasts flop and glide.

"I've missed this place." I gushed happily. "I came here only a handful of times since you left. It wasn't the same without you here … I missed you so much."

"I like to hear that." Vidar smiled, softly. "I have some gifts for you – I thought of you every day while I was gone."

I turned to him surprised and delighted, as we sat together on the edge of the clearing, our feet dangling. Vidar had pulled a few bundles from somewhere in the brush. He handed me the first bundle; it was small and wrapped in a strip of dark linen. I opened it to find a magnificently crafted ivory comb, carved from deer antler.

"I hunted the stag, myself, and made this for you." Vidar explained proudly.

Along the edge of the comb he had etched Nordic runes. I squinted at them through the darkness, slowly making out what they said.

Remember me, my love, I remember you.

It was wonderful. A warm smile lit up my face. I kissed him and uttered my thanks, reading the runes over again.

"I adore it!" I breathed, my face flushed pink.

Vidar beamed at me and took the comb from me, offering me the second bundle in return. It was very large and heavy and wrapped in the same dark linen as the comb. I pulled away the fabric and revealed a gorgeous garment – a gown!

I scrambled to my feet, holding the sunshine coloured dress out with trembling hands. It was a gorgeous Anglo-Saxon wedding gown! It was long, flowing and made of silk, with a scooped neckline, hemmed with a thick white trim, delicately embroidered with a simple yet beautiful silver pattern. There was an ivory girdle to tie around my hips that matched the patterned trim. It was exquisite – never had I imagined being wed in a gown so elegant.

"Where did you get this? Wait! I don't want to know."

"I take it you like it?"

"*Ja*," I gasped.

"Good! You can wear it on our wedding day." Vidar smiled smugly. "Now, the last gift …"

I held the gown against my body for a moment longer, reluctant to put it away so soon. With outstretched arms I gazed at it again, overjoyed and awed by the beauty of the garment before I folded it carefully and wrapped it back in the linen. I returned to my spot beside Vidar and he held out yet another gift, a small wooden box.

"I would pray to Frigg every day, asking her to protect you and watch over you. When I came across a forest of silver birch, I thought of Frigg and my prayers." Vidar said. "Immediately I stopped and prayed to her again, I made an offering to her, then cut down one of the trees before I made it into this for you."

Vidar had painstakingly etched images of whales, cats, trees and flowing water into the yellow-ivory box. Here and there I found a rune hidden amongst the pictures. I beamed at the box and opened it slowly, admiring all the intricate details he'd carefully carved. There inside was a simple, thin, silver ring.

"A ring?" I gasped, gaping at him incredulously.

"We don't use engagement rings, or fancy gowns for our marriages," Vidar said. "But I know your Christians do."

"But I'm not Christian – nor are you?"

"Your blood father was." Vidar answered. "I asked your father – Birger – to wed you, the Danish way. We'll marry the Danish way, raise our children the Danish way, live and die the Danish way. But I thought of your blood father … though he would not approve of our union, certainly not of me and my Nordic ways … I thought he must've dreamt of marrying you the Christian way.

"Family is important. Your ancestors, they are all significant to you, and as I am soon to be your husband, they are significant to me … You renounced your Christian faith, you left behind your Anglo-Saxon life, but I think your blood father would be proud to see you, dressed in this, with my rings on your finger – your Christian engagement ring and Danish wedding ring – knowing your life with them is not completely forgotten. You've merely moved on."

I was silent, rolling the ring between my fingers, the box rested on my lap. Vidar's words resonated within me, I was impressed and grateful that he had thought so deeply and thoroughly of marrying me.

Vidar had spent two years away from me, battling and raiding, but had clearly spent time carefully planning our wedding in a way to appease and respect both of our cultures. Vidar's reasoning was noble and admirable, and I was in awe that he'd considered my dead blood father's opinion on our union.

I wondered how well his father and certain townsfolk would feel about honouring my Anglo-Saxon culture on Vidar and my wedding day. In my mind, I decided to try to make the beautiful Anglo-Saxon wedding dress more acceptable to the Danes. Maybe I could add the turtle shell brooches with the amber beads that hung between them? A woollen cloak … and instead of the all-encompassing head-to-toe yellow veil of Anglo-Saxon women, I would wear a simple headband …

"What are you thinking about?" Vidar asked, a note of worry in his voice.

"I love you." I whispered.

Smiling, he took the ring and slipped it onto my finger.

Tenderly, we kissed.

***

Late Spring

THIRTY DAYS PASSED quickly, and I still hadn't married Vidar. Every spare moment was dedicated to readying the ships and the men to sail to Britain as soon as possible, to join Guthrum and defeat Wessex.

Most of our men would be leaving, except for Vidar and a few others – the best of our warriors would go to Britain with Alvar. Some of the wives and families would be accompanying their men, as well as a good portion of thralls. It was unsure how long they would be gone for, highly expected to be years, and many were planning on settling in Britain for good.

So close to conquering the entirety of Britain, Roskilde planned to give full force and aid the Great Army to the very end.

Ivar the Boneless, another of the great Ragnar Loðbrók's sons, had died the previous year, and now Olaf the White – who had ruled the Kingdom of Dublin beside Ivar – was dead. Olaf's son, Oistin had taken seat as King of Dublin, or Dyflin as the Danes referred to it as. There were rumours circulating that Halfdan Ragnarsson was not best pleased Oistin had taken the throne, but for now Halfdan focussed on defeating the Picts and the Britons in Strathclyde.

This information rolled around in my mind endlessly, as I watched the ships glide away from Roskilde. The longships appeared weightless, skimming the glittering waters with their oars and splintering the reflections of light upon the glassy face of the fjord as they swiftly propelled forward. Soon the longships were nothing more than smudges upon the glorious landscape of Roskilde Fjord. And then they were gone.

"You've been here for a while." Vidar commented as he sat beside me.

"I've noticed something." I did not look at him, I remained staring at the spot where the ships had disappeared. "You hardly greet me – you always start a conversation without saying hello. You seem to just pop up out of nowhere and speak."

"Is that what you've been thinking of, all this time?" Vidar laughed, leaning back on his hands, admiring the scenery before us.

"*Nei* ... I was thinking of Birger."

"Valhalla is where the warriors belong." Vidar commented, light-heartedly. "You've been here for nine years, you know that. That is where Birger belongs. He is a one-armed man, he has decided to fight with his men and die gloriously. This is his decision; you must accept it. He wants an honourable death."

I was a little shocked, but I said nothing, knowing everything he said was true. I was more surprised because he spoke the exact words Birger had uttered the night before he left.

Birger and I had argued. I hadn't wanted him to leave, but he was going to and he did, regardless of my wishes. He explained, word for word, everything Vidar had said.

"To Hel with your 'honourable death'!" I screamed at Birger hysterically. "I don't care whether your death is honourable or not, I don't want you to die!"

I collapsed to the ground and wept. Birger held me tightly as I sobbed into his chest. I cried until my eyes burned, and he patiently comforted me, silent but for an occasional soothing hush. Slowly, bitterly, I accepted that I could not convince him to stay.

"Aveline!" Birger suddenly cried brightly, beaming at me as I gazed up at him, my eyes puffy and sore. "I want you to make me a promise. After you have wed Vidar, I want you to have many children – sons, daughters, as many as you possibly can! And I want you to name your firstborn son after me. Can you promise me that?"

Stunned, I gaped at him, before I burst into laughter. As I giggled through my snot and tears, I agreed.

And now Birger was gone, and I expected never to see him again. Our home and land were now mine, alone. The sheep were mine, all his belongings were solitarily mine.

With no surviving blood kin of his own, Birger made sure to sort the contracts for Vidar and my marriage before he departed, but time was of the essence and there was no chance Vidar and I could wed before he left. Birger assured me that knowing I was going to marry well – and marry the son of his oldest, dearest friend – brought happiness to him, and peace to his mind.

"So, we ought to plan our wedding now." I mentioned, turning to look at Vidar.

"We ought indeed." He beamed. "Of course, we'll marry on Frjádagr – Frigg's day. I have a few things to settle in town now

I'm acting jarl, and I must travel to Ribe to trade and deal with a few other things there ... I think a month's time would be a wise time to marry."

"Then it's decided." I grinned, curling up against him.

***

"ARE YOU SURE you won't travel to Ribe with me? I can have a thrall tend to Svartr and your flock." Vidar offered yet again.

"*Nei*, I'm fine." I assured, kissing him once more. "Go trade! Be quick and return to me."

"You'd enjoy Ribe." Vidar pressed, pecking me softly on the lips over and over.

"*Nei*," I repeated firmly. "I'll be fine. Should I need for anything, I will ask Freydis."

"She adores you, you know?" Vidar commented, smiling.

"And I admire her greatly. Now get on your horse and go." I blushed, shoving him towards his steed.

He laughed, and we kissed once more before he mounted the handsome, iron-grey beast that huffed and grunted behind him. As soon as Vidar was upon the horse, the townsfolk behind him ended their conversations and quickly readied themselves.

There were two riders, not including Vidar, and there were three wagons pulled by a pair of horses each. The wagons were loaded with goods to trade – casks of ale and beer; a barrel filled with crispy smoked fish; a mountainous amount of furs and hides; sacks of goose feathers and dyed wool; and chests of precious whalebone and various sized turtle shells.

The third wagon was overflowing with thralls, squeezed together tightly, bound at the wrists and feet, scared and sorrowful, ready to be traded at Ribe. When Vidar and his men had returned from Britain, they had brought many poor Anglo-Saxons back with them.

I stayed as far as I could from them, not wanting to sympathise or empathise or even meet these poor, unfortunate people. None of them were to be as lucky as me, I knew that much for sure. I had already seen more than one of the women get raped; shutting my ears to the sound of their screams.

"Go." I repeated, tearing my eyes from the pathetic, pitiful thralls, crying with anguish over their fates. "I love you."

"I love you too, little fawn." Vidar winked, and then he left.

Reaching Ribe would take the group four, possibly five days of fair weather, due to the wagons and having to get passage over the sea. They'd spend a week or so in the Jutland town, before beginning their journey home.

It would be easy to sell the thralls – they were the most sought-after commodity the Danes had to trade, always high in demand, easy coin to make. The skins and furs would also be straightforward to be rid of. All the other items would be swapped for other food stuffs that Roskilde was short of.

Feeding an army had taken a lot of our food supplies, but luckily Roskilde still had reasonable stores left. Also, it was the end of spring, and with that our livestock had born plenty of offspring. We had harvested most root vegetables and leeks, our onions and garlic would be harvested in the following months; cabbages had already been sown, and beans would be sown soon. We were beginning to harvest our grain crops – our rye, barley, wheat and oats.

I realised how much work there was to do, with thralls being sold, and most of our men left for Britain, taking with them their wives and thralls, there weren't many people left to help harvest and sow the fields. I watched the wagons noisily roll away, staring shrewdly at the thralls. I noticed most were women ... I wondered if Vidar intended to trade them for more male thralls to tend to the fields.

The days seemed to skid away quickly, Vidar had already been gone for a week. I had many new lambs and had agreed to help Adhelin milk her many cows and churn some milk into butter. She had begun teaching me how to make cheese, I wasn't very good yet, but was getting slowly better.

"Aveline! Aveline Birgersdóttir!" I heard a voice call to me, as I passed through the marketplace.

I turned and saw none other than Freydis, with three thralls at her side. I smiled warmly to her.

"Good day, Jarlkona. What can I do for you?" I greeted.

"Have evening meal with me at the hall tonight." Freydis replied, her dazzling green eyes twinkling as she smiled at me. "You're soon to marry my son, I'd like to discuss your wedding with you."

"I would like that very much." I blushed excitedly.

We exchanged some farewell pleasantries before she left me, and I went on my way to Adhelin's farm, pleased to be in Freydis's good favour.

***

THAT EVENING I was exhausted. One of Adhelin's cows had been attacked by what we assumed were wolves. The cow's mangled carcass was found in the furthest end of the pasture. Two of her other cows had disappeared, recently, only their blood was found; great cold pools of stinking red soaking into the grass.

When Adhelin and I found the mauled corpse, she had panicked and rushed to make an acceptable offering to the gods to save what was left of her herd. She had sent her two thralls (her husband, Hefni, had left for battle taking their other three thralls with him) to gather the cattle and bring them to their pens for the night.

Usually, now the weather was warming significantly, she'd let them graze day and night in their pasture but terrified of wolves or whatever was feasting and stealing her livestock, she intended to keep a close eye on them, especially on the new calves.

I quickly went home after Adhelin had left and cleaned myself with cold water from the well. I paused and gazed up at the bright prickles of stars puncturing the navy sky. I felt sorry for poor Adhelin, alone, her husband sailing to fight across the seas; her livestock, which were her livelihood, being killed ...

I lowered my gaze and watched my sheep. They bleated at each other occasionally, their fleeces covered in dirt and grass, mindlessly grazing away at tufts of green. I decided it better to err on the side of caution and began to herd them into their pens in the house. I'd rather not be in a similar boat to Adhelin.

"I am sorry for my lateness, I had to bring the sheep in. Poor Adhelin lost another cow today." I apologised profusely to the Jarlkona upon entering the hall.

"Oh no, not another." Freydis sympathised, gesturing for me to take a seat at the table.

Freydis's dark skinned thrall, Aaminah, gently set my meal before me – a steaming bowl of cabbage soup, and a plate covered with warm slices of pork and rye bread. Aaminah's smile was laced with surprise when I thanked her gratefully and vividly, so eager to eat was I.

"Is there any damage to her fencing? I assume she's already sent a thrall to check for any breaches."

"*Já*, she has. So far, they can find none. This cow wasn't missing like the other two though – it was mutilated." I explained, dipping a chunk of bread into the soup.

"*Mutilated?*"

"She assumes it must be wolves so she's penning the rest of the herd overnight. I decided I ought to do the same thing, just in case the wolves come back and notice the cattle are gone and decide to attack my sheep instead."

Freydis glared past me for a few silent moments, her forehead furrowed, her thin pink lips pursed in a small frown.

"Why would wolves attack a cow when they could attack the sheep instead? Or even the lambs and the calves?" She asked, bewildered. "Wolves are not stupid animals; they'll attack the easiest prey because it'd be the quickest meal. Why would they take on a cow, rather than a calf? That doesn't make sense."

I felt rather dumbfounded for not realising the same thing.

"She didn't hear any howling or snarling. From what she said, the cows didn't make any noise out of the usual, either." I said, slowly.

Freydis's frown deepened.

"Hilda," she called – even hearing that damned thrall's name made me angry. "Fetch me Kolbrandr – tell him to bring his sons."

Hilda nodded and scurried off to do her mistress's bidding. The thrall had ignored me overtly since I'd arrived, but I did not care, it was better than her ignorant, resentful glares she usually shot at me.

"What do you fear, Freydis?" I asked cautiously.

"I do not fear," she replied. "But I wonder if man is the creature behind the cattle's disappearance and mutilation, not wolves."

"Who would do such a thing?" I gasped.

"An enemy, of course. Maybe she has had a feud with a neighbour." Freydis contemplated. "Though I've heard nothing from her. I'll have to ask her in the 'morrow. For now, all I can do is set guards on her land and hope for the best."

I nodded silently and slowly continued to eat my food. I hadn't seen Adhelin argue with anyone, Freydis hadn't heard of any feuds – usually these sorts of thing were brought to the jarl or jarlkona's attention, so the situation could be settled fairly and unbiasedly.

Adhelin hadn't spoken to Freydis, whoever she may have been feuding with hadn't either. Adhelin hadn't mentioned a feud to me, or anyone for that fact. Adhelin was not afraid to share her thoughts, nor was she afraid to fight – if she were feuding with someone, I'm sure the whole town would've known rather quickly.

Soon enough, Kolbrandr, a short but very strong farmer, about the age of Vidar, appeared with his sons. All of them had fair hair with dark brown eyes and scruffy beards. Kolsveinn was the youngest at fifteen years of age and towered over his father and brother.

There was a running joke around Roskilde that Kolsveinn was the bastard son of another man, but his face was identical to his father's, disproving the amusing rumour. Kolfinnr was seventeen, small and stocky like his father, but known to be swift and silent, hence he was known as Kolfinnr the Quick.

"Kolbrandr, Kolsveinn, Kolfinnr, thank you for coming to me." Freydis said. "I apologise for interrupting your evening meal."

"Not at all, Jarlkona." Kolbrandr replied, his voice was gruff, and he was seemingly oblivious to the spill of stew on his chin. "What can my sons and I do for you?"

"Two cows have gone missing from Adhelin's farm, and one was found mutilated at her home this morning. There were no breaks in the fencing, so we assume something devious is afoot.

"I'd like you and your sons to stand watch over her land tonight. The other cattle have been penned already, but I need you to watch should the perpetrator return. If it is a wolf, kill it and the pelt is yours. If it is a man, bring him to me as soon as you have captured him." Freydis said, her voice low and commanding, but her expression remained serene.

"Of course." Kolbrandr agreed, straightening himself to his full height, shoulders back and head high. "Come, boys." He said, turning to his sons. "Let's go."

Once they had left, Freydis and I resumed our evening. We finished eating and moved into the garden to admire her beautiful flower collection, examining each freshly bloomed petal and every sleeping bud. I saw the snapdragons and thought of Vidar.

As the night grew later the temperature dropped, and we moved inside, sitting together by the roaring fire. Freydis made a thrall bring out her weaving, and together we settled for the evening, weaving and spinning together by the fire, at ease with each other's company. The dark-skinned thrall, Aaminah, and a red-haired thrall worked at a loom together, while Hilda and a pale blonde thrall cleaned in the kitchen.

As the hours passed, I slowly readied myself to leave. It was extremely late, the black of night was completely upon us, and sleepiness, entwined with the delectable warmth of the fire, was making it difficult for me to do anything but murmur in reply to Freydis as she spoke to me.

"Mistress!" The blonde thrall yelped, running in from the kitchen. "There's commotion outside!"

Freydis and I glanced at each other before leaping to the door. We peered out from a sliver sized opening to see the orange glow of fire rising into the darkness, coming from Adhelin's farm. Screams shot into the air sporadically but within moments the town was filled with the howls of panic and alarm.

"Intruders!" A man bellowed.

And then we saw them.

Like a flood, a gush of men streamed through the streets, dressed in dark leather, the glint of firelight reflected on their blades. More and more fires began rising from different farms and houses. Roskilde men leaped into the street, defending themselves from the invaders, but they were not dressed for battle, they were geared only with basic farming tools, knives, whatever weapons they could get their hands on.

"Sword, bow! Sword, bow!" I chanted, trying to fathom what was happening. "I need a weapon!"

I began bustling through the hall, trying to find a weapon. Shock and determination surged through my being. My first home had been burned to the ground when I was a helpless, innocent child, but I was a woman now. I wasn't helpless anymore. I would fight to protect Roskilde, *my* Roskilde, until my last breath slipped from my lips.

I yanked a shield from the wall, found an axe by the kitchen door, and, upon great luck, found a bow made of yew, bullhorn and sinew, with twelve arrows, propped against Vidar's bed. I recognised it instantly; Vidar had taken me hunting more times than I could count, using this very bow.

I set the shield and axe upon the table, returned to the door, lifted the bow and nocked an arrow into place.

"Open the door." I whispered, drawing the bow.

The blonde thrall did as she was told, opening it a crack. I signalled impatiently for her to open it a little wider, and she did immediately. Carefully examining the crowd, I found my target across the way.

Fires had risen into an inferno that devoured my town. Plumes of steel and ebony smoke shimmered across the black night sky, which was lit up with an eerie copper and scarlet glow. The scolding air was thick and bitter on my tongue, burning my throat as I inhaled. Sharp, piercing screeches howled to the heavens, the clatter and noise of battle and death were deafening! My poor Roskilde was the embodiment of the Christian hell described to me when I was a child.

The invader I'd targeted was in battle with the blacksmith – the blacksmith had shoved him backwards with his shield, hard, flinging him a few paces, his arms wide open, his face perfectly clear with nothing to block his way. Silently I released the arrow, and it soared.

The invader dropped, the arrow had punctured him in the side of his face, diagonally piercing through his head and peeking out through the base of his skull; an instant death. I grabbed at another arrow, deftly nocking it and aiming again.

I had become automatic. My eyes darted to find a target, with a swift swoop of my arm I'd nock an arrow into my bow and with the lightest opening of my fingers I'd release the arrow. All thought fled my mind but a single chant: *target, aim, loose; target, aim, loose* ...

I saw my enemies frantically searching for the mysterious archer, following the direction of the arrows. Fortunately, a few townspeople fought them, taking advantage of the distraction to crush their skulls with axes or stab them through the belly with knives or pitchforks.

But my luck did not last long.

By the eighth arrow, eight perfect shots, eight enemies dead, a hoard of invaders trampled down and slaughtered the townsfolk fighting them in front of the hall. Four men, strong and burly, stormed to the hall doors.

"Get back!" Freydis hissed, dragging me away. "Shut it!" She ordered the thrall.

The thrall pushed the door quickly, quaking and horrifically pale, terrified out of her mind, but the door swung back, forcefully, smashing her into the wall. There stood the four men. They entered the room, but the last one paused, hearing the thrall behind the door whimper in her foreign tongue. He slammed the door on her again and again, until the poor thrall was bawling in agony. He banged the door shut, grabbed the sobbing thrall by the hair and impaled her onto his sword, snickering as he did so.

"Ah, Freydis, is your husband home? I wish to talk to him." Smirked the awful face of the leader of the invaders.

He was older, around fifty, light brown hair, deeply saturated with grey, that fell down his shoulders. His beard was long and neatly trimmed, his mustachio held its colour, whereas silver hairs framed his bottom lip, dripping down his chin into the wiry bush of brown and subtle red. His eyes were a deep sapphire blue, glinting with malevolence, and his mouth was twisted into a vicious grin, like the snarling chops of a wolf.

"He's not here. He's supporting *our kings* in their battle against Britain." Freydis spat disgustedly, glaring at him. "What are you doing here, Erhardt?"

Jarl Erhardt made his way to the table, shoving the shield and axe to the floor with a deafening clatter, and took a seat in front of the scraps left on my plate. Two of his men began searching the hall, in case we had anyone hidden and ready to attack them.

"Look what I found." Laughed one of them, coming from the kitchen with Hilda in his arms.

He'd already struck her; fresh blood was oozing from her lip. He threw her to ground at Freydis and my feet. Hilda spotted the murdered body of the thrall crumpled behind the door and proceeded to vomit into the packed dirt floor.

"Thrall, get me food." The Jarl of Aros barked at the red-haired thrall, ignoring Hilda's retching.

The thrall looked between Freydis and Erhardt, shaking like a leaf in a storm.

"*Nú!*" He bellowed.

The thrall squeaked with fear and scurried to the kitchen, quickly fetching him a plate of food with trembling hands.

"She's a pretty one, this." Erhardt commented, slapping her rear roughly, causing her to yelp with fear. "Tell me, little mouse, do you squeak like this when you're being fucked?"

She answered with tears. One of Erhardt's men, with long black hair and no beard, stepped forward.

"Jarl Erhardt, let me have her and we'll soon find out." He crooned darkly.

"*Nei*, please!" The thrall begged.

"Take her." Erhardt replied, waving a hand in the direction of the beds, before shoving a chunk of meat into his mouth.

The thrall girl kicked and screamed, hollered and yelped, shrieked and wept. I heard the rip of her clothes, the shuffle of him dropping his trousers, the *slap* of him grabbing the thrall girl and pulling her against him ... the squeak of her as he entered her, and his victorious laugh. Then followed the steady, hard thud of him pounding her, and her quaking wails.

"Ah, so she does squeak when she's being fucked!" Erhardt remarked, one eyebrow raised. "Such a pretty little mouse."

He noisily gulped down a few more bites, took my glass of mead and tossed it to the back of his throat.

"So, you want to know why I'm here." Jarl Erhardt said, beckoning Freydis to sit before him. She did so, hesitantly at first, but held her head high and shoulders back and took her seat gracefully. "I'm here, like every time, to ask you to divorce Alvar the First One."

"*Nei.*" She said curtly.

"As you say, every time." The Jarl of Aros waved his hand at her reply, as though he were bored with her answer. "So, I am going to take Roskilde as mine. I notice your dear son isn't here, nor are most of your men? I'm sure my men have slain most of your remaining warriors by now."

"You've been watching Roskilde for a while." Freydis remarked, eyebrows furrowed, and lips curled into a snarl towards the man sitting before her.

"For a little while now, yes. Thank you for that woman's cows, by the way. We were getting quite peckish. The fence was loose, so all we had to do was pick it up, let a cow out, then put it back, and she was none the wiser!" Erhardt chuckled into the cup. "That last cow, that was just for fun, though. We got what pieces of meat we needed – thought we'd leave the rest for the old dear when she woke up the next morn'."

The two other invaders laughed heartily. I scowled at them, disgusted, bile rising in my throat; these intruders sickened me.

"Tell me, my love, when is Vidar due to come back?" Erhardt asked casually.

"Tell me yourself, you've been watching Roskilde for long enough, perhaps you've already slaughtered my son?" Freydis replied acidly, tilting her head as she glared, her beautiful green eyes bulging furiously at the beast.

Erhardt paused for a moment and studied her expression before he continued.

"Well, I should've liked to, really I would've." He proclaimed. "But unfortunately, we arrived here a little too late to catch him.

Depending on the decisions made at this table, however, I will surely slit his throat next time I see him."

Freydis was unable to keep up her fierce charade, her mask of invulnerability. She gasped, her hands clenched into fists, and her lovely eyes began to glisten. Erhardt grinned victoriously at her, eating and chuckling as she tried to compose herself, his eyes not leaving her for even a moment.

"I have already told you I will never divorce Alvar." Freydis stammered. "You have already conquered my town, so I cannot bargain with that. What can I possibly offer you to have you leave and not harm my son?"

"There *is* something you can offer me."

"And what is that?" She growled.

"Before we get to that, I need to ask, who is this young woman here, with the bow?" He questioned, suddenly turning to face me.

The bow was still in my hands and Aaminah was at my feet, shielded by me. My fingers trembled, and my heart had thrust itself into my throat when he referred to me. I was afraid, terribly afraid, but motivated by revulsion. When Erhardt had promised to slit Vidar's throat, a scorching rage bubbled through my body, igniting every fibre of my being with seething loathing. I would murder Erhardt before he could touch Vidar.

"She is Aveline Birgersdóttir." Freydis replied softly.

"Birgersdóttir?" He asked. "As in Birger Bloody Sword's daughter? I thought his family died years ago?"

Freydis nodded slowly in reply, clearly unsure of the consequences of her admission. Birger was renowned for his skill in battle, even as far as Aros – the town of which the infamous Erhardt ruled as jarl.

Erhardt scrutinised me, combing every inch of my flesh and the features upon my face with his beady eyes. Suddenly his face lit up with realisation.

"I heard he took a thrall as his daughter – you're the Anglo-Saxon child that bewitched Bloody Sword for her freedom, are you?" Erhardt fell into a fit of laughter, pounding the table with his fist. "Well, girl! I was expecting something much different. Most casters of magic who walk Midgard are old and haggard – I thought you'd be a hideous creature! But I suppose not all witches are ugly. Freyja was indeed the most expert at *seiðr*, and she is of course the most beautiful of all the goddesses. You're pretty and have a hawk's eye and a warrior's aptitude for archery. Very impressive ..."

I had no answer for his rambling monologue, I only scowled at him, disgust dripping from my glare. He was clearly unconcerned with me and focussed on Freydis once more. As he did so, the invader with the long black hair returned from the sleeping area, but the red-haired thrall was nowhere to be seen. He winked at me as he entered the room, and I tightened my grip on Vidar's bow.

"Now, we were talking about what you can offer me. You want your son to live, correct? And you want me to leave Roskilde?"

"*Já.*" Freydis answered firmly.

"And you refuse to divorce the First One for me?"

"*Já.*" Freydis repeated.

"I want a peace-pledge, and I want her." Erhardt pointed his finger at me.

"*Nei!*" I shouted.

Erhardt's only reaction to my cry was a terrible smile that slithered slowly across his face like a fetid worm.

"Fine." Freydis said without even hesitating, maintaining unblinking eye contract with Jarl Erhardt, though I spotted a single tear slip down her pale face.

"I'm to be wed to your son!" I sputtered at her, betrayed and panic stricken.

"Even more of a reason for you to be the peace-pledge." The black-haired invader spoke up, garnering snickers from his comrades.

"Of course, since I am taking his woman to be mine, I will graciously offer a new bride in her place." Erhardt sneered, his deep voice drenched with sordid glee.

"Who will you offer my son in return?" Freydis demanded.

"My daughter." Erhardt said smugly. "I will have her here at sunrise."

"And these marriages will guarantee peace between our towns?"

"As long as no harm comes to my daughter." Erhardt said. "If even the slightest harm comes to her, I will cut open our bewitching little Danethrall from her cunt to her throat; burn this town to the ground with every man, woman and child in it. Then I will torture your son; I'll cut off his every limb and appendage and let ravens peck out his eyes. Then I'll slit your throat, after you've watched him die."

"No harm will come to your daughter." Freydis choked, her voice quaking violently.

"Let's discuss the terms of the marriages then, shall we?"

CHAPTER SIXTEEN

BY THE NEXT afternoon, I was officially betrothed to Erhardt. Negotiations and contracts had been agreed between Freydis and Erhardt, monies were exchanged, and I was sold into marriage to the Jarl of Aros.

Danish women had the right to approve and disapprove of suitors and marriage proposals, but both Freydis and Erhardt had thoroughly explained to me that the safety of Roskilde and its people depended on my agreeing to this match ... I had no choice but to accept.

I had argued, however. I had cried, quietly, watching the two haggle over my fate. Freydis avoided eye contact with me but managed to arrange an ample *mundr* to be paid to Birger on his possible return, and Erhardt's morning-gift to me was equal to my dowry. At first Erhardt had been angered by the prices of the *mundr* and morning gift, I was nothing more than a kinless thrall in his eyes, and he bartered with Freydis over me like he was purchasing meat from a butcher. But the dowry Freydis had offered him was extremely generous, and he accepted the terms soon enough. She vowed the dowry would come from her pocket and assured me that she would hold the *mundr* for Birger.

I scoffed at this promise. She and I both knew that Birger was not going to return. Birger and my sheep would be taken as part of my dowry, and our home would stand empty and rot to the ground.

After the wedding negotiations had been determined and confirmed, Freydis and the Jarl of Aros recessed and agreed to convene in the morning to begin the arrangement of Vidar and Erhardt's daughter's wedding.

Erhardt and his men had returned to their camp, and through the night Freydis walked the streets of Roskilde with Hilda and a few field thralls, ascertaining who had survived the attack and arranging burials for those who had not. The fires had mostly been put out, and the depressed townspeople were busy clearing the charred wreckage of homes and burnt bodies from the rubble.

Whilst Freydis and her thralls surveyed the wreckage and destruction from Erhardt's attack, I wept, wrapped in the sympathetic arms of Aaminah, while the poor red-haired thrall quaked silently across from us on another bench, refusing to be held or comforted by anyone.

I was forced to stay the night in the Jarl's hall, disallowed to go to my home in case I might flee. So, I whimpered and sobbed, as field thralls brought extra straw mattresses from the rafters and the storage shed outside and set them around the hall for the homeless townspeople who stumbled in, to stay until their homes had been rebuilt. Some laid on the mattresses, most just threw themselves onto the benches, huddled families with the same soot, blood and tear-stained faces.

The next morning Erhardt arrived at the hall with his youngest daughter, Ursula, by his side. Presumably she had been kept in their camp while Erhardt and his men attacked Roskilde until the time came when it was safe for her to arrive. The sly, cunning Erhardt had planned it all, maybe not originally planning on taking me, specifically, as his peace-pledge, but he had found me an adequate addition to his plot at any rate.

Ursula was invited into the hall and sat, smugly, beside her father as Freydis and he commenced discussion over her nuptial negotiations. The betrothals were agreeably arranged, but only Erhardt's and mine had been sealed with the *handsal* – a hand-clasp between Erhardt and Freydis (who acted on behalf of Birger since he, nor Vidar and Alvar, were present, and Birger and I had no living male kin), that confirmed the legal agreement of Erhardt and my betrothal.

Erhardt planned to return to Roskilde in two weeks' time to *handsal* with Vidar and seal his betrothal to Ursula. The Jarl of Aros had also proposed that Vidar and Ursula's wedding should take place during that very same visit, to which Freydis had reluctantly agreed.

After the negations had been agreed to, Erhardt, Freydis and I, along with Aaminah the thrall and Erhardt's beardless companion, went to Birger and my home to collect my sheep and my belongings.

On the doorstep I found the burned remains of my poor, tortured cat, Svartr. My poor innocent feline was almost unrecognisable, so badly scorched was his body. I fell to my knees and howled – in just one evening I had lost my love, my home and now even my beloved Svartr!

Aaminah held me tightly, stroked my hair and shushed me. As she quietly sung into my ear sympathetic sounding words in her native tongue, the cruel, heartless Jarl Erhardt and his man pushed by us and entered my ransacked home, determined to verify the number of sheep I owned and herd them to the longships.

***

"SORRY ABOUT THE precautions, but they're necessary, you understand?" Erhardt said to me, wearing a brief façade of sympathy, before he thrust me into the wagon.

My wrists were bound, and I landed flat on my face on the ragged, filthy, wooden floor. My face burned hotly as laughter erupted around me. I managed to scramble onto my knees, but was met with a swift, harsh slap on the rear which thrust me to the floor again. My bottom stung and my face was scarlet with embarrassment, as the beasts around me cackled.

"Now, be good to her, aye?" Erhardt scolded light-heartedly, snickering with his men. "She's only mine to fuck. She's to be my wife, you understand? The Jarlkona of Aros."

"*Já*, of course." The animal who'd struck me grinned, flashing a quick glance in my direction. "We won't mistreat our future jarlkona."

Erhardt swapped a few crude, degrading exchanges about me with his men, before he mounted his horse and began to lead the journey to Aros.

I clambered onto my knees again and, as the wagon shuddered and shook noisily, I clumsily crawled to the side and leaned against the rough wooden wall. I gazed at Roskilde as it quickly fell into the distance. Erhardt's men ignored me, engulfed in their menial conversation, and I was thankfully left to my thoughts.

Petrified of the unknown future I was heading towards, I realised the good fortune I had until this point and appreciated Birger for being the one who had taken me to Denmark, rather than any other Nordic raider. I was treated like a Dane, like a human, by most in Roskilde, but not anymore. My luck had changed – I would not be in Roskilde any longer. I was the forced bride of a man who'd taken me to spite his enemy and anger the son of his enemy.

I resented Freydis for agreeing to sacrifice me as peace-pledge, but I understood her reasons: she was saving her town and her son. At least, saving Vidar in the short term.

Erhardt, his men and I, and surely Freydis no matter how little she wanted to acknowledge it, knew the moment Vidar found out his love had been married off to the jarl his father had been feuding with for years – especially after waging a sneak attack on Vidar's undefended town – Vidar would be sent into a rage.

I was bait, I was being used to lure Vidar, outmanned and blinded by fury. To attack Aros would only ensure Vidar met his own slaughter.

Rarely was Vidar swayed by impulses, but he was still occasionally a victim to his emotions, like all men. The possibility of the wronged Vidar charging into an enraged attack of vengeance, thus leaping into the palm of Erhardt's hand, was such a very real likelihood.

It was common knowledge in Roskilde that Vidar was a remarkable warrior and a shrewd leader. I had received a sliver of insight from the many games of Hnefatafl we had played to realise how calculated Vidar was, but I had no idea how he would handle coming home from trading to find Roskilde in such destruction, many of his townsfolk murdered and his betrothed sold away.

Would he lunge immediately into an outraged counterattack?

Would he bide his time and avenge Roskilde when Erhardt came for his and Ursula's wedding?

The wagon jostled and rocked as it quickly rolled over the bumpy road. Roskilde was swallowed by trees and foliage, completely out of sight with only the faint, dirty scent of smoke betraying its whereabouts. My eyes were glazed over, staring hazily at the spot where the town stood in the distance, engulfed by the forest.

Though I feared the future I was entering, though I was terrified of what life was laid before me, surrounded by the vile monsters that were Erhardt's men; terrified of the Jarl of Aros himself … I hoped, deeply and truly, that Vidar would not fall into Erhardt's trap.

To all the gods, I hoped Vidar would create the most infallible plan to return me to Roskilde and into his arms … then destroy Jarl Erhardt and annihilate Aros.

***

AROS, DENMARK

THE LARGEST PART of the journey to Aros was via ship. I was tossed around as though I were a bag of grain. Occasionally Jarl Erhardt would pay attention to me, to the amusement of his men. I was not a bride-to-be; I was a puppet and a prisoner. Erhardt would yank me to my feet and ram his slimy tongue down my throat, my arms still bound behind my back, so I could not resist. I tried to turn my head away, at first, but with a vice like grip, he would grasp my jaw, his yellowed nails dug deeply into my cheeks as he forced me to face him.

Erhardt would cackle at me, press his lips against mine, and force my mouth open my squeezing my cheeks as hard as he could. I'd gasp as my mouth dropped, then splutter as his tongue licked mine, slithering inside my mouth.

I refused to scream.

I refused to cry.

I refused to show any weakness.

"Wait until we get to your new home, my little *Danethrall*, and we consummate our marriage." Erhardt grinned as he released my face and ran his hands down my neck and the front of my dress.

Jarl Erhardt mockingly toyed with the turtle shell brooches pinned upon my dress, sending ripples of foreboding trepidation skidding across my flesh. He grabbed one of my breasts and crushed it tightly in his filthy paw. I tried so hard to stop myself from wincing, but I failed; my face screwed up tightly, tears welled in my eyes and my teeth clenched agonisingly, but I made no sound. At the sight of my grimace, Erhardt broke out in jeering laughter and pushed me to the slick and slimy floor of the longship.

We sailed the whole day and into the night. The wind picked up later into the evening, the ship's large square sail was lowered, catching the breeze and quickly propelling the ship over the water, speeding up our course. I had no fur, only my woollen cloak, and I shuffled into it, trying to keep warm as much as I could. I watched the black smudge of the island Roskilde was situated on slip away and meld with the night. Tears began pouring down my face in cascades.

Under the cover of darkness, with nothing but the silver orb of the moon and the pinprick stars glowing above me, my fear was no longer concealable or ignorable. The horrifying realisation that Vidar, Roskilde, my home — everything was gone, sinking into blackness as we sailed away — it constricted my heart, icy tendrils of dismay seeped through my body and froze my veins. Silently I wept, a puddle of tears and snot soaking my cloak until, at last, I fell into an uneasy slumber.

By the early, misty hours of the morning, Aros was within close view — I could spot the grey shore, the juniper, sage and viridian land, and the charcoal wooden wall that enclosed the town. Everything was cast over by the shadowy haze of the pale sunlight. The town of Aros was much smaller than Roskilde, and much flatter. As we drew closer, I could see the cluster of dwellers' homes, farms and the few shops. It was quiet; like a ghost town. There were still a few of hours left until people would wake to begin the long day's work, igniting the place with bustle and life.

Aros was situated in a luscious green valley surrounded by woods and beaches on the northern shores of a fjord that offered a valuable natural harbour. Slowly, now, the longships drifted towards the fjord, gliding into it, silently. As we grew closer to the land, excitement riddled the air, radiating from the warriors and raiders eager to return to their homes, victorious. By command of Erhardt, the tall, dark haired, beardless Dane inhaled deeply and brought a large polished horn to his lips. He blew, the deep bellow of the horn resonated across the waters, announcing their arrival.

The nerves that had fled me as I gazed upon the land, suddenly rushed back through my body like a million bolts of lightning. I shuddered at the noise. Not long ago, the roar of the horn as it echoed over the waters was a welcomed, hopeful sound. Now, though ... Now it was an ominous noise that struck me with anxiety. Sullen and apprehensive, the daunting rumble of the horn finally silenced.

Slowly, with grievous anticipation on my part, the ships were moored to the shore. After a lot of shouting and scrambling, we were ready to disembark.

"Welcome home!" Jarl Erhardt exclaimed loudly, greeted by much adulation. He came to my side, gripped me against him and hissed into my ear: "And welcome to your new home, little *Danethrall.*"

I shuddered in Erhardt's arms as he dragged me off the ship. He barked orders to men while he led me up the shore, keeping me securely clamped against him as we walked.

Suddenly he stopped.

Erhardt grabbed my wrists, and I staggered as he forcefully spun me around. With his utility knife, he cut through the rope that had bound me and tossed it aside. Erhardt grabbed me again and shoved me through the tall gates into Aros.

My bleary eyes squinted through the morning mist at the town. A planked path encircled the town, and buildings were squashed together in some degree of order. I stumbled down the path and staggered along the planks beside Erhardt, struggling to match his long, quick paced steps.

Townsfolk had begun to waken at the call of the horns. Faces peered from doors, groggily watching their jarl stride merrily through the streets, his arm wrapped around an unknown woman. They welcomed their jarl warmly, until they spotted their loved ones in the crowd of crewmen pacing up behind us through the gates.

Erhardt led me down a path that curved passed farmhouses and longhouses. It straightened out as we reached the centre of the town where his hall was situated. Like Alvar the First One's hall was positioned in the centre of Roskilde, Erhardt's hall commanded the centre of Aros. However, instead of facing shops like Alvar's had, the hall of Aros faced a huge square of green, with two other houses on either side.

The whole town seemed very rigid in their grid, roads and paths sectioned off the house plots, farmers' homes and pastures lined the outer edges of the town, with the shops and homes in the centre – all protectively surrounding the Jarl's home.

Various shrubs and trees were dotted around the islet, but there was no forest – the woods and pastures were situated on the mainland. I assumed that one of the houses facing the green was Aros's ritual hall, and that their *blóts* and honourings to the gods happened on the large square patch of grass, or maybe the land was used as a burial plot for the dwellers?

I didn't have a chance to question this, though, as Erhardt ushered me to his home, shoving me over the threshold and slamming the door shut behind us. The *bang* of the door woke his thrall girls, who leapt out of bed and hurried to add wood to the fire.

"Food! Fetch me food, now." Erhardt snapped, throwing himself onto a chair at one of the tables.

His hall was much like Alvar's, minus looms or family paraphernalia. Erhardt's daughter had taken my place in Roskilde as Vidar's soon-to-be wife and Erhardt had prepared himself perfectly in his plan to attack Roskilde, all his daughter's belongings had gone with her; there was no trace of a woman living in his home, excluding the three thrall girls.

I stood a few feet from Erhardt, where he had left me, my shoulders were slumped, but my eyes darted around the building; I had no idea what to do. The thrall Erhardt had barked at, timidly walked by me, shooting me a quick nervous glance. I responded with a saddened one of my own; her expression moved to sympathy, but she hurried to take the bread and cheese and dried fruits to Jarl Erhardt.

"Danethrall, sit with me." He bade, beckoning me with a wave of his hand.

Slowly I made my way to Erhardt and sat opposite him. My stomach began to grumble, but he offered me no food, he just eyed me as he shoved cheese into his mouth.

"Thralls, come." The Jarl commanded, and all three girls scurried to his side.

I noticed on one of the girl's faces were the faded shadows of bruises and a scab encrusted half of her bottom lip. She felt my stare and shifted; her short, lank wiry blonde hair fell over her face and concealed her wounds from me.

"We will proceed with the wedding ceremony at midday today, as it is Frigg's Day." Erhardt announced, his voice calm and steady. "I don't want to wait. We will have a large, grand feast beginning this eve. Since contracts had already been agreed upon, the *mundr* and dowry have been exchanged, I see no need to wait to be married …"

A small smile crept upon Erhardt's face. It was cruel and twisted – as casual as his words were, they had a mocking undertone. He had seen the shock that flashed over my face at the idea of marrying so soon, and he took pleasure in my distress. Erhardt's smile widened as I glared at him: he knew he was under my skin.

"These thralls will be your attendants and ready you for the ceremony, and our wedding bed. I would offer you my first wife's bridal crown since you don't have your own, but I fear I am too superstitious …

"My first wife gave me two daughters before dying after birthing our third girl. My second and third wives each died – both birthing me daughters, who also died! Very unlucky." He snorted with bitter laughter. "Since they all wore the bridal crown, I assume the thing must be cursed. We will be omitting the bridal crown from the wedding ceremony, perhaps then we will break the unfortunate *tradition* I seem to have! Maybe you'll even give me some boys, aye?"

I pressed my hand against my abdomen. Inside my womb I already held a child – Vidar's child. Only Vidar and I knew, and I would not share the secret with Erhardt, for fear of what he'd do

… In a few months' time I would be obviously pregnant and Erhardt would hopefully believe himself to be the father. In the meantime, I would just have to pray to all the gods that Vidar would rescue me as soon as possible.

Erhardt watched me, waiting for me to answer him or make some sort of comment, but I didn't. Silently I stared at my lap, holding my small tummy under the cover of the table. I gazed at the thin, silver engagement ring that Vidar had given me. It sparkled and glinted … I missed Vidar so much.

An impatient noise sounded from Erhardt's throat. I glanced up at him and he continued his speech.

"After breakfast we will bathe: the thralls will clean you and dress you while I ready myself. I will have our wedding feast prepared. At midday I will formally introduce you to the townspeople, we will have the ceremony, begin the feast; then my chosen men and these thrall girls will lead us to our bed, and we will consummate." Jarl Erhardt continued, staring at me. "What's wrong with you, woman? Does your tongue not work? Speak!"

I jumped at his sudden bark. I stared at him for a few, panicked moments, before I answered him.

"What do you want me to say? We're being married. By the end of the day I'll be your wife. It's not like you or Freydis gave me much of a choice with this betrothal, what on earth do I need to say now?" I questioned quietly and coldly.

"Well, if I'd had my way, I wouldn't marry you so elaborately. Contracts are signed, money is paid, really I'd like to fuck you and be over with it." Erhardt spat. "You're a peace-pledge: you're a tool, an implement of mine to do with what I please, why on earth would I want to spend the time, effort and money on a huge Danish wedding for you? You're an Anglo-Saxon Christian thrall! The gods don't give two shits about Christians, why would they care about you?" He laughed spitefully.

My lips were pursed together tightly. Erhardt rose and stood beside me, grabbing my jaw and forcing me to look at him.

"*But* as jarl I owe my people the ceremony and the week-long feast. You're a peace-pledge and so this marriage needs to be done properly to be validated. No, you don't have a damned say. By marrying me, you'll gain great status, elevated from a thrall to a jarlkona! I paid a substantial *mundr* to marry you, far more than you're worth! I agreed to peace with Roskilde, my enemies! I've sacrificed my daughter to Alvar's son, and agreed to marry a thrall, all in good faith to keep that peace. You'd do well to appreciate everything I am doing."

Erhardt added more pressure to his claw-like grasp of my face, raising me to my feet. I cringed, eyes squeezed shut, panting from the pain.

"As for fucking you, though ..." The Jarl said, grabbing my rear tightly, and moving his other hand from my jaw to curl around my neck. "I could fuck you wherever and whenever I wanted, and no one would care; you could scream or cry, it wouldn't matter. You're a thrall!"

Erhardt cackled, sinister glee lit his face eerily. He rammed his mouth against mine, shoved his tongue against my lips and forced my mouth open as tears poured down my face. His grip on my neck tightened, and I pounded my fists against him as hard as I could.

Somehow, I managed to rip our lips apart. I scowled at him, my face burning red with rage.

"I don't care about the status or elevation this marriage offers me! And my *faðir* doesn't need your filthy *mundr*! If you hadn't cowardly attacked Roskilde when every warrior was gone, we would've slaughtered you! To hell with Aros, you *and* your daughter!" I snarled, digging my fingernails into the wrist of the hand choking my neck.

Before I knew it, he raised his fist and smashed it into my face. A flash of white blinded me, and I collapsed to the floor in a crumpled mess. I clapped my hands over my throbbing cheek as excruciating pain seared through my face, stabbing into my skull.

"Don't test me again, little Danethrall." The Jarl of Aros commanded darkly.

There was a brief knock and the beardless face of Erhardt's dark haired companion appeared at the door. He entered the room, amusedly glanced at me, and sat at the table. The blonde thrall rushed to the kitchen quickly, returning in moments with a plate of food for him.

"What can I do for you, Tarben?" Erhardt asked, still glowering down at me.

"I didn't mean to interrupt, just came to plan the day." Tarben answered light-heartedly, watching me snivel and writhe at Erhardt's feet, half of my face covered with Erhardt's scarlet fist mark. "Do continue."

"We have just finished." Erhardt smiled calmly, returning to his seat at the table. "Thralls, take my darling betrothed and clean her up. I want her impeccable for the wedding."

The thrall girls rushed to my side and lifted me to my feet. One of the girls – with light brown hair – slipped me a rag to wipe my face with and grabbed my arm, quickly pulling me away with her. I heard Erhardt and Tarben mutter something between themselves before they roared with laughter. My face burned with embarrassment and yet more tears gushed down my cheeks.

The thralls steered me to the back of the house, into the kitchen and out through the back door to the garden. There was a tall fence surrounding the sliver of land behind the Jarl's hall, nothing filled the land but overgrown grass and a well. The sun was climbing into the sky, its beams stretched across the land, radiating blessed warmth.

The blonde thrall and her companion brought a wooden tub outside from the kitchen and carefully placed it near me, before dashing back into the hall again.

"I'm Elda." Said the thrall who'd handed me the rag, breaking the silence. She had pretty brown eyes, light brown hair and was gaunt and skinny. "She's Estrith," she pointed to the emaciated, beaten blonde, who appeared with a steaming bucket in her bony hands.

"And I'm Burwenna." The small, scrawny third thrall smiled meekly, also hauling a metal bucket filled with steaming water.

I wondered if Elda and Burwenna were sisters – they had the same rich brown eyes but Burwenna's hair was darker and she was much younger. I watched the girl pour the hot water into the tub and noted the similar features Elda and she shared.

"It's nice to meet you." I replied, smiling warmly at the three timid, withered faces. "My name is Aveline Birgersdóttir."

Estrith, the poor woman, she was probably the same age as me, maybe a year or two older. She was so terribly starved, like the two others, and her light grey eyes bulged from sunken sockets. Deep shadows smouldered in the cavernous hollows below her cheekbones, purple and grey bruises splashed across her pale, dull flesh. She avoided eye contact with me, staring at the ground instead. Though all three thralls were gaunt, she seemed the weakest, the most damaged and broken ... I examined the contusions and wounds on her face and arms, all ranging from old and faded to fresh and nauseatingly bright. I wondered what other abuse that slight, cadaverous body had endured.

Elda squeezed my arm, gently, before leaving me to stand alone in the garden. I stared into the sloshing waters of the tub as the three women filled it with water heated from over the fire in the kitchen. I watched the thralls as, every now and again, they'd drag a bucket of cold water from the well and lug it into the house to boil. After a little while of this, Burwenna appeared by my side.

She tossed a few handfuls of fragrant herbs into the water of the full tub, swirling them with her hand, before looking up at me. Though her face was sunken and pinched, her stomach bloated from starvation, she smiled at me cheerfully.

"How old are you?" I asked, as she helped me remove my filthy dresses.

"I'm thirteen." Burwenna replied, clutching my dirty clothing in her arms as I stepped into the tub, carefully.

"You're so young ..." I sighed, sadly. "How long have you been here?"

"Four or five years, now." She said nonchalantly. "There was a huge army of Northmen that wintered in our town before they killed King Edmund. Jarl Erhardt and his men took a lot of people as thralls ... He wanted just Estrith and Elda, but Elda refused to leave me. He beat her in front of everyone, then laughed at her cheek and bought me, too."

"Is Elda your sister?" I asked.

"Yes, she's six years older than me. I used to have two older brothers, too, but the Danes killed them." Her voice surprisingly didn't falter. "Do you have any brothers or sisters?"

"I used to have seven older brothers, but the Danes killed them."

We glanced at each other for a moment and grinned, chuckling in dark humour. We fell into silence, privately reminiscing.

Elda and Estrith appeared a little while later, the former hauling a bucket of heated water, the other carrying a basket of oils and clothes that didn't belong to me. Elda slowly and carefully poured the boiling water into the bath while Estrith knelt between Burwenna and I, by the tub. She dampened the cloth in the bath water and began to scrub my arms.

"I'm ... I'm sorry he hit you ..." Burwenna murmured.

Estrith shoved her and glared at her forebodingly.

"Why did you do that?" I gasped.

"I – I thought it not prudent." Estrith recoiled and her soft voice wavered. She paused scrubbing my arm, shaking in trepidation of what I might do.

"Jarl Erhardt beats us if we speak out of turn." Burwenna piped in. "But, with how he mistreats you already, and what you said about your brothers ... I wanted you to know that we empathise with you and are here for you."

Alarm sparked on Estrith and Elda's faces. I understood their apprehension; they had not heard Burwenna and my previous conversation.

"Don't fear," I said, glancing between the two of them. "I am not cruel like him. Burwenna's right, he mistreats me already, and I'm somewhat comforted that you can empathise with me, but it fills me more with sorrow ... You're all from Britain, aren't you?"

They all nodded silently, eyes wide and staring at me. Only Burwenna's face held a faint, eager smile.

"I'm sure you heard him call me 'thrall'? Well, I was born in the Kingdom of East Angles. You three are countrywomen of mine." I revealed, speaking in my native tongue, a tiny smile curled at the corners of my lips.

The three thralls' mouths dropped.

"By the end of the day I will be Erhardt's wife, the *Jarlkona of Aros* ... I cannot promise you much, he has hit me without care of consequence which shows how little he regards me as a Dane, but I will try my hardest to care for you."

"Danes don't care for thralls." Estrith mumbled, staring into her lap.

"I don't know if I'll ever return to Britain." I replied, taking her horrifyingly bony hand in mine, surprising her enough to look me in the eyes. "But I liked my life in Roskilde, regardless of how I got there ... Not all the Danes are cruel. And I promise I will never raise a hand to you or hurt you." She nodded slowly at me, and I smiled mischievously at her. "I'm the *Danethrall*, remember?"

CHAPTER SEVENTEEN

I STOOD IN the shadows watching the crowds. People were merry, cheerful, happy. They drank deeply from their wooden and horn carved cups, firelight glinting on the polished surfaces. Their bellies were blissfully full of goat and swine – a sow and a boar – all sacrificed earlier that day to begin the wedding ceremony. Laughter erupted from various groups and clusters. Games were played, of drinking and chance; wrestling; insult contests; dancing. Couples kissed and held each other, embraced by the loving atmosphere … the celebration of a wedding filled everyone with an evanescent warmth of adoration and ardour.

I, the bride, was hollow and alone.

It was deep into the night, Erhardt and I had been married at noon and celebration had ensued for the rest of the day. After the traditional formalities had been honoured, the ceremonial drinking of the bride-ale and the ritualistic blessing of my womb, the feasting and merriment began.

It hadn't taken long for Jarl Erhardt to leave my side. He'd said enough pleasantries about me during the day to warrant abandoning me for the night. Last I had seen him, Erhardt had been necking a long horn of ale to the cheers of a cluster of men swaddled around him.

Some townsfolk had passingly congratulated me on the nuptials, but most had ignored me. I was a peace-pledge, and by this point all knew of my Anglo-Saxon blood. Those that had sacked Roskilde had obviously gossiped of the *Danethrall* to their wives and families. As much as a peace-pledge was welcomed, a rejoiced and revelled union, my being from Britain made me seem like an indecent, lesser match. I'd heard a few whispers from guests, stating I was an inadequate bride to be offered by Roskilde, and decided that Erhardt and my marriage would not be enough to uphold peace with the 'dastardly rulers' of Roskilde.

But I didn't care what they thought of me.

All I could think of was what my wedding was supposed to be like … I should have been dressed in my yellow gown, with Vidar standing beside me, his rings on my finger. I wondered whether he had returned to Roskilde, yet …

As I found myself doing so many times in Vidar's absence, I stared at the shining silver engagement ring as I twisted it around my finger. There was another ring upon that finger, now, a simple pale gold wedding band that proclaimed I now belonged to Jarl Erhardt Ketilsson of Aros. It had not caused any expense to Erhardt for it had a history: it had originally been worn by each of his wives.

Erhardt's ring was heavy upon my finger, laden with death. The rune etchings of the wedding band were so faded, I couldn't even guess what they might have read, and the metal was dull, marred by the ghosts of his three dead wives … would I be added to the list of women to leave Erhardt a widower? I glared at the damned ring and wanted nothing more than to hurl it into the darkness. It should have been Vidar's wedding ring on my finger – not Erhardt's!

Erhardt had married me for a reason – though my title was 'peace-pledge', I doubted very much that he married me for peace. I was a pawn in whatever scheme he had planned. Erhardt had proven very well that I mattered not … when would the time come that this wedding band would be snatched from my dead hand and shoved upon the finger of the next Jarlkona of Aros?

I gazed up at the shining ivory disc of the moon as it glimmered through the darkness, and in my mind, I prayed.

Mighty Frigg and your handmaidens, twelve,
Though my fate cannot be changed,
Stand with me through the horrors I'm doomed to face.
Grant me knowledge and courage to do what I must,
Give me strength and patience to endure the passing days.
Protect my unborn child and I from the wolves of Aros,

'Til we are returned to our family and home.

'Til we are returned to our family and home … to Vidar.

"You're lost in thought, Danethrall." A voice commented behind me.

I whipped around quickly, and my heart lurched – I half-expected to see Vidar, who had an ethereal tendency to appear when I thought of him. Of course, it wasn't Vidar who had crept up behind me – it was Tarben.

"I have a lot to think about, now I am the Jarl's wife." I scowled darkly at him, before I turned my back on him, to face the crowds once more.

Tarben took a step closer to me. I felt his long thin fingers slither through my hair, his other hand rested on my hip, as he leaned over my shoulder to whisper in my ear.

"Speaking of your husband, Jarl Erhardt has been looking for you." Tarben crooned, tracing his lips along the edge of my ear. He kept one arm coiled around me and took one of my hands in his other hand. I glared up at his gaunt, pallid face, repulsed by his leering grin. "He'd like to know where his beloved wife is, so together you can consummate your marriage."

"Well, I'm – I'm not ready yet." I stuttered as I attempted to pull away from his grip.

"But the Jarl is, so come with me, Jarlkona Danethrall." With a wolf's snarling grin upon his lips, his yellow fangs exposed, he forced me through the celebrators and towards Erhardt's hall.

I struggled against Tarben, tried to escape from him, but he was tall and strong. The people of the North were much taller than Anglo-Saxons, I was like a mouse in comparison to the sly, sleek panther whose clutches I was caught in.

"Jarl Erhardt! I have found your wife." Tarben announced, grasping me tightly still.

Erhardt and two other men were sitting at the table, while Elda, Estrith and Burwenna stood in the shadows. They were all awaiting my arrival. Murky blackness had engulfed the hall, only the pathetic dying glow of the main fire burned, but there was a torch lying on the table in front of one of the Jarl's companions. Erhardt rose and strode towards me, smiling softly.

"There you are, little Danethrall. You weren't trying to run away, were you?" Erhardt asked, running a finger over the huge bruise on my cheek.

"*Nei*, she was merely enjoying the festivities." Tarben replied on my behalf. "In fact, I found her reflecting on her wifely duties."

"Ah, is that so?" Erhardt grinned cheerfully. "I'm sure you'll please me. You've learned quickly from your lesson this morning – I'm very glad to hear that."

My heart began to race in my chest, and a knot formed in my throat.

"Thralls lead her to the bed." Erhardt commanded.

The three women moved to me, Elda offered me her hand, and we followed Estrith and Burwenna to the sleeping area. My hands had begun to shake uncontrollably, and my eyes welled with tears; I was terrified.

Silently, the thralls took me to the bed. Elda removed my gown and dressed me into a sheer white nightdress with a deep 'V' neck. Images of the god Freyr and his wife Gerd embracing were stitched along the hem of the gown's neck, sleeves and skirt, like the pictures etched on small golden plaques that decorated the bed. Tears dripped down my cheeks under the cover of darkness, and I continued to tremble, sat on the edge of the bed, waiting fearfully.

The three thralls stood anxiously along the wall on the far side of the bed. A few more moments passed before the flickering of torchlight drew closer to the room. The shadowed figures of the four men, menacingly lit by the orange glow of the torch, entered the room. Erhardt stood before me, that bloodcurdling smile still plastered across his face. His men stood opposite the thralls, staring at me intently.

"Usually this is where I would remove the bridal-crown." Erhardt said, his deep voice was low as he examined me hungrily. "But as my bride doesn't have one ..."

Erhardt placed a fingertip under my chin and pushed upwards, signifying his want for me to stand. I rose, squeezing my eyes shut.

He ran his finger down my neck, down my chest, between my breasts, before hanging onto the neckline of the nightgown.

The chill of the night danced upon my flesh, under the thin fabric of the nightgown. Goosebumps covered my skin and my nipples hardened, sore from the sting of the cold air. I felt the red burn of shame sweep over my face as the stares of Erhardt and his men rested upon my body, illuminated by the torch flame.

Suddenly, with a vicious rip, Erhardt tore open the front my gown, baring my breasts for Tarben and all the witnesses to see. The men laughed and cheered, and Erhardt chuckled, pleased with himself.

"We can now begin." He growled, pulling me against him.

"*Nej!*" I cried, losing all my Danish bravery and tearing away from him.

I scarpered to the door and crashed into the body of Tarben, who darted in front of me, blocking my exit.

"I thought you said she had been reflecting on her wifely duties, Tarben?" Erhardt snorted, watching me beat against his friend, twisting and writhing in his arms. "You realise this is one of your duties as my wife, Danethrall?"

Tarben, the two companions and Erhardt roared in laughter. Tarben clamped me tightly against his chest and carried me to the bed.

"She's a feisty one, this one." Tarben commented. "Every time she flails, she makes my cock harder!"

The men cackled again, as Tarben threw me onto the bed. The moment I was free from his clutches I crawled to the head of the bed and pulled my gown together to cover my breasts, sobbing and trembling.

Erhardt strode over to me and grabbed a fistful of my long chestnut hair, viciously dragging me off the bed and onto the ground. I whimpered, laying at his feet.

"Remember, Danethrall, this marriage is meant to create *peace* between our towns. If you want your beloved Alvarsson to stay alive, you'll do as you're told." The Jarl snarled, quickly undoing his belt and lowering his trousers. Erhardt grabbed my hair and yanked me up to my knees. "You *will* submit to me. If you don't,

I'll beat you and rape you, as will Tarben and every man in Aros, until you do. I advise you to yield to me now or suffer the consequences."

I met his glower with aching, bloodshot, misted eyes. Erhardt blazed with wrath and fury, and I knew he was serious with every word he'd uttered. I stopped crying, my shoulders fell, but I continued to shake. I held my breath and waited.

"Good." He sneered. "Now, open your mouth. And I swear to all the gods, Danethrall, if you bite me, I'll kill you."

I shuddered but did as Erhardt commanded. I screwed my eyes shut, parted my lips and began praying in my mind to any god who would listen, Christian or Norse – *any*.

Erhardt twisted my hair even tighter in his fist, jerking my head, until I weakly peered up at him. I was terrified, I was ashamed. I opened my mouth wider, as averse as I was to do so. Bile rose into my throat. He gripped his hard cock, and began rubbing my lips with its head, mocking and tormenting me.

"Stick out your tongue." Erhardt ordered. "Keep your eyes open! Look at me!"

I shuddered more violently but did as I was told; I held my tongue out over my bottom lip and my eyes burst with tears as I peered up at him. He wiped the head of his cock over my tongue, first side to side then up and down, glancing over his shoulder at his friends to guffaw with them, before pressing it deep into my mouth. I gagged and spluttered as Erhardt slowly thrust forward and backward, before suddenly slamming his cock down my throat.

I choked and retched, gasping for air but I received none. Erhardt wrenched and jerked my head with his fistful of my hair, ramming his cock back and forth in my mouth, hammering the back of my throat. My neck ached, eyes poured with tears, snot streamed from my nostrils. Finally, Erhardt stopped and threw me down as I coughed and wheezed in a pile on the ground.

The Jarl and his men laughed at me, cheering for Erhardt's accomplishment. They spoke, but I couldn't hear their words, too busy spluttering and spitting, choking up bile.

Erhardt's arms slithered around me, hoisting me to my feet. He ripped the remnants of my nightgown from me and hurled me onto the bed. I curled into a ball on the rustling straw mattress, arms wrapped around my knees as I cried. With a raucous *slap* he struck my rear, and pain shot through me. Erhardt seized my hips and dragged me to him, lifting me to my hands and knees. With fingertips dug into the soft flesh my hip, he grabbed his cock and pressed it between my legs, forcing himself into me.

I wailed as Erhardt entered me, screamed as he kept shoving into me, tearing me in half. He laughed victoriously, and began to pound me like a wild beast, pulling my hair so suddenly, my head snapped backwards. Erhardt pummelled me, thrusting quickly and brutally, my breasts slapped together from the violent motion. The assembled monsters vastly enjoyed the scene and moved around the for better observation, cheering and watching, their eyes bulging from their faces ravenously at the scene before them.

The torture seemed to last an eternity. I searched through the shadows and glimpsed the thralls, who stood by helplessly. Burwenna's trembling body was encased in Elda's arms, shielding my tormented image from the girl's eyes. Elda and Estrith gazed at me, crying silently, empathising – Estrith more than Elda – and pitying me. There was nothing they could do.

When Erhardt had finally finished, he sent Tarben and his friends away, ordered the thralls to leave, until it was just he and I who remained in the room. I laid in the bed, on my side, facing the wall that was hidden in darkness, Erhardt's seed spilling down my legs.

"If you'd not tried to run, we could've fucked privately, with no one watching." The Jarl of Aros whispered, running his hand up and down my body. "But you made me shame you in front of my men and my thralls. Don't do that again."

I said nothing.

Erhardt put a hand on my hip and pulled my body against his, curling around me, his sickening, stale, mead-ridden breath rasping loudly in my ear. His hand snaked up and clutched one of my breasts, his now flaccid member pressed against my rear.

"I said, *don't do that again.*" Erhardt spat darkly.

"*Já*, Jarl Erhardt." I whimpered.
"Much better. *Góða nótt*, my wife."

***

I HARDLY SLEPT that night, curled into a ball, my body aching. I watched as skinny fingers of sunlight slipped through the smoke hole. It didn't take long before the dampened sounds of the thralls preparing breakfast in the kitchen reached my ears. I rolled over and faced the doorway, attempting to devise a plan of sneaking out of bed and away from Erhardt.

Unfortunately, as if he could hear the thoughts whirring through my brain, he woke and gazed at me with his fetid worm smile stuck to his lips.

"You'd better get up," The Jarl recommended. "There is only one thing left to do to confirm our marriage. Company will be here shortly."

He smirked at me before he got out of bed and he pulled on his clothes quickly, leaving me alone slouched on the edge of the bed pitifully.

> *…Grant me knowledge and courage to do what I must,*
> *Give me strength and patience to endure the passing days.*
> *Protect my unborn child and I from the wolves of Aros,*
> *'Til we are returned to our family and home.*

I rose from the bed and spotted from the corner of my eye, a patch of red on the bedsheets. Blood. Alarmed, I ripped my skirts up and reached between my legs. Upon my fingers was a faint stain of scarlet. My knees wobbled, and I collapsed onto the bed, staring at my bloodied fingertip.

"Jarlkona?"

Burwenna appeared in the doorway with clothes and a finely pleated, white cloth – the hustrulinet – in her hands. It was the symbol of a married woman. I stared at the blood a moment longer before hurriedly wiping it on my gown.

"Y-yes." I murmured shakily.

Burwenna approached me, and I noticed a blue gown and white linen underdress in her arms.

"Whose clothes do you dress me in?" I asked.

"These clothes belonged to the previous jarlkona." She admitted quietly.

"He dresses me in a dead woman's clothes?"

Hesitantly the young thrall took a step closer to me, and I stood, allowing her to dress me. As she plaited my hair, I gazed at the blood on the bed. It was only a small amount – I hoped beyond hope that the child in my belly was fine. Though I ached between my legs, I felt no pain in my stomach.

> *... Protect my unborn child and I from the wolves of Aros,*
> *'Til we are returned to our family and home.*

Finally, Burwenna fixed the hustrulinet to my head, pinning it to my chestnut braids beneath. It took a while, but I was ready to enter the main room. I took a few steps forward, then halted abruptly.

'Vidar!' I thought desperately. 'Oh, Vidar! Please, Frigg, help me through this!'

Slowly, I entered the room. The thralls gazed upon me helplessly. Erhardt and the faces of Tarben and the men from the night before stared sneeringly at me. Erhardt grabbed my hand roughly and shoved a set of keys into my palm.

"There, you are the keeper of the keys now, Danethrall." Erhardt snorted. "You are officially my wife."

***

SEVEN DAYS AFTER our wedding, at the very end of the week-long celebration, Erhardt and a large group of his kin left for Roskilde to witness the wedding of Vidar and Ursula, Erhardt's beloved daughter.

I was not invited, for all obvious reasons, but remained in Aros with Elda, Estrith and Burwenna, under the sharp eyes of Tarben, who stayed to make sure I wouldn't attempt to escape. Tarben was Erhardt's right-hand man, though the Jarl did not lack loyal followers and retainers, he trusted no one more than Tarben.

Tarben, known as Tarben the Beardless, had a wife and a few children and was rumoured to have sired several illegitimate offspring with many an unwilling thrall. In this culture, the thralls were regarded similarly to livestock, their bodies available for sexual exploitation without punishment.

"You're smarter than I first thought, little Danethrall, it seems you took heed to our jarl's words. I'm surprised you haven't tried to flee." Tarben crooned snidely as he entered the hall. "I expected you would run away as soon as your husband departed. It's a shame, really ... I did *so* look forward to hunting and capturing you."

I scowled at him, then turned back to my loom. Estrith scuttled across the room and into the kitchen, quick to fetch Tarben his breakfast. I frowned as I watched the emaciated thrall girl tremble. Her quaking grew more violent the closer she came to Tarben. He laughed at the terrified girl and tossed his long, black hair, like a silken ebony sheet, behind his shoulder with one quick flick of his head.

"Fear not, little mouse, I'm not interested in you today." Tarben smirked as Estrith put his breakfast on the table.

Estrith's bony hands and slight frame shook and her narrow shoulders were hunched. Pale strings of her blonde hair hung over her gaunt face as she avoided meeting his eyes.

She scarpered away to the kitchen, a terrified rabbit in the den of a fox.

A smooth, liquid laughter streamed from Tarben's thin pink lips as he watched her. He dropped his long lean body carelessly into a chair and swirled his spoon in the fresh porridge on the table before him. Then he turned to me. He watched me in silence, stirring his porridge every now and again, but he didn't take a bite.

"Are you going to entertain your guest or not, Danethrall? You are the woman of the house, are you not?" Tarben asked, a slither of a smile painted across his porcelain face.

I ignored him and glowered at my weaving, attempting to concentrate on the pattern I was creating with black and white woollen threads. Unfortunately, in my peripheral vision I could spy his smug expression and it infuriated me. Elda delicately stepped into the room and set my meal on the table. Tarben grinned at the thrall and moved my bowl to the place opposite him.

"J-jarlkona, your breakfast is served." Elda stuttered, observing my lack of movement.

I glanced at the table. Tarben's long thin fingers were wrapped around a cup of ale, which he tipped towards me, his sickening smile glaring at me.

"Danethrall, join me." Tarben bade.

"I'm not hungry." I remarked stoutly.

Silence fell over us for over an hour, punctured by the hum of the thralls as they worked around the hall and the soft tapping and click-clacking of the warp-weighted loom. I worked diligently at the loom to avoid giving attention to Tarben. Occasionally he would utter a comment or two, but I refused to acknowledge him. Bored with me, he finally rose to leave.

"You're a terrible hostess, Danethrall." Tarben yawned.

"Then do not return." I suggested coldly.

"Oh, but I must! I promised your dear husband that I would visit you twice a day in his absence." He sighed mockingly, his eyes gleaming wickedly. "I will see you tonight, perhaps you will have found your tongue by then? Good day, Danethrall."

Tarben arrived for dinner that night. Elda tossed his food before him on the table and vanished away, leaving Tarben and me alone together. His only interest was to goad and aggravate me, but I continued to ignore him. It was the same the following day, snide comments fell from Tarben's lips and silence radiated from me.

It had been three days since Erhardt had left for Roskilde, and Tarben had quickly grown tired with my lack of reaction. He turned his attention onto the thralls – most specifically to poor Estrith. The broken girl trembled at the very presence of Tarben, when he spoke to her, her already sallow skin paled further, her grey eyes darted with fear and her bottom lip quivered uncontrollably.

"You're very jumpy today, Estrith." Tarben jeered, grabbing her skinny wrist as she set his dinner in front of him. "You're as skittish now as you were at breakfast! Come here, let me calm you."

He pulled the quivering girl onto his lap and began rubbing her bony back. Alarmed, I watched from beside my loom, frozen with trepidation. In a fluid, continual movement, Tarben stroked her back up and down, up and down, subtly and slowly sliding his hands over her hips, then up her back, down again, over her hips and along her thighs, then up her back ... Tears slipped down Estrith's face as Tarben's hands slid over her inner thigh, higher and higher, before she squealed with horror and tried to leap off him. Tarben forced her to stay seated on him, pinning her against him.

"Now, now, you might benefit from this." Tarben crooned, his hand tightly cupped between her legs, rubbing her through her rough flax tunic in small circular motions with his fingertips. "I know I feel better after I c—"

"Get off her!" I screamed, lunging at him.

I whipped the knife from beside the bread on the table and pointed it directly at him.

"Let her go!" I snarled.

Tarben stared at me – an odd mixture of surprise and awe lit up his face. Suddenly, his deep, smooth laughter poured from his lips as he tossed the weeping thrall to the ground.

"Ah! Now you're entertaining me, Danethrall!" Tarben the Beardless beamed, satisfied with finally infuriating me into the palm of his hand. "I'll leave your little slave alone. *But* you should be more playful; otherwise I'll get bored with you again and will have to find something more ... *amusing*, to play with – and she," he nodded his head at Estrith, "is *incredibly* amusing."

The knife still held tightly in my small hand, still pointed at Tarben, I commanded Estrith to leave. She fled to the confines of the kitchen, into the arms of Burwenna and Elda.

"Sit with me." Tarben smiled, pointing to the place opposite him, where my food sat cold.

Reluctantly I sank into the seat, but I didn't drop my glare from him, and I didn't drop the knife.

Tarben, seemingly overjoyed to have my full attention, spent much more time at the hall the following days. I was alert and watchful whenever he was around, always attentive to his every action, every word that fell from his lips, to his absolute delight. I couldn't drop my guard for even a moment around him. When Tarben arrived at the hall, I would send all three thralls from the house to tend to tasks and chores that kept them a safe distance away from him and the threat he posed.

It was early morning, and I sent Elda, Estrith and Burwenna, with shawls around their shoulders and baskets upon their arms, out to pick mushrooms and whatever edible flora they could find from the forests on the mainland surrounding Aros.

A short while later, Tarben let himself into the hall. Quietly he stepped in, and I said nothing to him. He strode around the hall, glancing through the doorway of the kitchen and pausing, listening carefully, before pacing again. Tarben stopped near me, by the fireplace and turned to me.

"Just us again, eh Danethrall?" Tarben asked mischievously.

"If my company isn't adequate for you, then leave." I spat, readjusting the loom to tighten the threads.

"Oh, but it is. If I didn't know better, I'd say you were purposely trying to get me alone with you." Tarben smiled slyly.

"Why on *earth* would I want to be alone with *you*?" I gasped incredulously.

"That's what I'm wondering," he smirked, sauntering over to me. "There's only one thing I could think of …"

Tarben reached his hand out and gently dragged the back of his finger down my cheek and across my jaw. I froze, stunned by his touch. His fingers were so cold.

"You're so still, Danethrall." Tarben whispered, stepping closer and placing a hand on my hip, pulling me towards him. "I prefer it when you're animated – like on your wedding night when you writhed and wriggled in my arms …"

Tarben gripped my hips and pulled me against him. He ran a hand over my buttocks and squeezed it tightly.

"What are you doing?" I hissed, struggling against his grasp.

"That's it – this is what I like." Tarben growled eagerly.

"Get off!" I yelped.

I squirmed and struggled before he finally let me go, sending me tumbling out of his arms and into the loom. He snickered at me, as I clutched my heart with my shaking hand, drawing breath in short gasps.

"What's for breakfast?"

Shamelessly, Tarben quickly took advantage of his time alone with me – he would touch me: caress my bare flesh, whether it be my fingers, hands, neck or face; graze against me as he walked by; press his body against mine; grope and grab my hips and buttocks. I couldn't allow him near my thralls and had no friend or ally to call upon to save me from him. I came to look forward to Erhardt's return, knowing that Tarben wouldn't dare touch me in front of him.

I suffered only three days of Tarben's molestation, three long, agonising days. It was early in the morning and Tarben had already come to the hall – I had to rush the girls out of the house within moments of his arrival. Tarben chuckled as he watched me shove the girls out of the house, their terrified faces glancing at him as they fled.

I slammed the door shut and turned to glare at Tarben. His long, slender body leaned carelessly in a chair at the table. I stomped to the kitchen and busied myself cooking, but the arrogant beast made idle conversation. Tarben began speaking of Erhardt, at which point I stomped out of the kitchen as the porridge bubbled in the cooking pot, and found him beaming at me, his lips curled into a menacing smirk.

"Speaking of our jarl, my husband is due to return tomorrow." I replied, wrinkling my nose at him. "You only have two more meals to ruin with your presence before I don't have to look upon your hideous face every day, anymore."

"Well, aren't you brazen, today?" Tarben snorted sarcastically. "I didn't realise my attending you was so abhorrent ... and here I was thinking we had become such *wonderful friends*."

I scowled at him, my arms crossed over my ribs, brow furrowed. Even the sight of him disgusted me. Tarben's eyes examined me expectantly. I stormed to the kitchen and fetched his meal, porridge with stewed apples. I dropped the large bowl sloppily on the table in front of him, before stomping passed him to my loom on the other side of the room.

I began weaving irritably, my every movement was sharp and brisk, seething with petulance. I heard him chuckling at me, angering me further, but I didn't say a word, my lips remained tightly pursed. Tarben ate his food quietly while I weaved.

"You're very angry today, Danethrall." Tarben murmured, suddenly behind me.

I flinched and gasped sharply as Tarben grabbed my waist and began massaging my back, firmly, with his thumbs. He pulled me against him, rubbing and stroking, caressing and squeezing. Tarben slid his large hands from my sides to my stomach, stretching the fingers of his left hand across my small tummy. His right hand snaked upwards, over my breasts and chest, onto my neck ... he held my jaw with a finger and thumb, turning my face to look over my shoulder. Stooping, he gently pressed his face against mine, breathing softly.

"Your belly is hard, little *Danethrall*, yet you haven't had anything to eat." Tarben whispered. "My wife's temper would fluctuate quickly, between joy and sadness, anger and calm, whenever she carried my children. I would never know if she was going to be pleasant or vicious, her mood would change so frequently."

My breath was caught in my throat, a horrible, tightly wedged knot of panic froze my entire being. Tarben dragged his fingertips along my jaw, to my breasts, enclosing one in his hand, kneading and squeezing it softly. Icy terror flooded through me, and I cried out as he pinched my nipple, gently rolling it between his finger and thumb through the fabric of my dress.

"My beloved wife learned soon into her second pregnancy not to snap at me though ... she may hold the keys to my home, but without me she wouldn't survive." Tarben murmured.

His other hand palpated my stomach. He grinned at me like a snake glaring down at a mouse, constricting me in his embrace. I turned my face away from him, shutting my eyes tightly. Tears poured down my cheeks and my body shuddered. Tarben alternated his play of my breasts, slowly increasing his pressure until I'd gasp or cry out. I could feel his torso reverberate in silent laughter, feel his pleasure hard against my buttocks, growing stiffer and larger with my every squeal.

"It's only been two weeks since you consummated your marriage with our jarl. I thought I'd watched him deflower you, but you must've been spoiled before the wedding, eh?" Tarben sighed, his breath tingling over my ear.

"I'm not with child! Take your filthy hands off me!" I finally barked, twisting in his arms.

I faced him and pushed against his chest with my trembling hands, stumbling backwards into the loom. Tarben snatched my wrists, saving me from falling, but I ripped away from him and staggered across the room, ensuring the table was between us.

"Don't touch me again!" I snarled darkly. "I am Jarl Erhardt's wife! I'll have your fucking hands chopped off if you even think of touching me like that again!"

Tarben examined me, scrutinising the fury upon my face, realising how serious my threat was. For many moments he stood there glaring at me, unspeaking.

"Remember, Danethrall," he finally whispered, his face bathed in shadow, his long ebony hair falling either side of his face like curtains of night. "As my wife's survival depends on me, so does yours. You do not want your secret revealed, now, do you? ..."

Tarben glowered at me for a moment longer before he glided out of the hall. The door slammed shut behind him and a wave of shuddering relief crashed over me. I laid a hand on my stomach as though I were trying to comfort the tiny occupant inside me. Of course, I felt nothing, I was perhaps nearly two months pregnant. My stomach had begun to feel firmer, yes, but there was no bulging belly yet.

My other hand travelled upwards to my aching breasts, my nipples throbbing. The same horror, fear and sickness that had consumed me on my wedding night with Erhardt rushed through my body as Tarben had grabbed me and touched me, and now ... the same overwhelming despair drowned me. I was mortified and disgusted, choking on the thick air of anxiety, agonising over what had happened and what could have happened ...

> *... Protect my unborn child and I from the wolves of Aros,*
> *'Til we are returned to our family and home.*

I fell to my knees and vomited violently.

CHAPTER EIGHTEEN

Summer

I CHANTED MY prayer every night. When Erhardt's snores filled the air, I'd close my eyes and pray to Frigg and her handmaidens to protect me and the child I carried inside me. As I prayed, a sense of calm would wash over me, and Vidar's smirking face would appear in my mind and warm my soul and ease me into slumber.

It had been two months since our wedding night, and Erhardt had realised I was with child. Never having witnessed my menses, he believed he'd impregnated me when we consummated our marriage. He bragged of his 'strong and potent seed' to all who would listen, which was a huge number of people considering his position as jarl.

I was now visibly pregnant; protruding from my belly was a firm, rounded bump, small but obvious. Since realising I was pregnant, Erhardt became somewhat considerate of the life I carried inside me. Though he still forced himself upon me, he beat me no more. This development drove me more obsessively to worship and pray to the Norse gods and goddesses – Frigg and her handmaidens had heeded my plea!

Ravaged by guilt but compelled by the need to survive, I learned quickly to lie down and accept whatever Erhardt did to me in our marriage bed. If I simply laid beneath him, eyes squeezed shut and reciting my prayer in my mind until he was done, copulation would be physically pain free and, mercifully, over quickly.

Erhardt, pleased and proud of impregnating me so promptly, and somewhat crediting me with a 'job well done', made no more comments about my Anglo-Saxon birth and heritage. I was his wife, I was carrying his heir, and that was that. He even referred to me as my birth name rather than the derogatory title 'Danethrall'.

The hot sun bore down on my back as I ambled around the labyrinthine town, Estrith at my side, glancing at farms and homesteads, longhouses and sheds as we passed them.

The air was clean in the summer, it was fresh. There was no need to burn the fires other than to cook, if one even chose to cook, so the stench of smoke was nothing more than a shadow once breakfast was over, and completely absent by afternoon.

I examined the sweating venders as they worked and called out their wares and smiled at the joyous faces of children prancing around the streets like baby goats. I placed a hand against my belly and daydreamed of the future. I imagined Vidar's beaming smile as he held his son in his arms, kissing me lovingly ...

"Jarl Erhardt wants more honey," Estrith mentioned meekly as we came upon the market stalls. "And fish for the feast tonight."

My fantasy dissipated, I acknowledged her, disappointed and reluctant to face reality, nevertheless I took heed of her. Though I wanted so desperately to, I couldn't stay in my imagination forever.

"I can't stand fish right now." I commented, taking her arm in mine. "But I suppose whatever the Jarl wants, he gets. Come along then."

Overwhelmed with delight at the possibility of having a son in but a few months, especially elated at believing he'd sired a child at such an old age as his, Erhardt had decided to throw a feast at his hall. He had invited not just Tarben, but Tarben's wife and children, also, as well his two daughters who lived in Aros, their husbands and children.

Erhardt's sister, his niece and two nephews, their respective partners and children would also be attending. Between the lot of them there was going to be seventeen children between the ages of two and twelve expected to fill the hall, and Erhardt's niece was grossly pregnant with her fourth offspring.

My head ached at the very idea of so many children bursting through the hall doors. The hall was large, but I didn't know how well it would hold with so many rampaging little ones stampeding through the place.

Excited though I was at the idea of motherhood, the feast made me feel nothing more than pre-emptive exhaustion and trepidation. I hoped beyond all hope that Erhardt's niece would not explode this evening and add another commotion to what I expected was going to be quite a tumultuous, chaotic affair.

Estrith was the only thrall who had come to the market with me, Burwenna and Elda were busy preparing the house for the many guests. During the morning, their duties included cooking breakfast, then cleaning and rearranging the hall. As soon as Estrith and I arrived home, the three thralls would be busy cooking for the rest of the day.

We were going to serve a lot of fruit and berries, both dried and fresh; baskets full of nuts; wild greens and eggs from chickens, ducks, and various seabirds (not to mention we'd be eating the birds, too); and copious amounts of fish cooked in various ways: boiled in rich stews, baked, smoked, salted.

Fish was in abundant supply and very inexpensive to buy. Half of our purchases today would be made for the feast, the other half would be smoked, dried and salted to replace the eaten food from our stores.

On top of all the food, we'd be serving mead, ale and buttermilk, and jugs of fresh icy water for drinking. Unfortunately, due to my pregnancy I'd become unable to eat most of the food we were going to serve this evening, enjoying only cold water and nibbles of forest greens and bland chicken.

Estrith and I ordered and paid for the fish, then wandered slowly around the market, enjoying the warmth, winding through the hustle and bustle. I bought two strings of pale amber beads from a vender, for Elda and Burwenna, and a set of brooches for Estrith.

Estrith gasped, astonished at the idea of me purchasing her a gift, she tried profusely to refuse me, but I ignored her. The beads and brooches were very inexpensive, but much grander than the girls were used to wearing.

I didn't care about their position as thralls, I'd come to adore Burwenna, Elda and Estrith as friends, and desired more than anything to have them happy. Slowly they gained weight from the meals I smuggled to them behind Erhardt's back. Erhardt believed in fear, in quelling his thralls into submission. They weren't human to him, they were slaves, lesser than livestock and he hated 'wasting good food' on them.

I'd never seen such a smile on Estrith's face when she wore the brooches. We pinned them to her gown then and there in the street, before continuing to the fish stall to gather our purchase. I paid the fishmonger a few extra coins to have his thrall carry the fish home for me.

"They suit you very well." The young, dark-skinned male thrall noted, nodding at Estrith's brooches, which glittered in the sunlight.

Estrith beamed at him, thanked him quietly and grinned the whole way back to the hall. When we reached the hall door, she nervously began to finger and stroke the brooches.

"It was my gift to you." I pointed out firmly. "You won't be in any trouble at all."

She nodded slowly, disbelievingly, and followed me in. Tarben was already there, leaning against a post, watching Elda hungrily. His eyes lit up as he noticed Estrith and me.

"Ah, welcome home, ladies. You've been gone for a while." He observed tartly. "We wondered if you'd arrive in time for the feast."

"How nice of you to scold in my own home." I answered acidly. "I thought Jarl Erhardt was my husband, not you." I added a little louder, catching sight of Erhardt entering the main room from the kitchen.

Grinning warmly at my comment, Erhardt stood by my side, placing a hand on my stomach and kissing the top of my head.

"Tarben jests with you." Erhardt chuckled patronisingly. "I'm glad you're home, but you are welcome to come and go as you may, your timekeeping is up to you."

I tiptoed upwards and kissed Erhardt on his jaw, my stare unbroken with Tarben's. Erhardt chuckled again, before continuing his way to the other side of the room, ordering Burwenna to the kitchen as he went.

"To think, you were like a terrified mouse only a few months ago and now you are a dutiful, loving wife." Tarben commented, one of his long, thin eyebrows arching upwards. "What a vast change there has been in you."

"I've learned." I spat.

And I had. Tarben smirked at me wickedly; I was as clear as glass to him, my manipulation of the Jarl amused him greatly, regardless that I used my talent to best him in Erhardt's esteem.

I'd come to realise how to influence Erhardt. Carrying his child not only prompted him to treat me kindly, but occasionally bestowing ounces of affection upon him gave me the power to sway him to my will.

At first it was difficult ... Guilt would weigh heavily on my heart, and a shroud of shame would envelope me. It took all my strength just to reach out and gingerly take his hand in mine. Like leaping from a boat into the middle of the icy fjord, I was filled with trepidation, but I forced myself to embrace Erhardt when he opened his arms to me.

With every peck and kiss and touch I meekly gave to Erhardt, I felt as though I were betraying Vidar. But survival was paramount. I'd shake away any thoughts of guilt, inhale deeply and feel Danish bravery ignite and burn away the darkness of shame inside me. Frigg had given me the knowledge I'd asked for, now I had to follow through, courageously.

"I do apologise, Jarlkona." Tarben sneered sarcastically, taking a step or two closer to me.

"Estrith, please show the fish vendor's thrall to the kitchen." I instructed Estrith, tearing my eyes from Tarben.

His stare had become too uncomfortable.

Estrith blushed warmly as she glanced at the thrall, his full lips curved in a small smile, before she ushered him to the kitchen. I watched them, grinning briefly, before I noticed Tarben had crept closer to me yet again. I scurried after the thralls into the kitchen, eager to be away from the Jarl's right-hand man.

***

ERHARDT AND TARBEN'S families arrived an hour or so before dinner commenced. As expected, the ridiculous number of children resulted in a copious amount of noise. I stifled my giggles as I watched the mothers chase their children, like herding cats.

The children were agile and swift, considering their short legs, with seemingly magical abilities to slip from their mothers' clutches. More than once had a child's raucous behaviour resulted in a little red, tear-stained face moping on a stool, bottom lip quivering, after being smacked on the rear end.

The noise from the children wasn't due just to misbehaviour, however, even the children's happiness was loud. As unused to a child's intensity and boisterousness as I was, it warmed my heart to bursting to see so many innocent little beings so happy in the hall. Knowing the struggles and hurdles I'd faced since moving to Aros and seeing my melancholy mirrored on my three thrall girl's faces … I was pleased to see such sincere bliss filling these walls.

The evening passed by deafeningly but uneventfully. It was awkward being introduced to Erhardt's daughters – by all legalities I was their stepmother, but they were older than me. Thankfully their children did not call me grandmother, respectfully referring to me as 'Jarlkona' instead.

The food was delicious, though I could not eat much. I'd lost a lot of my appetite since moving to Aros; even though my belly swelled with growing life, I was much leaner than when I'd first arrived, and very gaunt in the face. I'd formed dark grey smudges under my eyes, and to my surprise, Inga, Tarben's wife, had taken sympathy on me.

Inga doted on me, cared for me. I almost wondered if her sympathy was empathy in disguise … Tarben was merciless and cruel, especially towards women. I knew, first-hand, that the beardless Dane was possessed with an insatiable, compulsive lust to dominate women. He seemed to draw a depraved gratification, both emotionally and sexually, from abusing his victims … He bragged of controlling his wife with an iron first. I wondered if Inga recognised that I was trapped in a cold, loveless marriage – like her.

It was late, the moon was high in the sky and the stars twinkled like broken glass on a black veil. I was lying on the grass on a woollen blanket in the tiny garden, with Tarben and Inga's youngest child, their two-year-old son, in my arms. Inga and Agnes were sitting on chairs beside me, the fire roaring and offering us warmth and a fabulous orange glow to see each other by.

A shining thread of drool slipped down the boy's chin from his rosy wet lips. The little boy had crawled into my arms, rubbing his eyes, as Elda brought chairs out for Agnes, Inga and me to sit on. I remained laying on the blanket with the child, however, stroking his face with one hand, the other wrapped around him firmly and comfortingly, and he quickly drifted to sleep.

"Look who we have here." Tarben said, spotting his son in my arms and striding towards us from the backdoor. "Don't you all look comfortable?"

"Join us won't you, husband?" Inga invited, timidly patting my empty chair.

"I'd love to." He replied happily, though the unblinking glare he shot at me was anything but pleased. "What conversation did I interrupt?"

"We were only speaking of children, preparing Aveline for her coming child." Agnes grinned warmly, giggling at me.

"Ah, yes. Are you excited to have a new baby brother?" Tarben laughed. "What is it – a twenty-five-year age gap? You'll be a grandmother by the time your brother is a man!"

Inga and Agnes twittered and giggled, while I stared silently at Tarben. Our glances connected, and I saw the darkness in his eyes. Tarben took a hold of his wife's hand, squeezing it and stroking it. Inga was visibly surprised by her husband's affection; he had ignored her for most of the night.

"That's what we were laughing about!" Inga chuckled, gazing at her fingers entwined with her husbands.

"Speaking of babies and sibling, Agnes, have you heard from Ursula?" Tarben asked suddenly.

The women's giggles were quickly extinguished.

"Not recently, no." Agnes replied, glancing between Tarben and me.

"I wonder whether Alvarsson and her have conceived a child yet? It only took our beloved little Aveline one night to conceive a child with Erhardt. I wonder if Vidar and Ursula were so lucky?" Tarben said.

His tormenting words were smooth and deep, and smug satisfaction riddled his face as he goaded me. An inferno of rage engulfed me as I watched that damn sneer spill across his face. Shaking, I slipped my arm out from beneath the child, careful not to wake him, and rose from the ground.

"What's wrong, Danethrall? Surely you wish the couple the same bliss as you and your husband?" Tarben taunted. "A man needs an heir after all? Unless Vidar has an heir elsewhere that no one knows about?"

Blood beat in my ears and I knew my face was scarlet, I could feel the heat burning beneath my flesh. I caught a glance of poor Inga struggling to release her hand from her husband's grip, he was squeezing so hard she was wincing with pain.

"Of course, he doesn't, I'm sure we would've heard about it by now." I spat through gritted teeth.

"You and he were betrothed, were you not?" Tarben continued, ignoring his wife's whimpers. "Did you by chance give him a preview to what you could offer him in marriage?" He chortled snidely through his wolf-like snarl.

"And ruin myself before marriage?" I hissed angrily. I was lying but so full of fury I knew I must've been convincing to Agnes and Inga. "Jarl Erhardt is the only man to have bedded me. You were witness to that."

"So, the babe in your belly is the Jarl of Aros's heir? You were both blessed by the gods so quickly, it causes one to wonder what the truth might be." Tarben jeered, throwing his wife's hand down and rising to his feet. "You are showing rather soon considering how early you are in your pregnancy."

"That's enough!" Agnes cried abruptly. "You should be ashamed of yourself for speaking to the Jarlkona in such a way! In her own home, too! You must leave at once!"

Tarben's eyes darted disgustedly between the outraged Agnes's glare, his wife's tearful gaze and my seething scowl. His son had started to stir from his slumber thanks to the argument and began to moan. As he watched his son fidget awake, Tarben's expression began to calm, his eyebrows softened, and a smirk replaced his snarl.

"My apologies, Jarlkona. Thank you for a wonderful evening." He smiled, scooping his son into his arms, before turning to Inga. "Get the children, it's time to leave."

And he was gone.

Inga apologised, clutching her hand against her chest, before she rushed after her husband. Agnes and I watched them in silence. I dropped to my knees and held my head in my hands for a few moments, before lying down again. Agnes sat beside me, watching the backdoor, while I gazed at the sky.

"I hate that man." I murmured.

"I do, too." Agnes replied, making me snicker. "He's a fox. He's cunning and wise, stealthy and sly. He's an incredibly strong warrior, too, second only to my father. That's why my father keeps him close."

"There was nothing stealthy about him tonight – he quite obviously wants to create dark rumours about me." I sighed warily, closing my eyes.

"Freyja blessed you with bountiful fertility ... you carry my father's seed in your belly, hopefully his son and heir." Agnes said. "Giving him a child so quickly ... I haven't seen my father this happy in a long time. Tarben's probably afraid that a foreign-born girl will replace him in my father's admiration. I've seen Erhardt scold Tarben enough times in your defence this evening alone to know that Tarben is feeling threatened."

I laughed at her honesty and turned to look at her, propping myself up on my elbows.

"Though I enjoy the idea of Tarben feeling threatened by me, it doesn't put a stop to my fears." I said. "If Tarben convinces the Jarl that his wife is nothing but a thrall whore, pregnant with another man's child, I'm sure I would be killed. It's a simple but effective plan for Tarben to regain his position."

"I'd recommend you give my father a son." Agnes advised. "You'll forever be in my father's good graces ... and after giving Erhardt a son, execute Tarben."

I gasped, staring at her, my eyes as wide as plates.

"Tarben is a wolf and a fox! He is a scavenger that feasts on my father's scraps – whether it be women or glory – and he longs to be jarl." Agnes explained sinisterly. "My father is old, but still very strong; he could defeat Tarben in a battle, even now. But when he dies, Tarben will slaughter my father's bloodline – my aunt, my sisters, my children, all of us! – and then he will be jarl.

"Tarben is a threat ... My father is a dangerous man, but you need to wrap him around your little finger and use him to take down Tarben. Otherwise, Tarben will take down you."

***

AGNES'S WORDS ECHOED inside my mind for the rest of the night. She was right, and I was terrified.

Shortly after Tarben and his family had departed, the rest of the guests began to filter out. I excused myself and slipped away to bed while Erhardt was in deep conversation with his sister. The exhausted thrall girls were set cleaning the house, weakly bidding me goodnight as I passed them.

I laid in my bed, dozing fretfully but unable to fall completely asleep. Upon slipping into the soft sheets, I whispered my prayer to Frigg, as had become my custom, and closed my eyes. Immediately Vidar's face would appear in my mind, and memories would flood my brain. I sat up in bed, sadness tugging on my heart; I ached for him terribly.

An hour or so later, Erhardt drunkenly collapsed into bed, thankfully too inebriated to initiate intercourse. I praised small mercies and turned onto my side, staring into the night until I finally fell into an uneasy slumber.

We woke late the next morning, and from an epiphany borne in my slumber, I had created a plan. Tentatively and nervously, I began running my fingertips down Erhardt's chest, through his forest of grey and ebony curls, inching slightly closer to him, until my rounded tummy and legs touched his body.

Repulsion rose up in my throat, but I continued. I traced over his nipple, flicking it lightly, urging him to waken, and rousing his cock to stand.

"I don't think you've ever done this before." Erhardt grinned, his breath stinking of stale mead.

I propped myself up on my elbow, drawing closer to him, pressing my breasts against his arm. I pressed my lips against his shoulder, an illusion of a kiss, and ran my hand from his chest to the wiry down between his legs, taking his shaft and stroking it, timidly.

I said nothing to him, focussing on the task at hand. Giving him small tokens of affection offered me protection, I hoped that giving him my body willingly and generously would earn me more …

I brought myself on top of him, sucking on one of his nipples before lowering myself down between his legs. With a deep breath, I forced myself to lick him. Erhardt gasped ecstatically and gripped my hair roughly as my head bobbed up and down between his legs.

With a roaring moan he arched his back, body quivering. I clambered off him quickly and spat over the side of the bed. I laid back down on the bed next to him, wiping dribbles of his euphoria from my mouth with the back of my hand.

I was sickened, I felt filthy, but as he curled around me happily, I knew my plan was working, even if it was only beginning.

The next day I woke him the same way, and the next day, and the next. Quickly I noticed the effect my morning efforts brought me. When Tarben or any of Erhardt's men spoke ill of or to me, he would snap or roar at them, furiously defending my honour. I noticed Tarben back down reluctantly, darkly surveying me with curious, aggravated speculation.

***

Autumn

THE WEATHER HAD cooled, colour had faded from the trees and the brisk wind soared with a bitter coldness as it blustered over the rumbling waves.

"Our son will be born soon." Erhardt cooed, caressing my huge, naked belly, as we lay in the fur covered bed.

The hall was silent and shrouded in darkness but for the smouldering radiance of the crimson firelight glimmering across from our bed.

"I'd like to name him after my father."

"Which one? Your Danish father or your Saxon one?" He asked evenly.

"Birger." I replied.

There was silence for a while. My nipples stood erect from the cool night air; my small breasts were much fuller thanks to the late stage of pregnancy. Erhardt's hand drifted upwards and cupped one of my breasts, squeezing it gently.

"Okay." He answered simply.

I turned and faced him, searching his expression. He kissed me, his coarse beard scratching my face.

"Thank you." I whispered.

Gently, I pressed a hand against his chest, pushing him onto the bed. I sat up, slowly lifting myself onto him, taking his cock and angling it inside me. Gradually I began to thrust, his calloused grip on my breasts growing tighter and tighter as I increased my speed.

I watched him as I rode him, my breath quickening from effort. Between my legs was a man I never wanted to marry; a man I feared; a man I hated. Though my control of him improved with each passing day, I was scared that I would birth a daughter and all my hard work was for naught.

I closed my eyes and thought of Vidar, picturing his face.

It had been over half a year since I'd last seen him, but in my mind, his face was clear as day. The faint lines of age sprawling from the corners of his ice coloured eyes; his coy smirk curling the edge of his full, pink lips; the curve of his high cheekbones; the line of his strong jaw hidden beneath his soft, neatly maintained, sandy brown beard.

I loved stroking the lightly bristled sides of his head, where his hair was shorn to the scalp – I also loved removing the leather strip that tied back the glorious lengths of hair from the top of his head.

I would run my fingers through his thick tresses and admire all the different shades, the gold and ash, the honey and beige ...

Suddenly Erhardt grasped my hips, groaning and shuddering in ecstasy, and I cried out, sharply, clasping a hand to my belly as he jerked. I fell off him, biting my lip, but thankfully the pain was over quickly. He didn't seem to notice; he curled around me, grasped one of my breasts and kissed my head.

We spoke not a word as Erhardt caught his rasping breath. After a while, his breathing calmed and his grasp on my breast lessened as he began to drift asleep.

"What is childbirth like?" I asked quietly.

"Painful." Erhardt said after a long pause. "You're young and strong, though, so I wouldn't worry about the future too much. This won't be our only child, I'm sure."

I shuddered at the idea of birthing a child of Erhardt's, but I drew some comfort from his confidence in my strength – that I would survive birthing my child. Still, I could not shake the gnawing anxiety about the future.

Gingerly I laid my hand upon my stomach, where the pain had shot through. I felt the tiny child inside me move. A deep sigh fell from my lips and I silently prayed to my goddesses.

***

Late Autumn

A MONTH OR so passed, and we woke to yet another cold, wet morning. Rain bore down mercilessly from the steel and charcoal sky. The far-off bellow of thunder grew louder as the storm raged closer, and waves crashed and beat against the grey shores ruthlessly.

The unrelenting wind whipped and thrashed the hall, making the wooden abode creak and groan around me. My belly ached and throbbed, and I hoped to all the gods that these were not ominous indications of what was to come.

Recently, we had been harried by the weather. The delicious summer had soured into a furious autumn, which drowned most of our crops soon after we'd completed the seasonal blót. We feared the vicious hand of autumn and its hellish destruction, but with no sign of yielding, it proceeded with a terrifying ferocity. At this rate we had no idea how we'd survive through the fast-approaching winter.

"Are you okay?" Elda asked anxiously, watching me grimace and hold my tummy in agony.

"*Já*," I smiled weakly. "The pain passes quickly."

She scurried across the hall as I wobbled out of the bed and waddled into the main room to sit upon a fur covered chair in front of the fire. Burwenna appeared, draping a thick black fur over my enormous belly, concern pouring from her face. Elda soon returned, pressing a steaming mug of mulled wine into my hand.

Suddenly, with a crash the door slammed into the wall, flung open by Jarl Erhardt, in an atrocious mood. He was sodden, every inch of his body dripped with freezing rain, and Tarben following in behind him, shivering. Erhardt's fury seemed to be keeping him warm, I noted, watching him thunder back and forth, not caring about the state he was in.

"That's another damned longship destroyed since this fucking storm started." Erhardt growled. "Not only will half this town starve to death, but the other half will have no ships to sail in! Crops are drowned, cows won't produce milk, livestock won't stand on their damned feet, sickness is rampant, and now even more ships are being ripped apart!"

He smashed his fists on to the table, roaring as they collided with the hard wood. I leapt out of my skin, watching him rage. Erhardt glared at the tabletop, panting deeply, one hand gripping his chest.

"Erhardt?" I whispered.

"I'm fine." Erhardt answered gruffly. "And what of you, wife? Do you still have the pains?"

"*Já*, and they're growing closer." I replied apprehensively.

"I'm excited to meet our child, I assure you, but not yet, not this early – not until after winter." He commented lightly.

"I'm trying to keep him in." I smiled.

Suddenly a red-hot bolt exploded through my stomach. I doubled up in pain and dropped the cup clattering to the floor.

Erhardt rushed to me, grabbing my shoulders roughly.

"Aveline? Aveline?" He gasped.

"I don't know how well I'll keep him in." I whimpered, recoiling from pain.

"Thrall!" Erhardt screeched, pointing at the frightened Estrith. "Get runes! And we need offerings for Frigg—"

Blue sparks of lightning flashed across the hall from the smoke hole. In a whirl of panicked commands and booming roars of thunder, Erhardt tore the blanket from me and forced me to stand.

Tarben the Beardless was uncharacteristically silent. He sank into a shadowed corner of the hall, watching darkly, glowering at me as I clutched my aching stomach, Erhardt fussing over me wildly.

I staggered around the room, stumbling to the floor every time a shot of pain seared through me. Estrith crouched by my side, forcing runes into one of my hands, muttering words of comfort to me in our native tongue. Erhardt grabbed Burwenna and threw her into the storm to fetch someone, while I writhed on the cold dirt floor, agony flowing in a constant stream through my body.

"Aveline?" Erhardt said as he rushed to my side.

I rose to my feet clumsily, the palms of my hands slick with sweat, streams of exhaustion pouring down my face. I attempted to hold my head high, standing as straight as I could, my legs shaking.

"I think the baby is coming." I announced simply, smiling feebly. "You're right, it is very painful."

Erhardt stared at me incredulously for a moment before a rush of nervous laughter tumbled from his lips.

"Let's get this baby out of you as quickly as we can, then." He said, taking my hand in his.

Burwenna had returned, saturated in rain, her short brown hair stuck to her shivering flesh in sodden clumps. She'd returned with a cloaked elderly woman, who was knowledgeable, apparently, in childbirth.

While Burwenna shakily lit a white candle, the woman unwrapped herself of her sodden clothing and began chanting different prayers to Frigg, Freyja and the dísir, to aid me in the birthing process. As she chanted, she shoved a small set of silver keys into my free hand, before yanking me by the wrist to the table.

I pressed my fists into the hard, scrubbed tabletop, digging the sharp keys and smooth runes into my palms. My legs buckled and ached, but I stood nonetheless, desperate to get the baby out of me.

"Pray to the goddesses, girl!" The wise woman hissed, her skin hanging in sagging folds about her gaunt skull. Though she was extremely aged, there was an intensity that roared in her watery green eyes that commanded me to obey.

"Frigg, aid and support me!" I howled through gritted teeth. "Freyja, help me birth my child! Dísir, come to me!"

"They won't help you if you speak in your foreign tongue!" The wise woman snarled.

An hour or so had passed and finally I laid, freshly bathed, in bed, my clean, new-born son suckling from my breast contentedly, both of us snuggled together beneath a mountain of furs. I couldn't stop grinning, elated at my child, my perfect little boy!

"A son!" Erhardt cried out joyfully. "A son, finally!"

Erhardt was standing at the foot of the bed, with Tarben a few steps behind him. The moment my baby was born, and the wise woman had announced him to be a son, Erhardt had been elated. Tarben had left his place in the shadows at Erhardt's insistence, forced to admire the boy.

"Are you sure he's yours? He has blond hair." Tarben pointed out sharply.

"As did my damned father. The child has my eyes! He is definitely my kin." Erhardt spat, adding spitefully, "Go, Tarben. You're not needed here."

Tarben skulked away and exited the hall, slamming the doors behind him. My heart skipped a beat, delighted at the sight of Erhardt dismissing Tarben so curtly. Agnes Erhardtsdóttir was right, I had given Erhardt a son and cemented myself in his good graces.

I gazed at the baby, his delicate eyes were closed, and his long soft lashes curled like feathers of gold. There was naught more than a pale-yellow fuzz dusted on his head, and his eyes were the lightest blue, like ice.

He was new-born; truthfully, he looked like no one and anyone all at the same time, but I saw the few faint features he shared with Vidar already, and wondered how much like his father he'd look as he grew. Nervously I wondered how long I could keep Erhardt convinced that the baby was his, before he began to question my darling boy's paternity ...

"We'll gather witnesses and in a few days' time, I'll officially accept our son." Erhardt said softly, gazing at the baby in my arms. "Birger Erhardtsson ... I finally have my son."

CHAPTER NINETEEN

AROS, DENMARK
Spring, 876

"YOUNG BIRGER, COME and collect your toys!" I barked.

Young Birger had his back turned to me, contentedly playing with a single carved wooden longship. He sang indecipherable words, rocking his beloved ship through the air on invisible waves.

Young Birger was a year and a half old. His hair fell to his chin in soft yellow curls, his pale flesh was the purest white of fresh, undisturbed snow, and his cheeks held a constant warm, rosy glow. Despite Young Birger's cherubic appearance, he was mischievous and naughty, but was able to charm his way out of anything even at such a delicate age.

"Birger, what did I say?" I yapped, frustrated.

I strode over to the child and crouched behind him, grabbing his little shoulder and spinning him around. His piercing blue eyes gazed up at me, and the most heart-warming smile gleamed from his little pink lips.

"Okay, *mumie*." Young Birger cooed sweetly, before skipping off to the nearest pile of dolls and figures he'd littered across the hall floors.

I remained crouched, shaking my head, eyes closed, picturing Vidar in my mind. I'd seen that same expression emanate from Vidar's face many times before. I felt my face burn red and couldn't help but smile.

"You're just like your father, you are." I sighed, rising to my feet as the front door to the hall opened.

"What has my boy done now?" Erhardt grinned proudly.

"Ah, he's – he's just too charming for his own good." I stuttered hastily. "How was your meeting at the harbour?"

"It was fine. There are a few things that need to be handled, further, but all is well." He replied, waving his hand in gesture for me not to worry. "I do have some news however – we have a guest."

Behind him I noticed the exhausted face of a man with an uncanny resemblance to a lit candle stick – his flesh was sallow, almost yellow, with a mop of frizzy red hair upon his head, the exact colour as fire. His facial features drooped down his face like melted wax. Behind the odd-looking fellow were two equally exhausted thralls.

"Elda," I called, somewhat confused, "please ready some food. We have guests from afar, it seems."

"Thank you, Jarlkona." The stranger replied cheerfully, much chirpier than he looked, before he dropped into a chair.

"The kitchen is over there. Do help yourselves to food and drink." I smiled warmly to his thralls.

The men bowed their heads thankfully to me, then marched to the kitchen, hurriedly, stomachs roaring.

"This is Niklas. He is a good friend to me and my kin." Erhardt introduced, sitting at the table with the stranger. "He moved to Roskilde with Ursula – a familiar face, there to watch over her in her new home, comfort her, be an ear for her to speak to, you know."

My whole body stiffened; the soft, fair hairs on my arms stood on end. I pursed my lips together tightly, and raised a single eyebrow, examining Niklas. I was uncomfortable and suspicious of his presence.

"Oh yes?" I said shortly.

"*Já.*" Erhardt answered, cocking his head at me. "*Já* … well, he brings a message from Ursula."

"Uh huh." I murmured, scooping up Young Birger as he rushed into my arms.

"Ursula and her husband plan to come to Aros, to visit for a few weeks. Poor Ursula has been homesick for the last two years – she yearns to spend time in familiar surroundings with her beloved family, to cure her melancholy." Niklas explained.

I rolled my eyes at him inconspicuously, kissing the top of my son's head.

"Come, Birger." Erhardt called, opening his arms wide to the toddler who pranced over to him cheerily. "Your older sister is coming to visit! As is your brother-in-law." At this extra comment, Erhardt glanced at me quickly to gauge my reaction.

"Why did she send you ahead of herself? Why didn't she just arrive?" I asked.

"She has arrived. Her sisters saw her disembarking from the ship. She is currently talking with them, before she comes to the hall." Niklas replied, his attention drifted as his eyes excitedly followed the plate of food brought to him. "It won't be long, I'm sure – she is eager to see her father and meet her brother."

My jaw dropped. There was the reaction Erhardt was looking for. He didn't say a word, merely released the fidgety Young Birger, before folding his arms across his chest, examining me shrewdly.

"I'm glad to hear that." I stuttered unconvincingly. "I'll see the thralls ready more food. In case Ursula and – and her husband are hungry."

I whisked away into the kitchen, heart pounding.

Vidar was here! Vidar was in Aros. It had been two years since I'd seen him ... and Young Birger! Vidar has never met his child! I tutted, a trembling sigh tumbling from my lips. He wouldn't even be able to acknowledge the boy as his ...

"Are you okay?" Burwenna asked softly, offering me a steep cup of mead.

"*Já*, I'm fine, really." I spluttered, blinking wildly and taking the drink from her. I guzzled it down, quickly, wiping my mouth with my hand, before giving her back the cup. "We are expecting guests – many guests. I'm going to need more food made for them."

"Yes," she replied gently. "Niklas's thralls mentioned–"

"I'm sure they mentioned a lot." I scoffed, though not unkindly. "We'll need more beds set up. I'm unsure how many guests we'll be having, but ready a few anyway."

"Aveline, will you step outside with me for a moment?" I heard Erhardt's voice call from behind me.

"*Já*, of course." I replied nervously.

He strode over to me and ushered me towards the kitchen door to the back garden. We stood in the sun, side-by-side, basking in the warmth for a few moments.

"This is awkward for you." Erhardt said almost sympathetically – almost.

"I was betrothed to the man." I muttered.

"He's Ursula's husband. You're my wife." Erhardt's voice was stern and his expression was solemn.

"*Já.*" I confirmed apathetically. "And we have peace between our towns. We're fine. It just – it caught me by surprise."

Erhardt turned to me, swept a few stray hairs from my face and ran the back of his fingers over my cheek. I closed my eyes and saw Vidar's face, remembering when he used to caress me. In my mind I remembered being in Vidar's arms, remembered the subtle musky scent of his body mixed with the strong, clean smell of soap. I remembered the crease in one of his cheeks as one side of his lips rose and formed a smirk, not filled with malice but bursting with love; his eyes twinkling as he gazed upon me.

Slowly Erhardt dragged his hand down the side of my neck, stretching his fingers out to massage my shoulder. Erhardt placed his other hand on my hip and brought me to him. He kissed my forehead gently. We stood in silence for a while. I was uncomfortable, thinking of nothing but Vidar as I listened to Erhardt's heartbeat through his chest.

"If I catch you in his arms, I'll kill you both and burn Roskilde to the ground." Erhardt said quietly.

I stared up at him in shock. He simply stared at me, then walked back into the house.

***

IT HADN'T TAKEN long before Vidar and Ursula appeared in the hall. By the time I'd recovered from Erhardt's promise (for I knew it wasn't a threat), there they both were, a few thralls by their sides. Ursula glanced at me, possessively linking arms with Vidar.

Vidar stood before me. He was still as handsome as the day I'd first met him. He wore simple black trousers, leather boots and a thin black tunic that hugged his upper arms, tightly. His golden hair was plaited back, but I noticed a greasy glare to it. I was shocked – the Danes kept their hair clean devotedly, choosing to not wash it only when in mourning. My heart skipped a beat – who had died?

Beyond my sudden concern of who Vidar had lost, I couldn't help being maddeningly excited at his presence. I wanted nothing more than to throw myself into his arms and kiss his soft, pink lips, and yet I felt the same nervousness – almost fear! – of him as I'd felt when I was fifteen and had found myself alone in the wood shed with him …

Vidar glanced at me, his winter sky coloured eyes examined me thoroughly, but his face betrayed not even an ounce of emotion towards me. He nodded at me, cold and short, then turned and replied to Erhardt, continuing whatever conversation they had been having before I had entered.

Ursula grinned at me smugly.

Ignoring her, I took Young Birger into my arms and sat at the table, holding one of his little wooden toys and shaking it with my trembling fingers. I kissed him, squeezing my wet eyes shut, forbidding tears to fall and betray me.

"And this is my brother?" Ursula asked, stepping towards me. "What a handsome boy! And what is your name, my little brother?"

"This is Young Birger." I muttered icily. "He's named after my father."

"Your father?" Ursula stared at me blankly for a few moments before she burst into a titter of giggles. "Ah, you mean Bloody Sword! How foolish of me! Of course, he's named after Birger Bloody Sword – I would've been surprised if my father had allowed you to name his only son after your Saxon father … *Já*, a good Norse name like Birger … Bloody Sword is quite a man, too. A good name for the boy!"

I glared at her, outraged – her rambling infuriated me! Erhardt caught my gaze and shook his head slowly, warning me. I looked back at Ursula, who did not notice my livid glare, she was too preoccupied pulling stupid faces and cooing ridiculous noises at my son. I glanced at Vidar, quickly, and saw his smirk, the smirk I'd fantasised about only a short while ago. God, how I wanted to hit him and his disgusting wife!

I could spy Ursula Erhardtsdóttir's muddy coloured hair beneath her hustrulinet. Though she was only a few years older than me, she already had lines of age forming around her heavily hooded sapphire eyes and around her pinched mouth. She looked like her father. She was slim, but womanly, with large hips and ample breasts, but she had Erhardt's face. Had her facial features been more feminine, I'm sure she would've been beautiful, but she had a hard, square jaw, a bulging nose and skinny lips.

"We conceived him on our wedding night." Erhardt bragged proudly, puffing out his chest and beaming smugly at Vidar. "At my age! Can you believe it? Are you yet with child, my dear?"

"Not yet ..." Ursula replied stiffly, straightening up and glancing at the floor. "We – err – not yet ..."

"It's alright, my boy." Erhardt said as he clapped Vidar on the back, sympathetically, though he couldn't hide the gloating smugness that danced upon his face. "You'll get an heir. You're young – you'll have a child, eventually."

I watched the three. Erhardt's head was stuck in his own private cloud of conceit; Ursula was eyeing the floor with what seemed to be embarrassment and shame; and Vidar was staring at Young Birger. The tiniest hint of a smirk curled the edge of his mouth, as he looked between me and the boy. Then he winked at me.

"*Já*. Perhaps one day I will have a son, like yours." Vidar answered pleasantly.

I stifled my laughter with coughs, excusing myself to go and check on the thralls in the kitchen.

***

URSULA AND VIDAR had brought two more thralls with them, females – Ursula's personal thralls to tend only to her needs.

Niklas had two of his own, and Vidar hadn't brought a thrall, instead he'd brought Jan.

Though Vidar had welcomed me coolly, when Jan had seen me, he encased me in his arms, loudly decrying the time it had been since he'd last laid eyes on me. Jan sardonically congratulated Erhardt for managing to marry such a wonderful woman as myself. Though Erhardt did not catch the scathing sarcasm in Jan's tone, everyone else at the table seemed to have understood his meaning clearly.

The arrival of Vidar and Ursula had begun with discomfit and unease but had slowly unravelled into quite an uneventful night. Erhardt and Niklas drank deeply together at the table and swapped stories and jokes. Jan, cheeky and mischievous as ever, would pipe in with a teasing comment or mocking joke at their expense, without the two older men realising he was insulting them. Jan would catch my eye and wink at me, and I would stifle my laughter or turn away as he made his remarks.

Ursula was spinning with her thralls and they chattered quietly together about nothing important, peeping in, occasionally, with the men's conversation. I stood weaving at my loom, ignoring Ursula as best as I could, or I would scurry off to direct Elda, Estrith or Burwenna – whatever excuse I could get my hands on to escape Ursula, if she made any advance to speak to me.

For most of the night, Vidar laid belly down on the packed dirt floor, playing all kinds of games with Young Birger. He'd taken the young boy outside for two hours, playing together with woollen balls, or wooden toys, even battling together with small wooden swords.

An hour after they'd arrived, Vidar had presented Young Birger with a tiny bow and arrow set he'd made. The arrows were nothing more than sticks, blunt at one end, with feathers at the other, but the bow was finely made and perfectly useable, a miniature version of the very bow he owned. Vidar proceeded to swing the child onto his hip and rushed outside with him to teach him how to use it.

My heart burst with love and pride, seeing Vidar so affectionate and devoted to the son he'd only just met.

"Aveline, do come outside with me." Ursula pleaded, as I came out of the bedchamber from laying Young Birger down.

It was late. Young Birger had fallen asleep whilst eating some boiled fish, to the vast amusement of everyone in the hall. I'd slipped the boy into my arms and carried him to my bed. Burwenna, as usual, was laying with the child. If I did not immediately go to rest with him, Burwenna would take my place and curl up with the child in my bed, until I was ready to sleep.

Occasionally he would wake for a midnight feed – he was a year and a half and not due to be completely weaned until after he'd turned two – but thankfully he didn't wake that frequently to nurse. Most of the time, if he had me or Burwenna beside him, he would sleep soundly and happily for the whole night through.

As much as she was helping me, Burwenna loved to lay with Birger. It gave her a much-needed break from her duties and commands, and she'd also come to have a sort of sibling bond with the child. She played with him wonderfully and really seemed to care for him as though he were her own kin.

"Of course," I replied, half-heartedly, wishing I'd stayed in bed with my son.

Together we made our way to the kitchen, passing Erhardt and Vidar who were sitting at the table in the middle of quite a tense Hnefatafl game. Erhardt was glowering at the game board – he was losing. I peeped at Vidar's face and found him gazing at me. He had propped his elbows on the tabletop and held his entwined hands against his lips, hiding his gloating smirk from view. I couldn't help but smile at him, and he winked back at me.

Reluctantly, I broke our gaze and followed Ursula outside. Within a few moments she and I were settled on wooden chairs, and Estrith was setting up a fire for us. The pale orb of the moon shimmered in the darkening sky. The blue of day had waned into hues of lavender and grey as the sky slipped into night.

"Is it uncomfortable for Vidar to be here?" Ursula asked abruptly.

My eyebrows shot up my forehead and my jaw dropped.

"Why would you ask that?" I demanded, dumbfounded.

"Well, you were meant to marry the man, before Erhardt and Freydis's – ah – agreement." She replied stupidly, rolling her eyes at me. "Come now, Aveline, we are both adults and neither of us are fools. It's uncomfortable for you, is it not?"

"It is!" I snapped. "And it seems you are a fool – if you understand my discomfort, then why would you ask that?"

She ignored me.

"Was it hard for you to lay with my father on your wedding night?"

"What?" I gasped, horrified at her growing audacity.

She swallowed hard. Now she felt uncomfortable. In fact, I could see she was having difficulty to respond. Her face had gone an awful, ugly shade of maroon – she closed her eyelids, took a deep breath, stared me in the eyes and finally answered me.

"We have not consummated our marriage." She confessed in urgently hushed tones. "Vidar refuses to lie with me."

I gaped at her, astounded.

"Has he – has he laid with thralls? Other women?" I asked slowly.

"*Nei,*" she answered, her eyes flooding with tears. "It's as though he has no desire for sex at all!"

"I don't understand why you are telling me this. I've not spoken to you before tonight, and you are the woman who married my betrothed! Why would you share such things with me?"

"You married my father as a peace-pledge, and shared his bed though you didn't want to be his wife ... It's been two years and my husband refuses to share my bed ... Since Vidar willingly wanted to marry you, I thought you could advise me." She murmured. "I know it's difficult, but I hope you've moved on, especially now you've birthed my father's child ... I – I wanted to know ... did you ever lay with Vidar?"

"*Nei.*" I lied, adding sternly, "It's dishonourable for a woman to lay with a man before marriage."

"Of course, of course! I wasn't insinuating anything," she apologised hastily. "It's just ... I'm in such a horrid predicament with Vidar. I was just hoping – if you had shared his bed ... if you could tell me how I could get him to share mine."

I cocked an eyebrow at her. I was in complete disbelief. Was she really being this daring, or was she just so truly stupid?

"I've never shared his bed." I said firmly. "I know that he does feel the ... the urge for sex. But I could not begin to tell you how to get him to share your bed, for I do not know."

Ursula stared disappointedly at her hands tangled on her lap.

"I've not even shared a kiss with him, but for the one on our wedding day – if you could even call that a kiss ..." She whined. "But – it's just – I see how wonderfully he does with Young Birger! He'd make such a fine father! But why – why won't he share my bed?! He could have a son of his own! I know he wants one ..."

A heavy, uncomfortable silence blanketed us for what felt like an age. The sky was almost black now, and a handful of bats flickered wildly across the sky. I rose to my feet and began to make my way inside. I paused in the door frame, bathing myself in the saffron firelight.

"I'm sorry I couldn't be of more help." I said quietly, then turned my back on her, smiling to myself.

Vidar still loved me. And he had stayed loyal and faithful to me for two years, regardless of his marriage to Ursula! Vidar was still mine, thank the gods.

***

"DO YOU STILL keep sheep?" Vidar asked me at breakfast, a week into his stay in Aros.

"Of course, I do." I replied. "I could never get rid of Sven and Bjorn, Audrey and Aisly, Nelda and Kendra–"

"Okay, okay, I understand you still have the sheep." Vidar laughed. "How many do you have now?"

I paused in silence for a moment.

"The autumn when Young Birger was born was hard – it led into a terrible winter. Two of the sheep died, one went lame from hoof rot, so we had to kill her – and we had to kill three more for food. We only had a few lambs born the following spring, and, thankfully, most survived." I explained, counting the sheep on my fingers. "This spring we had a lot more lambs – I've been keeping an eye on them closely … I'd say, including the lambs, I have about thirty."

"Do you have names for all of them?" Vidar teased.

His eyes twinkled, and his subtle smile taunted me as he leaned closer to me.

"I have a name for you, right now." I said, pursing my lips together tightly.

Under the table, hidden from all view, he slipped his hand onto my leg and began stroking it, pausing to squeeze my thigh every now and again. My flesh tingled from his touch, and a delicious heat surged through me.

"*Mumie!*" Young Birger chirped, toddling over to me after wiggling his way out of Burwenna's arms.

Vidar took his hand from my leg quickly. I brought Young Birger onto my lap, slipped my breast from my tunic and angled my nipple towards the child's mouth.

"I remember when I was able to suckle on your breasts." Vidar muttered quietly.

"There wasn't any milk in them back then." I whispered amused, an electric thrill running through my body.

"And yet, I was still satisfied." He winked.

Together we laughed, foolishly, Young Birger's eyebrows furrowed as I bounced him from my laughter. Jan, with a bemused look on his face, approached us and sat opposite me at the table.

"What *are* you two laughing at? You're both red in the face." Jan questioned nosily.

"Old times." Vidar replied cryptically and simply, shooting another quick wink at me. "Aveline is going to give me a tour of Aros, today. Would you like to join us?"

"Oh, am I?" I interrupted. "I didn't realise I was."

"Of course, you are." Vidar answered, stretching out and leaning back in his chair, arms crossed behind his head, his hands gripping the back of his neck. "That way we can keep talking of the old days, before you were *Jarlkona of Aros*."

"I'd love to join you." Jan beamed, before falling into conversation with Vidar of the years before my forced move to Aros.

I had fallen into a sombre silence. It was hard to hear Vidar call me 'Jarlkona of Aros' – even if it was in a bitter tone. Sitting with him, holding our child in my arms ... it felt *right*. I suppose, for a moment I felt as though I had been transported into what I believed was my rightful existence – the life that was meant to have happened – and our marriages to Erhardt and Ursula were nothing more than awful, vivid nightmares. But when Vidar uttered those words ... it was real.

A deep, wavering sigh faltered from my lips. Young Birger had finished feeding and gazed up at me with his beautiful, large sky-blue eyes, full of sincere concern and wonder.

"It's okay, my wonderful child." I breathed, bringing his face to mine, and placing a delicate kiss upon his forehead.

"Are you alright?" Vidar asked gently, placing his hand on my thigh, again, hidden under the table.

"*Já.*" I muttered, clearing my throat slightly. "So, this tour of Aros, then?"

Ursula planned to visit her sisters, Agnes and Sighburgh, at Agnes's home, and had left with her thralls shortly after waking. This left Vidar free from any unwanted hassle and jealousy from his wife as to why he was going to be spending the day with me. Jealousy breeds well with suspicion, which explained why Vidar had invited Jan with us – he would be a witness to our innocence.

I decided to bring Young Birger and Burwenna to further refute any apprehension or misgiving Erhardt and Ursula might have. Young Birger was a baby and Burwenna was a female *and* a thrall, so they could not be counted as official witnesses, should we be accused, but hopefully Erhardt and Ursula would assume we wouldn't begin an affair in front of so many watching eyes.

Erhardt had disappeared to complete whatever work he was in the middle of. A leathery faced master shipbuilder, the shipbuilder's eldest son, and the malevolent Tarben had come to eat breakfast with us before leaving with Erhardt. I was intrigued – in hushed tones I'd heard them speak of shipbuilding, but that was all I drew from their slight conversation.

Erhardt had kissed me before he'd left – unashamedly and exaggeratedly – to an audience of smirks from his men and a stealthy dagger-eyed scowl from Vidar.

"Never would I have thought I'd eat a meal with Jarl Erhardt Ketilsson!" Vidar complained a few minutes after we'd departed from the hall.

"You can thank your mother for that." Jan laughed.

Vidar glowered darkly, knowing Jan's statement as true, but was displeased all the same.

"She did what she had to do." I comforted, gazing at Vidar with sympathy and understanding, though a stake of sourness stabbed into my chest.

"You know this isn't how things were meant to go?" Vidar continued, his voice brimming with ire.

"But this is what happened." I stated softly, squeezing Young Birger's chubby little hand in mine. "We just need to think of a way to fix it."

"Fix it?" Jan repeated curiously. "How do you think you can fix it?"

"How do you think?" I replied, darkly glancing at him from the corner of my eyes.

"You could divorce him for beating you?" Burwenna suggested innocently.

I answered her with a swift glare and hissed *shush*. Jan and Vidar, unfortunately, had heard her. They looked from Burwenna, to each other, to me.

"He beat you?" Vidar gasped, outraged. He grabbed me by the shoulders and glared at me. "Why didn't you tell me? The shameful swine beating his wife – he should be *killed* for that!"

"Be quiet, Vidar!" I growled, pushing his hands off me. "*That* is my plan to *fix* this situation!"

Young Birger fled to Burwenna's arms and hid his face in her skirts. The two of them and Jan, the surrounding houses; everything dissipated into nothingness. All I saw was Vidar, each of us glaring defiantly at the other.

"I can't divorce him; he'll wage war on Roskilde." I rumbled, barely louder than a whisper. "The only thing we can do is kill him.

Only some will care that he beat me – those who view me as a Danish wife. But here in Aros ... no one here will stand against Erhardt, they'll call me an Anglo-Saxon thrall, and beating a thrall means nothing!"

"I know!" Vidar hissed. His eyes darted around for a few minutes as he calculated a plan to murder my husband. "I'll burn him in his hall, with his daughter and thralls–"

"*Nei.*" I interjected sternly. "Not like that. There's one who will replace him who needs to be killed, too. Tarben ... He's younger and just as capable a warrior ... We also run the risk of being found out, if you and I, Jan, Birger, and my thrall girls sneak away all at once in the middle of the night. They'll realise our plan before the hall burns, and the town will wake and kill us all. No, we can't kill them in Aros ... we have to kill them in Roskilde."

"And how do you propose we do that? Invite him to my home – I'm sure Freydis would enjoy that." Vidar scoffed angrily.

"We'll find a way."

I turned back to the trio staring at us. I took Young Birger from Burwenna, silently, holding him close to me, his ear pressed against my chest, listening to my racing heartbeat.

We walked in silence for a while, our conversation buzzing around my mind like a swarm of wasps. How quickly the morning had gone from comfort and laughter, to fury and murder!

We finally reached the farm pastures at the back of the island. It was quieter here, though the farmsteads hummed with the steady noise of work and livestock, there was less chatter and bustle than in the heart of the island, filled with passers-by and listening ears.

"Erhardt owns this land, this farm ... we lease it to a family, who watch my sheep with their own." I explained to no one in particular, Young Birger cradled in my arms, tired from the walk. "I come here often, though."

I handed Young Birger to Vidar, carefully, before beckoning Burwenna.

"Where are you going?" Jan called.

"Announcing ourselves to the family, before they think we're sheep thieves." I explained over my shoulder as I looped my arm in Burwenna's. "We'll be back shortly."

We left the men and boy at the fence line of the sheep pen as we strode to the farmhouse.

"Don't speak out like that again." I warned the young thrall girl severely. "I know you were trying to help, but you didn't. Don't announce things – especially things like *that* – without my permission *ever* again!"

Burwenna's face had drained to the palest white. I saw her gazing at me in shock from the corner of my eye.

"I'm – I'm sorry, Jarlkona." She spluttered, nervously but sincerely.

"It's fine." I soothed, though my voice was still low and foreboding. "But never again."

By the time we'd reached the farmhouse, the farmer had already popped out to greet us. We conversed politely and pleasantly for a few minutes, before Burwenna and I returned to Jan, Vidar and Young Birger, who was calmly snuggled in Vidar's arms.

"The farmer is heading out to the market for a little while, so we caught him at the right time." I informed them. "He's left a thrall here to help us if we need it, but I'm sure we won't get into too much trouble with a few sheep."

We spent a reasonable amount of time talking and laughing in the field, the fat sheep trundling over to us and bleating madly. We found ourselves sat at the table in the farmhouse, sipping mugs of ale and snacking on dried fruit that the thrall had offered us.

Vidar rose from his seat and wandered back outside. Burwenna and the farmer's thrall were playing with Young Birger, joyfully, so captivated in their games that neither of them noticed as I slipped out of the house, following Vidar.

"Why did you look at me so harshly when you first entered Erhardt's hall?" I asked, standing by his side but not looking at him. Instead I gazed at the sheep and the lambs ambling over the grass.

"I was mad at you." He replied, plainly.

"For what? That was the first time you'd seen me in two years!" I retorted, stoutly.

"Exactly." Vidar said quietly.

I didn't reply. My heart sank deeply in my chest. The knot in my throat prevented me from speaking, so I silently watched my livestock mosey around and chew the grass before me, Vidar's reply echoing in my mind.

Silence had swallowed us for a time before we finally acknowledged each other again. Vidar laced his fingers in mine, neither of us even glancing at the other, just entwining our hands and squeezing, gently, lovingly, sadly.

Lost in thoughts of mourning, I surveyed the pastures, suddenly spotting the deep, sloping roof and low wooden walls of the little sheep shed at the end of the pasture. Excitement rippled through me at the sight of the shoddy little shed, and I began quickly walking towards it, tugging Vidar's hand to entice him to follow.

"What are we doing here, little fawn?" Vidar smiled amused and mystified.

He crouched down low to pass through the doorway, to avoid hitting his head on the frame.

"Your wife confided a secret in me ... she told me that you've never lain with her, and she asked me for advice to get you to share her bed." I said.

"Oh?" Vidar smirked, his eyebrows raised. "And what did you tell her?"

"I couldn't help her, unfortunately. I have never shared my bed with you ..." I grinned playfully. "I have only ever lain with you outdoors, but I didn't think to tell her that."

Vidar laughed at me and wrapped his arms around me. I took his beautiful face into my hands and we kissed each other thirstily. Releasing each other for a moment, but kissing each other still, Vidar yanked down his breeks, and I bunched my skirts up above my hips. His calloused hands raced over my body and wrenched me against him once more.

Our feet squelched in the filth of the sheep shed floor, my nostrils filled with the stench of shit, but I didn't care. I nuzzled against his shoulder, breathing in his scent. Vidar's every touch, every kiss, every nibble and bite, everything he did to me overwhelmed my senses, the awareness of our whereabouts quickly faded away.

The years that had passed had been long and wretched, I'd been beaten, raped and had my life threatened multiple times. I'd been forced to whore myself to Erhardt just to end his beatings. Young Birger was the only ray of light to shine upon the time I'd lived in Aros. And now, here I was, the man to whom my heart belonged making wild, frenzied, voracious love to me in the confines of a shit filled sheep shed. I couldn't have been happier.

"I have missed you dearly." I sighed, gazing at Vidar sadly. His icy eyes pierced through the iron grey shadows of the sheep shed that veiled his handsome face in darkness. "I hope we find a way to be together ..."

"We will, little fawn. We'll find a way." Vidar stated quietly, kissing me tenderly.

Together we left our unconventional haven and entered back into the harshness of our reality, mournfully making our way back to the farmhouse.

"Uh, Jarlkona, Young Birger wants you – what is that smell? *Oh!*" Burwenna gasped, her nose wrinkled.

As we entered the farmhouse, Burwenna's eyes grew wide and darted between Vidar and me, noticing the state of my clothes. She didn't say a word, but I could tell what she was thinking solely from her expression, "*What did you do?*"

"We must go home; I need to change. Come along, let's go." I said sharply, taking my son from her.

She nodded, speechless, chasing after me as I strode away, leaving Vidar to lean against the woven wooden fence of the sheep pasture. I heard Jan call something to Vidar from behind me before they slowly began to follow.

"Please don't tell anyone." I begged Burwenna, avoiding her gaze. "I love Vidar – he and I were meant to be together."

"I won't tell a soul." She promised. "But, please Jarlkona, if you flee with master Vidar – I beg, please take my sister, Estrith and I with you."

"I will." I vowed, taking her hand in mine. "I swear it."

CHAPTER TWENTY

UNDER THE PROTECTION of Lofn, the Nordic goddess of forbidden love, Vidar and I managed to escape our spouses and lay together on multiple occasions over the following weeks. Once or twice we returned to the sheep shed, but most of the time we found other secret havens, knowing that if we frequented only one or two places, we'd be easily found out.

Whether it was dawn, dusk or midnight, Vidar and I would find a way to be together. My loyal thralls, Burwenna, Estrith and Elda, would aid us: they would lie for us, watch Young Birger, act as lookouts … anything I asked of them, they did.

And Jan! The ever charming, enigmatic Jan would enthral Ursula's attention away from Vidar or whisk Erhardt into a game or conversation that the jarl could not rebuff. I prayed every day to Odin, Frigg, Lofn, to all the Nordic gods and goddesses that I could think of, thanking them for the good fortune bestowed on us.

Our unfaithfulness to our spouses was a hefty crime, punishable by law – if we were lucky, we'd face fines and divorce … If we weren't lucky, I could be legally slain for my adultery, and we knew that Erhardt would use our affair as a reason to wage war on Roskilde.

We should've stopped.

We knew our luck couldn't possibly last forever.

Regardless of the incredible risks and the lives we were gambling, we just *couldn't* stop! We were addicted to each other – the risk and the danger were nothing in comparison to the frantic lust and need for each other, that devoured us!

Birger's promise had brought us together like flint striking steel, igniting a spark between us that steadily burned its pale light. Gradually that little flame grew into an inferno, our two hearts had become one, burning together.

Our love had been smouldering all these years apart, radiating through the darkness of our separation and forced peace-pledge marriages. When reunited, those little flames blazed again, and we were unwilling and unable to extinguish them. Vidar's stay in Aros would be over soon, and then when would I see him? We fed our fires as often and as desperately as we could, our time was quickly fading away.

Every day went by and our feral thirst for each other grew. Even the mere brush of his fingertip would send my flesh quivering with goosebumps; would make all the faint, downy hairs on my body stand upright.

Vidar would test his limits, a quick caress of my thigh or a squeeze of my buttocks – in a room full of people! I was too timid to dare like he, so terrified of being caught … I would silently scold him, but fall to his alluring, seductive smirk and his mischievous wink.

"This place stinks of shit." I gasped, slicking back my damp hair from my sweaty forehead.

"We can wash in the sheep's trough before we go back to the hall." Vidar replied, clamping his hands onto my hips, prohibiting me from dismounting him.

His lips began to curl in one corner, as I tenderly ran my nails down his arms, winding my fingers around his wrists. I tried, half-heartedly, to pull his hands from me, but he resisted.

"I love being on you, but I'm covered in sheep shit and mud, I'd really like to wash." I smiled, running my nails up and down his arms again.

"You should've stayed on the blanket then, shouldn't you?" He chided softly. "I'm not covered in shit, and I'm the one lying on the ground."

I laughed and kissed him.

"Staying on the blanket wasn't at the forefront of my mind while I was riding you, I'm afraid." I giggled, still leaning over him, curled waves of my long chestnut mane, like a nest of snakes, tumbled over my shoulders.

"I'm glad to hear that fucking me takes your mind off sheep shit." Vidar smirked, cupping my breasts in his rough hands. "Don't get off yet, I just want to look at you for a little longer."

I straightened my posture and brushed my hair behind my back, resting my hands on my thighs.

"Do you like what you see?" I asked, pursing my lips together.

I raised my eyebrows slightly and stared into the darkness of the shed, posing for him.

"I love watching your breasts wobble when you push your hair back." Vidar said seriously, causing me to burst into laughter. I grinned down at him, happily. "Ah, that is my favourite thing to see."

As he said this, Vidar brought his hand to my face and slowly ran his thumb over my lips.

"I love your smile." Vidar almost whispered, gazing at me with adoration. "I love when you're happy – I love making you happy."

"I do, too." My smile faltered, however. Closing my eyes, I leaned into his hand for a moment, before taking his wrist and kissing his palm. "It's a shame," I continued, bringing his hand down to rest on his stomach, holding it there, gently. "That this won't last. You'll leave in two weeks and I'll not see you until when? Until your wife and you conceive a child?"

Vidar laughed, deeply.

"I haven't fucked the woman. I hoped she'd have divorced me by now for it. Why would I start fucking her now?"

"Well, until Erhardt and I conceive a child, then." I replied shortly.

"Young Birger is mine. I've been filling your belly with my seed for the last few weeks, if any child comes out of you within the next year, it'll be mine."

"And what? You'll come back every few years to get me with child, then leave?" I snapped, standing up and shuffling around the darkened pen in search of my clothing, tears blinding me.

"In a years' time, after you've birthed my son, I'll invite you and darling Erhardt to Roskilde to celebrate the birth of your second son. Then I will kill Erhardt, his men and kin, and lead an army to burn Aros to the ground." Vidar stated, his voice low and soft, his arms snaking around my waist and pulling me against him. Vidar kissed my shoulders lightly, resting his face against the dampened flesh of my bare shoulder. "And then we will marry and be together."

"And if I'm not with child?" I asked, voice quivering, gripping his arms tightly.

"Then I'll invite you both, anyway. The plan won't change – only the reason for the invitation." Vidar explained between kisses. "But you *are* carrying my child, I know it. Just wait and see."

I turned in his arms and kissed him deeply.

"I thought only women could foresee the future?" I teased.

"I do not know the ways of *seiðr*," Vidar answered coolly, not rising to my jesting jab. "But Odin has mastered that magic. I know you're carrying my child, because of him, and I know we'll have many more children together. Erhardt death, and the deaths of those that support him, will be sacrifices and honourings to the gods from us, for aiding us to be together once more."

"I believe you." I whispered.

In silence we dressed. With a final kiss, Vidar left the sheep pen regretfully and unwillingly, headed towards the house. The sheep bleated inquisitively at him, and I heard the splashing sound of him washing dirt and filth from himself. The splashing stopped, and I heard the soft tread of his leather boots through the grass and the quick creak of the gate as he began his journey to Erhardt's hall.

I sighed deeply and sadly and lifted my skirts high over my ankles. I stopped suddenly – in the darkness I heard the rowdy cawing of ravens. My body shivered as the horrid birdcall pierced my ears. I wondered if it was the half-blind raven from Roskilde. I shivered again and cursed that infernal bird under my breath as I began walking again.

"What—"

From the entrance of the pen a shadowed figure lunged at me, slamming all the breath out of me. I collapsed to the ground, the full weight of the large figure on top of me, crushing me. I couldn't scream – I could hardly breathe. The thick stench of sheep shit poured through my throat and nostrils as I gasped for air, before the sharp knuckles of a hard fist smashed into my face like a brick. Talons of pain ripped through my skull, tears streamed down my cheeks, agony seared in my chest.

"Planning to betray the Jarl are you, little Danethrall?" The acidic drip of Tarben's voice snarled into my ear, his breath was hot and held the faded stench of ale.

"Get off me!" I gasped, writhing to escape him.

Tarben kicked my legs apart and knelt between them. He grabbed a fistful of my hair and pulled me to my knees, taking my skinny wrists into one of his hands and yanking them above my head. With his other hand he fumbled onehanded with his trousers.

"*Nei*! Stop!" I begged hysterically, as he snatched at my skirts.

"I've been waiting a long time for this." Tarben growled.

I kicked and flailed as hard as I could. I wrenched an arm free from his grip and pounded on his head with my tiny fist, my legs still kicking. Infuriated by my flailing, Tarben lifted his fist high above his head. I flipped onto my stomach and attempted to crawl away frantically, but he struck the back of my thigh before I managed to escape.

I wailed and screeched as a flash of searing white lit up my clenched eyelids and agony erupted through my leg.

"If you don't shut up, I'll kill you!" Tarben hissed, grabbing my hips and wrenching me onto my knees.

Trying to stifle my tears, grunting and moaning uncontrollably from fear and pain, I bit down on my bottom lip until I could taste the copper of my own blood on my tongue. I couldn't stop myself from crying out as Tarben entered me. He cackled at my anguish.

Tarben coiled my hair around his fist and pulled me up, my back pressed against his chest. He released my hair and clamped his hand around my neck, small locks of my chestnut curls tangled between his fingers. I couldn't break free.

He tore open the neck of my dress and grabbed hold of my breast, squeezing it tightly, tugging at my nipple until I flinched and cried out, snickering at me as I wept.

"I don't know what I want more," Tarben sneered with sinister glee. "Do I kill you after I've fucked you, or do I hand you to your husband? ... *Oh*, it's such a hard decision! When Erhardt finds out you've been fucking Alvarsson, he'll want you dead! First, he'll kill your lover, then he'll kill your bastard son, then he'll destroy Roskilde. All the while, you'll be alive – fucked and beaten by every man in Aros! As much as I'd *love* to be the one to slit your throat, if I gave you to Erhardt, I'd get to rape you repeatedly ... Ah! And then – once everyone and everything you hold dear has been destroyed – then, he'll kill *you*!"

Tarben shoved me to the ground; my face slammed into the mud and sheep shit. He cackled and began thrusting deeper into me, back and forth, his malicious laughter rumbling from his throat.

Suddenly he stopped.

A sickening splash of warm liquid slapped onto my flesh and clothes. The heavy sweet and metallic scent of blood filled the air and with a thud Tarben's body collapsed to the ground.

I spun around to find Vidar, blood drenched knife in his hand, towering over Tarben's corpse.

***

"WHAT IS THIS?" Vidar roared as he stormed into the sleeping area.

The fire was low, but bright enough for me to make out movement and shadowed expressions. I watched the Jarl lurch up in his bed and squinted my eyes to see him glaring at Vidar through the darkness.

"What?" Erhardt grunted, irritation and sleep addling his voice.

Elda scarpered into the room with a torch blazing, holding it beside Vidar. In his arms he carried the dead body of Tarben.

"Your wife was raped!" Vidar boomed. "I caught him beating and raping your wife!"

"What?" Erhardt exclaimed, wide awake now.

"Can you say nothing more than that?" Vidar bellowed, tossing the body to Erhardt's feet. "This man raped your wife! How could you let that happen?!"

Erhardt leapt out of bed and stood over Tarben's body. With his foot, he shoved Tarben's head, the look of shock still fresh on the dead man's face.

"Where is my wife?" Erhardt asked.

"In the other room." Vidar spat, callously.

Erhardt stumbled into the main area of the hall, finding me gazing at him, despairingly.

"He killed Estrith." I whispered, pitifully.

Erhardt's jaw dropped the moment he saw me. My hair and clothes were caked in filth and Tarben's blood; my dress was ripped, and breasts still bared.

My head throbbed from Tarben's first punch – a bruise had bulged over my left eye and cheek, so large that I could hardly squint through the swelling. I could still taste the metallic sweetness in my mouth, could feel the scarlet flakes of blood dried to my lips.

"What did he do to you?" Erhardt asked faintly, rushing to my side and briskly stroking away stray hairs dried to my face by sweat and blood. "What happened?"

"I couldn't sleep," I lied quickly and quietly. "So Estrith and I went from a walk, to try to tire me ... I decided to check on the sheep since I was awake, so we walked over there a-and I heard a strange noise coming from the pen. Estrith waited by the gate while I went to check on it and – and moments later Tarben was suddenly on me, beating me ... then he – he–"

I choked, tears pouring, my voice shaking. Vidar paced the room impatiently, his boots crunching in the dirt. I glimpsed his face – he chewed his bottom lip furiously and his eyes darted around searchingly as he thought, assessing this evening over in his mind. His face was contorted by rage, and a violent tempest thundered in his icy eyes.

"I-I tried calling out for Estrith, but she d-didn't come. I didn't know until after Vidar had slain him, b-but Tarben had slit E-Estrith's throat before attacking me in the sheep pen." I paused and closed my eye, breathing in and out deeply for a few moments. "Her body is still there ... I-I couldn't carry her ..."

Elda, hearing the news of her friend's murder, fell to the floor and sobbed, stifling the noise as best she could. She was ignored by Erhardt and Vidar, but my heart wrenched for her. I wanted to hold her, to cry with her, but the atmosphere was tense and erratic – I was frozen to my seat, forced to watch the woman weep into the dirt floor, alone in her misery.

"Has he ever touched you before?"

"*Já...* while you were gone for Ursula's wedding." I admitted bitterly, shame flushing over me as I continued. "He never raped me but he'd – he'd grab me a-and touch me–"

"Why didn't you tell me?" Erhardt interrupted, rubbing his eyes and sighing disappointedly

"He said he'd kill me if I did ... He said I wasn't a real Dane so what he was doing wasn't wrong." It was a simple, honest answer, but I felt so embarrassed and ashamed of myself, I felt like a stupid tattling child.

"You should've told me."

"*Já*, Erhardt ..."

A heavy silence fell over us. Elda still sobbed quietly, her body still shuddered. Vidar had stopped pacing, he had his hands on the back of a chair, leaning into it, glowering ferociously at Erhardt.

"Why were you there?" Erhardt asked.

He didn't look at Vidar, but the question was obviously aimed at him.

"Why weren't you?" Vidar spat.

"Why were you there?" Erhardt repeated hotly.

"I woke and noticed your wife and her thrall were missing and decided to look for them. It's not safe at night for a woman." Vidar laughed darkly. "Obviously I was right! It is a good thing I went looking for them, otherwise your wife could be dead right now!"

"Good thing? If it had been a good thing, you would've got there in time to stop him from raping my wife." Spite oozed from Erhardt's voice. "But no. Her honour has been tarnished! You didn't even save her damned thrall. The only thing you did was kill a man who had his cock shoved into a woman!"

Vidar threw the chair across the room, smashing it against the wall. The commotion woke the sleeping occupants of the hall –

Jan, with his dagger swiftly in hand, and Niklas rushed to the main room, while Ursula's nosey face peeked out a few feet behind them.

"What's this?" Jan asked steadily, alarm plastered across his face and his dagger clenched tightly in his hand.

A scream pealed out from the sleeping area. Burwenna stood cradling Young Birger in her arms, pale and wide eyed, staring at Tarben's dead body, drenched in blood, his throat slit. She pulled my son against her, covering his face in her bosom, hiding the sight from his view.

Vidar didn't even flinch at her howl. Jan turned from the body to Vidar, confused and questioning.

"The Jarl's right-hand man raped Aveline and killed her thrall. I killed the Jarl's right-hand man, and now the Jarl is insulting my honour and shaming Aveline." Vidar seethed. He whipped his head around to face Erhardt, as did all the other shocked faces. "You dishonoured your wife by not protecting her – she was attacked and raped by your man, under your roof, and she was too scared and distrusting to tell you! You failed her as a husband – as her protector! You tarnished her honour! You!"

Erhardt was uncharacteristically silent and calm at Vidar's insulting accusations. Without even a glance at anyone in the room, he walked out of the hall.

CHAPTER TWENTY-ONE

AROS, DENMARK
Late Winter, 877

SAT BY THE fire, I held my small baby son to my breast, urging him to take my nipple into his mouth. He refused, shaking his little head, a squeaking cough resounding from his little mouth. He had been born only three months ago and had been small but healthy. My stomach had hardly protruded and signified my pregnancy before I'd suddenly entered a long and agonising labour.

Some had been shocked at the tiny size of my new-born son, some attempted to convince Erhardt to not accept the boy and abandon him, but thankfully Erhardt hadn't listened to them. Any son made him happy and proud, though the baby's cough, his constant cry and unwillingness to eat had been worrying him as of late; the poor child had been stricken with it for almost two weeks now.

Erhardt strode over from the sleeping area and paused behind me, placing a hand on my shoulder. I flinched noticeably at his touch, answered by a disgruntled sigh. He continued to the table and sat down, staring at me and the baby in my arms.

"He's sick, still." Erhardt noted, briefly nodding his head in the baby's direction.

"He's getting better." I replied stoutly, glaring at him.

"It doesn't sound like it to me – nor does it look like it. He still doesn't take your breast!" Erhardt pointed out.

I turned to the pale, blue-eyed baby and scowled, privately.

"It's alright, little Sander," I cooed softly, brushing my nipple over the boy's mouth again. "I'm sure you're hungry, come on now."

"He won't survive the rest of the winter if he doesn't eat." Erhardt continued, watching the baby turn his head from my breast yet again. "Look at him – he's nothing but skin and bone! I wonder if we should've left him in the forest—"

"*Nei!*" I snapped ferociously. "He's fine, he's just not hungry yet."

"We should try for another child." Erhardt proposed.

I shuffled my furs tighter around me, making sure to keep the tiny babe wrapped from the cold as much as possible. It was winter, the Jól celebrations had ended only a few days ago. Crystalline snow was piled thick outside, even with the orange fires burning hotly, every breath that slipped from my shivering lips was a pale cloud.

Burwenna slowly and steadily walked into the main room from the kitchen with a bowl of steaming oats in her violently shaking hands. Her entire body shook and shivered from the cold, but very carefully she placed the bowl on the table beside me without spilling any of the contents inside.

"Snuggle with Young Birger in his bed and feed him in there, make sure he's warm. Fetch one of my fur cloaks and wrap it around you both, you must stay warm, too!" I ordered, worried about the poor girl. "Build a bigger fire should you need to."

"Y-y-yes, j-Jarlkona!"

She scurried away eagerly to fetch Young Birger's oats from the kitchen, then rushed to the sleeping area where the boy was still laying, contentedly curled in a cocoon of furs.

I dipped a finger into the steaming bowl and blew on it a few times. I brought my finger to my baby's mouth and wiped the oats onto his tiny, wet pink tongue. He slurped at my finger, enthusiastically.

"A-ha! See? He just wants to eat food, not milk!" I cried, victoriously, dipping my finger into the oats and repeating the process, ignoring the chill air on my exposed breast.

"We should try for another child." Erhardt repeated, louder than before.

"I heard you." I replied stiffly.

"Birger is strong and growing well, but Sander is small and weak …"

I gazed across the room with glassy eyes.

"My son is fine."

"You are a devoted mother; you love your sons with a ferociousness I've never seen! I admire that ... but, surely you want more?"

"Not if it's because you want to throw one of my sons to the wolves!" I hissed.

"I won't do that." He assured me calmly. "I have accepted him; he is ours until death takes him from us."

"Or us from him." I growled.

Erhardt stood from his chair and moved behind me, bending over me and watching me feed Sander the oatmeal on my fingertip. Ever so gently, he reached over me and took my swollen, uncovered breast in his hand, gripping it softly. I froze, petrified by him. Though he was careful to cup my breast gently, his touch stung my frozen flesh.

I watched Erhardt dip his finger into the oats before he circled my areola with it, wiping the excess oatmeal onto my hard nipple. For a few moments Erhardt squeezed my breast until a dribble of milk spilled from my nipple, seeping over the oatmeal. He then took my breast to Sander's tiny mouth and pressed my nipple into it.

At first the baby began slurping the oatmeal. Then I felt the tight clamping of the Sander's gums on my nipple, felt the vacuum of his sucking, and the blessed, though painful, release of the milk that filled my breast.

I sighed deeply, happily, and smiled at Erhardt, relieved.

"When will you give your body to me?" Erhardt whispered longingly, dragging his hand from my breast and over my collarbone, gently stroking my neck.

My smile dropped, and my lips fell open from surprise.

"I can't ..." I answered awkwardly.

"I know." Erhardt's voice was firm. "That night ... that night was a long time ago. You lived! Now you must be alive; share your bed with me." He insisted, whisking around to stand before me. "I miss you!"

My gaze dropped from him to the floor.

"I can't." I murmured.

"You must!" Erhardt exclaimed, beginning to lose his patience. "A Danish woman is strong; she would not let this crush her. You lived – you lived and received immediate retribution. Your attacker was slain – please Aveline! You must move forward."

"I know." I whimpered. "I know!"

Erhardt gazed down on me silently, dropping to his knees. He snaked his arms around my hips, holding me, staring at me tenderly.

"I yearn for you, Aveline."

"There are other women in this city that you can bed, why not take them?" I whined, despairingly.

Erhardt sighed deeply.

"They won't give me heirs. You've given me two living sons – more sons than any of my other wives have given me. For that, I'm proud of you, and thankful! But ... many years ago – I think I was married to my second wife at the time? – regardless. Many years ago, a whore birthed me a son, my first male child! But the boy wouldn't suckle, he was small and weak like Sander ... he died six months after his birth." Erhardt explained. "Aveline, I will do everything I can to keep him alive, but we must prepare ourselves for the possibility that he won't."

Erhardt returned to his seat at the table and ate his oats quietly, leaving me alone by the fire to simmer.

"I'm confused – are you my loving husband pleading for me to share your bed because you want me and miss my touch? Or are you a heartless jarl trying to force me to produce more heirs and further your lineage? Do tell me which because I'm awfully confused." I spat bitterly.

"I am currently your loving husband begging for your body." Erhardt replied calmly. "But I have been more than patient and given you a long time to heal. I am the Jarl of Aros and your husband; it is your duty to give me heirs ... I will not ask you again."

***

Spring, 878

AND HE DIDN'T. Erhardt didn't press the matter of extending our family, he did not touch me nor try to persuade me to open my legs to him at night-time.

Since Young Birger had been born, I had only copulated with Erhardt a handful of times. Most nights, Young Birger would fall asleep nursing from me, forcing Erhardt to go to sleep unsatisfied. As my son grew older and started sleeping through the nights, Erhardt would attempt to initiate intercourse. Unless he was inebriated or exhausted, I'd have no choice but to lay with him.

Since the night Tarben had raped me, I hadn't even kissed Erhardt. After Sander had been born, little more than six months after Tarben had attacked me, Erhardt had begun trying to convince me to share my body with him. Time and time again, I would refuse him. The idea of being intimate ... I couldn't. My skin crawled as though covered in a swarm of insects, I would shake uncontrollably and break into tears if Erhardt touched me. His patience was running dry, and I didn't know how much longer I could avoid Erhardt's sexual advances.

I still prayed to Frigg every night, but I couldn't draw strength from my prayer as I had before. Erhardt had stopped pressuring me, though, for that I gave my thanks.

What I was most thankful for, however, was Sander. Sander had survived the winter! It had taken days of covering my nipples in warm, watery oatmeal or root vegetables boiled and mashed into a thin paste, before he'd finally nurse from my breast. But he did nurse, and he grew, and he survived.

Winter had melted away into a damp spring, and there was peace in the hall. The fields were gradually growing greener, the trees were already budding, but the wind remained chilled, especially on the sands of the coast that bordered the island.

The light brown sands crunched and slid beneath my boots. The aquamarine waves lapped the shore, lathering it with thick pearlescent foam, inching forward and dragging back, repeatedly. Above me the screeches of gulls cackled and called, and the voices and noises of sailors working on longships and boats echoed over the expanse of water.

I turned from the sea and faced the small cluster of trees that grew near the shore edge. Only a few feet beyond the trees soared the wall that squared around the entire city. In a sun glared spot between two of the trees lay a splash of dainty little flowers, bright and cheerful despite being towered over by the looming, skeletal trees.

"Let's look at the flowers." I suggested, readjusting little Sander in my arms.

Young Birger paused, whipping his head from left to right, trying to spot the flowers I spoke of. When he found them, he squealed with happiness and darted to them as fast as his small legs could take him. I giggled at the sight of him but picked up my speed as I followed him.

Together, Burwenna, Young Birger, Sander and I lolled on the grass. Young Birger was sprawled out on his tummy, forehead furrowed as he carefully and dedicatedly tugged the petals, individually, from one flower with his pudgy little fingers. I held Sander to my breast, who suckled serenely, and smiled at the boy before glancing to Burwenna.

The thrall girl was staring fixedly at the waters before us, her face bursting with what I could only assume was tough deliberation.

"What are you thinking about?" I asked gently.

"Oh, me?" The teenaged girl jumped. "Oh, I ..." and her voice trailed off nervously.

"Talk to me, Burwenna. There are no secrets between us."

"Well ... it's just ..." She spluttered, difficultly deciding whether to open up to me, or how to begin, I didn't know which. Eventually, after more stuttering, she sighed deeply and continued. "I was thinking of Estrith. And – and how she died."

"Oh." It was my turn to be speechless.

"She lived a terrible life ... I hope she's found peace now."

"Did she not live well in Britain?" I asked softly.

"She did for a while ... but she was taken by the Danes on her wedding day." Burwenna said, maintaining her unblinking gaze with the waves before us. "She was taken as a thrall to Aros, starved and beaten ... Tarben always touched her ... he had taken an interest – if you could call it that – in Estrith, and he raped her as often as he could. She birthed three of his children, you know?"

"What?" I gasped. "Where are her children now?"

"They died." A few tears slipped down Burwenna's pink cheeks. "She couldn't bear the thought of mothering Tarben's children ... she was forced to leave them in the forest ..."

I had no words.

"Will – when ... when will Vidar come to rescue you?" Burwenna asked, her big, brown, worried eyes glazed with sadness poured into me and wrenched at my heart.

"Hopefully soon. He said a year ..." I whispered, taking her hand and kissing it. "It's been almost that now; I'm hoping we will hear from him soon. Burwenna, when he comes for the children and me ... you know you'll be rescued, too? I will keep my promise to you."

The girl said nothing.

"I've tried to protect you as much as I could. I failed Estrith, and for that I'll never forgive myself – but I refuse to fail you and Elda! When Vidar's invitation comes, I will take you both with me to Roskilde, and there you'll live in my old home ... it will become your home. You'll be free! I'll find two good Danes to marry you both to, and you'll be free to live however you wish, never as thralls again!" I vowed passionately.

"Do you think you and Vidar will be successful?" She asked, her tone was doubtful, but her eyes betrayed her hopefulness.

"*Já*," I said firmly. "I am sure of it."

***

IT WAS LATE, my sons were both tucked away in bed with Burwenna and Elda, and I could hear the faint snoring of Erhardt. I had stayed awake passed everyone else, busy at my loom, but darkness had swallowed the hall and as the night grew older, I halted my work, unable to see even with the pale glow of the fire beside me. I sat on the raised stone edge of the pit, lost in thought of Vidar, watching the smouldering embers flitter between colours as they died at the edge of the small flames.

On nights like this, when nothing but the soft sound of slumber filled the hall, it was easy for my mind to fall on Vidar. I thought of the night he woke me and led me on a mad dash through the night to the clearing in the forest, to watch the whales splash and play. I thought of his face, remembered every expression, every line, every detail. I thought of his body, strong, muscled, the silky down of fair hair that lightly spattered his chest, almost unnoticeable. I thought of the softness of his flesh, as I ran my hand over his torso, wrapped in his large, strapping arms ...

"Are you coming to bed?" Erhardt asked, standing in the archway to the sleeping area.

"Uh, in a little while ... don't stay up on my account." I replied quickly, attempting to feign wifely concern for him.

He ignored me and walked to my side. He took my hand and pulled me to him.

"The boys and the thralls are asleep." Erhardt said pointedly. "We're alone ... together ..."

Erhardt lowered his head to kiss me, but I twisted in his arms. His hands still gripped my wrists, and excuses dashed through my mind. Irritated, he yanked me against him again. He took me by the shoulders and shook me roughly.

"How can I convince you to lay with me?" Erhardt demanded. "I've asked, begged, pleaded! I've given you time to heal from the incident, and I've tried to romance you! You used to lay with me willingly, now you won't even kiss me?"

Suddenly, Erhardt shoved me to the ground.

"On our wedding night, I had to beat you into submission. I was hoping not to have to do that – it's shameful for a man to beat his wife. You were nothing but a damned foreigner and a thrall to me back then – a useful pawn in an age-old feud – but a thrall, nonetheless. Beating you was inconsequential back then, but you've risen in my esteem over the years ... you became my Danish wife – a proper Jarlkona!" He growled. "But your behaviour has deteriorated since Alvarsson came to Aros; you're acting like a foolish thrall *tik*, again!"

"I was raped!" I hissed.

"So, you and Alvarsson say! Tarben and the thrall were the only witnesses, and they both died."

"What are you insinuating?" I demanded through gritted teeth.

Erhardt said nothing. He placed a fingertip under my chin and pushed upwards, signifying his want for me to stand. With a stab of fear in my heart, my wedding night flashed before my eyes. I rose to my feet, his finger trailed down my chin, my neck and between my breasts, before he ripped open my gown with a violent swipe.

He took my breasts, hard and swollen with milk, in his hands and squeezed them, palpating them until pinpricks of white began trickling from my erect nipples.

"Please, leave me be, I have to wake Sander to feed him." I begged, uncontrollable tears streamed down my face as I pushed his hands from my body and stepped back.

Abruptly, Erhardt lunged forward, smacking my face with the back of his hand. I yelped as I fell to my knees, sobbing. Ignoring me, he grabbed the hustrulinet pinned to my hair and dragged me to the table. While I was still on my knees, he ripped the pins and fabric from my hair and tossed them to the ground, unbinding my hair from the many plaits and braids until my curls were wild and loose. Taking a large fistful of hair into his hands, he hauled me to my feet and threw me onto the table.

"This reminds me of our wedding night." He grunted darkly, pulling down his breeks. "It also brings to mind the last time you laid with me … it was the first night that Alvarsson and Ursula came to Aros …"

He kicked his breeks to the floor but left his tunic on. Hurriedly, he focussed on me, tearing my dress and undergarments from me until I was naked on the table, like a prized swine at a feast.

"They were asleep at our feet, and I started stroking your legs." He reminisced. His hands slithered over my trembling thighs as he spoke. "And you kicked me away!"

My legs dangled over the edge of the table and my arms were crossed over my chest. I couldn't avoid him or refuse him any longer, but I couldn't make a noise and wake my children. I didn't want Young Birger to stumble into the room and watch the man he believed to be his father beat and rape his mother …

Erhardt took one of my breasts to his mouth and sucked, hard. I felt milk escape from my nipple and into his mouth. My breasts had ached from their fullness, and now I was filled with a nauseating relief at their release, angry that the respite came from Erhardt's mouth, instead of my infant son's.

Milk had begun pouring from my other breast, streaming down Erhardt's hand that gripped it. With a loud smack, he stopped suckling my breast, turning to the other one and sucking it instead.

"By the damned gods, you *hrafnasueltir* – let go of me!" I cried in disgust.

Erhardt stopped suckling and slapped his hand to my throat.

"I realised instantly why you didn't want me to lay with you. You didn't want Alvarsson to wake and see me fucking you … I had to hold you down by your neck, like now … then you were still and quiet, like a fucking corpse." He snarled. "You weren't as fun that night, as you were on our wedding night – when you wriggled and flailed – but, you know? As much as I did enjoy our wedding night, over the course of our marriage I have found I much prefer it when you lay with your legs wide and do as you're told!"

I grabbed his hand with both of mine and dug my nails into his flesh as hard as I could.

"This reminds me of the night Tarben raped me!" I hissed. "You were so angry that he'd dared to force himself on me – but you're no different from him!"

"There is a difference, my love." Erhardt rumbled. He pulled me off the table by my throat, flipped me around and slammed me, face down, onto the tabletop. "You are my wife, not his. Only I have a right to your body. We blessed your womb on our wedding day so that I may fill it, no one else!"

"Ha!" I sneered hysterically. "And beating me? You beat me just as he did! You dishonourable swine! You *argr* dog! You dastardly wolf!"

I heard the whoosh of his tunic sleeve as he swung his arm, and with a deafening crack! his hand hammered down upon my naked rear. A shrill wail burst from my lips – I clapped my hands to my mouth, trying to silence myself – I couldn't wake up the children!

"I should kill you for speaking to me like that." Erhardt snarled, his sharp fingertips digging into the soft flesh of my hips. "When you behave like a Dane, I never raise my hand to you, but when your Anglo-Saxon heritage shows I'm forced to discipline you like the thrall you were born!"

He kicked my legs apart and forced himself inside me. I whimpered as he entered me and yelped when he snapped my head backwards by my hair.

"Ah, just like our wedding night!" Erhardt jeered as he shoved himself deeper into me.

It only took a few moments of brutally pounding me until his lustful hunger was satiated. Erhardt pulled his cock out of me and snatched up his breeks, staring at me as I laid on the table, still and motionless, his satisfaction oozing down my legs.

A terribly heavy silence fell over us both. I wrenched whatever clothes were within my reach and tried to cover myself with them. My body shuddered, snot and tears streamed down my face, my hands shook violently.

"I don't want it to be this way, Danethrall," Erhardt murmured. "I don't want to discipline you and force you to lay with me. You were doing so well – you learned, quickly, you were such a good wife for so long!" He sighed deeply. "A thrall from Ursula arrived today, inviting us to Roskilde, they want to celebrate the birth of Sander ..."

I stared at Erhardt in shock.

"But I am faced with a problem ... I don't know if I want to take you to Roskilde since Alvarsson has had such a bad influence on your behaviour."

My jaw fell in horror. My tears had halted, but my small, quaking body still shuddered.

"I'll make a deal with you, Danethrall. Willingly give yourself to me when I want you, and you'll go to Roskilde with me and our sons. But, if you deny me even once, no matter when or where – if you make me raise a hand to you – you'll never see Alvarsson or leave the walls of Aros ever again."

"I promise." I whispered.

CHAPTER TWENTY-TWO

ROSKILDE, DENMARK
Summer, 878

WE ARRIVED IN Roskilde a few days before *Midsumarblót*. Anxiety ate at me and my nerves were in tatters. As our ship sliced through the fjord, Roskilde rose before us, the sun's golden rays set the town alight. Erhardt sat beside me and took my hand.

"Danethrall, you must not look Alvarsson in the eye." He said simply.

I didn't question him, just nodded shortly in agreement.

"You've been behaving well as of late, you've been a good wife. I hope I can trust you to do as I ask." Erhardt continued condescendingly, stroking a few stray hairs from my face.

I nodded silently, again.

"I've not had to discipline you at all, since our ... *understanding*. I praise you for that – I really don't want to have to discipline you again." Erhardt persisted, his tone low so only I could hear his words.

I was still, listening to every patronising syllable that fell from his lips.

"You will lay with me tonight, whether Alvarsson is awake or not. You are my wife; your body is mine. No one will deny my right to you."

"*Já*, husband."

Seemingly satisfied, he rose and stomped back down the longship to converse with a few *holumenn*, crewmen on the ship.

Erhardt had not even looked me in the eye since that spring night ... He hadn't touched me, nor had he forced himself on me or even beaten me. Erhardt had hardly even spoken to me since then.

But that night, our first night in Roskilde, I laid with him.

It was pitch black, except for the smouldering embers in the fire pit, and the pale ivory moonbeams that dimly gleamed through the smoke hole. The soft sounds of slumber permeated through the familiar hall, from the many sleeping occupants. Straw beds covered in sheepskin were littered around the sleeping area, filled with resting bodies, and upon the platforms in the main room slept Vidar's exhausted house thralls. Only the bed closet that belonged to Alvar the First One and Freydis was empty.

Young Birger and Sander lay nestled between Elda and Burwenna at the foot of Erhardt and my bed, and to our right Ursula and Vidar shared a bed. The straw crunched and rustled deafeningly as Erhardt heaved himself onto me, kneeing my legs apart as he rammed his mouth against mine.

I did not stop him. I gripped the hair of the sheepskin beneath me and did not interfere or try to stop him. I laid there and allowed him my body.

All the while, through the darkness Vidar watched. His livid glare blazed through the night, sickened by the sight that met his eyes. Sorrowfully and deeply filled with shame, I could not meet his gaze, and he mercilessly would not tear his sight from me. I squeezed my eyes shut and clutched the sheepskin tightly in my fists until Erhardt finally rolled off me.

Morning came, and when I awoke, I met Vidar's venomous stare piercing me through the dim morning light. My body jolted with shock, but he did not flinch.

"What's wrong with you, woman?" Erhardt grunted.

"Nothing, go back to sleep." I muttered, peeling the linen sheet from my sweat drenched limbs, my night dress uncomfortably stuck to my flesh.

I crawled out of the bed and stumbled through the hall, passed the thralls sleeping upon the hard-wooden platform. I saw the blonde head of Hilda poking out beneath an old sheet, and the bronze flesh of Aaminah as she gently shifted in her slumber. I wondered what happened to the red headed thrall from those few years ago, as I silently slipped into the garden.

To my shock and sadness, the flowers were all dead. Freydis's once gorgeous garden was nothing more than heaps of black, rotted plants, overgrown grass and long tangles of feral vines. Slowly I stepped towards the plot where the snapdragons used to thrive.

"Oh Freydis." I whispered, running my hand over the top of the unkempt mess.

"She took no joy in maintaining the garden after you left. I suppose the guilt of selling you off was too much for her."

I lifted my head and saw Vidar leaning in the doorway.

"Where is she?"

"She left a few weeks ago. She went to Hedeby to stay with friends. She said she couldn't be here to see you and Erhardt."

"I understand that." I replied, turning away from him.

"She can't stand sharing a house with his little rodent of a daughter." Vidar smirked, taking a few slow steps towards me. "Can't say I blame her, I avoid the woman as much as I possibly can, myself."

"Mmm, hmm." I mumbled, staring at the knots and snarls of wild flora that roared in front of me.

"Freydis wanted you for her daughter-in-law. She still cares for you, deeply. She sincerely regrets what she did. I haven't found the strength to forgive her yet, but I understand her actions." Vidar said.

"How long will she be gone?" I asked.

"I don't know. A few weeks, months – maybe she'll come back after Alvar returns from Britain." Vidar replied, following me as I attempted to slyly maintain distance between us. "Aveline, look at me."

I froze, unable to do as he asked, terrified that Erhardt might be snooping somewhere watching and waiting for a reason to make true his threat to me …

"I hated watching him take you last night … I plotted his death in so many ways." Vidar said as he stepped closer to me.

Suddenly his hand clasped mine.

"Please, don't." I begged under my breath.

"He's still asleep." Vidar whispered. "Why are you afraid of me?"

"I'm not afraid of *you* …" I replied quietly, my voice trailing away as my heart raced from his touch.

Vidar slipped his hand on my hip and gently pulled me to him.

"You're afraid of him … but you're home now, tell me when to kill him, and I will."

"Not yet ..."
"When?"
"Soon."

I turned around and gazed up at him, steadily, his icy blue eyes filled with passion and determination. Gently I placed a kiss upon his lips, then darted inside before anyone could catch us. I slipped back into the straw bed beside Erhardt and heard the slam of the hall door as Vidar stormed away.

***

"*FADIR,* COME WALK with me." Ursula pleaded playfully that morning. "It's beautiful today, we've had a wonderful breakfast, let's walk along the fjord."

"Will your husband be coming?" Erhardt asked.

"*Nei*, just you and me." She beamed. "He woke early, for business I expect. He won't be back until late. It's been an age since we spent time together, do come with me!"

"Wouldn't you like your stepmother to accompany us?" Erhardt said carefully.

"I'd much rather it just be us – it's been so long! She can stay here with my brothers and join us next time." Ursula replied, tipping her head to the side and pushing her bottom lip out.

For a few heavy moments Erhardt contemplated. He saw the pleading pout on his daughter's face, shot a nervous glance at me, then gazed back at Ursula.

"Alright, but we can't be too long." Erhardt replied. "And you said your husband wouldn't be back until late?"

"*Nei*, he never is when he leaves this early." Ursula explained nonchalantly. "We may even see him on our travels, he's usually working on the ships or in meetings with his council. With *Midsumarblót* so close, I'm sure he's tied up planning the ceremony."

"Of course, of course." Erhardt exhaled deeply, relieved by her answer. "Let us go, then."

Erhardt and Ursula left after a little hustle and bustle, taking Hilda with them. Hilda the thrall had been bitter and hateful towards me, as well as reluctant and grudging to serve me when I lived in Roskilde; and she hadn't changed much at all. It was only the morning of the second day of our stay in Roskilde, and her coldness was substantial, she hadn't looked at me or uttered even a single word to me.

I wondered if she was still resentful at my rising in the ranks of the Danes; I'd literally leaped up the social ranks since I'd been brought to Roskilde. Hilda, however, had been taken as a thrall, raised as a thrall and remained a thrall.

She knew my rise to jarlkona had not been of my will, she knew nothing of my life in Aros, but I wondered if she even cared …

I wondered if Hilda remembered my attempt to defend the hall – including her! – from the Aros savages? I wondered if she remembered my screams and tears as Freydis sold me away to Erhardt, a month after my and Vidar's wedding announcement? I wondered if she still viewed me as a betrayer … I betrayed Britain by embracing the Danes. I betrayed Roskilde by becoming jarlkona of Aros. I betrayed Vidar by marrying Erhardt behind his back …

I didn't feel the same hatred towards her as I'd once felt. There was a strange heaviness I felt when I watched her. Time had not been kind to her. She had aged badly, her nose was bulbous, permanently damaged from the broken nose Tarben had given her all those years ago. Her face was creased with lines she was too young to bare, and grey bags hung thickly beneath her eyes, like charcoal coloured slugs. She was still unwed and childless …

Though Vidar and Freydis were extremely kind masters, their thralls were well fed, and the house thralls especially were cherished, Hilda, Aaminah, the thralls that tended the land, they were all still thralls. Their lives were still hard and tiring, and it showed so very clearly on their flesh.

Aaminah had greeted me warmly. She had aged, but not as badly as Hilda. I wondered if the resentment and loathing that eroded Hilda's heart was what ailed her flesh …

Aaminah's beautiful face glowed with happiness when her big, deep, onyx eyes laid upon me. Her brown-pink lips curved into a huge grin and her long, thick, sharp eyebrows arched in surprise, as she flung her arms around me.

I had laughed and held the woman tightly, as a whirl of foreign words spilled from her mouth in a praising, grateful tone. I didn't know which god or gods she was thanking, but I closed my eyes briefly, and sent a quick prayer of thanks to them, too.

Thinking of her, I turned and looked at the thrall. Aaminah was sat on the floor, cradling Sander in her arms, grinning her big wonderful smile, and singing to him in her native tongue. Young Birger had Elda and Burwenna throwing a ball in the garden with him, I could hear their laughter and his squeals of delight.

"Where are you from, Aaminah?" I asked.

Aaminah looked up at me surprised, her eyes twinkling, my son smiling silently up at her.

"A land far, far away from here ..." She cooed dreamily. "I was taken, when I was a young child, to the edge of the Caspian Sea from my home in the city of Gurgan and sold as a slave to the Varangians. From there, I passed through many hands along the Caspian Sea to the Volga River, until I was finally traded to Jarl Alvar. I've been in the Dane's lands ever since."

"Do you miss it? Your home?" I asked as I watched Sander's eyes droop sleepily.

"I was so young; I hardly remember the place ... I do remember the hot, dusty sand beneath my toes and the heat blazing down on me as I ran and played with my brothers and sisters, and I remember the coldness of the night ... I remember the tranquil smile on my mother's face, and I remember my father bouncing me on his knee, or holding me, like this," she gazed at Sander lovingly. "Singing these songs to me."

"They're beautiful." I smiled.

Aaminah grinned back at me, a pale rose blush subtly glowed on her brown cheeks.

"I suppose I miss many things. But they would have changed by now, it's been so many years ... My father died two years before I was sold, and my mother had died a year and a half after him. My brothers and sisters and I, we were all quickly sold away after my mother's death. I don't know where they are, whether they're alive or dead ... with my parents being long dead would my land still be my home?"

I gazed at the floor sadly, feeling her words, deeply, in my heart. Though we were from much different places, countries separated by inordinate amounts of land and sea, I understood her.

"But the way I see it." Aaminah continued brightly. "The lands and my life may have changed, but I'll forever hold those happy memories of my family, etched inside my soul, so there isn't really much I need to miss – I have all the important things inside me. Outside of memories, master Vidar allows me to clean myself and pray when I need to, I remember every word of my mother tongue, and I've not forgotten any of the prayers for my god."

"In the land I was born, they worship only one god, too." I said. "But here, they have so many, male and female!"

"And who is your god?" Aaminah asked. Sander wiggled in his sleep and slowly nuzzled Aaminah in search of her breast. "Do you worship your homeland's god, or those of the Danes?"

I stared at the watered-down ale inside my wooden cup.

"Since I was brought to Roskilde, I lost my faith in the Christian God. I would pray often, every day, and He would never answer. So, I stopped praying to him.

"When Birger came back from Britain gravely wounded, it was the Norse gods who I prayed to, and his life was saved. In Aros, I prayed to the Norse gods for courage and strength, for the safety of my children … and they gave it to me." I said. "I'll be forever thankful to them."

With that, Sander let out an enormous howl, and I rushed to him. Urgently, I opened my dress and brought him to my breast.

"Maybe one day you'll find your faith again." Aaminah remarked, brushing the dust from the back of her skirts as she stood. "But to me it sounds as though you already have."

"*Já.*" I smiled. "I have."

***

VIDAR ARRIVED BACK at the hall a little while later, sweating lightly in the midmorning sun. He was accompanied by Jan, who held a few half-carved branches in his hand, and a knife.

"What are you both doing here?" I asked, surprised.

"Aaminah, take Sander outside to with his brother." Vidar ordered quickly. "Don't come in until I say so, tell Burwenna and Elda the same."

Aaminah immediately took the baby from my arms and did as she was told without question, nor even so much as a puzzled look.

"What's going on?" I asked, bewildered.

Without saying a word, Vidar pulled me into his arms and pressed his lips against mine in a thirsting kiss.

"By Odin, you're finally home!" Vidar exclaimed, beaming at me. "On *Midsumarblót* we will kill Erhardt Ketilsson and the rodents from Aros." His grin lit up madly, and his ice blue eyes glinted with bloodlust and excitement. "Three more days, my little fawn. The end is near!"

I was unnerved by him, shocked by his announcement, but his exhilaration was infectious. He whisked me up into his arms and carried me into the sleeping area.

"We're going to start a war." I cautioned.

"*Já*, we are." Vidar beamed.

CHAPTER TWENTY-THREE

"AVELINE, PLAY *HNEFATAFL* with me." Vidar said brightly.

Erhardt glared at me, alarmed. I didn't meet Vidar's gaze but continued to stare at the wad of fleece I was combing.

"Maybe another time." I said.

"Ah, but remember how much fun we used to have?" Vidar persisted, leaning on the back of the empty chair beside Erhardt as he gazed at me, a faint smirk playing at his lips.

"She said no, Alvarsson." Erhardt reproached gruffly.

"Have you ever played *Hnefatafl* with your wife?" Vidar asked, turning to the Jarl of Aros.

Erhardt irritably shook his head and drank deeply for his cup of ale.

"You have missed out then, Jarl Erhardt. Aveline is a wonderful player – she has even bested me on occasion. Remember when you lived here, Aveline? Remember all the nights we would spend together, laughing and drinking and playing *Hnefatafl*?" Vidar sighed reminiscently as he dramatically threw himself into the chair next to Erhardt. "What fun we used to have!"

"Well, things have changed since then." Erhardt muttered under his breath.

"*Já*, they have." Vidar said, glaring at Erhardt briefly, contempt flashing dangerously across his icy eyes. Vidar turned to me again, his wonderful smile lighting up his face. "Remember when I would teach you to swim?"

"Mmm, hmm." I rolled my lips together to hold back my grin.

Through my peripheral vision, I watched Vidar place his hand on Erhardt's shoulder and shuffle closer to him. Grinning at me mischievously, Vidar leaned towards Erhardt, making sure the Jarl of Aros would hear his every word.

"Aveline would take off her dress and, in nothing but that thin linen shift, she would slip into the cold water of Roskilde Fjord."

Vidar's voice was low, as though he were sharing a secret, but loud enough that every word he said was unmistakably clear.

Erhardt's face grew redder as rage boiled inside him. I stared at Vidar, astonished that he was riling Erhardt up so deliberately. Vidar caught my eye and smirked, winking one of his dazzling eyes at me.

"She was terrible at swimming – at every lesson I would have to dive in and pull her out of the water." Vidar laughed, resuming his normal tone. "But, *oh*! It was worth it just to see her shift turn sheer and cling to her dripping body, revealing all her beautiful curves – her lips quivering, her soft skin rippled with goosebumps, her nipples erect and pressing against the soaking fabric …"

Erhardt's hands began to shake violently, and a vein throbbed in his forehead.

"What fun we used to have! If you change your mind about *Hnefatafl*, Aveline, let me know. I'd love to relive some of the good old days with you." Vidar said. "Ah, Aaminah is here with dinner! It smells delicious."

I stayed true to my word to Erhardt and refused to meet Vidar's gaze, (in front of Erhardt, at least), and answered Vidar with nothing but a noncommittal noise or a few passing words, but Vidar …

Vidar had become so audacious and daring! He would kiss me, both tenderly and passionately in front of the thralls, stroke my hair and my face in front of his wife, Ursula, and taunt the furious Jarl Erhardt with tales of our past love …

Vidar had settled on the date of Erhardt's death; no longer was he concerned by repercussion. In his excitement for the fast-approaching end of our insufferable circumstances, he didn't care to be discreet with his affection for me, anymore. In his mind, he was invincible!

Vidar was a spider, he'd waited, patiently for a very long time, watching Erhardt flitter and fly freely before him, slowly edging closer to Vidar's web. Erhardt had no idea that he was caught, and it was just a matter of time before Vidar would pounce, wrap Erhardt up in his plan and destroy him, once and for all.

Vidar spent a lot of time visiting with Jan, and a small group of other men. Vidar had referred to these men as his 'council'. The men were a mixture of talented warriors and ship makers. The men of Vidar's council were all skilled. Alvar was wise, he knew not to take every fine warrior and craftsman to Britain with him and leave his town unprotected.

Unfortunately, the raid Alvar had feared had become reality whilst he was supporting the Danish kings in their war against Britain; his remaining men in Roskilde had been outnumbered and unprepared when Aros had attacked, and many had lost their lives. But Vidar was preparing to avenge his town, and his men were ready to avenge their fallen companions and kin.

During the brief moments we were alone together, Vidar would not tell me what he spoke of at his meetings. No, he'd kiss me and take me to his bed saying not a word. I was tense, apprehensive and fearful, wanting so much to talk to him, have him comfort me and wash away my anxiety. Instead I fell into the whirl of passion and ecstasy, free, for a while, from the world around me, until the inevitable moment came when I'd leap from his bed, pull on my clothes and rush away to find an excuse to hide behind when Erhardt or Ursula or one of their people would appear.

And there was Hilda, watching but not talking. Inconspicuously paying attention to us, without saying a word.

I wondered if I trusted her.

I wondered if we should kill her.

But I said nothing, choosing to wait until Vidar's plan came to fruition. I would decide then whether her blood would be shed or not.

Hilda had not betrayed us in the days leading up to *Midsumarblót*, and those days dragged, immensely! Seconds felt like centuries, minutes like millennia. The town of Roskilde buzzed with activity, I was kept busy with preparation of the hall for when the doors would be flung open and the townsfolk would fill the walls. Busy as I was with work and my sons, the days were incessantly long.

"Erhardt, come to the council at the ritual hall with me, today." Vidar said at the table the morning before *Midsumarblót*. "The festivities have been planned, as have the rituals and the sacrifice, but I have decided that you should officiate the event and spill the blood of the sacrifice, since you are the honoured guest here, as well as Ursula's father."

Erhardt's eyebrows zipped up his forehead, and he glanced at Vidar, quite surprised. He caught himself quickly, however.

"Of course." Erhardt replied, matching Vidar's cool tone.

"Hurry eating, then, so we can be off."

Sour at being told what to do by Vidar but pleased to have been offered such a respected position in the *blót*, Erhardt shoved his bowl of stew aside, only half eaten. Vidar smiled smugly, then together the two men left.

"I'm so glad *faðir* and Vidar are finally doing something together!" Ursula sighed happily and loudly.

"Oh, yes?" I answered.

"*Já!*" She gasped, not seeming to pick up on my aloof, impassive tone. "Vidar has been ... short, lately. The only kindness I've seen from him was directed to your sons ... *Faðir* has been very offended by Vidar's behaviour towards him, not respecting his position as father-in-law and jarl ... But I suppose the *blót* has just had him so busy and exhausted, maybe that's why he's been so ill tempered and terse."

"Mmm, maybe." I murmured, rolling my eyes. "Or perhaps it was the ransacking of his home, murder of his people and selling of his betrothed ..."

Ursula didn't hear me. As I muttered under my breath, the hall doors had opened, and Jan had stepped inside.

"*Góðan morgin!*" Jan announced loudly.

"Ah, Jan!" Ursula beamed. "Would you like some food? A drink? Vidar and *faðir* just left."

"I'm actually here for Aveline." Jan smiled warmly, running a hand through his long tawny tresses. "I haven't seen my old friend for a time, I'd like to take her and the boys around."

"Oh? Of course." Ursula blushed, a little dejected, but ever the polite hostess. "I have much to do here, anyway."

"I thought you would. The Jarlkona of Roskilde is always kept busy – I'm sure your husband has you all wrapped up with tasks." Jan winked.

"Oh, well – he's not–" She stuttered, her face a shocking shade of magenta.

"Continue on your hard work, my dear. I'd be glad to fetch you anything you need from the market." He offered.

"We're fine, *pakka*." Ursula gushed, staring at him avidly, her hands clutched together against her breast. "I appreciate your kindness!"

"If you change your mind, just send a thrall to find me." Jan continued, brushing a stray hair from her face as he passed her. "Young Birger! Where are you, boy?"

The toddler rushed towards Jan from the far platform where he had been playing.

I struggled to stifle my laughter. Ursula was intensely smitten by Jan! But most people were. He was smooth, seductive, handsome. Jan was charming and charismatic, and so, *so* funny. He had a comment or phrase that would have all his listeners fall to the floor in hysterics.

I remembered the dinner at this very hall, years ago, when Vidar and Freydis had introduced Jan to me, as a suitor. Birger had desperately wanted me to marry Jan, but I couldn't. Had things been different, had Kainan and my affair not existed, had Vidar not confessed his love for me, then I would've married Jan.

The rays of daylight shone brightly through the smoke hole, lighting Jan's alabaster flesh brilliantly. He looked like a feral angel; pure, pale skin the colour of stars, deep sapphire eyes, and the moment his soft rose lips curved into a smile happiness would radiate from him. His fair brown hair was long, cascading down his back like a fine cloak, and he wore a thick beard, popular amongst the Norsemen. His beard was well kempt, and he kept three braids in it, and his mustachio was also neatly trimmed.

Jan was grace and elegance blended with blood thirst and battle skill; he was beauty and magnetism, and a true Danish warrior. Jan was Freyr!

Jan lifted Young Birger into the air and the delighted child squealed with happiness.

Yes, I would've married him if it had come to it, and I know I would've been happy. But I thought of my love, my Vidar. I thought of his sun bronzed flesh, his rugged handsomeness, the faded lines around his piercing icy eyes that sparked intensely with every emotion. I thought of his arms around me, my favourite place to be ...

Vidar was maddening.

In one breath he was safety to me. I knew I was protected and secure by just being in the same vicinity as him. He would gaze at me with infinite love radiating from his being, that I could even feel it!

In the same breath he scared me. His willingness to kill and the thrill he seemed to gain from killing was terrifying. I remembered the sacrifice, all those years ago, as he murdered the thralls, dutifully hauling them into the air by their throats, his eyes had glinted with enjoyment, and a smile had curled his lips ...

That same trait also comforted me. He promised to kill Erhardt for me, and Vidar was a man of his word. If he saw to do something, he would do it at all costs. But there was always a shadow upon his words, a darkness I could feel.

Though I supported it, his plan to kill Erhardt frightened me, and his excitement scared me even more-so. I wondered whether my Christian upbringing was quietly rearing its ugly head – maybe deep down I feared for my soul?

Vidar was two minds caged in one body. He was a highly intelligent, sly, manipulative warrior and murderer, easily consumed by jealousy. Vidar was extremely faithful and committed to his family and his people. He was a seducer, and a tender, passionate, considerate lover.

Vidar had abandoned his womanising, flirtatious ways, solely devoted to me – he had not shared his wife's bed, nor any other bed, for four years, adamant that doing so would betray me.

Though I realised the joy that marrying Jan would have brought, I did not regret my choice – I did not regret my heart's choice. I loved Vidar. Every contradiction and every harmony; every danger and every safety; every smile and every tear. Vidar was flawed, he wasn't a perfect hero from tales I'd been told as a child. Vidar was flawed, he was human, he was Norse, he was mine.

Our souls were two halves made whole when we were together, and our hearts ached when we were apart. I was the naivety and innocence that balanced his experience and darkness. We were contrary forces, complementary and interdependent, giving rise to each other.

"We're ready." I peeped.

I covered my breast, and Sander's little lips smacked together happily as he dozed in my arms.

"Would you like me to attend you?" Burwenna asked as I rose from my chair.

"*Já*, please." I replied, turning to Elda. "Elda, please help Aaminah with anything she needs."

"Yes, Jarlkona." Elda smiled.

Elda, Burwenna and Aaminah had become very good friends. I would hear them bickering in hushed tones, when the delicate topic of religion arose among them, but otherwise, the three women were amicable and contented together.

Elda and Burwenna would gaze in awe at Aaminah as she prayed to her god. Aaminah would lay down a special mat and raise her hands, fold them over her chest, bend, prostrate and rise repeatedly, all whilst praying in her mysterious tongue. It was truly fascinating to watch, as though she were in a trance, so captured in her concentration.

"We'll return shortly." I said to Ursula as I walked past the lovesick puppy, her infatuated gaze following Jan across the room.

Jan held the door open for Burwenna and me, one of his large hands engulfing Young Birger's tiny hand. I nodded to Jan and smirked as I went by him.

"She seems to have quite a shine for you, Jötunnson." I commented.

"Are you jealous, my dear?" Jan winked.

"How does Vidar feel about his wife's affections for you?" I teased.

"He's quite pleased, actually. It keeps her away from pestering him, though she hasn't tried since that little *altercation* that happened between them, a few months ago. He's not fond of the woman; you know? Very resentful towards her. I feel sorry for her, trapped in a loveless marriage – and that bastard of a father of hers ... I don't think it hurts to show mercy." Jan explained casually.

"Altercation? What altercation?"

"That's not my place to tell, little lamb." Jan said lightly. "I'm sure Vidar will tell you soon enough."

"Nevertheless, you sound quite interested in her." I said, though inside I couldn't quell my curiosity over the mysterious 'altercation' between Vidar and Ursula.

"*Nei*," Jan replied, wrapping his arm around my shoulders. "Not at all. I'm just a kind, thoughtful young man I'll have you know."

We laughed together, striding down the dirt road away from the hall. We chattered meaningless conversation, teasing one another, speaking of what had transpired over the last year since we'd seen each other. Again, Jan glossed over the mysterious altercation. I tried hard to manipulate the conversation and trick him into sharing his little secret, but he would not budge, he would not tell.

We spent a short while glancing through the marketplace but found ourselves wandering to the shore. The briny tang of the fjord wafted over us pungently, with every calm breath of the blissfully cool breeze. The sun was blaring down upon us, and beads of sweat trickled down our foreheads and necks. I heard a quiet noise above us and gazed up towards the bright, beautiful sky. There, in the distance, I saw the black smudges of birds soaring high above.

"That damn bird follows me everywhere." I cursed and shook my head in disbelief.

"What bird?" Jan asked, squinting upwards and following my gaze.

"There is a raven blinded in one eye ... I see it frequently." I blushed, I felt stupid to admit I had a crippled bird stalking me.

"Maybe Odin has sent one of his ravens to watch over you?" Jan suggested, a smile played at his lips and his eyes twinkled.

"Oh yes, I'm sure the Allfather is incredibly interested in *me*." I scoffed. "Let us rest for a while. These boys are exhausting!"

I hoisted and rearranged the wriggly baby Sander, who watched his brother, eager but unable to play alongside him. Young Birger had spent his time climbing all over Jan, hanging from me or leaping around the shore with Burwenna at his heels, pausing every now and again to swipe shiny rocks from the muddy coastline.

"Let's sit over there." Jan suggested, grabbing Young Birger by the waist and heaving him up a grassy slope.

The emerald blades sparkled in the light, glittering from the tiny diamonds of sea spray scattered upon them. Jan found us a relatively dry spot and together we sat. Young Birger rambled down to the coastline again, picking up stones or racing the waves. Burwenna was by his side, playing and laughing along with the child.

Jan and I watched them, sat in comfortable silence but for the noise of Sander grabbing tufts of grass in his tiny little hands and ripping them out with all his might. He amused himself with this for a while, before he pulled at my dress, rooting for my breast.

"All this boy does is eat!" I complained, but really, I was glad of it.

Not long ago, Sander's lack of appetite had me fearing for his life. Now his rosy cheeks were plump, his small fingers were pudgy, and he yowled like a cat, impatient for his meal. He squirmed on my lap as I unpinned a strap from my apron dress and shuffled open the slit of my underdress. As I slipped my breast out Sander squealed happily, and I laughed as I lifted the hungry child to my swollen nipple.

"I think motherhood suits you." Jan commented as he watched me.

"I'm pleased to hear you say that." I smiled.

"You do have wonderful breasts!" He winked, a grin creeping across his face.

I laughed wholeheartedly and blushed fiercely at his comment.

"I'm assuming you didn't bring me, my children and my thrall here just so you could complement my breasts, Jan Jötunnson."

"*Nei*, though seeing your breast is definitely a highly appreciated addition to this little jaunt of ours." Jan grinned. "I brought you here to give you a message. Vidar asked me to meet with you since he won't have a chance to be alone with you until tomorrow ...

"The *blót* tomorrow … you must stay at the hall. As soon as Ursula and Erhardt have left your side, you must return to the hall as fast as you can. Vidar will meet you there as soon as he is able."

The seriousness of Jan's message destroyed the light-hearted atmosphere, bringing goosebumps to my flesh.

"What is he planning, Jan?" I whispered.

"The *blót* will begin as usual, but with Erhardt residing instead of Vidar. He and I will slip away as the ceremony begins and make sure you're at the hall. Keep the boys and the thralls there with you. Once we've been assured that you're safe, he and I will return to the *blót* in time for the sacrifice … and that's when Erhardt and his men will die."

***

I COULD HARDLY sleep that night. Again, Vidar's intense gaze stabbed through the dark, watching Erhardt take me, as he had every night since arriving in Roskilde. I was sure Erhardt felt Vidar's stare, too, and copulated with me nightly out of spite, rather than out of physical urge, pleasure or obsession to produce heirs.

Whatever the reason, this would be the last time that Erhardt would share my bed. That knowledge thrilled me, though the heavy cloud of guilt and fret hung over me, darkly. I had no doubt that Vidar's plan would succeed. What struck unease inside me was knowing Erhardt's blood, and the blood of all his men, would be on my hands as much as on Vidar's. Though I had killed many men in Roskilde's defence the night Aros had attacked, this felt different.

That night, I had killed to protect.

This was murder.

CHAPTER TWENTY-FOUR

"WAKE UP! NOW, woman!" Erhardt commanded, shaking me from my slumber.

Startled, my eyes shot open, and I gazed groggily at him.

"You've slept so long; you've almost missed breakfast." He reprimanded disapprovingly. "Come, you must ready yourself for the *blót*."

"Mmm, yes." I murmured, slowly sitting up in the bed.

Erhardt glared at me for a moment before leaving me alone in the room. I flung my feet off the bed and paused to rub my eyes. As I glanced at Burwenna, Elda and my sons' bed, I noticed that Elda and Young Birger were absent. I smiled warmly, however, at the sight that met my eyes: Burwenna and Sander were curled together happily snoozing away.

I rose and found my clothing, dressed quickly and took a brush through my hair. I heard Sander shuffle and squeak, signifying his awakening, and I turned and beamed at my darling son.

"*Góðan morgin* my little one!" I cheeped quietly, fluttering to him. I carefully scooped him up without waking Burwenna and cuddled him against me closely. "And what a good morning it is!"

Sander grinned and gurgled at me, grabbing for my breast.

"Hungry already, are you? You've slept so long, I'm sure you've quite the appetite." I giggled, unfastening my dress and slipping out my breast.

Milk had already begun to dribble from my nipple, which he engulfed ravenously. My mind drifted to Erhardt's doubts of Sander's survival ... I thought of his utter conviction that Sander would die. I remembered his attempts to ready me for the death of my 'weak' child ... Erhardt was wrong. With glee and satisfaction, I gazed at my son. He once refused to suckle but now sucked milk from my breast with gluttonous enthusiasm.

Sander was strong.

I supposed I should've thanked Erhardt – if he had not wiped oatmeal on my nipple, would Sander have latched? Or would he have starved to death like Erhardt was so convinced of? It did not matter. Sander was strong, Sander lived!

"*Góðan morgin!*" I announced as I strode into the main area of the house.

There I saw the thralls: Aaminah and Burwenna were spinning while Elda and Hilda cleaned – even the sight of Hilda did not spoil my mood. Young Birger was squealing and playing with his carved horse and man, and Ursula was sat at the table fiddling with the *hustrulinet* pinned to her hair.

"You are cheerful today." Ursula remarked. "Did you sleep well?"

"Very well!" I smiled. "Today will be a good day."

"I agree," she said, pleased with my unusual pleasant disposition towards her. "Today we celebrate Baldr, so a wonderful day it will certainly be."

"Baldr?" Young Birger peeped.

"*Já,* my love!" I exclaimed, sitting down and swooping him against me with one arm. "Today is *Midsumarblót*, we celebrate the god Baldr today. Baldr is the second son of the Allfather, Odin, and his wife, Frigg. He is the most treasured and beautiful of all the gods! The epitome of joy, innocence, and everything that is pure and uncorrupted."

Then it struck me, the irony of this day. Today Vidar planned to take Erhardt's life and the life of his supporters, on the day of Baldr, who, amongst many other things, was the god of peace ... I didn't know whether to laugh, or fear the possible impending wrath of the gods ...

"Vidar and Erhardt left a little while ago." Ursula explained cordially, sitting beside me. "I plan on meeting Niklas soon, so we can walk with my father and husband to the ritual grounds. I didn't want you to be alone when you awoke, however."

"I appreciate that." I said, sincerely surprised.

At first Ursula had struck me exactly as I'd expected, she was self-righteous and disapproving of my heritage. She had been smug and spiteful, but why wouldn't she? She had married my former betrothed. I'd been so hateful and resentful towards her and had taken immense pleasure from her troubles with Vidar ... But the simple-minded Ursula had soon softened towards me. She had come to respect my role as her stepmother and confided in me her troubles. I almost felt guilty at the revolt Vidar had planned. Almost.

"I'll be taking Aaminah and Hilda with me," she continued. "Would you and my brothers care to join me?"

"*Já!*" Young Birger grinned, climbing on to her lap.

"Actually, no." I corrected firmly. "We will make our way there in a short while, I have a few things I'd like to take care of first."

"I go with Ursula?" Young Birger begged.

"You will stay with me." I chided. "Elda, Burwenna, please prepare a bath for Young Birger."

The small boy began to cry and whine angrily. Burwenna whisked him up, scolding him under her breath as she forced him to the garden.

"Oh, what I would do to have a child." Ursula sighed, watching Young Birger disappear outside with the thralls.

"You and – how are you and–" I spluttered awkwardly.

"I try to please him, but I've long since given up on taking him to my bed." Ursula admitted softly, her tear-filled eyes staring at the tabletop. "I fear I'll have to divorce him; I know my father would not approve ... but–"

"Do not think of your father." I interrupted sternly, before adding encouragingly, "Your husband has refused to go to bed with you in all the years you've been married. That is a fair and just ground for divorce!"

"I know." Ursula whispered, her voice drifting. "One day you'll realise why this union between Vidar, and I had to happen ... Aaminah, Hilda, come."

I watched her hurriedly make her way to the door, wondering what on earth she meant. Hilda quickly stood beside her mistress and Aaminah slipped in from the garden, her hands wet, perspiration dotting her forehead.

"Are you sure you wouldn't like to join me?" Ursula offered again. "I could wait a *little* longer."

"Oh, I would, but I have to bathe the boys and myself, we will take much too long, I wouldn't want to interfere with your arrangement." I stuttered, snapping out of my thoughts. "But, please, one moment, could I borrow Aaminah?"

Aaminah paused, looking from Ursula to me. Hilda glowered silently.

"Of course." Ursula smiled.

I beckoned the thrall to me and led her to the garden. The moment we'd stepped foot outside, out of Ursula's earshot, I gave Sander to Elda and grabbed Aaminah's hand, pulling her close to me.

"When you have the chance, come back to the hall." I whispered, watching the doorway carefully.

Aaminah looked at me confused, opening her mouth slowly.

"Don't question me." I ordered in urgent, hushed tones. "The moment you can slip away, do so! You must be back before the ceremony begins."

"Yes, Jarlkona." She replied, puzzled.

"Don't speak a word of this warning, just heed it." I commanded. "*Please*! Return to me as fast as you can."

"Yes, Jarlkona." Aaminah repeated, her voice was stronger this time. "I will."

"Thank you!" I whispered, placing a quick kiss on her hand.

Aaminah was shocked and exceptionally confused, as were Elda and Burwenna, but none of them questioned me. I stepped back into the hall and Aaminah slowly followed behind.

"Would you like her to help you with your *hustrulinet* before we go?" Ursula suggested considerately.

"*Nei, pakka*, I'm fine. I don't think I'll be wearing it today." I answered quickly, holding the door open for them. Before the quizzical Ursula could say another word, I began closing the door on them, catching Aaminah's gaze. "We will see you in a little while."

And they were gone.

I leaned against the door, breathing deeply. Midday was not a long way off, and the town had begun assembling on the streets, awaiting the procession that was led by the musicians, Vidar, and

Erhardt. The townsfolk would take their places in the procession and march towards the forest. At midday, Vidar's plan would begin.

"Jarlkona, may I ask … why must Aaminah return so quickly?" Burwenna said, meekly appearing in the doorway.

"You'll know when it happens. You're safe here, with me, and I want her to be, too." I answered obscurely. "For now, it's best you don't know. Anyway, we must bathe the children."

I strode passed the bewildered girl and retrieved Sander from Elda. I thanked her quietly, as she stared at me questioningly for a few moments, before fetching another bucket of water from the well. Young Birger was standing naked by the tub which was filled only a few inches with cold water, while a pot bubbled over the fire. He shivered, glaring at me, still furious that I wouldn't let him go with Ursula.

"My child, you may look at me like that all you want, it won't change a thing." I scolded, but added softly, "You'll see Ursula later."

Young Birger wasn't pleased with my answer, but soon forgot it as Elda poured another icy blast of water into the tub, spraying him. He squealed loudly, but was somewhat relieved when Burwenna waddled over carefully, a steaming pot of boiled water clutched in her hands. She slowly poured it into the tub.

"There, that should take the bite off." Burwenna smiled. "Climb in the tub now, Birger."

***

MY SONS AND I had been bathed, dried and dressed in fresh clothing by the time Vidar and Jan arrived. Sander was napping in Elda's arms and Young Birger had settled down to play as Burwenna and I spun. The moment Young Birger saw Vidar he leapt to his feet.

"Vidar!" He exclaimed, rushing and hurling himself at him. "Come play!"

"My boy!" Vidar grinned, just as excited as the child in his arms. "Unfortunately, I do not have much time, and I must talk to your mother."

He set Young Birger down and noticed the disappointment on his face.

"Don't worry, my son, I will play with you later." Vidar promised, his voice soft and earnest. "Let me speak with your *móðir*, first."

"I'll play with you," Jan offered, beaming at the boy who readily accepted his offer.

When Vidar referred to Young Birger as his son, I glanced at him, alarmed. Vidar's paternity of the boys was still a well-kept secret; I was shocked to hear him speak such a risky phrase to Young Birger. At the same time, butterflies whisked around my stomach, I was so delighted to hear him speak those words aloud, even if it was just a passing phrase to soothe a saddened child.

"What is happening?" I asked, slightly concerned, as Vidar approached me.

Vidar snatched my hands to his lips, unleashing a flurry of kisses upon them before pulling me against him. I giggled softly as he placed my hands onto his shoulders and wrapped his arms around me, pulling me in to a voracious kiss.

"The *blót* is underway, so we have only a short time to be together. I thought we could make the most of it." Vidar winked.

I laughed and kissed him as we stumbled to the sleeping area, so focused on the taste of each other and the freedom of being together in his hall, without being sneaky or secretive. We crashed upon his bed, ripping and tearing clothes from each other's bodies, gusts of fabric hurtling across the room as we carelessly threw them aside.

Vidar knelt between my legs as I laid beneath him in the centre of the bed, my arms snaked around his neck. The soft graze of his beard against my face, the gentleness of his lips against mine, the warmth of his flesh pressed against my naked body … God, how I'd yearned for these sensations!

Vidar rose abruptly, staring at me for a fleeting moment of silence.

"What's wrong?" I whispered.

"This is how it was always meant to be." Vidar replied quietly, triumphantly, his smile growing. "And now it has happened, I'm finally sharing my bed with my true wife."

I blushed heavily, beaming at him. Vidar lowered himself upon me and kissed me deeply. Gradually his lips left mine, trailing down my jaw, down my neck, kissing along my collarbone. I squeezed my eyes shut and ran my fingertips over his sides, sliding my hands up his arched back, over his broad shoulder blades.

Vidar slipped further down, his legs between mine, his upper body rested on me, the heat of his flesh pressed against mine. He cupped my breasts in his hands, licking my nipples in turn, with short, quick lashes of his tongue, before settling on one and sucking it tenderly. He gently rolled my other nipple with his thumb and squeezed the small globe of my breast.

I felt his warm breath dance upon me, the flicking of Vidar's tongue on the tip of my nipple, encased in his mouth. Tingling explosions radiated through my body; my breathing quickened. Vidar turned to my other breast, sucking, licking; squeezing the other and brushing his thumb over my saliva-dampened nipple.

Quietly I gasped, sensation permeating through my body. With a *smack* of his lips, Vidar looked up and smirked, kissing the tender flesh between my breasts and lowering himself even further down my body. All the while, his soft beard swept over my skin as he placed a trail of kisses and nibbles over my ribs, my stomach, my hips, inching his body further off mine, until all that remained was his head between my legs.

My knees were bent over Vidar's shoulders and his hands were wrapped around them, gripping them open. Vidar shot me another smirk, his icy blue eyes twinkling.

Sharply Vidar flicked his tongue over the soft pink folds between my legs, twice, three times; my body jerked uncontrollably with each lash of his tongue. Vidar stopped, snickered under his breath, then slid his smooth, flat wet tongue over me, applying a slight pressure. He pressed his mouth against me and glided his tongue over me in a continual gentle motion, delicately sucking, lapping me like waves on the shore.

Vidar was patient, the movement of his tongue was constant, with every stroke ripples of euphoria rushed through me, growing into a crescendo that crashed through me from between my legs to the tips of my fingers and toes. I gasped, overcome by the bliss that surged through me.

Victoriously, Vidar rose and crawled upwards, wiping my wetness and his saliva from his mouth with the back of his hand. He pressed a passionate kiss upon me, and I kissed him back with fervour, the tantalising scent of soap and musk filling my nostrils. I shuffled upwards, tried to rise to my knees, but he wouldn't let me.

"What are you doing, little fawn?" Vidar whispered.

"It's my turn." I replied huskily.

Vidar allowed me to push him onto the bed, allowed me to straddle him, our kiss virtually uninterrupted. I slid my body down him, but he lifted his knee and blocked me.

"*Nei*, I want to be inside you." Vidar said in a hushed, eager tone.

I smiled as I shifted and eased myself onto him until he filled me. A muffled moan rolled from Vidar's lips and he arched his back in pleasure. He grabbed my breasts in his large hands, my nipples lightly pinched between his thumb and forefinger. I pushed against his pectorals, gradually gaining speed as I steadily rode him, feeling him so deeply inside me.

I gasped, panting, heart racing. Vidar slapped his hands upon my thighs, gripping tightly, his body twitching, his pelvis jolting from his euphoria. With every jerk of his body, his cock throbbed inside me as he unleashed his satisfaction, I cried out, unable to stop myself, his sudden lurches sending pulses of pleasure through me.

Finally, Vidar's body calmed, and together we panted, catching our breath, hearts pounding. I collapsed beside him on the bed, one of his arms under my neck, my flesh drenched with perspiration. I pressed my buttocks against him and rolled onto his side and brought his other arm over me, holding me against him.

We were silent, tranquil, *happy!*

"I have to leave soon." Vidar said softly.

"Please, just a few moments more."

He kissed my shoulder and squeezed me briefly. We laid in silence for a while before I interrupted our peace.

"Vidar ... what 'altercation' happened between you and Ursula?" I asked quietly.

"*Altercation?*" Vidar pondered for a moment. "Ah …"

Vidar paused, stroking me gently with the tips of his fingers, and a deep sigh rolled from his lips.

"I raped Ursula."

"What?" I cried out.

I leapt up in the bed and glared at Vidar, shocked, appalled, sickened. I hadn't expected to hear those words come from Vidar's lips.

Vidar gazed at me, still, silent. I couldn't read his expression. My heart was racing painfully in my chest and bile was caught in my throat. My hands shook as I pulled the sheet over me, covering my naked body from Vidar's view.

"Aveline—" Vidar reached out for me.

"Don't touch me." I snapped. "What happened to *not supporting rape* or *only take a willing woman to your bed*?"

"I was mad." Vidar replied nonchalantly.

"*What?!*"

"Aveline, when I returned to Roskilde and Freydis told me what happened, and what was yet to come, I was furious. I had half a mind to burn Roskilde to the ground myself! I agreed to marry Erhardt's daughter, only to give myself time to think of a plan." Vidar explained, eerily calm. "I refused to take her to my bed, even on our wedding night. I was betrothed to *you*, and I honoured that commitment thoroughly.

"Every day she tried to seduce me. She would flaunt herself; she would plead and beg; she would try to ply me with mead to warm me to her … but I refused. She demanded to know whether I was taking other women, and I told her I was not – there was only *one* woman I would take to my bed, and she wasn't in Roskilde anymore.

"When she and I returned to Roskilde a year ago, she had grown more desperate. One night, she stood blocking the bedroom door, uttering the same rant yet again. '*Do you not want any children? Do you not want an heir?*'" With a whining tone he mockingly imitated Ursula's voice. "As she spoke, I held onto the back of a chair and didn't say a word to her, waiting for her to give up, but the stupid woman wouldn't shut up! She was as exasperated by me as I was by her ... but this time, she finally went too far. '*What will it take for you to share my bed?*' she screamed at me, '*Do you need a man's tending to make your cock stand?*'."

Vidar paused and laughed bitterly, rubbing his eyes with one hand.

"Ah, if only she had stopped talking! If only she had shut her mouth! She accused me of being *argr* – for that slander I should've killed her where she stood! But I knew if I'd killed her, I would've sentenced you to death ... But I couldn't do nothing, otherwise I would've proven her right – a man could be outlawed for not retaliating to such an insult!"

I stared at Vidar wordlessly. Erhardt had said the same thing to me when I had called him an '*argr* dog' ... just as Vidar had raped Ursula as punishment, so had Erhardt brutally raped me ...

"'*Your Danethrall isn't here anymore! You're my husband and you need to act like it – otherwise I'll tell my father and he'll kill your Danethrall and destroy Roskilde!*'" Vidar continued quoting Ursula in that mocking tone. "When she said that, I finally realised that there was only one weapon that I had.

"I smashed the chair against the wall and lunged at her. I grabbed her by her throat and told her that Roskilde could burn for all I cared, she would never be my wife. Only my *Danethrall* could fill my bed, only my *Danethrall* could fill my heart ...

"In fury and wrath, I tore her clothing from her, I told her if she wanted me to lay with her so badly, then I would, then I threw her to the ground." Vidar rubbed his eyes again, a pained smile twisting his lips as they opened and closed – he was struggling to continue. "She was my enemy – the daughter of my enemy. She had insulted me in the worst possible way.

"Her father robbed me of you, and she tried to rob me of my honour! ... She accused me of *argr* because I refused to enjoy her body. In madness, so crazed by fury, I told her that she'd been wanting me to share her bed for so long, I would finally take her and prove her accusation wrong.

"She was so afraid ... she begged me to stop, *she had changed her mind, she was sorry* ... I ignored her. As I raped her, I told her that if I couldn't have my Danethrall as my wife, then I would never be anyone else's husband ... I could never love anyone but you. She couldn't hear me, she just screamed and cried ...

"I couldn't stand being inside her any longer; I took her out of rage, not out of passion. I could not even spill my seed; I was so infuriated by her! A blessing really, I did not want a child borne from her."

Vidar sighed deeply. I watched him, he was as still as a statue, even the rise and fall of his chest as he breathed was faint. He stared at the blanket, and in his glassy stare I could tell he was reliving that night in his mind. Slowly I stepped towards the bed and sat on the edge, my back turned to him.

"I have never cared for the rape of women – thralls or foreigners from raids ... After I saw that wolf in Aros rape you – seeing your fear, seeing your hopelessness – I could see him break you with every movement he made ... It seemed almost worse than killing you ... I thought I could never do that to a woman.

"But she ... I wanted to break her. I wanted to shatter her ... I should've killed her for what she called me, but I couldn't risk Erhardt killing you in retaliation, Aveline. He had stationed too many of his men in Roskilde – he would've heard I'd killed his daughter and he would've slain you in vengeance faster than I could slay his men. I am not ashamed for giving up my moralities and raping her ... It was all I could do in retribution for her accusation without risking your life."

Tears cascaded down my cheeks, I threw myself into his arms, clutching him tightly. His revelation alarmed me – I, too, did not think that Vidar could be capable of such an act ... but he *was* a Norseman. Norsemen raped – even the sweet, charming, enigmatic Jan had fathered children with thralls he had raped.

Norsemen raped, pillaged, raided and killed ... It was a fact I had struggled to come to terms within my years of living in Roskilde. How could I love a people who lived such a sinful, murderous way of life? But I did love them. Alvar, Freydis, Birger, Jan, Vidar ... they were mine.

I had never believed that Vidar could be capable of such an act, but my life in Aros had shown me that even I was capable of doing the unthinkable. In the years of our separation, we had both been forced to do whatever it took to survive. Shamefully, I had used sex as a tool to control Erhardt – to save myself from beatings and rape. I had given my body to Erhardt countless times, I had pleasured him. I had betrayed Vidar just to survive.

Vidar had risked his honour; he had stayed true to me for as long as he could. When Ursula accused him of *argr* Vidar had the right to kill her with legal impunity – but he didn't. His hands had been tied! Vidar had risked so much by not killing her for such an insult but did so to save me. I was more important to him than his morals, more important to him than his honour.

Vidar was flawed, he was human, he was Norse, he was mine.

"But ... I shamed myself Aveline ... I killed that wolf in Aros for what he did to you – and it sickened me to know that I had become just like him ..."

"You're nothing like him, Vidar." I whispered, kissing him gently. "You never will be. You're mine, *my mighty Ullr*! I love you."

Vidar smiled and laughed sincerely. He bent his head down to mine and kissed me tenderly on the lips.

"And I love you, my little fawn."

A high-pitched scream erupted through the room.

I leapt up in the bed and stared at the doorway – there stood Ursula, pale as winter's snow, engulfed in horror. Jan stood panicked, gripping her shoulder, and smirking victoriously beside Ursula was Hilda. I glanced between their faces, alarmed – I tried to flee the bed, all I wanted was to dress and run, but Vidar pushed me down and leapt over me.

"I told you!" Roared Hilda. "I told you they were scheming behind your back!"

"What in the gods' names did you do?" Ursula bawled, her whole body shuddered. "What did you do?!"

Vidar said nothing.

His every movement was swift and precise. It took him only a few strides, and he was before her. With one great sweep of his hand Vidar grabbed an axe that leaned against a chest next to the door, brought it high over his head and, with a glint of steel, Vidar buried the axe into his screaming wife's head. A deep *crack!*, a sharp gasp, and Ursula dropped to the floor.

The room was stunned, still and mute; the very air seemed to congeal and tasted like death.

Vidar stood over Ursula's body silently for a moment. He grabbed the axe's handle. Ursula's body twitched and flopped limply as he wrenched the axe from her skull. Vidar knelt beside her corpse, laying the axe on the floor. Scarlet poured from the wound that split her head, rushing like a flooded stream, spilling over the expression of appalled shock frozen to her face; drenching her clothes. Vidar reached out a steady hand and closed her eyelids, calm in his retribution.

Hilda screeched in horror, shattering the silence. She was rooted to the spot, ashen in terror, her eyes bulging from their sockets. I flinched at the thrall's fearful scream, but my eyes only rested on her for a moment, before darting back to Ursula's body.

"What did you do?" I gasped, sitting on the edge of the bed, sickeningly echoing the last words of his wife.

"It's begun." Vidar replied coolly, scooping his clothes from the floor and hurriedly dressing.

Hilda suddenly lunged towards the door, but Jan caught her and raised the flailing thrall off her feet. She kicked and shrieked, writhing in his arms.

"You will all burn in the lake of fire and brimstone for the rest of eternity!" Hilda screeched. "*And if he smites him with an instrument of iron, so that he dies, he is a murderer: the murderer shall surely be put to death!*"

Hilda continued to damn us; her shrill cries pierced the air and throbbed inside my brain agonisingly. Her noise was overwhelming! My head spun – her voice resounded in my brain – she blared so loudly, I could hardly make sense of anything!

"God will deliver you all to your enemy for your villainous ways, and your punishment will be death at Erhardt Ketilsson's hand!" Hilda thundered.

I leapt from the bed and lunged at the howling thrall. She released another hideous screech, and I ripped the utility knife from Jan's belt and thrust it into her stomach.

"Here is the vengeance I vowed upon you all those years ago!" I hissed.

Hilda glanced at the knife then stared at me, stunned. Her body convulse, and the colour drained from her face. Consumed by rage, I brought my face inches from hers to watch the life fade from her. My fist trembled, wrapped around the hilt of the knife, but I kept the weapon firmly within her, remorseless.

"Adulteress! Murderess! The fiery wrath of vengeance will hail upon you, Babylonian harlot, and upon your godless fiend of a lover!" Hilda raged, spitting in my face. "Just as Sodom and Gomorrah, you will suffer eternal fire!"

Her spittle dribbled down my face, but I ignored it.

"*Knowest thou … the rejoicing of the wicked is short, and the joy of the hypocrites is but a moment.*" I whispered.

I twisted the knife and shoved it deeper inside her. She gurgled as blood oozed from her mouth, pouring down her chin, but she continued to glare at me with loathing until her last struggling breath ebbed from her lips. Hilda began to suffocate on the mass of blood in her throat; she choked upon it, spraying my face, until the glare of her soul dimmed from her eyes, and, at last, it was gone.

I pulled the knife from the thrall and tossed it to the ground. I staggered back to Vidar's bed and slumped down upon it. Vidar looked quickly to Jan, who nodded to him. He tossed Hilda's corpse upon my sons' bed, before turning his back on us and rushing away. Silently, Vidar pulled Ursula's body from the ground and threw it atop Hilda's corpse.

Bile rose into my throat and I struggled to swallow it down. Vidar strode to me, knelt between my legs and kissed my knees.

"It's time to free us, little fawn." Vidar said, staring me in the eyes with urgency and determination. "It's time to kill Erhardt. Jötunnson told you the plan, *já?*"

"*Já* …" I muttered meekly.

"Will you stay here?"

"*Já.*"

"I'll leave you a sword, a bow and a quiver full of arrows."

"I'll keep our sons safe."

"I know you will." Vidar said warmly.

He placed his right hand on my jaw, slick with Ursula's blood, and pressed a kiss against my forehead before he rushed to the doorway.

"Vidar!" I called out.

"*Já?*" Vidar replied, sticking his head through the doorway.

"You didn't tell me you were going to kill Ursula." I said weakly.

"You didn't tell me you were going to kill Hilda." Vidar answered, the smirk returning to his face.

"It was all I could think to do."

"Killing her was all *I* could think to do, I can't marry you if my wife lives." Vidar replied.

"She was considering divorcing you."

"Well, now she doesn't have to." Vidar said flippantly, moving into the room and staring at me, perplexed. "I love you, Aveline. I told you I'd kill *all* Erhardt's kin and followers. She was one of them. Do you regret this plan? You know it's too late to back out, now?"

I shook my head vigorously.

"*Nei, nei, nei!*" I gasped, gazing up at him, my eyebrows furrowed. "I have spilled blood for us now, too. I was just ... shocked. A lot of secrets have been revealed tonight and – and ... I'm with you until the end, Vidar Alvarsson. But don't surprise me again. We vowed never to keep secrets from one another, don't hide things from me again."

"Never again." Vidar approached me and placed a warm kiss upon my lips. "You're shaking." He whispered.

"I've never stabbed someone before." I said.

"It gets easier with time." Vidar soothed, stroking my hair. "I wish I had time to comfort you, little fawn–"

I rose from the bed, quickly found my dress and hauled it over my head.

"I'm fine." I said as I smoothed the garment down over my thighs. "Let's slay Erhardt and the rest of his people."

"*Já*, let's." Vidar grinned excitedly, kissing me yet again, before he dashed through the hall after Jan.

CHAPTER TWENTY-FIVE

"WHAT'S GOING ON?" Begged Aaminah as I rushed into the main room, my hand dripping with blood.

"Your mistress is no longer Jarlkona of Roskilde: she's dead." I answered, every word, every syllable, was precise and firm. "As is Hilda. Vidar and Jan are going to kill Erhardt. We're to stay here and wait for their return. I need you to keep the boys safe – *stay inside!*"

Her jaw dropped. I heard gasps from Burwenna and Elda from the other side of the room. I didn't bother to face them, maintaining fixed eye contact with Aaminah, whose face had lost all colour.

"You are safe, *we* are safe." I reassured.

We were safe.

The roar of the attack had not begun, all the townsfolk were still at the forest celebrating the god Baldr, making their sacrifices. It would be awhile before we would hear the battle, the cries, the dull *clink* of metal on metal, the heavy thud of an axe as it pounded against a wooden shield, the deep *crack* of skulls caving in or the wet rip of flesh being slashed … if we'd even hear anything at all.

We waited.

Burwenna occupied herself with snuggling or playing with Young Birger. Elda and Aaminah busied their shaking hands with cleaning, and I spun wool, maintaining a strong, calm and stable composure, whilst inside I was drowning in fear and anxiety. The shock on Ursula's dead face and the rage upon Hilda's both glared at me as I worked. Sander slept soundly on a bench, snuggled into soft furs, not a care in the world. His face was the epitome of innocence and peace, he had no idea that the world around him was quickly slipping into chaos.

As time went by my baby woke and I held him tightly in my arms as he nursed from my breast. My eyes darted between the faces that surrounded me and I wondered whether the hall was the safest place ... I wondered how many of Erhardt's followers and supporters were hidden in Roskilde, and whether I should've taken my thralls and my children elsewhere. But where? No, we were safe where we were. We'd be fine.

We heard noise.

Deep, dull, distant noise. But it was rising, it was loud! Alert and afraid, like rabbits in an open meadow hearing the crunching of grass from a fox nearby, the thralls and my ears pricked and keenly we listened, eyes wide, mouths drawn identically into tight, anxious frowns.

The noise was constant, varying slightly in rhythm, with one huge eruption of raucousness, followed again by the deep, dull drone.

Suddenly we realised, with panicked glances passing between us, that the noise was nearing ever closer, close enough that I could distinguish it to be human voices, but far enough away that I could not recognise what they were saying.

"Do you think ... it's victory?" Elda questioned nervously.

"I hope so." I whispered back, staring at the closed door.

The thunderous voices had reached the walls of Roskilde. I could hear the horns and drums and bone flutes, slicing through the air in their haunting tune. The song – prayers to the gods and goddesses, songs of praise celebrating Baldr! The steady thump of the march as the townspeople steadily strode through the streets in strict, meticulous order.

"My wife!" Roared Vidar triumphantly, bursting through the door.

The thralls and I leapt out of our skins at his arrival. He was covered from head to toe in blood, his fair hair was scarlet, his body dripped, his flesh was red, so saturated in blood was he. Only his light blue eyes shone from the crimson, they sparkled with glory, mischievousness and dark glee.

I rushed to him.

Standing before me was a devil sprung from the depths of hell, but I ran to him. I soared into his arms, flung mine around his neck and plunged a deep, impassioned kiss upon him. Vidar returned my kiss, just as fiery, just as zealous, just as crazed. I tasted the thick metallic flavour of blood as it smudged against my face, onto my lips, upon my tongue. The sickly-sweet scent filled my nostrils and my head spun, drunk on the smell and the adrenalin that pumped through my body.

"You killed him?" I gasped, giddy with excitement.

"His retainers and kin, too!" Vidar grinned wildly.

"You must wash," Jan interrupted, slipping through the door behind Vidar, pressing his hand onto his friend's shoulder. "Your appearance is alarming the children."

I turned to my sons, seeing their little quaking bodies and pale faces. I released Vidar and took a few steps closer to the boys but paused when I noticed my gown. I was covered in blood imprinted upon me from Vidar and my embrace. Quickly I began pulling the outer dress off, wiping my hands with the fabric.

"Elda, Burwenna, run a bath for Vidar." I commanded, hurriedly. "Sander, Birger, come my children."

Burwenna brought Sander to me, putting the baby into my arms. I held him tightly, kissing his soft round cheeks, gently. Birger reached up to me, gripping my skirt in his little fists.

"*Mumie?*" Young Birger said, his big blue eyes gazing up at me.

"Son," Vidar said.

Vidar knelt on the ground and took Young Birger's hand and pulled the boy to him.

"*Nei!*" Young Birger exclaimed, attempting to pull away from Vidar's grip.

"There's nothing to fear, child." Vidar continued, his voice steady and firm, his hand still grasping the boy's skinny wrist. "The blood that covers me is an offering to the gods, this came from the lives of beasts we have sacrificed in their honour. The gods have aided us, me, you, your beloved mother and brother."

Young Birger stopped tugging away from Vidar. He stared at Vidar with his big, glittering eyes, listening to every word of his explanation. Vidar lightened his hold on the child's arm, softened his gaze, a small kind smile etched upon his blood-stained face.

"Today is *Midsumarblót*. You know, the blessed god Baldr was slain around this time, a long time ago, a grievous blow to the Æsir

... But they recovered, they continued to live their lives, as will we. Remember that, my son. The gods recovered, as will we." Vidar brought Young Birger against him, held him close and kissed the top of his head, tenderly, smudging our son's fair hair with red.

The celebration was well under way outside, music resonated through the air, harmonised with voices and laughter. As time went by the delectable scent of food began wafting through the crevasses of the hall, intermingled with the thick, pungent, bitter smell of smoke from the many bonfires. All the while, Vidar bathed, I changed and washed the blood from Young Birger's hair. The poor child still didn't know that the man he had called father was dead.

There was a strange sense of calm that had settled inside the hall. Jan had removed the two women's corpses earlier, presumably he had taken them to the ritual hall to burn alongside the other bodies on the pyre. The thralls and I had not spoken of the deaths, of the murders of Erhardt and Ursula and their people. Nor was any word uttered regarding Hilda's death.

There was a sort of freedom that had come from Vidar's shocking, bloody entrance and his crazed announcement. Elda and Burwenna would not return to Aros – they were finally free from the dark memories of Estrith's murder and the abuse they'd suffered there.

I carried Sander, who giggled and wriggled in my arms, outside. The sun glared down upon us, the radiant blue of the sky stretched out, unblemished, as far as the eye could see. It was, indeed, a beautiful day.

Before me I saw Vidar, eyes closed and head back, relaxing in the tub. He had rinsed Erhardt's blood from his body and now sat in fresh waters, but his skin and hair still held unusual rosy hues. I watched him for a few moments, gazing at the droplets sprinkled across his gorgeous flesh, the white reflection of the sun pooled around him on the face of the water. He was stone still, but for the slow rise and fall of his chest and the subtle dancing of his beard and mustachio hairs from the steady waft of his breathing.

"Elda, please take Sander inside." I asked, as she brought a bucket of water outside.

She did as she was told, leaving me alone in the garden with Vidar. He turned and beamed at me, eyes squinting slightly from the brightness of the sun.

"Are you going to tell me what happened?" I asked as I knelt beside him.

A deep purr resonated from his throat as I ran my hands through his slick, wet hair. I took the bar of soap from the ground beside the tub and rolled it between my hands, bubbles and suds quickly covering my hands. I began scrubbing his hair gently with the suds while I waited for him to reply.

"Of course, I will. Where would you like me to start?" Vidar replied, peacefully.

"From when you left the hall." I pressed, rolling my eyes at his casual, relaxed attitude.

"Well, when we left the hall, Jan and I ran to the forest. When we arrived, I slunk back to my spot behind Erhardt whilst Jan took his place with the other men. He nodded to them, the signal to confirm our plan, as Erhardt finished speaking. Your darling husband looked like a fat pig on its hind legs, puffed up and red in the face." Vidar snorted.

I smacked him on the forehead, angrily.

"Stop referring to him as my 'darling husband'." I snapped. "Get on with your explanation."

"Calm yourself, little fawn, I'm only teasing." Vidar laughed. He glanced at me, spotted the seriousness on my face, briefly cleared his throat and continued. "Anyway, instead of the animals being led to the nooses, his men were grabbed and thrust towards them. Niklas was first ... Erhardt had begun to shout, but I leapt upon him and held him tight. I made him watch as Niklas was pulled into the tree, then each of his other men in turn until they were all lifeless, hanging from the branches.

"Erhardt was howling by then, writhing in my arms; quickly I pulled my knife from my side and pressed it against his throat. He twisted around and faced me, hissing all sorts of empty threats and begging pleas while Jan completed the final prayer to the gods. Then I slit Erhardt's throat as he stared me in the eye, watching his life rush away as his blood sprayed over me." There was a maddened glint in Vidar's eyes as memory flickered across his vision.

"Then what?" I whispered, no longer soaping his hair.

"Then the *blót* continued as usual, our sacrifices were made, our thanks given, then we returned to town." Vidar finished, anticlimactically, shrugging his shoulders and shutting his eyes.

I pulled my hands through his hair again, gently scrubbing his scalp with my fingertips.

"And the bodies will be burned on the pyre?"

"*Já.* Would you like to pay your last respects to your husband?" His voice was soft and prickly.

"I'm washing the hair of my *husband*; I just have yet to marry him." I answered, tugging roughly on a lock of his hair.

Vidar turned and gazed at me, taking my face in his damp, sweet smelling hands.

"You don't regret a thing?" Vidar asked, examining my expression desperately.

"The only thing I regret," I smiled, kissing him softly. "Is not having wed you yet. But I am truly thankful that now I finally have my chance to."

Vidar beamed and kissed me.

"Now turn around so I can rinse your hair."

***

"LET ME HOLD my son." Vidar said, quietly, from behind me.

I had left his side after washing his hair, hearing Sander's cry. Elda had given my son to me, who cheered up quickly upon seeing me. I had nursed him and danced with him around the table, singing quietly in a soft, out of tune whisper. It had been a while until Vidar had returned inside, dressed, dried and clean, the strong scent of the soap radiating from him.

"You love to sneak up on me, don't you?" I smiled, turning and carefully giving him the happy baby.

"You once compared me to Ullr the mighty hunter, remember?" Vidar winked, grinning at Sander who had immediately began pulling Vidar's beard. "And you are my little fawn."

Rising onto my tiptoes, I kissed him.

"Come here." I ordered softly, taking Vidar's hand and pulling him towards the table.

I pushed him down into a chair, Sander still in his arms. He set the boy onto the tabletop and pulled silly faces at him while I swept across the room, taking a comb from the cupboard. I stood behind him, carefully pulling his damp hair behind his ears, so it fell, sleekly, down his back. Gingerly I drew the horn carved comb through Vidar's hair. He straightened his posture, shoulders back and head high, pleasurably enjoying my outward show of tenderness and affection.

"You washed my hair, and now you comb it, you are spoiling me." Vidar commented, delightedly.

I smiled smugly in reply, carefully tugging and pulling snares and tangles from his beautiful locks. After a time, I managed to plait the long golden lengths of hair from his face and tied it with a thin strip of leather.

The stubble on the back and sides of his head was longer than he usually kept it, but there wouldn't be time to shave it. As acting Jarl of Roskilde, Vidar needed to show his face at the celebration soon, I was sure the townsfolk were waiting with bated breath to hear Vidar's explanation as to why he'd just struck war upon Aros.

He rose from the table after I'd finished his hair, kissed me gently on the forehead, then beckoned all in the hall to heed him.

"It's time." Vidar said simply, his lips twisted into an excited smirk, eyes glittering cerulean and silver.

Vidar still held Sander in his arms, and I brought Young Birger to my side, holding his hand tightly. Aaminah held the door open for us and together, Vidar, Sander, Young Birger and I stepped into the streets, ready to reveal our family unit to the world, our thrall girls following, timidly, behind us.

"Are we all enjoying the celebration?" Vidar bellowed, joyfully, gazing upon all the townsfolk that covered the bay of Roskilde Fjord.

Not too far from us laid the almost phallic shaped maypole. Beautiful women and sweet young girls piled various brightly coloured flowers, vines and other decorations to adorn the pole after it had been raised. I smiled, looking at the wives with their white veils and headdresses pinned to their heads, and the young maidens with flowers crowning their long hair that fell down their shoulders and backs. The flower crowns signified their readiness to wed – today there would be much discussion of marriage, and a lot of deliberation over contracts.

Bonfires burned: men stood laughing and drinking beside mountains of sticks and twigs sat near large stone circled pits, whilst small children dashed around with arms full of bundles of kindling and baskets of tinder.

I spotted a gaggle of married women sitting on the grassy banks beside a bale of straw, giggling and gossiping as they created corn dollies to hand to the children, ready for them to burn later in the evening. Happiness rippled through the crowds of people, like the gently sloshing waters of the fjord. There was not a sad face that I could see.

When Vidar had announced our arrival, the many faces stared at us, cheering and roaring with delight at the sight of Alvar's son. One man, however, stared at me and my sons with surprise and confusion.

"You have the pig's wife and children in your arms, Jarl Vidar?" He exclaimed, supported by a few grunts of sceptical celebrators.

"Aveline Birgersdóttir has been betrothed to me for many years, Rikulf." Vidar replied. "And these boys are my sons."

Vidar released my hand and scooped Young Birger up, now holding both the boys in his arms. He strode towards the man, Rikulf, smirking at him.

"Look at these boys faces; which man do you see in them? Erhardt or me? You truly believe that old swine could suddenly conceive two sons, in just as many years?" A wave of snickering laughter washed through the crowds, Rikulf couldn't help but grin. "That man couldn't even conceive a son with a damned thrall – his cock ran dry long ago. I planted my seed in Aveline before she'd even been stolen from me: these children are mine."

Vidar began pacing around the crowds, showing the boys to the people of Roskilde, pausing to allow them to scrutinise and examine his and his sons faces. Comments of amazement were made, nodding heads admitted that Young Birger and Sander were mirror images of him.

"How did you do it?" Rikulf marvelled as Vidar made his way back to my side.

Vidar turned to Rikulf, his eyes narrowed and his crooked smile glowing.

"Erhardt, the níðingr, thought he had bested me when he stole my betrothed behind my back, but the fool didn't even notice me bed his wife right under his nose." Vidar winked.

Triumph blazed from Vidar's face as he returned to me amidst applaud and cheers. He gave Sander to me and turned to face his townspeople again.

"Look! My wife and sons are returned to me!" Vidar roared, flapping his hand to beckon a horn of mead from a passing thrall. He thrust his horn into the air, his people followed his suit, raising theirs. "Praise the gods, my family is united, and Roskilde is victorious! On this Midsumarblót we thank the gods, both Æsir and Vanir alike – we thank them for their aid, for the strength of patience they encouraged in us to survive Aros's oppression, until the perfect moment of revenge revealed itself! We celebrate our quick victory! The swift death of Jarl Erhardt Ketilsson of Aros, his foolish followers, and, soon, the end of the feud between Aros and Roskilde!"

Vidar tossed his head backwards, guzzling the mead from the horn until it ran dry, his people cheering, drinking with him. Vidar threw the horn down and beckoned for another quickly, still staring at the townsfolk, his eyes darting from one to another to connect with them all.

"Today is the longest day of the year, a day of celebration and merriment! But the days will soon grow colder, and night will grow longer ... As such, today marks the time to be daring, a time for risk and action! To fearlessly reach outwards!" Vidar thundered on, answered to a tumultuous applaud and cheer. "Now that our crops are safely planted, we would normally sail forth and raid foreign lands! But!" He paused, gazing across the eager faces that focussed only on him. "But the battle has been brought to the very shore of our Roskilde, when Jarl Erhardt and his men raided our lands, those few years ago! When he burned down our homes and slaughtered our kin! Today, his death marks the end of his tyranny, and the beginning of our revenge! When the first rays of morn' shine onto our beautiful Roskilde, we will take to the fjord and set aflame the town of Aros, as they did to us! But we will not spare any life! We will not barter with them; we will slay them!"

The bay was alive with passion and support for Vidar. When the cheering and applause faded, he stared at his people and a bizarre silence settled on the beaches. Not a word was spoken, not a movement made, all gazed at their champion, at Vidar Alvarsson, waiting eagerly to hear each and every syllable to fall from his lips.

"Erhardt kidnapped my betrothed and stole her to his lands. There, over the years she was held captive, he beat her and raped her. Erhardt raped my woman! As did his men!" Vidar spat, quietly and regretfully, anguish carved across his face. "They raped your wives and daughters when they attacked – they raped Roskilde citizens and freewomen and went unpunished for so long! For that I am sorry. I failed you as your jarl, I failed to protect you, my people."

Vidar turned to me and took my hand in his.

"I failed to protect you, little fawn. I hope I can earn your forgiveness one day." Vidar apologised.

"You already have." I whispered.

"The death of Erhardt and a handful of his men is not enough to earn forgiveness for everything you've been through – for everything Roskilde has been through, thanks to my absence." Vidar said to me sadly. He kissed me quickly, my hand still clutched tightly in his. "I will take the lives of every single soul in Aros. Then, I will deserve your forgiveness."

Vidar turned the town, holding his and my clasped hands high into the air.

"Then I hope I will deserve all of your forgiveness!"

The town roared and bellowed and thundered with cheer, men began lunging forward, clapping Vidar on the back, thrusting drinking horns into his hand.

"We failed to protect our women, also, Jarl Vidar!" Some of the men remorsefully confessed. "Together we will take Aros and murder all those guilty of hurting our women and murdering our companions and kin!"

"Together, then!" Vidar beamed. "Together we will destroy Aros! By tomorrow's eve, they will all be dead, and Roskilde will never fall again!"

CHAPTER TWENTY-SIX

ROSKILDE, DENMARK
Summer, 879

AND AROS DID burn. By noon the following day Vidar and his fleet had arrived upon the shore of Aros and began setting flame the farms and steads that they passed until widespread terror and panic had erupted throughout the town.

Ultimately, Vidar and his men did not burn every single home to the ground – instead, they slaughtered those who chose to battle. They offered freedom to those who switched their loyalty to Vidar, but those who staunchly supported Erhardt and refused Vidar's new rule were herded into Erhardt's hall and the hall was set alight. Young or old, man or woman, Erhardt's loyal supports were killed by blade or by flame.

Danish custom dictated that harming a woman was a grave dishonour, so Aros women and their crying offspring were invited to stand by unscathed and watch their husbands and male kin burn in the hall. Most women mournfully accepted the offer, whereas a few loyal women stood by their husband or families and burned to death with them.

I regretted their deaths, I wished they would have traded their loyalties for the sake of their lives, but these Norse were a proud and loyal people.

"Their deaths were honourable, they supported their jarl and went to the afterlife for him." Vidar had admired.

Whilst Vidar and his men seized Aros, the Midsumarblót festivities continued in Roskilde regardless of the lessened numbers. In fact, the celebrations seemed more joyful – the thrill of freedom shocked through the town like lightning. On the last day of the festival, Vidar and half his men returned. Jan had been left in Aros with the other half to control the surviving peoples.

At the final feast of Midsumarblót, blazing fires roared around. A vivid indigo sky hung above us in the heavens, and Vidar delighted the townspeople of Roskilde with his exciting testimony of the vengeance exacted on Aros.

It had been a year since that night, and Vidar and I had still not married. Our time had been consumed by the two towns we now ruled. Freydis had not returned and Alvar and his men were still at war in Britain.

The survivors of Aros had been assimilated into Roskilde, either as thralls or they had willingly remarried our people and maintained their standing as karls, though we would watch them carefully, lest they planned vengeance. When he had finished overseeing the many weddings, Vidar had carefully split what little men we had between Roskilde and Aros.

Thankfully, Vidar had convinced many of the Aros residents to accept him willingly as jarl. Thus, Aros was rebuilt, slowly, clearing the damage Roskilde's attack had wrought. We built a new hall, a grand, elegant hall with fine carvings in the wooden beams, sheep pens at one end, which opened into the pasture we'd fenced behind the building.

This new hall was to be ours.

Erhardt's hall was nothing more than ash, dust and blackened nails. The remains of the scorched and charred corpses had been buried deeply on the mainland, far from Aros. I hadn't watched Erhardt's death, nor his cremation, I refused to speak his name or even Hilda's. I tried to not waste too much time thinking of them, but it was of my highest hopes that, Christian or Nordic, they both were rotting in a hellish afterlife.

Ursula however ...

Ursula had been rude and foolish, but that was not a worthy reason for her untimely death ... No, she had been Erhardt's daughter and although she could not control her parentage, unfortunately her kinship and her loyalty to her father had been enough to condemn her to her death ...

Regret hung heavily over me ...

Ursula had suffered at the hands of Vidar and for that I pitied her. She had sought solace and advice from me and was answered with coldness and lies.

I regretted Ursula's rape.

I regretted Ursula's death.

I couldn't change the past, but I dearly hoped that Ursula was at peace in Helgafjell ...

With closed eyes, I wiped the sweat from my dampened brow on the back of my hand.

The thick, piquant aroma of freshly turned soil wafted up my nostrils. I breathed it in deeply, comforted by the musky odour. I opened my eyes and stared at the scene before me. I had managed to singlehandedly tackle the wild chaos of weeds that had devoured Freydis's garden flowers. A mountain of unwanted vegetation towered beside me, drying in the sun.

My hands were stained black, chunks of soil were wedged beneath my nails, but I was successful. The horror of Freydis's abandonment, her guilt and sorrow, was finally gone. I didn't know whether I would plant any new flowers yet, but for now at least the jungle was gone. The nakedness of the rich brown beds relieved me enough, for now.

"Out here again are you?" Vidar's voice purred behind me, softly.

"What do you think?" I smiled, rising from my knees, my back still turned to him.

Vidar's hand slinked over my hips, and he pulled me against him, placing a kiss upon my head regardless of how sweat drenched it was.

"I think you're beautiful, even when you're covered in dirt." Vidar smirked, wiping a smudge of soil from my forehead.

"I meant the garden." I pressed, rolling my eyes.

"It's wonderful." Vidar replied sincerely and sweetly.

I finally turned and faced him. Vidar's gaze was fixed upon me, and when I looked at him, I saw that his expression was serene and truly, truly happy.

"What are you thinking about?" I couldn't help but smile – his contentment was infectious!

"I think it's finally time we wed." Vidar replied, almost in a whisper.

I gaped at him and threw my arms around his neck, pulling him into a deep kiss.

"I agree!"

***

Autumn

"AND NOW THE feast may begin!" Vidar announced, to vast cheers from the densely occupied hall.

The double doors had been opened and faces were squashed together, watching the blessing of my womb. I gazed down at the little silver hammer lain across my lap. It was finely detailed with intricate shapes and runes, I wondered if Thor's Mjölnir was as grand …

Of course, on this, my wedding day to Vidar, everything seemed inordinately beautiful and significant. A week before our wedding day arrived, Vidar had surprised me with the gorgeous sunshine yellow silken dress he had acquired for me from Britain – he had kept it safely pristine throughout my time in Aros. Though I had born two children since he'd given it to me, it fit perfectly, like a second flesh. Aaminah had delicately affixed the turtle shell brooches my darling Birger had gifted me when I was but a child, with the amber beads hung between them.

It saddened me that Birger was not here to witness the union he was so surprised and thrilled by. But here I sat, beside my husband. Though Birger's absence saddened me, I was gloriously content.

Upon my freely cascading, waist length curls was a beautiful silver crown, garlanded with flowers. The headpiece was both simple and stunning in appearance, and I wore it with fierce pride – looking forward to the day I'd pass the crown down to my daughter for her wedding day …

"So, Vidar, you realise you were meant to stab the ceiling, not destroy it?" Jan laughed beside Vidar.

I glanced between the two men, giggling. Vidar smirked and snickered but continued eating his food thoughtfully. It was true, by custom after he'd led me over the threshold into the hall, Vidar was meant to plunge his sword into a ceiling beam and the depth to which the sword sunk into the wood was supposed to symbolise the length of his and my union. When Vidar had thrust his sword upwards the blade not only sliced through the wood, but it had split the beam entirely, showering himself with sharp shards and splinters.

"We will fix it in the 'morrow." Vidar finally commented, unconcerned. He tossed a small hunk of meat into his mouth and clapped his friend on the back warmly. "Tonight, I celebrate my marriage; I do not wish to think of carpentry."

"Regardless of fixing the beam, I believe our marriage is to be long, indeed." I purred, leaning against Vidar's arm.

Vidar chuckled as he chewed and pulled me into his arms.

"Ah, but what of the splinters and the split?" Jan pushed, mischievously. "Surely they signify something?"

"Do be quiet, Jan!" I ordered, gruffly. "This is Vidar and my wedding day – don't ruin our joy with your horrid omens."

"Pay no mind to him," Vidar said, kissing my forehead. "Jötunnson is jealous of our union. So jealous, in fact, he hasn't noticed the beautiful young women gazing at him from across the room …"

"Where?" Jan demanded, his eyes darting across the crowd before us. "Ah, Vidar, you're fooling me – there are many beautiful young women here tonight! And I cannot see a single one gazing at – ah … I see."

Across the room was a gaggle of young women, between the ages of fifteen and twenty, dressed beautifully in the hopes of attracting male attention. All six of the women were blushing pink and gazing adoringly at the handsome Jan.

"I will return in time to lead you to your room." Jan promised, his voice drifting – he was so absorbedly, hungrily eyeing his flock of admirers.

With that, he skilfully and gracefully leapt around the table and swiftly made his way to the blushing young women. I watched, intently. I couldn't hear the words Jan said, but even from this distance I could read the young women's expressions. Jan oozed charm and charisma – he had said something witty and funny, and all six women were tittering at his words, and gawping at his handsomeness. Ridiculously large, infatuated smiles covered their magenta flushed faces.

"Which do you think he will lay with tonight?" I asked Vidar, crawling into his lap.

"All of them."

I stared at him, horrified, but together we burst into laughter. Vidar placed a tender kiss on the tip of my button nose, we pressed our foreheads together and smiled contentedly at one another.

"Oh, darling, look!" I cried, grinning over Vidar's shoulder.

Young Birger and Sander were curled together, asleep, on a pile of furs behind us. They had played hard all day and had finally managed to exhaust themselves. Vidar looked at his sons and chuckled.

"Leave them there for now, they are comfortable ... In fact, maybe you and I shall complete the next legal requirement of marriage a little sooner than expected – before they awaken ..." Vidar suggested, winking at me.

I grinned as he brought me into a deep, sensual kiss. His hands squeezed my body, holding me tightly against him, and a wave of cheers boomed around the hall at our spectacle.

Then suddenly, the hall fell silent.

Vidar and I glanced around and stared at the double doors.

The crowd had parted and there stood Freydis.

Faces whizzed between Freydis, Vidar and me. She stood there, alone, not even accompanied by a thrall. A pale mint coloured cloak swathed her body, she lowered the hood and gazed at us with watery eyes. Her beauty had faded, beneath her hustrulinet her hair fell limp, pale as the winter's moon, no ounce of gold left upon her strands. Lines of guilt, sorrow and age were engraved deeply into her flesh.

I studied her intensely.

I had expected to feel hate, resentment or rage at the sight of her. Though I had understood her reasoning for marrying me off to Erhardt, I couldn't help the bitterness that ate at me whenever I thought of her or heard her name.

But now Freydis was before me, physical, real ...

"It's lovely to see you again." I said as I walked towards her. I took her hand in mine and gently kissed her cheek. "Come, I have two very important people to introduce you to."

I led her to the main table where Vidar still sat, motionless but for his eyes that followed his mother and me.

"This is Sander." I scooped up the young boy and handed him to Freydis.

Light snores drifted from his lips, his slumber undisturbed. Freydis gaped at the little boy in her arms as I lifted my firstborn son from the fur.

"And this is Young Birger," I introduced. "Sander will see his third winter this year, and Young Birger will see his fifth. There are only two years and some days between the boys."

Young Birger blinked drowsily, flashing his blue eyes at Freydis as he regarded her with drowsy vision. He laid his head upon my shoulder and fell back to sleep, his silky blond ringlets tumbling over his face.

Freydis was confused and lost for words. Her eyes glided between my sons and me. Yes, the boys had some of my features, my nose and pointed ears, and Young Birger even had my curls, but they were strikingly fair with eyes the colour of ice.

"They are your grandsons." Vidar said quietly, a subtle smile playing over his lips as he placed a hand upon his mother's shoulder.

And then it struck her.

Not one ounce of these children was even a shadow of the swarthy, boar-like Erhardt. No, the boys were glowing resemblances of Vidar!

"How? But – oh Vidar ... they're wonderful!" Freydis wept joyfully, sweeping Sander with kisses, stroking Young Birger's cheek with a quivering hand.

"Come, share food with my wife and me," Vidar offered. "We will explain what you have missed."

"Wife?" Freydis whispered.

"Welcome to our wedding celebration."

***

THROUGH THE EARLY morning rays, I saw Vidar deep in thought, staring at the ceiling. I curled around him and he squeezed me gently. Our flesh glistened with thin sheets of sweat – we had retired from our wedding celebration many hours ago and consummated our union thoroughly. Nine years ago, Vidar and I spoke to one another for the first time in the shadowed confines of a woodshed. That meeting had led to our romance, and the tumultuous years of struggle and separation, but now we were finally husband and wife.

There was an occasional slip of laughter or a muffled conversation from groggy, drunken voices that resonated to our room. Most of the guests were snoring, fast asleep where they had stumbled and fallen.

"What does the shattering of the beam signify?" Vidar asked, his voice almost a whisper.

"I'm not a seeress, I don't know what it signifies." I replied, unintentionally shortly, so surprised by his unexpected question.

"Maybe Jötunnson crawled under my skin too deeply … but, I do wonder if he's right. If it is an omen…" Vidar's tone was light, but his words weighed heavily upon me.

"What do you think it means?" I asked meekly.

"I wonder if it … if it signifies the end of our marriage." Vidar admitted, shuffling slightly under the bed sheet.

"*Nei.*" I said firmly. "You buried your sword deep into the beam – that prophesies a long union, correct?"

Vidar murmured a noise of agreement. I thought carefully for a while, before I continued.

"I don't want to believe it's suggesting the end of our marriage … In fact, I believe with all my heart that we will be married for a long time." I explained slowly. "Our romance has spanned nearly a decade, and for that whole time it had been fraught with difficulty – but our love thrived and survived. Maybe the shattering beam signifies that our struggle is not over?" I gazed up at Vidar and found him smiling down at me. "I don't know … What I do know is that a broken ceiling beam will not decide the end of my marriage to you. The only thing that will end our union is death!"

Vidar snickered at me.

"For once in my life, death is not a thought I'd like to dwell on. As exciting a prospect as Valhalla is, I'd like to enjoy my life in Midgard for a time yet." He smirked.

"For a long time yet." I corrected sternly.

CHAPTER TWENTY-SEVEN

ROSKILDE, DENMARK
Spring, 880

FREYDIS SETTLED INTO her role of grandmother quickly and easily. She was tender, doting and loving, and the children adored her. With the help of her cherished young grandsons, she quickly filled the empty flower beds of her precious garden.

It had been less than a year since her return to Roskilde, but her garden flourished, even in the crisp, drizzly morning. The flower beds poured out with a vibrant spectrum of brightly coloured flowers and plants. Rain droplets twinkled on the delicate blossoms and on the dainty yellow-green buds that sprouted from the fingers of tree branches, robbed of their leaves by the brisk autumn winds two seasons ago.

Rain pitter-pattered down from the cloud covered sky and glittered in the streaks of the tepid sunlight that whispered promises of a temperate day. Through the hazy grey light, shadows appeared in the distance upon the fjord. Quickly they glided closer and horns echoed across the bay. My heart lurched in my chest at the deep billowing noise.

Vidar caught my glance and dashed to the water's edge to join the throng of puzzled and excited onlookers, as I scurried with Freydis and my children back to the hall.

By early afternoon the tender showers of rain had stopped, and the soft clouds had been wafted away by the gentle breeze, exposing the fresh powder blue sky. As it had slowly scaled into the sky, the pale sun had brought greater warmth and the beautiful afternoon it had hinted in the rain sprinkled morning. And beautiful it was, for the longships that had slipped across the fjord were none other than Alvar the First One and his men!

I leaped out of my skin when the double doors of the hall burst open and Vidar and his father, exploding with joy, tumbled through the doorway.

"I am home!" Alvar roared happily, holding his arms up high.

"Alvar?" Freydis gasped as she dashed into the room from the garden.

"My love!" Alvar cried, holding his arms open to his wife.

As they embraced and kissed one another I saw all the lines and signs of stress and age vanish from their flesh. I blushed as I watched them, unable to tear my eyes from the beautiful sight before me, husband and wife, lovers for decades, finally reunited.

"Aveline!" Alvar bellowed, a huge grin spread across his aged face that was split with cuts and scars, his arms still wrapped around Freydis. "My son tells me you are finally his wife?"

"I am," I replied warmly. "Welcome home, Jarl Alvar!"

"No need for titles now you are my daughter." Alvar beamed, stepping momentarily away from his wife to pull me into him with a bear-like grip. "I am glad my son has wed you at last. There is good news all round!"

I wrapped my arms around the huge man as best I could, returning his embrace affectionately. A warmth filled me from his kindly words, but there was still a disquiet inside me.

"A-and my *faðir*? Did he – is he with you?" I spluttered hopefully.

The beaming grin fell from Alvar's lips suddenly, and his shoulders dropped. For a few moments his lips subtly moved, but no words came out. My heart sank.

"I'm sorry, my child." Alvar said at last. "Birger was slain soon after we arrived on the Anglo-Saxon shores. I vouch that his was an honourable death. Be happy and proud, sweet Aveline, for he fought with formidable strength and aptitude, right down to his last dying breath. Birger Bloody Sword most certainly sits in Valhalla now."

I frowned, my eyes prickled with sadness at the confirmation of what I had already expected. My Birger, my darling faðir, was dead. Vidar took my hand and squeezed it, and, with melancholy, I nodded to Alvar.

"So, was the – was the raid successful?" I asked awkwardly.

I stepped aside and offered him a seat at his table. He had not seen his home in six long years. Sympathetically, Alvar kissed the top of my head and sat close to the fire as Aaminah brought us each a deep cup of mead.

"Unfortunately, many warriors met their deaths, the fleet is half the size of when we departed. But we were successful – half of Britain is now under Scandinavian rule – and Roskilde's few remaining longships are filled with vast amounts of treasures and bounty." Alvar explained.

"*Amma*! Come play again." Exclaimed Young Birger and Sander as they appeared in the kitchen doorway.

"*Amma?*" Alvar gasped and stared at the boys who glared back at him. Alvar gawped at Freydis, "You are a grandmother?"

"I'd like to introduce you to your grandchildren." Vidar smirked. "My sons, come here – I'd like to introduce you to your *afi*."

"He's a golden bear!" Sander exclaimed, pointing at Alvar incredulously.

"Come give the old bear a hug!" Freydis giggled, beckoning the boys to come closer.

Young Birger bravely stepped over to Alvar and surveyed him with a frown.

"And what is your name, young man?" Alvar asked, aghast.

"I am Birger Vidarsson. Who are you?" Young Birger demanded, his eyes still narrowed at the man before him.

Alvar boomed with laughter, frightening Sander who jumped into Freydis's arms. Young Birger didn't move a muscle.

"I am Alvar Kulbenson, your father's father." Alvar smiled at the boy. "By the gods, you look just like Vidar when he was a child. How many winters have you seen, boy?"

"Five." Young Birger replied, puffing out his chest. "Are you truly my father's father? Or are you a pretender?"

"I am Vidar's father; I am your *afi*." Alvar confirmed, nodding his head firmly though a shadow of confusion whispered across his face at the young boy's fierce interrogation.

"Then I will hug you." Young Birger decided after a thoughtful pause and opened his arms to Alvar.

Curiosity stole at Sander as he watched his brother embrace the 'golden bear'. He slinked out of Freydis's arms and meekly stood behind his brother.

"I am Sander Vidarsson. Are you my *afi* too?" The young boy questioned.

Alvar nodded, beaming, and scooped the boy into his arms. I couldn't help but smile at the sight of the grandfather and his grandsons, and crept to the bed chamber, my eyes still bristling with unfallen tears. I cleared my throat pointedly as I entered the main room again, holding a bundle in my arms and a secretive smile upon my lips.

"And this is Æsa," I announced as I offered the tiny baby swaddled in silk and linen to the shocked Alvar.

"Another?" He gasped as he took the little babe from me.

Alvar the First One gazed upon the infant in his arms, absorbing the beauty of the delicate new life he held. Timidly he stroked one of his massive calloused fingers over her soft, chubby cheek and like a candle flame flickering in a breeze she opened her amber eyes and stared at him. His breath caught in his throat when he saw her fiery irises. Small and pristine, the precious baby was the embodiment of splendour, her eyes were glistening ambers, her thin lips were the colour of rose quartz and her flesh was the palest gold.

"She has your hair!" Alvar beamed to his wife, his light blue eyes shining with happiness.

Freydis grinned silently and gently stroking the snow-white strands upon my daughter's head.

"Her naming ceremony was but a few days ago." I said, overflowing with pride.

"You have given my son three wonderful children." Alvar gushed, gazing upon his grandsons and the granddaughter in his arms. "Well done my dear daughter-in-law – well done my son! Birger, Sander and Æsa …"

Alvar was overjoyed at the boys' names. As I had vowed to him, Young Birger was named after my late Danish father, Alvar's truest companion and longest friendship. Sander was named after Alvar's late brother who had been a warrior in the army Ragnar Loðbrók had sailed with to Britain early in the year 865. Sander Kulbenson was slain by King Ælla of Northumbria's soldiers after the longships had shipwrecked upon the Northumbrian coast, leading to the deaths of the Scandinavian warriors and the demise of King Ragnar himself.

Alvar squeezed his grandsons tightly, overwhelmed with pride; promising me over and over that Birger would've been honoured and delighted with Vidar and my sons.

And Æsa – our beautiful, newest babe – many a kiss was pressed against her little forehead. My labour with her had been swift, she had been small but not as worrisomely tiny as Sander had been at his birth. I had named her 'Æsa' meaning 'god', for surely based by appearance and the blessed ease of her birth alone, she must have been a gift from the gods.

***

"AND GUTHRUM HAS abandoned our people – his people! – and joined the Anglo-Saxons and their Christian God. He goes by the Christian name Athelstan now, and rules the damned Kingdom of East Angles. *The Kingdom of Guthrum.*" Alvar spat angrily at the evening feast. "The whore's son willingly gave that wretch, King Alfred, men from his army as hostages – free to kill should Guthrum break his oath to him."

Jarl Alvar slammed the rest of his mead to the back of his throat and crashed his cup down onto the tabletop. He had completed his avid account of the happenings of the Great Army in Britain and shocked us with his revelation.

A deep tone of panic had struck through Alvar and many others, sickened by Guthrum's betrayal. Alvar the First One had returned his fleet to Denmark two years after Guthrum's defeat, keen to stop the disease of Christianity from infecting his people and spreading to his lands.

The riches laden in the longships had been welcomed, but Jarl Alvar's announcement of Birger's death was bittersweet, as were the deaths of the countless other Roskilde warriors.

Though it hadn't been my home for fifteen years – I had spent most of my life in the Norse lands – the news that the Kingdom of the East Angles, my old home, was changed, left me with a bizarre feeling inside. I had been gone from there for so long and so much had changed in my absence …

Aaminah had said the same thing to me, years ago. Her parents were dead, she had no clue where her siblings were, and she realised her lands had changed in the years she had been away from it.

"The lands and my life may have changed, but I'll forever hold those happy memories of my family, etched inside my soul, so there isn't really much I need to miss – I have all the important things inside me."

And I would hold the memories of my family inside my soul, too. My land had changed, and so had I. I was a Dane now, a mother and a wife. I had a new focus in life, a purpose. I was eager for the future, and I had long since let go of the past.

"In spite of Guthrum cowing to the Anglo-Saxon king, almost half of Britain is now under Scandinavian rule." Alvar sighed, accepting another cup of mead from Aaminah. "Tell me, son, other than the great union between Aveline and yourself, not to mention the births of your three wonderful children – what news do you have of the years I have been absent?"

Freydis, who sat between her husband and son, moved to one of the empty chairs beside me. Young Birger and Sander had sat beside me at the table but had long since retired to bed, their poor little eyelids had drooped heavily from the lateness of the hour. I clutched Æsa to my breast as she suckled occasionally in her drowsy state, anxious at the loaded question Alvar had asked his son.

Vidar sighed heavily. He brought his polished wooden cup to his lips and deeply gulped the contents.

"A month after you departed for Britain, I rode to Ribe for trading." Vidar said calmly. "Whilst I was gone, Erhardt of Aros attacked Roskilde. He had slaughtered many of our men and left a large contingent of warriors to guard Roskilde whilst he shipped Aveline to Aros. I returned to Roskilde a few days later than I had intended and found Erhardt and his daughter sat at our table. Aveline was gone and the swine jarl was in control of Roskilde."

At Vidar's words, Alvar's face drained from colour. He took a few moments to process what his son had said, and his face gradually transformed from white with shock to scarlet with rage. Vidar shifted his back to his mother, his arm rested on the table, bodily sheltering her from Alvar's view.

"He demanded a peace-bride and chose Aveline when he found out she was betrothed to Vidar. He offered his daughter to Vidar, in Aveline's place. If I didn't agree to his terms, he vowed to burn Roskilde, slaughter the remaining townspeople and murder Vidar. So, I agreed." Freydis admitted in a small voice as she stared at the tabletop.

Ashamed and afraid, Freydis shrank behind me. Alvar swelled with fury. His huge paws curled into shaking fists upon the table.

"You handed Erhardt Ketilsson my son's betrothed and my town?" Alvar growled furiously as he glared at his wife; his tight lips barely moved as he spoke.

"When I arrived," Vidar continued, attempting to draw his father's attention from his mother. "The dastardly boar dictated to me what would have to happen to save Roskilde from being destroyed and save Aveline from being killed. And I agreed to his terms, as well."

"What?!" Alvar roared in disbelief, rising to his feet and hurling his cup across the hall.

His wooden cup smashed against the wall. Silence shocked through the townsfolk in the hall from Alvar's outburst, and the terrified Æsa wailed in fear.

"The vile son of a whore trapped us in the palm of his hand!" Vidar hissed at his father, shooting to his feet. Both men ignored the sea of faces staring at them. "He bestowed an ultimatum upon my mother that she couldn't refuse – if she had, your town would have been burned, people murdered, and Aveline and I would've been killed! Freydis accepted his offer to save our people.

"We suffered four years under his reign, and it was well worth the bloodshed that was avoided. Erhardt had attacked us unawares, he had already slaughtered so many of our people – if we had fought him further, we would be dead, and you would have returned to ashes, not a town!"

"I am ashamed of what I did!" Freydis cried vehemently, tears cascaded down her face, but her voice remained strong. "But many lives were saved and Erhardt is dead!"

Alvar stared at her.

"I am the Jarl of Aros, now." Vidar announced.

Alvar was dumbstruck. He collapsed into his chair and gaped at his son.

"Tell me everything."

"After Ketilsson dictated to me what was to happen. I followed his commands to give me time to formulate a plan of my own. I married his daughter and a week after the wedding Erhardt returned to Aros.

"His man, Niklas, and his contingent remained in Roskilde to quell any revolt we might plan – to remind us we were under Erhardt's control. Niklas lived in the hall while the wolves of Aros stole homes and farms, killing those who fought. We lost many more townspeople. If any words were spoken against Erhardt – no matter how meagre – his men would cut out the tongues that said them." Vidar spat.

Vidar paused his account. The townspeople in the hall had begun to murmur to one another, the steady hum of their voices filled the hall, melded with the tinkering of knives on plates and alcohol swilling in cups and horns.

I flinched at every tap-tap as Vidar knocked the metal fork against the wooden plate, fidgeting in silent rage and shame. After a few long, heavy minutes of difficult silence, his livid scowl began to soften into a sly, dark smile.

"Two years after Erhardt had besieged Roskilde, his daughter and I visited Aros. There he introduced me to his firstborn son ... Little did he know, the child Aveline had born was mine."

Vidar and Alvar caught each other's eyes and smirked faintly to each other.

"What happened next, son?"

"By that point I had finally formed a plan to reclaim Roskilde from the villain, rescue my love and my son and end the feud, for good."

I beckoned Freydis to follow me to the bedchamber as I went to put Æsa into her cradle. I had soothed her back to sleep and needed, now, to soothe the grandmother of my children.

After laying Æsa down, I turned to face Freydis and found her sat miserably on the edge of Vidar and my bed.

"I didn't want you to be hurt." Freydis sighed. "I just didn't know what else to do."

I sat beside her, took her hand in mine and squeezed it tenderly.

"Had I been in your place, I would have made the same decision." I whispered.

"I am so sorry, Aveline, I truly am." Freydis wept.

"Ssh ... I forgave you a long time ago."

We sat together in silence for the longest time. The thick curtains draped over the doorway dampened the noise from the hall.

Sander and Young Birger were sprawled at opposite ends of their bed, snoring in unison, and not a sound escaped from Æsa who slept in blissful peace. Occasionally I heard the distant sound of the hall doors, creaking open and banging shut, with every scrape and slam I was stirred from my thoughts.

"I must sleep, my daughter-in-law." Freydis muttered as she rose and stepped towards her bed closet, her voice hoarse. "Thank you for staying with me."

I nodded to her and left the room, slipping through the curtains like a ghost. The hall was nearly empty, but for the many drunken bodies snoring where they had collapsed.

I walked by Aaminah and spotted heavy black bags hung beneath her bloodshot eyes. I ordered the poor, shattered woman to bed. Gratefully, exhaustedly, she followed my command and stumbled to the bench. She collapsed onto an empty spot on the sticky bench in her filthy clothes and her eyes slammed shut immediately.

I took my place beside Vidar at the table where he and his father were still sat, locked in heated conversation away from the realisation of time.

"–And if Aveline can forgive my mother for selling her to Erhardt, then you and I can hold no reasonable grudge against Freydis." Vidar finished, entwining his fingers with mine without breaking the stern, determined stare he maintained with his father.

For a long time Alvar stared at his plate, contemplating, and like a statue Vidar gazed at his father, waiting patiently for a response. I rested my head on Vidar's shoulder, feeling the soft rise and fall of his breathing and found myself drifting in and out of sleep.

"Okay, Vidar." Alvar said at last. "Okay."

"Enough of the past. We own Roskilde *and* Aros, now, we need to look to the future!" Vidar grinned, his mood lightened.

Vidar and Alvar entered a long and excitable conversation. For hours, they described and considered various actions for the two towns, now both were under their family's control. Alvar was proud of Vidar for rising above hardships and obstacles to not only earn his own jarldom but also that he had built up Roskilde and its riches.

It brought no end of pleasure to Alvar to realise the busy market town that Roskilde had become. Merchants and traders had begun passing through Roskilde to sell their wares, expanding the town's prosperity as well as population. Aros was quickly becoming a vast trading town, and Vidar had many comprehensive proposals and detailed strategies to build the two towns into rich, prosperous assets.

Unfortunately, as the father and son began to delve into those proposals and strategies, I fell asleep, leaning on Vidar's shoulder.

***

A FEW WEEKS had gone by and Vidar, our children and I were finally preparing to leave Roskilde. We stood by the bay and our elegant ship bobbed on the fjord before us, waiting for us to embark. Crates and chests of our belongings were being loaded onto the longship, not just ours – a few Roskilde families had decided to move to Aros with us.

Aaminah stood on the dock beside our longship with Freydis, who held Æsa in her arms sadly, not wanting to bid farewell to her darling grandchildren. Both women smiled with watery eyes at Vidar and me as we approached. Elda and Burwenna, my dear friends, stood on the shore with their husbands, waiting to bid farewell to us.

As I had promised, I had gifted Elda and Burwenna with Birger and my farm and had married them to two good Danish men. Since Burwenna's marriage six months ago, only Elda, her husband and their small daughter lived in my old home. Burwenna, who had married Jan's younger brother Jakob and carried his child in her belly, lived in Jakob and Jan's family farm.

"I will miss you!" Burwenna wept, throwing her arms around me. "And the children!"

"We will miss you, too! You will have your hands full, soon, with a child of your own." I smiled, touching her belly gently and pressing a kiss on her cheek. "Do send a message to me when the baby is born!"

"We will," Jakob promised, embracing me in farewell.

"Oh Elda, I will miss you also!" I cried, holding her tightly. I kissed her young daughter on the cheek. "I will see you again, little Marta!"

Once I had bid farewell to my friends, their partners and children, when they had kissed my three children goodbye, I stepped, sadly, to Vidar's side. He was in the middle of a deep conversation with his father.

"Our gods are stronger than theirs, remember?" Vidar smirked, taking Young Birger from me and setting him on his shoulders.

"Their god might not be as feeble as we first thought. Guthrum is a king, Vidar, he is meant to be strong. With their god behind them, a few penniless, rag wearing monks and an illness-stricken weakling convinced a great Danish king to abandon his gods for their own!" Alvar cautioned his son.

"The sickly weakling was a king, just like Guthrum – he may not be strong of body, but what he lacks in muscle, he owns in intelligence. And those penniless, rag wearing monks must be more cunning than you give them credit." Vidar laughed. "I do not believe their single god is more powerful than our many gods ... Guthrum is not a stupid man – he agreed to their terms and gained a kingdom."

"And has forsaken his people and his gods in the process of his greed." Alvar growled.

"We hold much of Britain, correct?"

"*Já*, though the Kingdom of East Angles is now 'the Kingdom of Guthrum'." Alvar grumbled.

"Regardless, we still hold power. Christian or not, Guthrum has succeeded in gaining a kingdom and that may be advantageous for us, should this religious conversion be a ruse. With the Great Army still stationed there, and more Scandinavians settling in Britain, we are stable, we are strong. We will regroup and launch another attack upon Britain, we will take it wholly and completely." Vidar said passionately.

"Is that what you intend to do, eh, son? Jarl Vidar of Aros! Now you have conquered your own kingdom, do you plan on conquering Britain, too?" Alvar chortled. "When you sail to Britain, you don't intend to become Christian, too, do you?"

Vidar snorted with laughter and shot a beaming grin to his father.

"As jarl, I plan on growing Aros, making sure my hold on it is firm and my followers and retainers are trustworthy and loyal, before I can begin raiding or battling." Vidar explained, wisely. "And," he continued, sparks of mischief glinting in his eyes. "I plan on further expanding my family, by taking my wife to bed as often as I'm able!"

Vidar and Alvar laughed heartily together, and I blushed heavily at his statement.

"Speaking of your wife," Alvar said, glancing at me. "I'd like to talk to her before you set off, if you don't mind."

"Of course, go ahead. I'll ready the children." Vidar smiled, hoisting Sander onto his hip, his other arm tightly gripping Young Birger's leg.

Freydis carefully stepped on to the longship, cuddling her granddaughter, as Vidar set down his sons. Immediately the two boys began running around the longship squealing happily. Vidar chuckled and wrapped his arms around his tearful mother.

Alvar and I had walked a while before he shared any words with me. Apparently waiting until we were out of earshot of anyone, he finally began.

"I don't think we have spoken alone since Birger's sickness." Alvar commented as we strode down along the fjord's edge together.

"I believe you're right." I realised, surprised.

"He was always so proud of you." The Jarl of Roskilde smiled. "He loved you, dearly. He despised the circumstance that brought you both together, he hated the hurt you had to suffer, but he did not regret a thing. You were his daughter, and he loved you."

A smile rose upon my lips, remembering the gentle face of my beloved *faðir*.

"Birger should've died from his wound. No man has survived a wound like that." Alvar reminisced. "But Birger did. You saved him – you saved his life, you saved him from spending the rest of eternity in Hel. You bought him more time to earn his spot in Valhalla, where I know he is sat drinking now. Birger and I had been friends since we suckled from our mothers' tits, he was a brother to me, Aveline, and you saved him. I'll be forever grateful to you, for everything you did for him."

"You killed my brother, you know." I said quietly. "When I was nine, and you attacked the Kingdom of East Angles ... I watched you kill my brother, Kenrick. You cleaved an axe through his head. The sound of my mother's screams as she was raped in our home rang in my ears as I watched you murder him ... I ran. I ran and ran, but Birger caught me and stole me away to your longships."

I glanced up and examined the solemn, steady expression on Alvar's face.

"I was scared for such a long time. Every time I saw your face, I saw the metal blade of the axe crack through my brother's skull, like a knife through an eggshell. Every time I looked at Birger, I was sickened ... I hated him for stealing me. I wished I had died with my family, wished I could have been in heaven with them ... But ..." I sighed, the shadow of a smile played on my lips. "It's funny in a way ... I never would have thought I'd laugh in comfort with my brother's murderer – would never believe his murderer would one day become my kin! Nor could I believe I'd love so desperately the man who stole me from my home. I did hurt, dreadfully and for a long time ... but I am glad to be Aveline Birgersdóttir."

"Do you want vengeance?" Alvar asked softly.

"What?" I asked, startled.

"Vengeance. Do you wish to take vengeance for the deaths of your family?" He reiterated.

"Once upon a time I did." I replied honestly, staring across the glassy surface of the fjord. The gentle breeze blew dancing strands of my chestnut hair across my face. "But no, no I don't want vengeance anymore."

"You've forgiven me?" Alvar asked lightly, his tone was a mixture of amusement and curiosity.

"*Nei.*" I surprised even myself at how quickly that single word had fallen from my lips. "*Nei*, Alvar ... and I don't think I ever will. When Freydis gave me to Erhardt, she was protecting her people and family – she was protecting her son. I understand what she did – during my marriage to Erhardt, I had to do many abhorrent, shameful things for the safety of my children, too. When you killed my brother and my people, you did it for riches and spoils. You killed them to take what treasures they might have had. I can't forgive you for that ...

"But I cannot change the past, and what good would vengeance be? It wouldn't change a thing."

"You're entitled to vengeance when one wrongs you." Alvar the First One pointed out.

"Would killing you or taking compensation bring my family back from the dead?"

"*Nei*, it would not."

"It might break the family I have now though, correct?"

"Possibly."

"And that is why it's not a hard decision to make. I don't need vengeance, Alvar. I craved vengeance once, but not anymore. Bitterness is a heavy burden to carry, and Birger's love and the family I have made here relieved me of that terrible load."

"Is this home to you, now?" My father-in-law asked.

"*Já.*" I admitted. "It truly is."

Alvar smiled warmly at me as we settled onto a felled tree that lay by the water's edge. In the branches of a nearby tree, I heard the throaty cawing of ravens. I turned and saw Huginn and Muninn perched together on a branch, ruffling their feathers and staring at us with their glossy black eyes.

"I asked you to join me for a reason." Alvar said after a while. "After the ordeal of being sold as peace-bride to Erhardt, I believe you deserve an explanation."

I nodded silently, my lips drawn together and eyes somewhat narrowed, apprehensive in my anticipation.

"This feud with Aros ... it all started decades ago. Freydis, she ... she was betrothed to Erhardt many, *many* years ago. She was born and raised in Roskilde, and I was infatuated with her for as long as I could remember. When she was sixteen years of age, she was taken by her father to Aros and quickly engaged to Erhardt.

"She was so beautiful – golden like a summer's day, with those gorgeous, meadow-green eyes! She took my breath away. She was kind, she was gentle, loving ... I was mesmerised by her.

"When she returned from Aros, betrothed to Erhardt, the swine, I was furious. Erhardt was not worthy of a woman like Freydis – but I believed I was. So, I wooed Freydis and quickly convinced her to wed me instead. And she did – upon Erhardt's arrival in Roskilde, the day they were meant to wed, she was already my wife, not his ...

"Then the feud began ...

"So, I ask you again, Aveline Birgersdóttir, do you wish for vengeance? I sit beside you, the killer of your kin, a dastardly fox and oath-breaker – for I was as the one who convinced Freydis to break her promise to wed Erhardt, so I am equally to blame. I am the man who began the feud that led to your suffering. *Do you wish for vengeance?*"

Alvar stared at me, a cold, stony expression etched upon his pale, aged face.

"*Nei.*" I repeated firmly. "I don't. Vengeance would not bring my family from the dead, and it would not change the things that have happened. I do not want to lose another family; I wish no revenge on the grandfather of my children, the father of my husband. I am tired of fighting and grudges, Alvar … I do not wish to waste my time on hatred."

"You have done well adapting to the Norse ways, but there is some Christian remaining inside you, Aveline." Alvar winked as he nudged me with his elbow and smirked at me.

I grinned heartily back at him.

"I suppose that's why they call me Danethrall."

***

WE MADE OUR way back to the longship. Everything was set for Vidar and me to depart back to our hall in Aros. Carefully, I climbed into our vessel, spotting my children being cared for by a few of Vidar and my companions while waiting for me to return.

When I stepped into the ship, Vidar swiftly wrapped his arms around me and sharply pulled me against him. I giggled and threw my arms around his neck, kissing his neatly trimmed beard covered jaw quickly. He gazed at me, lovingly, pressing a tender kiss against my forehead before we turned back to the dear faces of our loved ones on the shore.

"Thóra – are you sure you wish to remain here with Jötunnson? You could be free of him now if you get on to the longship!" Vidar called to the ebony haired girl wrapped in Jan's arms on the shore.

Thóra was one of the many girls who had admired Jan at Vidar and my wedding. She and Jan had married not long ago, and her belly swelled enormously from the life of Jan's child inside her.

"I think I am trapped with him now I carry his child!" She quipped back, a hand rested on her belly.

"My apologies to you, then, dear girl!" Vidar laughed, kissing my head, gently. "Treat her well, Jötunnson, my brother! She is the only woman left in Roskilde who is mad enough to take you as a husband!"

"I am following in your footsteps, Vidar!" Jan called back. "Seduce a young, beautiful woman and impregnate her so she will not run away!"

Thóra and I caught each other's gaze and rolled our eyes to each other, grinning.

With jubilant laughter echoing across the bay, Vidar held me close, kissing me between our giggles. He beamed down at me as our longship sliced through the waters of the fjord swiftly, easily, quickly. Not much time had passed before the faces dotting the shoreline were already blurred from sight.

"Vidar, when you do raid ... I want to go with you." I declared suddenly.

"Wherever I travel, I want you by my side." Vidar agreed. "We have spent too much time apart ... I want to show you the world – I won't be able to do that if you're locked away in our hall."

"Where will we go first?" I whispered excitedly.

"Iceland, Francia, the Iberian kingdoms, wherever you want to go." Vidar smiled. "Where would you like to go first?"

"Home." I replied, snuggling against him. "With you."

Printed in Great Britain
by Amazon